NIHPLOD

by Jill Mercer

Best Wishes

Jill Mercy

© Jill Mercer 2019
ISBN 978-0-9570693-1-2

Cover illustration: Heath Hearn
Book design by Topical Design

Printed by CLOC Ltd, Unit 10 Milmead Industrial Centre
Mill Mead Rd, Tottenham, London N17 9QU
www.clocbookprint.co.uk
Winners of the Green Apple Environment Award

info@seesawpress.co.uk

FOREWORD

by Claire Wallerstein (Rame Peninsula Beach Care)

As more and more people are becoming aware, plastic pollution poses a major and growing threat to marine wildlife, from the tiniest organisms such as plankton up to the largest whales.

The plastic waste we humans produce, mismanage and dispose of on land can now be found locked into Arctic ice and at the bottom of the deepest ocean trenches, endangering life throughout all of the seas that cover 70% of the planet we mistakenly call 'Earth'.

The United Nations estimate that at least one million seabirds and 100,000 marine mammals are killed each year by plastic in the sea, either by mistaking it for food or becoming entangled in it. This needless death and suffering comes on top of the many other issues threatening sea life, such as ocean acidification, over-fishing, noise pollution and habitat destruction.

I see the effects of plastic pollution every day in my work running Rame Peninsula Beach Care, a beach cleaning and marine conservation awareness-raising charity operating around the same areas of coastline where the 'real life' action of Jill Mercer's book Nihplod is set.

Over the past seven years, our wonderful local community volunteers have removed many thousands of sacks of hazardous plastic waste from this tiny slice of the Cornish coastline, found dead animals entangled in balloons and ghost fishing gear, campaigned for change and contributed to scientific research to further our understanding about the source and impact of marine plastics.

One of the most heartwarming aspects of my job is working with schools and other groups of young people and children, all of whom have been born into the Plastic Age with its brightly-coloured conveniences and distractions, and yet who are usually so quick to grasp the seriousness of the issue and question how we could allowed things to have become so bad.

Just as Swedish teenager Greta Thunberg has had the bravery to stand up alone to challenge corporate greed and government inaction on climate change, so it is brave and passionate young people – like Imogen in the story of Nihplod – who will be our biggest hope in the battle against the plastic polluted world they are set to inherit.

In fact, climate change and plastic pollution are more closely connected than many people realise. Production of plastic – which is made, of course, from oil – will increase fourfold by 2050, with its extraction, refining, manufacture and transport accounting for a huge 13% of all climate-changing emissions.

So much destruction has been committed in the name of profit, greed and convenience against our planet's air, land and sea, creating a way of life that has drawn many people away from understanding that we are a part of, and completely dependent on, Nature for our own survival.

All of this has happened in the blink of an eye in planetary terms, and yet we have reached the point now at which our young people are facing a future that looks scary and bleak. Facing up to this reality can be very overwhelming, so it is unsurprising that some people choose to put it out of their minds and continue to live as if the Earth's limited resources can be abused and poisoned forever.

However, I hope this book will help to inspire many young people to become the much-needed environmental champions of tomorrow, who will fight to save and restore the ecology of this beautiful planet – our one and only home and life support system. It's important to remember that the positivity of action, no matter how small our actions may be, will achieve so much more than negativity and despair.

The scary headlines may make it seem pointless to take small personal steps to combat issues such as plastic pollution – for example by using a refillable bottle instead of buying plastic bottled drinks, stopping using straws, or using a bamboo toothbrush. But just imagine what a difference it would make if everybody in the world did the same thing….

As a wise man once said, each journey of a thousand miles starts with a single step. We must all use our voices to speak out, spread knowledge, encourage our friends and family and refuse single use plastics.

Want to get involved? A great place to find some serious inspiration, with loads of ideas about everything you can do to help in the battle to protect the planet from plastic pollution, is right here: http://www.kidsagainstplastic.co.uk/

It's never too late to make the world a better place!

illustration by Hayley Gibson

'Skyscraper' (the Bruges Whale) in Belgium, was developed as a reminder that 150 million tonnes of plastic waste still roam in our waters. The colossal installation leaps from the Bruges canal with four stories worth of plastic reflecting in the calm waters. 'Skyscraper' is visible near Bruges' Jan Van Eyck statue as part of the Bruges Triennial 2018.

AUTHOR'S NOTE

I was inspired to write Nihplod by the work of Greenpeace and Rame Peninsula Beach Care, and by Sir David Attenborough's BBC series, 'Blue Planet II,' which showed vividly the devastating effects of plastic pollution in our ocean. Another inspiration was Brian Cox's 'Human Universe,' which explores through science how we, planet life and the Universe are all connected.

Although Nihplod is a fictional adventure story, there are many facts and scenes based on true events which are woven into the plot, such as the leaping rays which startle Lowen and Imogen, and the ways that dolphins often help us humans. The Pacific Ocean garbage patch scene, which Imogen gets caught up in, and the way plastic pollution is starving and stupefying sea creatures and fish, are also based on true life.

I'd like to say an extra big thank you to all the children who read the early version of Nihplod and took part in surveys - you helped me shape this story. Another big thank you to all of you who have so generously given your time to proofread and give feedback, Claire for her foreword and Viv Calderbank and Hayley Gibson for producing some wonderful illustrations for this book - check out Viv's dolphin flick animation.

If you have purchased this book, you have already taken action against plastic pollution - at least 30% of all book sales will be donated to environmental charities. But don't stop here, there are lots of ways you can be a champion for our planet and your future.

CHAPTER 1

Waves thundered down over our basket raft, tearing at the flimsy sail.

'Nihplod!' I screamed as another wave tossed us like a ball across the dark sea. I tried to move to the other-side, next to him. He was waving his arms and shouting something, but I couldn't hear him. In a flash, he grabbed my arm steering me away from a huge curled wave, just in time, he pushed me onto the basket floor. In that moment Nihplod was gone — the wave caught him, and threw him overboard.

Trembling, I crouched down and held my breath. I stayed like that, frozen until the storm subsided. I was tired and exhausted from clinging onto the bottom of the basket raft. There was no sign of Nihplod and before I fell into a disturbed sleep, I remembered how the day had begun, with my dog Paddy not wanting me to go. Did he have a sense of the dangers that awaited?

* * * * *

Dazzling sun-rays had found a gap between my curtains and danced across my face and pillow. I pulled the duvet over my head to block out the mischievous sun and snuggled back down to sleep. Just then my dog, Paddy, bumped hard on the door and barged in. He jumped on my bed, snuffled my hair and sat on me. Not his usual routine of waiting outside my door.

'Imogen! Are you up?' called my mum from the stairs.

'I can't. Paddy won't let me.'

'Don't be ridiculous. Come and have breakfast, before you go off kayaking with your brother.'

'Yeah. I'm off in ten, and not waiting for you again,' shouted Lowen,

I tried to push Paddy off, but he resisted by making himself heavy on me and thumped his wagging tail on my bed like a drum.

1

'Paddy! Get off!' I said irritably, while giving him a huge shove.

With a hurt expression, he slid clumsily off the bed and proceeded to lick my toes as soon as they touched the floor. Bleary-eyed, I pulled open the curtains to check the weather and, to my surprise, I saw a massive white bird fly past. It wasn't a seagull: it was much bigger. I opened the window and stuck my head out in an attempt to see where it went. There was no sign of it, only a herring gull sliding down a neighbouring roof to pull up moss from the guttering. Mum called me again, this time sounding impatient, so I left the window, pulled on my shorts and grabbed my T-shirt. In the bathroom, I gave my teeth a quick brush and headed downstairs, followed at heel by Paddy.

'There was an enormous white bird flying around,' I said to stony ears.

'Yes. Here,' said Dad, with no interest, while putting a bowl of porridge on the table for me.

'I'd prefer toast. Suppose Lowen's pigged the last piece as usual?' I said, taking a bottle of juice from the fridge.

'So what? You need to get up earlier. Anyway, I'm off,' said Lowen, picking up his paddle from the hall.

'Don't start you two. Wait for your sister,' said Mum. 'Imogen! How

2

many times do I have to tell you not to put plastic in the rubbish? Take that bottle out and put it in the recycling bag.'

I finished half a bowl of porridge, but didn't take the plastic bottle out of the bin because I wanted to catch up with Lowen, who was already out of the door. Anyway, I didn't get all the fuss about recycling.

Bye,' I called, picking up my paddle and heading to the front door to catch up with Lowen.

When I arrived at Kingsand quay, there was a huge commotion and more people there than usual. I couldn't work out what was going on. Lowen was already down on the beach. He had at least taken my kayak off the hook for me. I was pleased, because it's quite heavy and I always struggle with lifting it off the wall. One of the children, who I didn't know, was launching her kayak in the water and shouting.

'Look! Look! Quick, there they are.'

I looked to where she was pointing and just caught sight of them. Dolphins had leapt out of the water in unison and were taking a nose-dive.

'Come on Imogen,' called Lowen, looking back at me.

'Wait for me!' I pleaded, dragging my kayak heavily behind Lowen and another boy, who had reached the sea.

'Get yerself dreckly in that water, me lovely,' encouraged a rugged-faced man on the quay.

Most of the others in kayaks were already paddling frantically against the waves. Those with small sails used their paddles to gain extra speed. The children were shouting excitedly as they drew closer to the majestic pod of smiley-beaked dolphins. Their voices were carried like chimes by the wind over the sea. Two of the dolphins, enjoying their popularity, had broken away from the pod. They joined in the game by leaping high to nose-dive, disappearing... then breaking the waves minutes later, on the other side of the bay.

By the time I had launched my kayak into the water, Lowen had cleared the rocks and was heading out toward the Plymouth side of the bay. I moved my paddle competently. Twisting it in my hands, pushing the water to one side, then the other, making sure I didn't let my kayak lie side on against the waves. The sea lapped at the fibreglass kayak, while moving swiftly out into the bay. My shorts and T-shirt were drenched in cold salty water, thrown up by my determined paddling. I had my sights on the two dolphins and thought I knew where they would pop up next.

'Lowen, you're going the wrong way,' I shouted. 'This way, they'll come up by Edgcumbe rocks.' But Lowen couldn't hear me. He and the others were heading in another direction. In my determination to prove I was right, I had paddled unthinkingly out of the bay and beyond the sight of Kingsand quay.

* * * * *

I was eleven years old then, and my brother Lowen was thirteen. We tolerated each other in a competitive sort of way. Normally, I would have been pleased at him getting into trouble, but that day when he returned home without me, I wished more than anything that he had been with me.

I was right though, the others had gone in the wrong direction. The two dolphins popped up almost within a paddle-length of my kayak. I was so excited that for a moment I forgot to breathe in case they vanished. One of the dolphins looked straight at me and opened its beak and made a little chuckle... Oh, I can't tell you how brilliant that was, I laughed along with it, and then they were gone.

I stopped paddling to look for them, and there they were again, leaping out of the sea in unison, not too far from the coastline but going towards Rame Head. So I started paddling as fast as I could. Then they leapt again and one - I'm pretty sure it was the one that had looked at me - showed off by doing a half-twist in the air.

I can't quite remember when I realised I had lost the others. I was so caught in the moment of dolphin playtime that distance had been left

4

behind. Funny, I don't usually take risks, but I wasn't scared of being on my own: well, not until I lost sight of the dolphins. I had followed them for several leaps, I'm not sure how many — obviously more than I realised. I thought I had followed the coastline and was near Whitsand Bay, but then I scanned the sea to its horizon and saw neither dolphins nor land. In fact, at this point I had totally gone off the dolphins and was wishing I had followed Lowen and the others.

My stomach lurched and I felt that prickly sensation when you feel unnerved. I didn't understand how I could have gone that far out. My breathing quickened and the paddle started to feel heavy. I was sitting on the vast sea alone, in a single fibreglass kayak. I tried to talk to myself, to quieten my breathing and to decide which direction to paddle. It wasn't as simple as turning my kayak round because I wasn't sure which way was back towards Kingsand, nor was it obvious by the waves — you think waves just go in the direction of the shore, but they don't. I remembered what my dad had told me and Lowen several times over: 'Always hold on to your paddle, no matter what happens, because you can hold your paddle up to be seen if you ever need to be rescued.' Of course, I thought, they would rescue me if I couldn't find my way back to the shore... 'Don't panic Imogen,' I told myself... 'Don't panic'. Well, I did panic, but not until it started to rain: not hard, but enough to make my hair wet and dripping down my neck. I was trying not to hold my breath — something I did when I got scared. The wind got stronger and although I had been paddling for what seemed like ages, there was still no sign of land or the familiar chapel, which looked like a dark cherry on a cake at the top of Rame Head. I was hungry too. By now it was time for our tea and my best friend Katy was coming round with her iPad — I wasn't allowed one until I reached twelve. I never understood why — it would be outdated technology by then.

The sun was still there somewhere behind a cloud, so that helped when it peeked through a couple of times, to warm me and bring a faint rainbow. It was difficult to keep my mind on other things and I was soon back to thinking what I would do if it got dark and I still wasn't rescued. Then, oh, just then, as I was thinking bleak thoughts and feeling scared, I saw it... A helicopter... I jumped up and nearly toppled over so sat down again quickly, steadying my kayak and then holding up my paddle. 'Here, over HERE... Here I am!' I shouted waving my paddle, being careful not to drop it. The helicopter wasn't close but it looked like it was getting closer. Then it turned and circled in another direction. That's when I started to cry. Distracted by my tears I let go of the paddle. As it slid off the kayak, a translucent white gloved wave came and snatched it. I stretched out my arm in an attempt to grab the paddle, but with that movement I didn't think of the consequences and let my kayak turn side on to the waves. It happened so fast — my kayak kicked against the wave and flipped me into the sea. I thrashed out, trying to grab hold of the kayak, but it slipped away from me. I started to swim towards it, then my foot got caught up in something. Looking down, I saw that tangled rope and plastic fishing line had wrapped round my left foot. I couldn't shake it off and with my attempt to free it by using my right foot, that too got caught. Unable to swim, I panicked and found myself being dragged down below the waves.

CHAPTER 2

Lowen paddled towards the shore and jumped off his kayak while talking to Jack, a friend in his year at school.

'Are you going up to Maker later?' asked Jack. My dad is playing guitar and I think Haunt the Woods and the Trees may turn up.'

No, I have to stay in. We're going roller-boarding at Edgcumbe tomorrow and I have to take my pesky sister.'

'Hey, Lowen,' called another friend from the quay steps... 'Brilliant wasn't it? See you tomorrow.'

Lowen dragged his kayak over the stones to the harbour wall and attached it to a hook. He noticed Imogen's kayak hook and looked around. He spotted one of Imogen's friends...

'Oi, P,' he shouted, 'have you seen Imogen?'

'No. I loved the dolphins, didn't you Lowen?'

'Yeah, great.'

'Fancy an ice-cream?' called Jack from the quay.

'No, I've got to find Imogen... Will you text me if you see her?'

'Sure.'

Lowen walked round into West Street and knocked on Katy's door. Mrs James opened it.

'Hello Lowen, come in. Look at you, you're soaked, been kayaking?'

'Yes,' replied Lowen dolefully. 'Is Imogen here?'

'No, Katy left to go round to yours for tea, only five minutes ago.'

'OK,' he said. 'No, I won't come in: better get home.'

'Yes, you'd better get out of those wet clothes. See you, bye.'

Lowen went back to the quay, picked up his paddle and took one last look round the bay and out to sea before heading home. He walked up the cobbled street, holding his paddle in one hand, the other fist clenched deep in his pocket. When he arrived at his door it was the first time he noticed the dirty brass door knocker. It was a dolphin.

'Ah, here they are,' called Lowen's mum cheerfully from the kitchen, on hearing the front door rattle open, 'just in time for tea, and Katy's here already.'

Lowen left the paddle in the porch and walked heavily into the kitchen.

'Hi Lowen,' she said, wiping her hands on her linen apron and bending enough to allow a kiss on the cheek. 'Imogen,' she called, 'come and give your mum a kiss.'

'She's not here.' said Lowen in a quieter voice than normal.

'You didn't leave her struggling to hook her kayak up did you?'

'No,' he replied in a slightly indignant tone, 'no, she's not there.'

'What do you mean, not there? You went kayaking together didn't you?'

'Yes, but when I got back she wasn't there.'

'Is her kayak on the hook or on the beach?' she asked in a concerned voice, taking off her apron.

'No. And I've looked everywhere for her, I thought she'd come home.'

'You were supposed to wait for her.'

'I did, but she's so slow and there were dolphins in the bay.'

'Oh, Lowen,' she said irritably, 'stay here and keep Katy company, and get out of those wet shorts.'

She picked up her mobile phone, 'Hi, Helen, so glad you're home. Would you pop round and keep an eye on Lowen and Katy for me? Thank you… Erm, well not really. Imogen hasn't come home after kayaking. Yes, I'm sure she's OK, but I'll notify the coast guard just in case. Any idea what the number is at Rame Head?… yes, or the emergency services. See you in a minute. Thanks again, Helen.'

She rummaged through some papers looking for the local directory, before picking up the phone and dialling 999. She felt irritated by all the questioning, having to give details of who she was, where and when she last saw Imogen... 'I'm sorry if this sounds rude, but I've answered enough questions, can you just put me through to the coastguard at Rame Head pleease!...Yes, if you say this is important, but my eleven-year old child

8

is probably in trouble in her kayak out at sea!' As she voiced her fear she suddenly realised this was more than likely and she found it hard to hold back the tears. In a shaky voice, she thanked the operator, who was trying to console her by saying he had already contacted the coastguard and alerted other emergency services while they were speaking.

Helen arrived when Kim was speaking to the coastguard and put a comforting hand on Kim's shoulder. 'Don't worry, Mrs. Trevelyan,' the Coastguard was saying, 'we have most of the details and if she's out there, we'll find her. The alert is out, we have powerful telescopes up here and the helicopter is taking off as we speak. Now can you ask your son Lowen to try to remember as much detail as he can?'

Lowen came to the phone with watery eyes and spoke to the coastguard.

Sorry,' he said, 'I didn't see which way she went out of the bay but it must have been toward you at Rame... I think Mum told you what she was wearing... no, she didn't take anything off.'

Kim gave Lowen a kiss on the cheek and ruffled his hair before leaving the house. She asked Helen to phone Heath, her partner at the boatyard, to tell him what was happening, and that he should come home.

'I'm going down to the Quay and will ask Dave if he'll take me out in his boat. Bye.'

Katy was crying now and Helen put her arms round her and Lowen.

They'll find her,' she said softly.

CHAPTER 3

For once, my habit of holding my breath when I got scared was a good thing. My record was one minute ten seconds. That wasn't long to get my legs untangled from rope and plastic fishing line. Try not to panic, I told myself, while I wiggled my toes round a piece of rope and tried pulling it away. I was fighting against the current of the water which was twisting it round my foot faster than I could loosen it. If I could only get one foot free, I thought as I used my arms to push up against the water in an attempt to surface. As I slowly let small amounts of air out, I was beginning to despair, when I suddenly felt something tugging at the rope and plastic line. I didn't dare look down to see what it was. Then, like magic, my feet were free and I whooshed to the surface, with legs frantically kicking. I took a grateful lungful of air before looking to see who my rescuer was. To my surprise I was being nudged and clicked at by a dolphin. I thought it must have been one of the dolphins I had been following, so felt it wasn't a stranger. Without thinking I put my arms round it to hold myself up. It didn't seem to mind and it kept still and just looked at me with a smiley eye. I was shivering with cold and shock from almost drowning; this dolphin was a comfort to hold on to. It took a few minutes for me to calm myself and to think straight. Still holding on to the dolphin, I looked around for my kayak and there it was, just a couple of metres away, bobbing on the waves as if nothing had happened. I could just about hear a helicopter, but only faintly — it sounded a long way away. I was just thinking of letting go of the dolphin to swim to my kayak, when a thought that wasn't mine popped into my head.

'Do you want an adventure?'

I thought the shock of nearly drowning, or water in my ears, was making me hear voices. But the same silent question came again.

'Do you want an adventure or not?'

I looked hard at the dolphin and it opened its beak and made a

clicking sound at me. Then a thought came like conversation.

'Yes. It is me talking to you.'

It was, believe me, that was dolphin talk, it talked inside my head. Any other time, I would have jumped at an adventure with a dolphin, but I was still feeling pretty shaken and unsure how I would get home.

'Do not worry, I will bring you back home,' said the dolphin in its thought language. 'Would you like to come with me on a voyage of discovery, today?'

I said 'no' out loud when I was really thinking 'yes.'

'Let's go then,' said the dolphin. It knew what I was thinking, not what I said.

I still wasn't sure. I knew Mum and Dad would be worried, but how often do you get a chance of an adventure with a dolphin?

'OK,' I said. 'But I mustn't be too long.'

The dolphin nodded its head again. 'You're cold.' With that thought it blew a huge bubble from its blowhole, which popped as it touched my head and sprinkled me with thousands of tiny soft bubble-beads, which crackled around me. It felt like I had been put in a big fluffy towel and warmed by a wood-burning stove.

'Climb on my back and hold on tight.'

Still holding on to its head I moved round, and as I did the dolphin immersed itself a little more into the water so it was easy for me to get on to its back. We swam to my kayak and, to my surprise, there was my paddle, lying on top of my kayak. I couldn't understand how it had got there and even more surprising, we were in sight of Rame Head.. The dolphin made a little chuckle sound and blew another two bubbles: one fell over me, the other on my kayak and paddle. I turned round to look at the kayak and paddle as we sped away — both were shimmering, then faded to a shadow and disappeared.

'Wow!' I said out loud. 'You're brilliant. How did you do that?'

Annoyingly, it didn't answer my question but did one of its chuckles and just said in its thought language to me:

'Your humans will worry more if they find your kayak and paddle and not you — they will stay invisible for a while.'

I was so caught up in the moment of adventure that I had forgotten how worried they would be, and thought I really should ask the dolphin to take me back to Kingsand.

'Tell your mother you are safe and will be home soon.'

'How?' I asked.

'Just as you are talking to me... Concentrate and think the words to her — you humans have always had the power of telepathy but rarely use it.'

That was easy for a dolphin to say, when it was almost pulling my thoughts out as fast as I thought them, but I gave it a try. I had only just finished thinking hard, 'I'm OK, Mum, don't worry. A dolphin will bring me back after our adventure,' when the dolphin took a dive. In that moment I was looking at fish and at the sun's rays lighting strands of water, forming small patches of rainbow colours. It was beautiful, I had never seen the sea from within it before. I couldn't wait to tell Katy and Lowen: they would be so jealous.

As we were gliding through the water something felt strange, and I looked down to see a huge dark grey shape a few metres below us. I sensed the dolphin was unhappy and even confused. We were being drawn towards the thing like a powerful magnet, but at the same time I knew the dolphin wanted to get away.

CHAPTER 4

This time I said it out loud instead of just thinking it, 'I'm frightened! What's that below us?'

'It's a human thing that uses sonic sound like us: this confuses us and it's piercing painfully through my brain ... I'll be alright as soon as I change direction. It sounded like a dolphin in distress and it has taken me off course.' Imogen took another look at the dark grey shape that was now more in view.

'It's a submarine!'

The dolphin blew a spurt of water from its blow hole.

'What are these submarines?'

That wasn't an easy question to answer. To a dolphin they must look like huge metallic fish. I thought for a moment and then said,

'They are underwater ships that hide from other ships and the enemy...you know, like in war.'

It sounded a bit silly but this was the best explanation I could come up with. I hoped the dolphin wasn't going to ask what war meant. Instead it just went quiet and didn't share its thoughts with me. Then almost flippantly came a thought.

'Perhaps you would explain, and ask them to use a different frequency when you get home.'

'Yes, I'll try, They probably don't realise what they're doing to you. But it's not just our navy that have submarines.' I felt like I was making an excuse for not doing anything, but I was not sure anyone would take me seriously.

Then the dolphin swam away from it as fast as it could, leaping out of the water, and nose down just under the surface to gain speed. Holding on tight to its fin, I laid my head low, as close as I could to help the dynamics. So incredibly amazing doesn't begin to describe what it felt like almost flying through the waves and skimming the surface. I had watched competent surfers on their boards down at Whitsand Bay. I guessed they must feel something similar to what I was feeling, but they only had fibreglass boards to ride on and I was riding the waves on a dolphin. It must have been the magic bubble over me that allowed me to breathe underwater, because I couldn't hold my breath for as long as the dolphin when we dived deep into the sea. I saw fish I had never seen before: one with a fat pink face and spiky back; it came and swam alongside us for a while. A shoal of pale yellow fish swept past in front of us, then turned like swallows and circled back. Octopuses and squid of all sizes swam like dancers and hid under rocks waiting for prey. We sped up to the surface and leapt out of the sea to nose-dive with barely a splash. It was brilliant, better than any waterpark ride.

Then, just ahead, I saw a small pod of dolphins that had formed a circle round one which was sinking. They were all making clicking noises, and my dolphin clicked back as we swam towards them. The dolphin in the middle was being patted with the other dolphins' tail fins, while two were pushing it with their beaks to the surface. It didn't look well — limp and not moving. Then a dolphin swam up with a lobster in its beak and placed it over the sick dolphin's blowhole...

'What's wrong with it?' I asked.

'It can't breathe and is suffocating. We're hoping the lobster can reach in and unblock its blowhole.'

I wanted to laugh because it looked such a funny sight, but it wasn't a funny situation. The lobster peered in with one of its wobbly stick eyes, then put one of its smaller pincer legs down the dolphin's blowhole, like a surgeon with a probe. Then it leaned back on its flat tail and pulled. Success came, with a whoosh of air and water spluttering out of the dolphin's blowhole, the lobster fell back, still clasping something in its small claw. Finally, the lobster let it go as it toppled off the dolphin's back. The partly round object floated past me and then I saw what it was...

'Plastic!'

14

'Is that what you call it? We call it death snot.'

'Death snot,' I repeated, without being able to stifle a laugh, when really this was nothing to laugh about.

'It is a terrible problem, not only for us dolphins but for every living thing. Many die or get sick. This must be affecting you humans too because you eat fish, and every fish now has some death snot in it.'

'Well, we do recycle,' I said weakly. 'But, we've got to do more,' I added, as I watched another clump of debris, tangled with bits of yellow plastic and straws float past.

The dolphin chuckled and gave the sick dolphin a friendly nudge with its beak. We raced each other, jumping and riding the waves, and I realised they did this for the fun of it. Swimming and playing with the dolphins was amazing! At that moment I knew this would be something I'd remember all my life.

We swam for a while with the other dolphins and a few smaller fish joined us for the ride. They swam close so they could be drawn along in the current of the dolphin's speed.

'Wow!' I said. 'Look at the fish swimming with us. Aren't they afraid you might eat them?'

'No', replied the dolphin in our thought language. 'They know when we are hungry and we do not eat these fish.'

We left the pod of dolphins, and swam so fast my hair was drawn backwards. When we dived down near the sea bed, I saw a long row of lobsters. They looked so funny, marching awkwardly along with their pincers raised above their heads, I wondered if the lobster which had helped clear the plastic out of the dolphin's blowhole was with them. After looking at other sea creatures of all sizes which lived on the coral and sea bed, the dolphin speeded up. We swam so fast everything flashed past me. It was like trying to look out of the window of an express train, but even faster than that.

'Why are we going so fast?' I asked in our thought language.

'There is something I want you to see, before taking you to our destination.'

Then we slowed, and came up just under the surface of the water. I thought we had swum into a giant soup of slimy junk, and was glad the dolphin had put a protective bubble over me. The sea was full of thousands of bits, that looked like it went on for miles. We brushed against a huge clump of rubbish. Yellow and blue tiny plastic beads all tangled up with fishing rope and plastic string, blobby sludge and some seaweed. It rode on the waves and swirled around us, smelling like dirty wet socks. The stuff looked disgusting, a bit like my dog Paddy's sick. It felt eerie and I started to hold my breath.

'I don't like it here. Let's go.'

'Not many humans see this and there are more places in our oceans that are the same. I wanted to show you, Imogen, so you understand the enormity of the problem. It is death to us and destroys food, by blocking the sun that allows plankton and algae to grow. It is also being used by a dangerous force.'

I wasn't sure why the dolphin wanted me to see the gunge, it wasn't as if I could do anything about it. This was something I found out much later.

It was too much to take in and I just wanted to get away. It wasn't anything like the brilliant sea I knew, to swim and kayak in. I was surprised to see any fish choosing to swim in it. They all looked a bit weird, and the weirdest of all were two whales, moving slowly among the debris as though they were in a trance. The whales were much bigger than my dolphin, but not as huge as ones I'd seen on TV. Neither took any notice of us, even though my dolphin was clicking at them. Then one turned to look at us and made a small haunting sound like a peacock with a sore throat. My dad used to have a pair of peacocks, but Mum didn't like the noise they made, so Dad took them off to live in a park.

'What's wrong with them?' I asked

'They have eaten too much death-snot and now cannot swim to

normal depths. The death-snot you call plastics, makes them float.'

'Why do they eat it then? That's stupid.'

'Many whales are starving and some death-snot looks like food to them.' As if to demonstrate the point, what I thought was a jellyfish floating past us, was a thin plastic bag.

We bumped into an empty oil drum, and a clump of plastic mixed with seaweed had wrapped round my foot. It was difficult for my dolphin to swim in all this junk and I was hoping it didn't open its beak and accidentally swallow any. This was more like a nightmare than an adventure and I just wanted to get away from it all. The dolphin was pretty smart at reading minds even when I wasn't trying thought language.

'Don't worry, we will go now,' it said, followed by a chuckle. It seemed to take ages to swim out of the plastic soup, but finally the last clumps of floating gunk drifted away in another direction. I felt a bit dizzy and realised I had been holding my breath for too long.

'Have you always done this 'holding breath thing' when you are frightened?'

I didn't like being questioned about it. Mum and Dad decided a long time ago to ignore me when I started doing it to get their attention. Then I couldn't stop doing it whenever something scared me or when I was upset. Lowen teased me, but none of my friends, not even my best friend Katy, asked me about holding my breath. Although I had caught them sniggering sometimes and I hated that. So someone I didn't even know asking, and it being a dolphin, made me feel embarrassed.

'No.' I replied. 'Not always.'

'We dolphins have funny habits too sometimes. One I know that likes to show off, started doing belly flops to splash us. He did it so often it became normal for him and it slowed his swimming down. The other dolphins in the pod got tired of waiting for him to catch up. He was then on his own and became very lonely. I swam with him for four moons, until he retrained his brain into thinking how to swim properly again.'

'Did the pod take him back?' I asked.

'Yes, of course.'

I don't know why, but I liked this story about the dolphin. We swam on in silence after that and I had lost all sense of time when the sea went dark and the dolphin told me not to be afraid.

CHAPTER 5

'What's happening!' I screamed, when I saw through the darkness a swirl of rainbows — as we whooshed up out of the sea. We were cloaked in a cloud of cold, dense, light grey mist. The only sound I could hear was my own breathing as we drifted, not swam, through the mist. Then I saw a faint glow of white light in the distance. We were moving slowly towards it. As we got closer the mist thinned and started to clear. That's when I saw it. A vivid green island with a small wonky castle on its hilltop. The glow was coming from the sparkly white sandy beach.

'Where are we?' I asked.

'Nettogrof,' the dolphin said with pride.

'Netter what?'

'Nettogrof,' repeated the dolphin.

I thought it was a weird name for an island, but It looked amazing and I wanted to go exploring. Then I thought there might be fierce animals or snakes on the island. That was when I really missed Lowen, I would have felt a lot safer exploring the island with him.

'You don't need to be afraid,' said the dolphin. 'There are no fierce humans or animals that would hurt you, and you will be invisible to all but me and the trees.'

The dolphin swam as close as it could to the shore, for me to get off and swim the short distance to the white sandy beach.

'Where will you be?' I asked, feeling nervous, and uncertain about leaving the safety of my new friend.

'Don't worry, I'll be here whenever you want to come back.'

'You, promise?' I said, climbing off, while still holding on to the dolphin's fin.

'Promise. This is the start of your adventure. Nettogrof will be special to you.'

I was only a few swimming strokes away from shore and couldn't wait to start exploring. I said goodbye and patted the dolphin's head. When I reached the shore I was surprised at how soft the white sand felt under my feet. Not soft like sinking soft, soft like caster sugar but slightly springy underfoot. Before walking up the beach I turned round to look for my dolphin, and to my relief it was still there. I laughed when it ducked its head and waved a tail fin at me.

'See you soon,' I shouted, 'don't go away.'

CHAPTER 6

This was the weirdest place I'd ever seen — the beach dazzled me. It sparkled bright, like powdered glass catching the sun's rays. Just ahead was a shingle path that led from the beach through vivid green bushes and thin trees to the castle. It was much warmer than at home and the heat from the sun got to work on drying my hair and clothes. I stood mesmerised for a while, looking up at the weird-looking castle and wondered what the people were like. I thought of myself as an explorer as I marched up the shingle path. I was just thinking how much Paddy, my dog, would love Netter whatever it's called, when I came across a funny little fat man with a red face and pointy beard. He was holding some sort of thin stone, like slate, which he was writing on. I went to hide behind a tree, but tripped over a shrub and fell on to the path. It was then I realised he couldn't see me, so I got up and carried on walking slowly up the path. As I got closer I could hear him.

'twegh, seyth, eth, naw, deg...' Each time he pointed his stick-type marker at something, he bobbed up on tiptoe.

He was such a comical character, I thought I'd follow him. I soon got bored because he walked and bobbed along so slowly while counting plants and trees, so I ran past him. It was really weird being invisible... How brilliant it would be if I could be invisible whenever I wanted! I stopped running and looked back. I couldn't see the dolphin any more but was sure it was still there. The funny little man hadn't got much further up the shingle pathway than when I first saw him. He was counting one of the tall thin trees, with branches that hung down like a willow, when it gave him a whack on the back of his head. I was so startled I thought I was seeing things, until the man shook his marker at the tree and gave the tree a kick. They have really weird trees here, I thought. Then I remembered what the dolphin had said and I wondered if the tree had done that for my benefit... It did make me laugh, and I'm sure I saw the tree shake its branches when it whacked him, as though it was laughing.

The shingle path led to an open field with different crops growing on each side. I recognised one that looked like corn, but the others looked strange to me. There were orange and lemon trees and cactus. I moved carefully past a cactus to pick an orange. It had very thick peel and wasn't smooth like the ones from home. I gave up trying to peel it after squeezing some of its bitter juice into my mouth. There was a bonobo up a tree collecting fruit from high branches. To my surprise when it came down with an armful, it gave four to the people waiting at the bottom and only kept two for itself.

Then I saw it: a real-life magical castle... 'Wow!' I exclaimed aloud. I was so excited. I had seen programmes on TV about castles, but most of them looked much the same. Mum told me about her travels seeing wonders of the world like the ancient city of Petra, and the Pyramids, but this had to be better than anything. It wasn't made of stone or brick. It was like massive woven flat baskets, joined together and piled high with woven stairs and open windows. Vivid, wonky, green beans had been used to decorate and form part of the little turrets. I stood looking at it, completely mesmerised, and not aware at first of a small group of people, with a goat, who had emerged from the field and were on their way to the castle. One was so close that she nearly bumped into me, as they walked past where I was standing.

'Hello,' I said.

I so wanted to speak to them, but they not only couldn't see me, they couldn't hear me either. I could hear them though, and to my surprise I could understand what they were saying.

'I'm hungry,' said a dark-haired boy, wearing only straw-coloured shorts.

'Me too,' I found myself saying, in unison with the girl I had nearly bumped into.

'Yes,' I thought, as I followed them into the castle, 'I'm hungry

and thirsty.' They were talking excitedly about how well something was growing, and laughing about someone called Etarip who had been annoying the trees by counting them every day.

'Even the goats are getting fed up with him, tapping them on the head each time he counts them. One goat has gone boss-eyed and another ate Etarip's hat in protest.'

'I've tried suggesting he counted everything only on a new moon,' added one of the girls. 'But he said he needs to keep records and daily counting was necessary. He is a funny old thing, but he did invent our sun oven.'

They all laughed in that infectious way and I found myself laughing, almost hysterically, as we walked through an arch, made up of small bendy trees. This led to a banqueting hall. In the centre was a huge woven table, laden with food and six ceramic jugs placed between platters and bowls of fruits. Most of the food looked strange to me. There were small brown flat pancakes and things of all shapes and colours. Figs I recognised and honey, the most delicious honey I had ever tasted. I was careful to take food when everyone else was engrossed with eating or talking, so they wouldn't notice. Otherwise, it would look to them like floating food that was disappearing. I greedily dipped my pancake into the bowl of thick dripping honey, making my mouth and fingers sticky. As I was trying to lick it off my fingers and round my mouth, it made me think of Paddy when I smeared Marmite on his nose and I instantly felt homesick. Surreptitiously I drank a gulp of fruit juice from the furthest jug, near the end of the table where no-one was sitting, before making my exit.

When I left the banqueting hall I heard voices. I couldn't see anyone at first, so I walked through the courtyard, round to the other side of the woven tree-like wall. The wall had bright blue berries growing on it, like those I had seen on the banqueting table. A small group of people and two bonobos were gathered in a circle looking at something a girl, around my age, was holding. It was difficult to get close enough to see what it was without barging into the circle. I still wasn't used to the fact that I was invisible to them. Whatever the thing was, it was causing a lot of debate. It was difficult to hear what they were saying, so I cautiously got closer. Just then the funny little man, Etarip, arrived, bobbing along from tiptoe to heel, counting each step. He barged his way into the group and snatched the thing from the girl.

'Etarip!' said the girl in a cross voice. 'Give me that and go back to your counting.' He looked at her with a red temper face, puffed out his cheeks and said something I couldn't understand,

'Biwoto, whiffen ballow! aso.' Or something like that. He studied the thing for a moment, then just as the girl tried to take it back, he put it in his mouth. It was then that I saw what it was — a crunched up clear plastic bag.

'Etarip!' They all shouted in unison.

I couldn't help myself, I too shouted, 'Etarip! You can't eat it. It's plastic, stupid.' Of course none of them could hear me, except maybe one girl, who turned and seemed to look straight at me. I smiled, but she just looked and turned back. I watched with frustration as the funny little man tried chewing it, his face going more red with every chew.

'Please don't try to swallow it', I said without effect. He did try, then started gagging and spluttering as he spat it out and exclaimed, 'Atikats!', before stomping off.

They all looked down at the chewed up, spit-riddled plastic. I guessed no-one fancied picking it up. Then a goat, which had been watching the scenario, stepped in casually and ate it. They all just stared at the goat which did a little bleat after swallowing it whole and looked round at them all with a look of, 'So what?' I wanted to talk to the girl, who I thought perhaps could see me, and nearly tapped her on the shoulder. Instead I walked round and stood in front of her and said, 'I'm Imogen, what's your name?' She couldn't see or hear me and looked straight through me. I felt pretty silly and was glad no-one could see that I had gone red-faced with embarrassment.

Seeing the plastic bag made me think of home. I so wanted to tell Mum and Dad about Nettogrof and the goat with the plastic bag, but knew I couldn't. No-one would believe me, not even my best friend Katy. I began to feel homesick and thought I should get back home and wondered what time it was. I looked around me and up at the castle wall, but there were no clocks or even a sun dial here. The group dispersed — I was thinking of heading back to the beach and my waiting dolphin when I heard singing: a beautiful voice backed by melodic humming. I looked around and couldn't see her at first, then I spotted a girl, not far from me. She was sitting cross-legged under one of the trees. There was a small fish laid out on a piece of cloth in front of her and she seemed to be singing to it. I couldn't see who was humming or making the shushing musical sound, but as I looked closer, I thought, 'It can't be?' The hum and music backing the girl singer was coming from the tree. The tree was tapping and rubbing its thin branches together, sounding like maracas. It was so funny, I burst out laughing. I wondered why she was singing to a fish. I walked over to where she sat and so wanted to ask her, but knew she couldn't hear me. She had long dark hair and looked a bit older than me: not much, maybe twelve or thirteen. I sat down next to her and looked at the fish. It looked like a pretty ordinary fish. It was pale yellow with red gills, about the size of a mackerel. I didn't know the song she was singing and could only catch a few words, something about the sea and the moon. Two boys walked through the courtyard and came to join her. One of them nearly sat on me, and would have if I hadn't been quick enough to move out of the way. They joined in her song. One boy had a wooden flute, the other boy sang and I hummed along too. Then something started tapping me on the shoulder! It made me jump like a grasshopper. I looked round and realised it was the tree. To my surprise it put two sticks in my hand for me to tap together. I know this was weird, but it felt natural to tap the sticks and hum along with them. When the song ended, they all looked at the fish and It was only then that I noticed they all had tears in their eyes. I thought it must have been a sad song, but couldn't work out what part the fish played. Crying over a fish? I so wanted to ask them, but made up

25

my own answer instead. They must be vegetarians or vegans, was the only explanation I could think of.

As I moved away from them and headed toward the shingle path, I wished Katy or Lowen had been with me to talk to and see this amazing place. It's funny being on your own, something I've never really done before. Not being able to talk to anyone was so difficult for me — Dad always called me a chatterbox. Chatterbox? I wondered where that word came from: perhaps it had something to do with silent movies. I thought that was something else I would check out on the Internet when I got home. At least I could talk to my dolphin, even if it was only in thought language. I wondered if anyone else had discovered this island, Netter whatever. Then for no reason, I gave a skinny-looking tree a hug and to my surprise, it crackled with electrical flashing and gave me a slight shock. I stood back and looked at it, crossly.

'That wasn't very nice,' I said looking up at it. The tree was different from any of the others and I made a mental note, to avoid any like this one if I ever came back.

I was so full to bursting with questions for the dolphin I started to run down the path to the beach. Then I stopped in my tracks when I heard a voice call,

'Hello there.'

I looked around and saw a boy of similar age to me, maybe a year or so older. He had dark, almost blue-black hair, and was wearing shorts and a baggy top. His clothes were made of what looked like a loose-weave pale yellow cotton. I thought he couldn't be talking to me as no-one could see me, but looking round, I couldn't see anyone else near us.

'Yes, you... Hello there... Wait, wait for me.'

He was talking to me, he could see me! For a moment I stood frozen like a frightened rabbit and held my breath, then let the air out with almost a splutter. I looked hard at him and frowned, trying to work out if he could really see me. Then he waved at me.

'It's all right.' he called, while walking in my direction. I moved slowly

26

off the path and hid behind a tree. The tree made a little sighing noise and stroked my hair with a thin branch. I was in high alert, so being stroked by a tree at that moment wasn't soothing. I pushed the branch away from my hair and ran as fast as I could towards the sea. To my horror, when I arrived at the shore, out of breath, I looked wildly around for my dolphin's fin and couldn't see it anywhere.

'Dolphin! Dolphin, here, I'm here, want to go back home now. Dolphin, where are you?' I shouted as I waded into the sea. I looked behind me and there was the boy walking towards me smiling and waving. Even if I could outrun him, there was no escape off the island unless my dolphin arrived.

CHAPTER 7

'It's all right. Please don't be afraid,' called the boy. 'Look. I'll wait over here. I only want to talk and get to know you. No-one has ever visited our island before.'

I was up to my waist in water, and didn't really want to go much further if my dolphin wasn't there to take me home. I stood still for a while looking hard at the open sea — the thick mist was still there so I couldn't see beyond that. There was no sign of my dolphin between the mist and gentle waves that trickled to the shore. I just wanted to get away so swam a little further out. I knew this was pointless, I couldn't swim home so I swam back, still scanning the sea.

'Dolphin!' I called weakly, one last time before turning round to look at the boy.

He was sitting under a willow tree on the edge of the beach, looking back at me. The tree seemed to be twiddling the boy's hair with one of its long thin branches, the way my mother would do to me when I sat on the floor by her feet. These trees are definitely weird, I thought as I walked out of the sea towards him. The boy jumped to his feet, smiling at me with crisp white teeth. A piece of his hair was sticking up where the tree had twirled it round. He looked friendly, and I needed someone to talk to now my dolphin had gone.

'I need to get back home,' I said when I got closer.

'I am so excited,' said the boy. 'Tell me, how did you get here and where are you from?... Or are you a sea fairy?' I thought he might be a bit bonkers if he thinks there are sea fairies.

'Cornwall,' I said, and went on to explain how I had followed the dolphins in my kayak.

He didn't know what a kayak was, and that was more difficult than you would think to describe.

'Cornwall,' he repeated in a quizzical way. 'So this Cornwall is

beyond our mist. We have a great affinity with the dolphins, they used to help us fishing, by driving shoals of fish into our nets. But why would a dolphin bring you here to Nettogrof?'

'I don't know,' I said irritably. 'Look, I have to get back home. Do you have any boats to take me? And a phone so I can call my mum and dad?'

You would think these were simple questions, wouldn't you, but not to someone who has never heard of boats or phones, let alone ever seen either. Trying to explain these things when I just wanted to be home was irritating. Then fear crept over me when I allowed the thought in that I was stuck in this strange place: Netter, whatever it's called, which has no boat to take me back home, or phone to make a call — I might be stranded here forever. When I slowly sat down on the sand and sobbed into my hands, he stopped asking questions.

'Don't cry,' he said, gently patting me on the shoulder. 'I have just finished building my raft, I can take you back to Cornwall on that. I was going to venture past the mist in search of knowledge, but you can come with me and we will go to Cornwall.'

It's funny how someone being a bit nutty can make you instantly alert, and in my case I stopped crying. I looked up at him through tear-blurred eyes. He was taking off his top and handed it to me as I stood up.

'Here,' he said, holding out his funny-looking T-shirt to me. 'You can have this, it's dry and I have more clothes in a bundle with my raft. Follow me, I'll show you.' With that he turned and started walking towards some black rocks.

I hesitated a while, holding his T-shirt away from me as though it was contaminated, but not for long — it felt so soft. I hurriedly peeled off my wet T-shirt and put his dry one on, it was light in weight and so soft. I felt instantly warm. I took one more hopeful look at the sea but my dolphin wasn't there. I couldn't believe it had abandoned me like this, but I had to think of a plan. If we weren't too far away from Kingsand, maybe a raft would get me home, or at least the helicopter might spot us.

'Wait for me,' I called, and ran after him. I climbed over the black rocks, still holding onto my wet T-shirt. He was just ahead of me and he turned to wave.

'Nearly there,' he shouted.

I caught up with him just as we reached a small cove. He had started to lift some yellow grasses and moss-looking stuff off something.

'Help me clear this off the raft,' he said. 'I needed to hide it from my uncle Etarip.'

I draped my wet T-shirt over a rock, to dry in the sun, and helped clear the raft of its camouflage.

'Etarip! I exclaimed. 'That funny little man who ate plastic?'

'Plastic? What is plastic?'

I was about to try explaining what plastic was, but thought this might take too long and I really wanted to get back home.

'Where are we?' I asked.

'Here,' he replied. 'Nettogrof.'

'Yes, but where is Nettogrof?'

'Here,' he repeated. I could tell this was going nowhere and wasn't sure if he was just trying to be funny or didn't know where we were. I just hoped he knew how to get to Cornwall. Then we both got caught up with his excitement of revealing the raft.

'Look! It has taken me over 12 moons to build it and, over here is the mast and sail,' he said, unfolding some fabric not much thicker than his T-shirt.

The raft looked a total mess. I was expecting to see logs neatly roped together, but this looked like a version of their castle, it was a big woven basket with stuff growing out of it. I felt a sob about to bubble up, but instead I laughed. The basket-type raft made me remember a book my grandmother gave me when I was little, called The Owl and the Pussy-Cat. He started laughing too, and our laugher encouraged each other to laugh more, until I'd forgotten what I was laughing about.

'We can go to Cornwall soon if you like,' he said looking at me seriously. 'I had planned to sail off today. You can help me to find out what

30

is happening to the fish. See, here I have food and juice of fruit and if we run out we can eat this.' He pulled a piece of green weed from the raft and popped some in his mouth, while holding out a piece for me.

'Yuck, no thanks,' I said. 'I'm not that hungry.'

I was so caught up with the idea of getting back home that I agreed to board his organic raft. Besides, what else could I do? No-one was going to find me here. I wanted to ask him about the girl singing to the fish, but thought this could wait until we were on our way.

'OK, let's go,' he said cheerfully.

We had dragged the basket-raft down the beach and I helped him attach the raft and sail. The shallow basket-shaped raft was lighter than I expected and floated like a rubber ball. I couldn't wait to get in and try it out. There were two paddles, made of what looked like giant bamboo, which had been squashed and beaten to make a flat paddle at one end. We took one each and paddled out toward the mist. This reminded me of my kayak and I felt really happy. It was only when we were paddling through the thick mist that a prickly feeling crept over me and I suddenly felt panicky.

'Where did you say Nettogrof is?' I asked in a suspicious voice.

'Somewhere in this Indian Ocean, I think,' he replied cheerfully while concentrating on paddling. 'We can raise the sail when we get through the mist. I feel so exhilarated, I have never been beyond the mist before.'

I stopped paddling and was speechless for a moment while I played back what he had just said.

'You idiot!' I yelled. 'Have you totally lost it? Turn this thing round. This place isn't even in the same sea as Cornwall.'

I could have ranted on for ages: fear had been replaced with fury, not just with him but with myself. Why had I been so stupid, to sail off in a floating basket with a boy who thinks knowledge is a thing hiding in the sea?

CHAPTER 8

We had just come out on the other side of the mist, where the waves and the wind were stronger. He stopped paddling too and looked at me with such a hurt look, like my dog Paddy would look at me when I told him off. 'Bad Paddy!' I would say when he stole part of my breakfast off my plate, and he would hang his head, looking up at me with sorrowful eyes, and I'd end up giving him another small piece of bacon.

'Please let's go on, I am sure we will find your island, Cornwall,' the boy said in a humble but confident voice. 'It cannot be so far away if the dolphin brought you here this same day.'

That was difficult to argue. The dolphin had brought me here and it didn't seem to have taken that long, maybe not even an hour, I wasn't sure. Funny how it's hard to guess the time by events, especially when you're having fun. The sun was still in the sky, but it was lower. I was rubbish at geography but I knew enough to know the Indian Ocean must be near India and that's miles away.

'Cornwall isn't an island, stupid,' I said unkindly, and immediately wished I hadn't. 'I'm sorry. I just want to get home and I can't see it happening in this thing, but we may find somewhere that has a phone and proper boats.'

He jumped to his feet beaming at me, with a white-toothed smile that stretched the width of his face.

'You won't regret it,' he said. 'Come, help me pull the sail up, we will go fast with this strong wind.'

We talked while we ate some fruit and more of those flat bread things. He looked wide-eyed when I tried to explain about cars, and how phones worked, and I realised I didn't really understand how phones worked either. Neither of us could pronounce the other's name. We fell about laughing in the floating basket trying to say Nihplod — that was his name — and he pronounced Imogen like he had a cold, Imohen.

He told me his uncle Etarip was not his real uncle. His grandfather found him washed up on the beach and barely alive. He was not more than a small cactus high but he punched and kicked my grandfather when he recovered.

'Etarip was only a boy then, not much older than I am now. My father was pleased at first to have a brother, but Etarip has always been a strange person and not much fun.'

I found out that neither of Nihplod's parents were alive.

'My mother died not long after I was born and my father died with others in the fish poison plague over 15 moons ago. Fish were plentiful and an important part of our diet but now we can't eat them.'

It made me think of death snot but I decided not to confuse things by telling him what I had learnt from my journey here with the dolphin. Besides we still eat fish at home and don't die.

CHAPTER 9

I was listening intently to Nihplod telling me about the legend of Nettogrof. He had got to the part about how their tribe was being attacked by a hostile tribe wanting to kill them and take their land, when something started pushing our basket-raft sideways. Then we started spinning round, first one way then the other. I was about to start screaming when it suddenly stopped. We were sitting at opposite ends of the basket-raft, facing each other and hanging on to the side. I thought my eyes must be as big and startled as Nihplod's as we looked at each other. I realised I had been holding my breath, and blew out the air and just as I did, I felt something slimy touch my arm. That was it. That's when I started screaming, in a pitch so high I didn't know it was possible. I whipped my arm away from the side of the raft in a flash, shaking my arm to rid it of the invisible slime which had slithered away. Terrified, I looked over at Nihplod with clenched teeth. I mumbled, 'Help.'

He was just sitting there, looking back as calmly as Paddy by the fireside.

'It's alright Imogen,' he said. 'It's only an octopus being playful.'

There were three long, dirty, pink arms — two were holding on to the side of the raft as if to steady it, and the other was tapping Nihplod on his shoulder. Then its bulbous head emerged between its own legs and the octopus rolled back its eyes. I felt another scream waiting to fall out, but something in Nihplod's look made me calm down and I let my breath out with a long hurr!

'I think it's trying to tell us something,' said Nihplod. 'I haven't communicated with an octopus before, so I need to concentrate. Are you less fearful now?'

I just nodded and watched, feeling repulsed, as Nihplod touched heads with the octopus. They were like that, with their heads together

34

for what seemed ages, but was probably less than a minute. When they drew apart I realised I had been holding my breath again and my ears crackled with little pops under the strain. The octopus vanished with a splash, sending tiny drops of water over us in a spray.

CHAPTER 10

Nihplod looked up at the sky and I followed his gaze. There was a big white bird flying overhead, like the bird I had seen at home when I drew back the curtains. It was much bigger than a seagull and looking majestic, with its wings spread to ride the breeze. I felt uneasy when Nihplod's eyes dropped down and he looked at me — the carefree sparkle in his eyes had been replaced with an adult look of concern.

'What?' I asked.

'The octopus came to warn us of an angry storm coming and there is trouble in the seas. It said that we need to turn back from the sun and follow the albatross to get to the nearest land.'

'Wow! That's what it is, an albatross', I thought, not properly taking in the implications of the pending storm.

'So the albatross is going to lead us to land?' I asked. 'How cool is that!'

'Yes,' said Nihplod firmly. We used our paddles to turn our raft.

'We should keep paddling to help the wind take us,' said Nihplod, in a commanding voice I hadn't heard him use before.

The sun was getting lower, nearer to the sea. The sky was still clear, all but a few light grey clouds, which floated quickly by as if in a hurry to get somewhere. The albatross held its head straight and moved its giant wings majestically, waving in the air. We followed in its direction, in our scruffy edible basket-raft. Oh how I wished that Mum, Dad, Lowen and Katy could see me... They're never going to believe this, I thought dreamily, in happy ignorance of the dramatic changes soon to hit us.

CHAPTER 11

My arms were beginning to ache with paddling, so I stopped for a while to watch the sun getting closer to the edge of the sea. Then I saw, in the distance, what looked like a heavy dark blanket, starting to be pulled over the sky by invisible ropes. It was coming closer at an alarming speed and I saw that Nihplod was watching it fearfully too. The warm breeze had turned to a chilling wind and I shuddered under its icy breath, as the first slash of rain hit my face. The sail had caught the heavy wind and it billowed out like a frightened toad.

'Hang on tight,' called Niphlod, as our small lightweight craft raced over the fast-growing waves.

The rain fell on us in bucket-loads, instantly soaking us, and the sky broke into crashing bangs and crackling lightning. Nihplod was shouting something to me but I couldn't hear him.

'What?' I called.

He was gesturing with an outstretched flat hand, but I didn't understand what he wanted me to do. I thought of going to sit next to him so I could hear what he was saying. I also needed a reassuring arm around me. As I tried to stand up I was wishing he was Lowen.

'Noo!' I heard Nihplod shout as he lunged himself towards me.

In that second a huge wave tossed our basket like a rubber ball, throwing us to another wave which caught us and threw our basket back. In the dizzy confusion I didn't see what happened but Nihplod had disappeared. I lay as flat as I could on the bottom of the basket-raft, clutching on to its weave with the tips of my fingers. The waves crashed over me and thankfully drained almost as fast through the porous raft as quickly as it was filling with water. So, as ridiculous as it looked, the basket-raft was better than any boat, which would have filled and sunk like a stone. My only comforting thought was hoping Nihplod was hanging on to the raft on the other side, but really, I knew this was unlikely and

I didn't dare move to try and look. You would think I'd be screaming, but I wasn't. It's funny, how, when you are on your own, in real danger, your mind sharpens. Although my heart was thumping in my ears, I surprised myself with my clear survival instinct. I realised this was what Nihplod was trying to tell me — to lie flat on the bottom. The sun had long disappeared and the storm went on for what seemed like hours. I was feeling very weak. My fingers were numb with cold and wouldn't straighten, from hanging on to the raft for so long. The noise of the storm was fading: like a gang of hooligans, it was leaving to go and menace someone else.

'Nihplod,' I called weakly, getting to my knees and peering over the edge of the raft while holding on. I looked hard into the sea, and felt all round the outside of the basket-raft, which was squishy to the touch, but there was no sign of him.

'NIHPLOD!'

The rain had stopped and the moon had taken its place in the sky, giving enough light to see that the albatross had also disappeared. I crawled on my hands and knees, checking the basket-raft for any damage. Surprisingly, although it looked like a straw hat that seagulls had been pecking at, the storm had just rushed through it without tearing any bits off. The sail, however, hadn't fared so well — it had holes the size of a football, and it drooped like a Cinderella rag dress. The remains of our food had been thrown out, but there was always the weed, and there was one paddle left. I pulled off a bit of the weed and chewed. It tasted salty but I didn't care: it was a small comfort. The gentle rolling sea rocked the basket and although I was trying hard to keep awake and think what I should do, exhaustion and sleep were stronger than my fear. I curled up on the bottom of the raft, holding my knees close to my chest and drifted off into sleep.

CHAPTER 12

Meanwhile, back in Kingsand Kim had gone out with Dave in his boat, in the hope that they would find Imogen. Looking at the vast open sea, Kim's heart felt heavy. Dave's boat was so much bigger than Imogen's single kayak and even his boat felt dwarfed and vulnerable by the enormity of the ocean. It was while they were following the coastline, that Imogen's voice came into Kim's head as clearly as if she was speaking to her.

'I'm OK, Mum, don't worry. I'm just going on an adventure with a dolphin and will be home soon.'

'OK, darling,' said Kim instinctively, which startled Dave.

'What's that?' he said.

'Oh. Nothing. I was thinking of Imogen.'

Kim didn't want to tell Dave, so she just asked if he would turn back to Kingsand.

'You know, Dave, I think perhaps it may be better to wait for news at home.'

'Sure thing. Whatever you think's best,' said Dave, turning the boat round.

Heath and Lowen had come down to the quay to wait for Kim. When she joined them, they had a group hug before heading up the stone steps and back home. Heath spoke quietly to Kim so Lowen wouldn't hear,

'Helen said the coastguard can't see any sign of her or her kayak. It's a bit odd, don't you think?'

Kim took a short breath, 'Yes, but something weird has happened. Erm... I'm sure she's alright.'

'What do you mean?' asked Heath, looking puzzled.

Kim replied in a quiet voice, 'I think we should go home and wait and I'll tell you there.'

'What are you talking about?' asked Lowen, feeling left out.

'Nothing much, only that we're sure the coastguard will find her,' said Heath putting an arm round Lowen's shoulder.

When they arrived home Kim took Heath's hand and led him into the garden.

'Tell me,' Heath said looking intently into her eyes, 'What weird thing happened?'

'You're going to think me nuts, or that it's just wishful thinking, and maybe that's it.'

'What? Tell me.'

'Well, this very powerful thought came to me from Imogen. She was telling me that she was OK and that a dolphin would bring her back after an adventure. Don't look at me like that, I told you it was strange. But, seriously, I immediately felt calm and I asked Dave to turn the boat around.'

CHAPTER 13

Heath gave Kim a lopsided grin.

'I haven't lost my marbles!' she said indignantly, pulling away from him. 'Why would that thought so strongly come into my mind? I heard it in Imogen's voice... It, it could be telepathy,' she said cautiously. 'Of course I was frantic with worry and still am in a way, but honestly Heath, I somehow know she's alright and will be home soon.'

'OK, darling.. Oh,' he sighed, 'I do hope you're right, because there's no sign of her kayak.' They put their arms round each other and hugged tightly before walking back into the house.

'Erm, I don't think you should mention this to the coastguard or anyone just yet... What do you think?'

'No. I won't, don't worry. I'd like to tell Lowen, he's so distraught and blaming himself, it may comfort him.' Heath agreed.

They walked into the open kitchen, where Helen was making everyone tea. Lowen was talking to one of his friends on his mobile phone, while pacing up and down the hallway.

'Tea?' asked Helen.

Heath nodded and Kim said, 'Yes please.'

Helen poured tea from a large pot and handed Heath a cup. His eyes filled with tears at this small kindness, as he took the cup unsteadily in his hand. By now, other friends and neighbours had come to give their support and the house hummed with quietened voices. Lowen had finished talking on his mobile and followed Kim out to the garden.

'That sounds totally bonkers mum!' he protested, after Kim had explained her telepathic moment.

'I know it sounds a bit nuts..'

'Just a bit,' he said, interrupting Kim. 'You're only saying this to make me feel better... I, I should have waited for her,' he said, bursting into tears, and burying his face into his mother's shoulder while she held him tight.

'It's not your fault Lowen,' she whispered softly into his ear. 'Imogen is very wilful and she would have gone her own way, even if you had waited for her... When has she ever done what you tell her? I know this does seem incredible, but there are lots of stories about people having telepathic experiences, so it's possible isn't it?'

Lowen nodded into her shoulder and let go to wipe his eyes.

'I guess so,' he said, 'but I still think you've lost it.'

'Oh, we're all a bit nuts at times. Come on you, let's go and rescue your father from Mrs Kindle.'

Kim had seen Mrs Kindle, one of their neighbours, through the French doors. She had pinned Heath down, getting him to sit next to her and no doubt wanting every detail so she could be first in the village with the latest gossip. As Kim approached she heard Mrs Kindle saying to Heath.

'It's been over two hours now... Oh, dear, you poor things.'

'Hello Mrs Kindle, thank you for your kindness, but we're coping alright. Sorry to interrupt but I need to talk to Heath.'

'Oh, of course,' she said, only half apologetically, as Heath stood up and looked at Kim with knowing gratitude.

Kim phoned the coastguard again while Heath and Lowen stood closely by her side, straining their ears to listen to what the coastguard was saying.

'Still, nothing... No, I see, only a pod of dolphins... Yes, we'll just stay by the phone. Sorry to keep bothering you. Thank you.'

When Kim hung up, Heath suggested taking their mobile phones with them and walking back down to the harbour.

'I can't bear just hanging round here and not doing anything', he said, as he caught hold of her hand.

'OK,' said Kim, ' I'll make up a sandwich to take with us first, Imogen must be starving.' Heath thought that was a bit pointless but went along with it.

'It's got so crowded in here, with half the village wandering around

42

with cups of tea,' said Heath.

'They mean well, but I wish they'd all go,' agreed Kim in a quiet voice. 'Go and find Lowen will you? We should take him with us.'

Heath left the kitchen, trying to avoid being engaged in conversation with anyone. Kim warmed up some carrot and coriander soup which she poured in a thermoflask, and wrapped up a marmite and cheese sandwich in tin foil. She asked Helen to take charge of any landline calls, and to phone her mobile if the coastguard or police phoned.

'We're just going down to the harbour for a while. I'd really like to be there when they bring her back.'

'Of course you would,' said Helen, giving Kim a comforting hug. Kim went to look in the living room, then the garden, where she found it hard to extricate herself from a well-meaning friend.

'Have you seen Heath and Lowen?' Kim asked a tall thin man who was standing holding a mug of tea in the hallway.

'I haven't seen Lowen, but saw Heath go in the kitchen a minute ago.' She thanked him and went into the kitchen.

'Let's go', said Kim impatiently, 'Where's Lowen?'

'I don't know. I've tried his phone and looked everywhere for him, his bedroom, garden... He's not here or picking up on his phone.'

'Oh no!', said Kim in a slightly exasperated tone, 'What's that silly boy up to? We can't lose them both.'

She banged the flask down on the kitchen table and let the sandwich drop on the floor as she started to sob uncontrollably.

CHAPTER 14

Lowen

Lowen's mobile phone was ringing. He took it out of the pocket of his jeans — Dad's name showed on the screen. 'I'm not answering,' he said to himself, and let it go into voicemail. He had taken his paddle from the hallway, jumped on his bicycle and was heading back down to Kingsand Quay. As Lowen dragged his kayak down the beach, Dave spotted him and called.

'Hey Lowen. You OK? What you doing?'

'It's OK, Dave. Not going far.'

'Hang on. I'll take you in my boat.'

'No. You're alright. Prefer to go it alone.'

'You be safe now,' shouted Dave, as Lowen launched his kayak into the sea, digging his paddle into the water and pulling back with all his force. He ploughed through the sea at a speed he had never reached before.

It wasn't long before he was in sight of the rocks at Rame Head. Only then did he slow his determined paddling, to scan the sea for his sister and her kayak. He stopped paddling and shouted over the gentle draw of the sea.

'IM! IMOGEN! Where the hell are you!'

All he could see were two sailing boats and a ferry heading towards France — no sign of Imogen. Lowen sighed heavily and felt defeated. He had such a strong feeling that he would find her by the rocks at Rame Head. Trying to decide whether to go back to Kingsand or go on round the headland to Whitsand Bay, he gazed at the cluster of rocks. In his stillness he saw a seal: first its head, then, pushing itself up with its flippers, it bounced out of the water and flopped onto a rock. Then came another seal, and another, until Lowen could see at least four seals all jostling for a space on the rocks.

'Awesome,' Lowen said out loud. He took his phone out from his

44

pocket and took a photo. What he saw next made him think the sunlight flickering on the sea by the rocks was playing tricks on his vision. He closed his eyes tight then looked again. No, it was still there. Something blue-black, similar to the seals but much bigger. He took another photo and noticed Mum had called. He hesitated, but decided not to call yet and put his phone back in his pocket. Just then came a faint sound of an instrument which sounded like a harp, mixed with the lapping of the waves, then someone singing. It didn't sound like English or any song he had heard before: the voice drifted in and out of his ears with the sound of the waves. ... We travel the seas, musicians are we (Spanish) ... He sat bolt upright in his kayak, trying to get a better look at the thing he was seeing. He couldn't work out if the music and song was coming from the thing on the rocks. Tentatively, he used his paddle to move nearer, but as he did, one of the seals turned and looked in his direction and swiftly slid off the rock into the sea. Then another followed, and another, until there was just one seal left with the dark thing. He still couldn't make out what it was. The thing seemed to be doing something to the seal — it was pulling at something round its neck. Then, in a flash, the seal was free and it wobbled and bounced off the rock, with a plop, into the sea. It was then, the thing turned round to look at Lowen. He was so astonished, he let his kayak turn side-on to the waves and he toppled over into the sea. Still holding his paddle, he managed to grab hold of the kayak and from that position, in the water, he gazed mesmerised at the most beautiful woman he had ever seen. She threw her gleaming black hair over her shoulder and laughed: not a mocking laugh, but friendly as if they were sharing a joke. Lowen smiled and called,

'Hi.' What an idiot, he thought. Hi, who says hi to a mermaid?

'Hi,' mimicked the mermaid, with an accent, and beckoned him to join her on the rock.

Lowen smiled and waved at her before managing to pull himself up back on to his kayak. He felt his face flush with colour as he paddled slowly towards the rock. As if to help him feel more at ease, the mermaid picked up her small harp and sang to him. He didn't understand a word but he didn't care: it sounded awesome. Lowen wedged his kayak between two rocks before joining the mermaid on her rock. She smiled at him with her deep blue eyes and carried on singing.

'That's such a cool tune,' said Lowen. 'I'd love to learn how to play it.'

With that, as if by magic, an instrument appeared in his hands. It wasn't a guitar, not like he was used to playing, but more like a ukulele, with six silver strings instead of four. Although smaller than his guitar, it was similar and he managed to pick up the set quite quickly. This was brilliant, he thought.

'I've got to play this up at Maker, it'll blow them away,' he said, turning to look at the mermaid. She just smiled at him and carried on singing. Lowen was so engrossed with playing this new instrument, his mind had floated away from thoughts of home and finding Imogen. Then, as if breaking free from a trance, he stopped playing and turned to the mermaid.

'I have to go,' he said. 'My sister, Im, have to find her.'

He offered the silver-stringed instrument back to the mermaid, but she shook her head.

''Esto es un regalo,' she replied with an enchanting smile that made Lowen blush.

'Urm... I don't understand,' he said. 'Do you mean,' pointing to the instrument then at himself. 'I can keep it?'

'Si,' replied the mermaid.

That he understood and beamed a boyish lopsided grin at her.

'Wow! That's so cool, thanks, um.. Gracie or whatever.'

Then a thought came to him in a female voice.

'Do not worry, your sister is safe. She is with a friend of the ocean.'

Lowen turned to the mermaid with a puzzled look.

'Si. Soy yo.'

'It's you talking in my head, in English? How? No forget it. I must go.'

Holding on to the instrument, he picked up his paddle and turned to

46

climb back on to his kayak. Just as Lowen was about to step off the rock, the mermaid shouted, 'Lowen, parate! Peligro.'

He soon understood what she meant when a giant tentacle sprung from the sea and lashed at him. The mermaid moved, as quickly as the wind, to pull him back onto the larger rock out of reach. Then it lashed at Lowen again and the mermaid grabbed the tentacle before it struck. She dived into the sea, still holding on to the giant octopus. Lowen wanted to help, but didn't know what he could do. He pulled his phone from his pocket, hoping it really was waterproof. It seemed OK.

'Dad!' he shouted down the phone. 'Get help quick. A giant octopus has got the mermaid.'

There was a silence, before his dad replied.

'If this is some kind of joke to get you off the hook, forget it. Where the hell are you?'

CHAPTER 15

Imogen

It was seagulls that woke me, caw, cawing and laughing just over my head. For a moment I thought I was back home in bed, with the window open and being greeted by seagulls on our neighbour's roof.

'Nihplod!' I called, remembering him being thrown to the waves by the storm and disappearing.

I hated the thought of him being swallowed up by the dark angry sea. My only comforting thought was the hope that he had been picked up by a passing ship. This adventure had turned into a nightmare and I felt grumpy with the dolphin for taking me to Nettogrof.

My mouth felt dry, and I would have given anything for a hot bowl of porridge, that I'd usually push away ungratefully, in favour of whatever Lowen was having for breakfast. Warm toast dripping with butter, marmite and home-made peanut butter was his favourite. My stomach groaned at the thought of such luxury, as I looked grumpily at the salty weed. I stuffed a bit of it in my mouth and chewed while picking up the paddle.

'Which way?' I said out loud.

Wearily, I looked up to see if the albatross had come back, but there was no sign of it. The seagulls that had swept down near me had moved on, after realising it wasn't a fishing boat that might have easy pickings of fish guts for them to eat. Then I saw the majestic white wings. The albatross had returned. I jumped up and waved my arm, not my paddle this time.

'Hello, Albatross,' I called excitedly, as though it was a familiar face. 'I'm here ready to follow you.'

My arms felt heavy and ached when I started to pull at the water with my paddle. It was much harder to do on my own. Then I spotted a fin, not far ahead in the water. I leapt up with excitement, punching the air, as I shrieked at it.

'Dolphin! Dolphin! You've come back too.'

But as it got closer, I could see it was bigger, much bigger than my dolphin. It moved slowly with a look of purpose towards me. I caught my breath and held it, hoping that if I didn't breathe and kept very still, it wouldn't know I was there. Moving slowly through the water, it came alongside my little basket-raft. It was enormous, at least four times longer than the raft, and its sinister bulk of a dark blue grey body showed a flash of white. It came very close, so close it lightly bumped the edge of the basket. That small touch pushed the raft unsteadily, like a bully bumping you in the playground. I gasped, trying to stifle a scream. 'Oh, dolphin, please, please come quickly,' I thought hard with an intensity I never knew possible. As the giant sea monster brushed past, I blew the air out of my lungs with relief. I turned my head slowly to look where it was going and, with horror, I watched it gradually cut through the water curving its massive body round to come back. My eyes were transfixed by it. I stared wide-eyed like an unblinking owl before thinking to drop to my knees and hide in the hollow of the basket raft. I wanted to cry and

scream for help but knew it was useless. Cold sweaty beads sprung from my face as I hugged my knees tightly. I felt another bump, harder this time as it brushed against the raft.

'I'm done for,' I thought. 'Dolphin, dolphin, please make me invisible, please save me.' It bashed the raft again and showed its giant face - shiny black and white with a cold beady eye. Water poured off its head as it rose out of the water. That did it. I couldn't hold back the scream that had welled up in me, the sound from me pierced my ears and I screamed like a siren.

When I stopped screaming everything was still and I hadn't been eaten. I moved my head slowly to look up over the basket. No, the sea monster's face had gone. I crawled to the side of the basket and peered over the edge. There it was, moving slowly away, and just behind it I saw something wonderful. I rubbed my eyes to make sure. Yes!

'Ha! DOLPHIN! Dolphin. It's you.'

The little fin and small body didn't look a match for the massive orca, but there was my dolphin chasing him away.

'Yeah,' I shouted. 'Go get him.'

I was a bit disappointed because I thought the dolphin was going to bash it up with its tail, instead it just gave the orca a nudge with its beak and it looked as though they were in conversation. The dolphin stayed still, blew a little water from its blow hole, then turned toward me and the basket raft. It cut through the water with lighting speed. Watching the Ocra disappear with a boom as its massive body moved and sunk into the sea, I squealed a high pitched 'Dolphin!' As it came alongside the basket and raised its chuckling beak, looking at me with that friendly eye, I patted its head and leant over to hug it.

'Come, hop on.' It said breezily in its thought language.
I didn't need much persuading to leave the floating basket. Throwing one leg over the side I wrapped my arms round its neck and climbed on. It blew another one of those magic bubbles from its blow hole over me and we dived into the ocean.

CHAPTER 16

It was brilliant going to Nettogrof, but the storm and frightening orca had left me feeling exhausted and homesick. I was so relieved to be rescued by the dolphin who I knew would take me back to Rame Head and my waiting kayak, that for a moment I had forgotten the boy. Then, while watching an octopus glide past us like a ballet dancer, with its long arms held neatly together, I thought, 'Nihplod!'

'Dolphin, we've got to find Nihplod!'

Silence. No thought-speech came back to me at first and I started to explain who Nihplod was. Then a thought came to me, reminding me of what the dolphin had said.

'No, it's impossible... Only the trees and I can see you on Nettogrof, is what you said. Nihplod could see me.'

This dolphin is a bit weird with its magical bubble stuff, but I didn't get how it could change into a boy.

'Are you Nihplod?', I asked tentatively.

'Yes. The biggest clue was in my name. You have worked that part out. It is difficult for you humans to understand — you are not ready for the knowledge, or to travel through time. I am Nihplod, once a boy, but I decided to become more dolphin when I found the knowledge many moons ago. You crossed a time zone when you touched the special tree on your way back down the path on Nettogrof. You were destined to meet me, Nihplod, as a boy, and to meet one other.'

I was trying hard to think back to when I first saw Nihplod, and what tree he was talking about. I remembered a tree twiddling my hair, but that was after... then I remembered the skinny tree that gave me an electric shock.

'Yes, that is the tree,' said the dolphin breezily. 'It has special cosmic powers.'

So much didn't make sense. I decided to ignore the tree for now, I was more interested in Nihplod.

'How could a boy become a dolphin?' was my next question.

The dolphin went on to explain, 'When the raft was attacked by the storm and I was swept away, an enormous wave crashed down on me, then another, until I was pushed further into the sea's belly. I couldn't breathe and my lungs had started to fill with water. My head spun and I think I lost consciousness, so I am not sure how long it was before I was rescued. In that moment, when I thought I was almost dead, I was swept up by three dolphins who carried me up to breathe air. These dolphins were descendants of dolphins that had been the protectors of Nettogrof. Their ancestors created the mist to hide the island of Nettogrof from other humans in the world. The dolphins that saved me had followed the basket raft. I could now breathe and I was riding on the back of one of the dolphins, as you are now. They took me to the Well of Knowledge. It is in the deepest part of the deepest ocean and swirls like a rainbow whirlwind. In there, I travelled through time and saw the origins and destruction of everything.'

'Wow! Like Doctor Who,' I interrupted. 'That's so cool.'

Although Dr Who is only fiction, somehow time travel didn't seem so incredible. I noticed the dolphin didn't ask about Dr Who, which was just as well because I didn't fancy trying to explain. Instead of continuing the story he said.

'I can show you part of what I saw in the Well of Knowledge if you like?'

'How? Err, but I don't fancy going there.'

'No need. I can take you in thought, like a dream.'

'OK,' I said, and then in a flash I felt like I had been catapulted into another world.

It all looked a bit scary. I was in the sea but all the creatures around me looked really weird, hundreds of them, including prehistoric fish with long snouts and razor teeth. I was crawling out of the water onto the shore with giant lizards. Then there was another flash and I was round a camp fire with a group of hairy people and some small bonobos and a group of giant lizards. At first they all seemed to be working together,

making shelters from palm leaves and branches and foraging for nuts and berries. Suddenly there was a loud bang of thunder, which rang in my ears. The sky was ablaze with lightening and crackled with electricity and I was thrown by a lightening bolt into the air. When I landed everything was white and frozen and I could hear animals and humans screaming with rage and pain.

'Nihplod!' I shouted. 'Get me out of here!' I felt dizzy and the ground seemed to be sinking. I started to hold my breath, then another flash catapulted me back to the present.

'My apologies,' said Nihplod. 'It was perhaps too much to experience.'

'Yes, too much,' I said, trying to breath normally again. 'What was happening? I don't want to see, just tell me.'

'You saw early humans and dolphins emerging from the sea like giant lizards. We all lived on land then and ate only vegetation and fruits. But during the first ice-age some species turned aggressive. As humans began to evolve we knew we could no longer live on land together as friends. So the dolphins went back to live in the sea.'

'So what I heard, was that humans attacking early dolphins?'

'Yes. Food was scarce and some species grew long trunks or necks to reach fruits and leaves. Others like the bonobos were apt at climbing trees, but humans couldn't climb as well and they turned to anger and started killing.'

I thought how sad that was and was glad I didn't witness anymore in the dream. I had learnt some things about evolution, but experiencing what it felt like emerging from the sea was awesome.

I was quietly reflecting on how amazing it is that dolphins still seem to like humans and thought about stories Mum had told me of dolphins rescuing fishermen. One time they protected a family who were out swimming, from a killer shark, by forming a circle round them until the shark swam away.

'We're still friends aren't we...dolphins and us.' It was more of a statement than a question. 'Even though you live in the sea now.'

The dolphin nodded its head,

'We are still friends of humans and sometimes they join in our play, like you and your brother did. We are sad that humans have so much fear and lack of knowledge. This makes them damage each other and our oceans. I will always be your friend Imogen.'

It was a lot to take in and I was in my own thoughts for a while. The bit about damaging each other made me think of all the wars in history and those like in Syria, that are still going on. I could see why dolphins think humans... I mean some adults are weird. Everyone could do with a dip in the Well of Knowledge.

'It's brilliant that you'll always be my friend. Did you become a dolphin in the Well of Knowledge?'

Dolphin, or Nihplod, I get that now, went on to tell me that all living things are made of the same cosmic stuff. I was interested in science but hadn't done much at school, so all that he tried to explain about particles and atoms was easier to understand as just stuff.

'I had a choice to make: the transition from boy to dolphin whenever I wanted,' he said. 'It was in my name and history, my destiny. So becoming a dolphin wasn't so impossible for me and the Well of Knowledge also held a powerful magic.'

I imagined becoming a super-brain or a wizard, if I ever went to the Well of Knowledge. Then I had a sudden scary thought. What If the dolphin picked up that thought! I didn't fancy going there today.

'You are taking me back home aren't you?' The dolphin made a chuckle as it broke through the waves and surfaced to breathe.

'Yes. Do not worry, I am taking you back to your kayak. It is too soon for you to enter the Well and the guardian... well, I will not worry you with that for now. Perhaps one day you will, your adventure has already extended your knowledge.

CHAPTER 17

That's when it happened. An enormous wave, bigger than The Shard in London — it was heading straight at us.

'Hold on tight', said the dolphin, just as the wave loomed over us, poised to crash down. He took a nose dive at such incredible speed, I felt the skin tighten on my face. It must have been the wave crashing down into the sea that catapulted us off course, into what seemed like boiling water. 'Dolphin, Nihplod!' I screamed.

'Just hold on. Don't let go.' As if I would!

'What's happening?' I asked while clinging on tighter than ever.

'I am hoping it is not what I fear,' came the thought from Nihplod.

That was no comfort, he could have at least said not to worry or something. Oh, I so wanted to be home. The sea wasn't hot, but it was bubbling and swirling around us. It was as if we were stuck helplessly in a giant boiling kettle. Just as I thought it couldn't get much worse, a roar thundered round my head. It was so loud I thought my eardrums would burst. Then I saw it just ahead of us. A fanged head that looked like a cross between a lion and a seal. A ginormous octopus had one of its arms wrapped round the sea lion's neck and they thrashed at each other in battle. The sea lion bit hard down on a different tentacle and the octopus released its grip. We were stuck in the boil of their raging battle.

'Can't we get out of here?' I pleaded.

'I am trying,' said Nihplod. 'It is as I feared.'

'What are they?' I asked, while trying hard not to start holding my breath in fear.

'It is the guardian of the Well of Knowledge under attack from the Grey Force. The Grey Force wants to seal off the Well of Knowledge forever.'

We were stuck in the swell of their battle and Nihplod's efforts to swim out of it seemed feeble. Then we got caught in a sea whirlwind and started to spin. I felt dizzy and it was hard to hold on. When Nihplod's body went limp, I thought this was it: we were so close to home and I was going to die. I tightened my arms round him and thought so hard the words were bursting like balloons in my head.

'DOLPHIN! Wake up! NIHPLOD! HELP!'

Then we suddenly stopped spinning, we had dropped to the bottom of the whirlpool and fell out of it.

'There was no need to yell thought at me', said Nihplod.

'But I thought you'd fainted,' I replied calmly.

'Fainted? What is fainted?'

How could I explain what fainted meant? Even brilliant magical dolphins don't know everything.

'Like being asleep', I said.

'I was not sleeping,' replied Nihplod. 'We needed to sink down to get out of the whirlpool.'

As Nihplod, dolphin was being so chatty I thought we must be safely out of their battle, but we weren't. The tip of one of the giant octopus's arms thrashed past us and nearly hit me. I wobbled a bit and drew in a sharp breath. It didn't hit me, thanks to the magical air bubble over me, which was still intact from the battle. Nihplod reacted quickly, turning and cutting through the sea at an amazing speed, out of reach from the giant octopus. I could tell it was difficult to get away into the calm water, which was so close. Nihplod nearly made it, but we were caught in a strong current, which was pulling at us. The sea around their battle scene was sucking and spinning everything into their frenzied fight, and I could feel we were being drawn backwards.

'Dolphin, Nihplod,' I pleaded in our thought language. If we were ever going to get out of this, I needed to get used to calling my dolphin, Nihplod. Before Nihplod responded, I could see what he was looking at. Dolphins, lots of them. They were coming towards us in a line, holding each other's tail fin in their beaks, forming a chain of dolphins. It was the weirdest thing I'd ever seen, but I was so glad to see them I gave them a

56

cheer, 'Yeah!'

When the lead dolphin got to us it gently held Nihplod's tail fin in its beak. I wasn't convinced this was going to work, but it did. We slowly moved backward, it felt like being drawn out of a hurricane by an invisible hand. The suction force of the battle scene made my hair stick straight out in front of me and Nihplod's beak looked stretched. It made me think of black holes in space, where the force of gravity pulls everything into the centre. Fish that were caught in the pull dashed past us, some upside down, while others, trying frantically to swim away, were being drawn backwards. A crab bounced past us with its claws flailing, and a whole shoal of fish which looked like mackerel were being sucked nearer to the raging battle. When we finally popped out into calm waters I realised I had been holding my breath and let the air out with a deep hurr. The dolphin chain broke their hold and after lots of dolphin chatter and a few of them nudging Nihplod with their beaks, we all did some leaps and dives. It was like doing high fives after winning a game. I thought this was so amazing and Lowen was never going to believe me. I wasn't sure what had just happened. As I patted Nihplod's head and gave him a hug I asked,

'What was that? That Grey Force octopus and why does it want to close the knowledge well thing?'

'It is the Grey Force of Ignorance and it has taken power over the giant octopus to help its cause. Giant octopus are intelligent, with good humour and usually have a determined mind of their own. So to take power over it, is an achievement for the Grey Force. The Well of Knowledge is a serious threat to it. While it exists the Grey Force's power is weakened.'

'But why? What does it want?'

'It wants to take over and rule our oceans. We do not know its reason or what controls it, but we do know it is a friend of your human's death snot.'

'Death snot, plastics. How can it be a friend of plastics? Plastics aren't alive, and don't think.'

'Not friends as we are, but friends as an ally or helper. Death snot

57

is a silent killer that has invaded our oceans and poisoned us and our plants. In this way it is a powerful friend of the Grey Force. It wants us weak and as you say, stupid, to make its task easy. It is also trying to turn us against each other like you humans do with war.'

'I don't like this Grey Force whatever it is. Do you think the sea lion is winning?'

That seemed a bit lame, but I didn't know what to say. This was serious stuff that was hard to understand. I'll never look at the sea in the same way again.

'The guardian will save the Well of Knowledge from the Grey Force today, but I am sad as this is the start of a battle that should never happen and will not be easy to win.'

The other dolphins were still in the water, and quiet while Nihplod talked to me in thought language. Their silence reflected the gravity of this battle they were all involved with. Then Nihplod did a little nod of his head to them and they all clicked noisily and looked cheerful again. It's funny how I understood a dolphin's mood: they don't have obvious facial expressions like dogs and cats, they express with their whole body and tiny movements. The sea where the battle was, had stopped boiling and was calm. Somehow Nihplod knew the guardian sea lion had won the day.

We said our goodbyes and I patted each dolphin's head as they came up to me, raising their beaks. Nihplod did a final clicking noise and the pod of dolphins swam away with leaps and dives.

'Phew! I can't wait to get home. We are going now aren't we?'

'Yes. I know you feel you have had enough adventure for today,' he said and made a chuckle before taking a dive. 'You will be home very soon.'

CHAPTER 18

An enormous wave rose up from the sea forcing Lowen to jump back onto a higher rock and he nearly dropped his phone. He could hear his dad still talking...

'Just get yourself back here now! We have enough drama going on without you kicking off.'

Soaked by the spill-off from the wave, he put the phone close to his ear...

'I'm not joking Dad! Come and get me off the rock... I'm at....' Then looking at his phone he realised there were no bars and he had lost the phone signal.

'Damn it!' exclaimed Lowen, looking angrily at the phone.

Keeping one eye on the unpredictable sea, he held the phone up above his head and moved slowly round. One bar blinked up, but vanished as soon as he pressed the call button. Trying to keep calm, he took a deep breath and looked round to take stock. Remarkably his kayak was still there, wedged between two rocks. But he had dropped his paddle when the giant octopus lashed out at him, and it was caught on jagged rocks close to the sea, which looked impossible to reach. There was no sight of the instrument — an overwhelming feeling of disappointment fell over him. It wasn't as if the instrument could help him get back home, but this little bit of magic had been short-lived and he felt the loss. He checked his phone again and sat down heavily on a rock to decide what to do. The sea looked weird, mostly smooth as a pool, but only a few metres from the rocks it was bubbling like a boiling kettle. Then he noticed something beneath the waves, moving slowly in his direction. Transfixed by this menacing-looking bulk, which was still hidden and getting closer, Lowen was frozen with fear and hoped, by not moving, that whatever it was wouldn't notice him crouched down on the rock.

'Please, please go away,' he whispered, more to himself.

Then the thing rose from the sea and looked straight at him. Lowen jumped up, and, as he did, the instrument magically appeared in his hands. Although struck by fear, as he looked back at the menacing giant octopus, Lowen somehow began to play. He felt his fingers moving over the strings as though they were being guided through the chords. From the instrument flowed an enchanting melody which was having an effect on the giant octopus. The triumphant, menacing look was fading to a dazed, mesmerised stare. Its massive head moved slowly from side to side as if conducting a symphony orchestra. Lowen's heart stopped thumping like a drum in his chest, as he started to feel more in control. Just then, to his delight, the mermaid appeared. She popped up close to the giant octopus and smiled at Lowen.

'Phew! Am I glad to see you,' he said while his fingers carried on playing.

'No dejes de tocar. Don't stop playing', she said first in Spanish, then as thought language in English.

'No way', replied Lowen firmly. 'Not while that thing is still there.'

She threw her head back laughing, and patted the octopus on the top of its massive head as if it was a cute pet, like their family dog, Paddy. As she lifted her arm, Lowen noticed a wound across her back and shoulder — red raw tentacle sucker marks.

'Woo', said Lowen 'That looks nasty. You OK?'

'Ah, that is kind, but do not worry. We mermaids are made of tough stuff,' she replied in thought language.

Lowen was dying to check his phone for a signal, but didn't dare stop playing. He had taken his eyes off the head-swaying giant octopus, to look dreamily at the beautiful mermaid. He drank in her beauty, in the hope that, when he got home, he would be able to conjure her image in his mind before he slept and when he woke.

'I must take this lump away to a safe place, before the trance wears off,' said the mermaid looking playfully at Lowen.

'Urm. yeah, cool,' replied a red faced Lowen. 'How about me? Are you coming back?'

'No. There is no need, it is safe. You can go to find your sister, she is returning now.'

Lowen felt deeply disappointed and just smiled at her. He wanted to ask if he would see her again, but didn't. The mermaid dived and picked up one of the giant octopus's arms and led it away, like a puppy on a lead.

Lowen carried on playing for a while until they were out of sight. Only then did he retrieve his phone from his pocket — still no signal. He rested the instrument on the rock before looking at his kayak. To his surprise, not only was the kayak there, but his paddle was lying next to it. He looked to the jagged rocks where it had been before, and sure enough it had somehow moved.

'Mermaids are brilliant,' he said out loud to himself.

He picked up his magical instrument and, with agility, moved swiftly down on to his waiting kayak. Lowen took one last look to see if the mermaid was in sight before he pushed off. Skilfully, he used his paddle to move around the rocks until he was heading back towards Cawsand and Kingsand. Remembering what the mermaid had said about Imogen, he stopped paddling to look out across the sea, but there was no sign of her.

'Imogen!' he shouted. 'Come on Im, where are you?'

Lowen was reluctant to go home on his own. He thought, at least if he turned up with Imogen, he would be seen as a hero rather than the idiot who went missing and phoned his dad about a giant octopus and a mermaid. The thought of trying to explain that call made him feel uncomfortable — they both thought Mum had lost it about hearing Imogen speaking to her. Lowen took his phone out of his pocket — he saw he had missed calls from his dad, mum and friend, Jack. He decided not to call anyone yet: instead he shouted Imogen's name across the waves, and decided to wait a while in the hope that she would turn up. Lowen thought he might as well learn how to play his new instrument while he waited. He laid his paddle across his lap and picked up the ukulele-type instrument and started plucking at the silver strings. The sound that came from its base was amazing, and his fingers seemed to find chords and notes that he had never played before. He beamed from ear to pimple at his own musical accomplishment, and began to hum while thinking of words to fit the tune.

While carried away with the incredible instrument, Lowen was oblivious to all else. Then he suddenly became alert to something close by. He stopped playing and looked just ahead of him at something shimmering on the surface of the sea. It looked as though it was going to form into something solid, but stopped when he stopped playing. He played a few more chords and the thing continued to slowly take shape. Lowen didn't get a sense of danger, but after his experience with the giant octopus he thought he should get further away from it. So he picked up his paddle and put an extra two metres between himself and the thing. It was still shimmering in the sunlight, a bit like a mirage of water you sometime see on hot days where the road dips. Feeling confident he was far enough away to make an escape to the shore if necessary, he picked up the instrument and continued playing. The shape grew, it was quite long and thin, a bit like his kayak. Then the shimmering stopped and the thing fully showed itself.

'Yeah!' exclaimed Lowen excitedly. 'IM! It's you.'

He laid the instrument down and picked up his paddle, but as he got closer he could see clearly it was Imogen's kayak and paddle, but there was no sign of her. Lowen pulled his kayak alongside Imogen's and scanned the sea in the hope of getting sight of her.

'IMOGEN!' he shouted before slumping down further onto his kayak.

Then a thought struck him. If his new ukulele-type instrument could mesmerise a giant octopus and conjure up Imogen's kayak, then why not Imogen herself? With that thought, he continued to play while looking out across the waves to the horizon. While Lowen played, he saw a small pod of dolphins in the distance, and wondered if Imogen had been following them and fallen off her kayak. He remembered stories of fishermen being rescued at sea by dolphins and wondered if it could be true. After meeting his mermaid, Lowen was open to believing almost anything. Just as the pod of dolphins disappeared into the horizon, a single dolphin came into view. It seemed to be heading in his direction. He stopped playing to take a concentrated look. As the dolphin popped up from a dive he thought he could see another shape. Was there something, could it be? No, he thought, it's not possible.

CHAPTER 19

I could feel the sea had got colder and it wasn't long before we surfaced again. I looked up and saw land in the distance. Green and yellow splashes of colour over the fields and there it was, that familiar dark dot on Rame Head. The little ancient chapel where we sang carols at Christmas and wild ponies took shelter in storms. I was nearly home. It had been an incredible adventure with no ordinary dolphin. Nihplod, my new amazing friend. I really wanted to tell Mum, Dad and Lowen, but knew I couldn't, they would never believe me. Then another thought slowly dripped through — that weird tree. Had it really zapped me into another time in history, before Nihplod became a dolphin? It must have, if when we left Nettogrof in the basket raft, that all happened years ago.

'Erm, did you get that thought?' I asked.

'Yes,' replied Nihplod.

'Yes!' I said, 'just yes?'

'Yes,' replied Nihplod.

'Woo, that's awesome!' I said, and punched the air with excitement. 'I'm the real new Dr Who.'

I could tell by the silence that Nihplod wasn't impressed by my excitement. But then he did do a little chuckle, so I knew I hadn't seemed totally uncool.

'I still don't get it. When you rescued me from the orca as Nihplod the dolphin, what time zone was that?'

'We were between times in history. This happened when you slept in the raft. It is difficult for you humans to fully understand this. Your destiny could have gone one of two ways. Fortunately, it was to be saved.'

Well, I was glad about that. The other destiny didn't sound so good. It was a prickly thought and realised I was starting to hold my breath, so decided not to dwell on that thought.

We swam on the surface so I could see where we were. He only

dived below the waves when we got too close to any boats or the Navy's frigate. A plastic bottle floated past as a reminder of what I needed to do.

'I'll try and help about the plastic. We've done projects at school.'

No thought-language came back from Nihplod. He understood that I really felt this was something too big for me. We both knew I would try, and I really would.

CHAPTER 20

Seagulls cawed and swept low as they passed us, as if to welcome me back. It was great to see proper boats again and I was sure I heard a helicopter, although looking up I couldn't see any sign of one. We were getting close to where I had left my kayak when I suddenly saw Lowen, keeping his kayak steady with a paddle. He seemed to be playing a musical instrument. The tune was beautiful and it made me smile — I used to think Lowen was rubbish at guitar, but this sounded awesome.

'Lowen!' I screamed, waving my arm at him frantically.

He had found my kayak and was looking round with a look of bewilderment.

'Lowen! It's me, look! Over here on Nihplod, I mean the dolphin.'

As we swam up to him, I could see he had been crying. My big brother who I thought didn't like me. He had come to find me. He stopped playing and laid the instrument across his lap.

'Imogen, Im, you idiot! Get off that dolphin! Everyone's gone crazy - they've even got a helicopter out looking for you! What you doing? Get off it!'

Then Lowen patted Nihplod's head and the dolphin gave him a chuckle and nudged his hand.

'Wow!' he said. 'It's really friendly.'

'Do you want a ride?' I said.

'No!' he replied angrily. Then added, 'Yes. Yeah, OK, but we mustn't be long and there's some weird stuff going on in the sea. You've been gone hours, Im. And got me in big trouble.'

I gave Nihplod a hug then climbed off onto my kayak.

'Thank you,' I said in my thought-language, 'It was awesome. I'm really going to miss you lots.'

I held on to Lowen's kayak, as he carefully put the musical instrument down and climbed on the dolphin.

'Im. Don't let that fall off my kayak,' he said pointing to the instrument.

'No. OK. Anyway, where did you get it? I asked quizzically.

Before he could answer, they were gone, making little leaps and shallow dives. As I watched them I had a terrible thought.

'Nihplod,' I called, 'don't take Lowen to Nettogrof!' Then I worried that they might bump into the giant octopus. But they were soon back, and I held Lowen's kayak steady as he climbed on.

'That was so cool!' he said, patting the dolphin, and I reached out and patted him too.

Nihplod looked at us both with his sparkling fun eye and gave a chuckle and nod of his head. As he swam away, gliding through the sea, he gave us a tail-wave.

'Ha, ha! Look at that Imogen,' said Lowen. 'It's waving to us.'

'Yes,' I said. Then in thought-language to Nihplod, 'I'll do what I can about death-snot, promise. Will I see you again?'

'Thank you, I know you will, and yes, we will meet again,' came the reply.

'Come on you, tell me about that dolphin later,' said Lowen. 'I've got to get you home, it'll be dark soon.'

Lowen looked hard to the open sea and horizon, in the hope of seeing the mermaid one more time. He wasn't sure whether to tell Imogen about the mermaid and giant octopus - remembering, she had never been good at keeping secrets. For now he wanted to avoid questions about the musical instrument until he could think of a plausible explanation. He still didn't know what he would say to his dad about his phone call, but knew Imogen coming home would take precedence and hoped his dad would forget about the call.

'You know it was a weird thing finding your kayak. I was sure I went past that same spot at least twice before I found it,' said Lowen, before Imogen could ask again about the instrument.

'Well, it may have been hidden by a wave,' I said, while trying to keep a straight face.

We paddled at a slow steady pace alongside each other. Lowen seemed quieter than usual. I was expecting him to have hundreds of questions for me and I wasn't sure how much to tell him. I looked over at him in his kayak and saw he had wrapped the instrument in his T-shirt.

As we paddled our kayaks into the familiar Kingsand bay, within the crowd of people I could see Mum and Dad waving frantically as they ran down the stone steps to the beach. Mum was holding a blanket in her other hand ready to wrap around me. I reached the shore just before Lowen and as I climbed off my kayak, she came running towards me and nearly slipped up on seaweed. Lowen caught up with me before Mum reached us.

'You better not do that again Im,' said Lowen. 'You made Mum go a bit nuts, hearing voices and stuff. Heard you talking to her.' Voicing this got Lowen thinking, about how he talked to the mermaid, and then his mum's experience didn't seem so weird.

Before I could answer, Mum had wrapped me in the warm blanket. She was hugging me so tight it was hard to breathe. Dad took my kayak, ruffled my hair and Lowen went back to pretending he didn't care.

'She's alright,' he said flippantly. 'She's just been playing with one of the dolphins. Stupid.'

'Lowen!' said Mum, then turned to me. 'Take no notice, he's been as worried as we were. I'm so glad you're safely home darling. And you,' she said looking at Lowen.

Tears welled like little springs in the corner of her eyes and I felt bad that I had worried her so much. Funny, I never really thought much about Mum's feelings. Now I understood what empathy meant.

'Me too,' I said. 'Sorry, Mum,' I said, attempting to give her a hug, under the constraints of the blanket.

I turned to look for Lowen. He had hung his kayak up on the harbour wall and was hugging his T-shirt with a benign look on his face.

'Hey Lo,' I called. 'Thanks for coming to find me.'

He didn't reply. I wasn't sure he'd even heard me. When he came to join us, he had a private joke smile on his face and nodded at me. As we walked together up the stone steps of the quay, I turned and took one last look at the sea and sighed heavily. Before my journey with Nihplod, I had no idea what was hidden below the waves and that somewhere out there was Nettogrof, that amazing quirky island where I knew, one day, I would return. I had to do something about death-snot, I mean plastics, but for now I was just enjoying being loved. When we reached the top step, the crowd started to disperse after giving cheers and kind words. My friend Katy came and hugged me in the blanket, before being led away by her mum.

'You must be exhausted!' said Dad. Then turning to Lowen, 'What was that about a mermaid?' he said laughing.

'Nothing,' said Lowen. 'It was a joke.'

We soon reached our house and for the first time I noticed our brass dolphin door-knocker. Helen opened the door to us and wiped her eye on a tea-towel she was holding.

'What a relief. Am I glad to see you.'

'Yes.' said Dad, looking first at me, then giving Lowen a quizzical frown.

'After tea, a hot bath and bed,' added Mum, still holding me and the blanket close to her.

I looked at Lowen and silently mouthed the word, Mermaid? He grinned at me and mouthed back, Nihplod.

CHAPTER 21

The same night Imogen had returned from her adventure with the dolphin, Nihplod, Lowen pulled out from under his bed the musical instrument he had wrapped in a T-shirt. The house was finally quiet. After tucking Imogen up in bed, both parents had stayed up talking until past midnight. Lowen had left his bedroom door slightly ajar so it didn't make a noise when opening. He used an old guitar case to put his new instrument in, but it was far too big, so he padded it out with a T-shirt. Putting his mobile phone in his pocket, he picked up the guitar case and moved stealthily onto the landing. There was enough moonlight coming through the landing window for him to see his footing on the stairs. He just reached the bottom step into the hallway, when there was a low gruff, 'Woof'.

'Shush, Paddy', he whispered. 'It's only me.'

Paddy bumped open the kitchen door and came happy-faced into the hall sideways, thumping his tail against jackets flung over the bannister. Lowen gave Paddy a rough head-and-back rub, before taking him by his collar, back to the kitchen. He found a doggy treat to keep him quiet before closing the door. Lowen stood like a statue outside the kitchen for a minute, to check he hadn't been heard. No-one seemed to stir, so he headed for the front door, picking up the guitar-case on his way. When the front door closed with a loud click, he hoped everyone was sound sleep. His bike was floodlit by the full moon. He jumped onto it, and pedalled down the cobbled lane. He hesitated at the bottom of the lane, still undecided whether to head for the harbour and his waiting kayak, or to cycle up to Rame Head, where he could try climbing down to the small cove and rocks. He slightly favoured Rame Head, as, from there he could have a good view over the sea, especially under the light of the full moon. When he arrived at the carpark, he looked to see if anyone was working in the lighthouse.

Certain no-one was there, he lifted his bike over the gate and startled one of the sleeping wild ponies. It whinnied at him before walking off. He cycled over the bumpy grass, down the slope and stopped by one of the benches on the coastal path. There he sat and opened the guitar case and began to pluck and strum the silver strings. The music that flowed was magical, it spread out over the cliff and down to the sea. He soon had an audience of wild ponies, rabbits and various birds. They kept a safe distance, but Lowen was astonished at the effect and hoped the mermaid was in range to hear. He was so enthralled by his own playing, he didn't hear the crackle of bracken being trodden underfoot, and not by a pony. Suddenly something leapt out on him, making him jump and he dropped his musical instrument. He looked with horror as it tumbled down the cliff.

'Paddy!' he shouted. 'You idiot. Get off me!'

'Sorry Lo,' said Imogen.

'What! It's you. Look what you've done now!'

'Sorry,' repeated Imogen. 'I heard you go out and was worried. Thought that instrument had done something funny to you.'

'When did you start worrying about anyone?' asked Lowen, angrily. 'I was OK till you turned up. Go home, and take this stupid dog with you.'

He looked over the cliff hoping to see the instrument and Imogen joined him. Paddy, sensing something was wrong, sat quietly by Imogen's feet and stared with them at the moonlit sea, hoping it might be a ball that they were looking for. Then something sparkled just for a second.

'Look. There,' Imogen said, pointing at some bracken more than half way down the cliff. 'I'm sure that's it.'

Lowen stared hard to where Imogen was pointing, then, without a word, he started to climb down.

'Lo! Don't,' shouted Imogen. 'It's dangerous.'

He ignored his sister's pleading and continued down the cliff, his foothold slipping between the bracken. Paddy couldn't retain his silence and started barking and looked up at Imogen with doleful eyes before he headed after Lowen.

'No. Paddy, Lo. Stop!'

But they were as stubborn as each other and completely ignored her pleas. Paddy was more sure-footed than Lowen — for such a big, slightly cumbersome dog, he managed the descent with ease. Paddy was just a head behind Lowen when Lowen's foot slipped on the dry earth. Imogen screamed as she saw her brother tumble down the cliff, desperately trying to grab at ferns and bracken to stop his fall. Imogen pulled the mobile from her pocket and was about to call 999 when Paddy leapt into hero mode. He raced down the cliff partly sidewards, like a small bear, and grabbed Lowen by the seat of his jeans. Together they slid gently to a standstill. Looking at the pair of them, Imogen was torn between laughing and crying. For a moment Lowen was dangled by the seat of his jeans in Paddy's mouth, before getting a foothold on the roots of bracken. He sat down and hugged Paddy, who showed his triumphant pleasure with licks and tail thumping.

'Lo!' called Imogen. 'Are you OK?'

'Yeah. Think so,' replied Lowen. 'Nothing broken.'

He was a bit wobbly as he tried to stand, so sat down again.

'Stay sitting,' pleaded Imogen. 'I can get someone to get you.'

'No!' insisted Lowen. 'Don't. I can climb up OK and look there,' he said pointing to the instrument, which was only an arm's length away.

Paddy also looked to where Lowen was pointing and took that as a retrieve command and promptly moved and grabbed the instrument, by the neck, in his soft mouth, and gently dragged it over to Lowen. Lowen took the instrument from Paddy and looking up at Imogen, they both burst out laughing.

'Now what?' called Imogen. 'Shall I go and find some rope?'

Lowen hugged his instrument on one side and Paddy on the other, while he paused in thought.

'Well?' Imogen shouted. 'I need to do something. We can't stay like this all night.'

'Hang on. I'm thinking. I'm closer to the sea. I could slide down slowly with Paddy.'

'OK. I'll phone Dave and we can get you in his boat.'

After Imogen suggested calling Dave, they were both quiet for a while, thinking that idea through. Imogen looked at the time on her phone — it was 1.55. She tried to imagine how the conversation with Dave might go.

'It's a bit early,' called Imogen.

Lowen was obviously having the same thought. 'Yeah. Maybe later, 6ish would be better. Go home and get a blanket and some toast. You can roll it down the cliff to me.'

'Toast!' shouted Imogen. 'No. I'll get a blanket, but I'm not making toast. Mum and Dad will hear me.'

Lowen laughed. Paddy snuggled up as he started to play his instrument. Imogen looked at them and instead of feeling jealous of Paddy's affection for Lowen, she felt glad that they had each other. She was about to get on her bike when Lowen stopped playing and shouted.

'Im! Wait. Look.'

Imogen put her bike down. First looking down at Lowen, then out to sea. There were two fins heading towards Rame Head. As one leapt out of the water, she recognised Nihplod and the other larger fin, which was giving a wave. This brought Lowen to his feet with a small leap of excitement.

'Careful Lo,' shouted Imogen and Paddy woofed as if in agreement.

'It's her,' called Lowen in an excited voice that was new to Imogen. 'My mermaid!'

Imogen smiled, and as she watched them swim closer to the rocks at the foot of the cliff, she concentrated on sending Nihplod a thought message.

'Nihplod, is this really you? Have you come to rescue Lowen?'

'Why ask a question that you know the answer to?' came the reply.

Imogen felt a bit hurt by Nihplod's reply. Of course, he was right, she did know it was him, but thought he could at least have said something nice.

'The mermaid will talk to Lowen. He is to climb down to the rocks and I will bring him into the bay. There you can meet us. We have things to tell you both.'

Imogen decided not to sulk or hold her breath, instead, she felt energised to be trusted and part of something that sounded important.

'OK,' she replied, and gave Paddy a whistle. 'Come on Paddy, here boy.'

But Paddy was torn between Imogen and Lowen, who by now was working his way down to the sea and rocks on his bottom. He looked from Imogen to Lowen and was obviously wishing they were together. When Lowen's foot slipped and he went down the cliff faster than he wanted, Paddy made his choice and bounded up to Lowen offering his sturdy body as support. Imogen sighed as she mounted her bike — she knew Paddy had made the right decision.

'You are finding some of the knowledge already,' said Nihplod in thought language. Then came a happy chuckle, which made Imogen laugh too as she pedaled up the hill. A few ponies watched her as she cycled to the gate, and one whinnied a greeting to her as it moved to let her by. The moon looked huge in the clear sky, flooding her way with its cool white light. This was the time when the seas swelled and the mackerel would swim close to shore and leap — making an easy catch for children's waiting hand-held nets. Imogen pedaled as fast as she could along the narrow gravel lane leading to Rame Church, past the farm and on to the fort road leading to Cawsand and Kingsand bay. She rested her bike by the harbour wall and raced down the stone steps to the stony beach. There they were: they made a strange and

funny sight. Lowen sitting on Nihplod, holding both Paddy and his instrument. Paddy's ears flapped in the breeze and his top lip was slightly curled back, showing some of his yellow teeth. As soon as they were close enough to the shore, Paddy made a leap and swam under his own doggy-paddle to the shore and, after a quick shake, he raced to greet Imogen. Imogen laughed.

'It's alright, Paddy,' she said, giving him a good rub. 'Now stay here, I won't be long.'

CHAPTER 22

Imogen stripped off her jeans and T-shirt leaving just her knickers and vest and waded in. Paddy barked at her from the shore. She swam out to the rock on the edge of the bay, where the mermaid and Lowen were sitting. Nihplod was still in the water, with his head lifted just enough to nod at Imogen as she climbed up onto the rock.

'This is my mermaid,' said Lowen proudly. 'She speaks Spanish and I'm the only one who can understand her.'

'Really', said Imogen, with a hint of sarcasm. 'Hola,' she said turning to the mermaid.

'Hola,' said the mermaid with an enchanting smile, then added. 'No estropees este momento para tu hermano.'

Lowen laughed and, to Imogen's annoyance, Nihplod gave a chuckle. She smiled at the mermaid and then challenged Lowen.

'OK. Clever pants. What did she say then?'

Before Lowen had a chance to react, Nihplod talked to Imogen in thought.

'She said, don't spoil this moment for your brother and she is right. Let him be the clever one with something special as you feel your friendship is with me.' Imogen knew Nihplod and the mermaid were right.

'No worries. You got me there. She's amazing Lo. Where did you meet her?' said Imogen.

Lowen explained to Imogen that he met the mermaid out at Rame Head when he went looking for her in his kayak and that the mermaid had given him the silver-stringed instrument.

It's magical,' he said, giving the strings a light strum. When Lowen got to the part about the giant octopus, Imogen squealed in recognition.

'The giant octopus attacked you! That thing is seriously dangerous. It's been taken over by the Grey Force and was trying to kill the Sea Lion that protects The Knowledge. We got caught up in a battle on the

way back.'

Nihplod interrupted. 'This is part of what we need to talk to you both about. We need your help sooner than we thought.' Imogen could see, by Lowen's serious expression, that the mermaid must be telling him the same thing.

'We need humans to catch the giant octopus and keep it safe for 10 moons. The guardian of the Knowledge Well, Lion of the sea, was badly injured in the recent battle and needs this time to heal. If you can keep the giant octopus in a trance for 3 moons this will release it from the power of the Grey Force.'

For once Imogen was speechless. What Nihplod was asking seemed impossible, so she just looked from Nihplod to Lowen, the mermaid and back to Nihplod. The mermaid had just finished explaining what was needed and Lowen looked hard at Imogen with a troubled brow.

'Why does your mermaid speak Spanish?' asked Imogen.

'What? Didn't your dolphin just tell you we've got to find a way to capture that octopus?'

'Yes, but I want to know why Spanish?'

'I'll tell you later,' said Lowen irritably. Then, seeing the disappointment in Imogen's face, said. 'She was one of the Spanish musicians that got shipwrecked years ago, so she speaks Spanish.'

'How did she become a mermaid?'

'What! I don't know. Shut up about my mermaid. We need to talk about the octopus.'

Nihplod chuckled and the mermaid threw her blue-black hair back and laughed. Imogen and Lowen stared at them, then Nihplod said they must go and he would speak to Imogen tomorrow. The mermaid blew a kiss, with the wave of her hand, and said, 'Adios.' In seconds they were gone, leaving Imogen and Lowen on the rock looking at the disappearing fin.

'We better get home fast Im. Are you OK?'

'Yes. It seems too much, I'm only eleven.'

'Yeah. I know. But you didn't start holding your breath.'

'No. I didn't did I? We can get that stupid octopus.'

Paddy, seeing the dolphin and mermaid had gone, started barking and ran into the sea.

'It's OK, Paddy,' shouted Imogen. 'Stay! We're coming.'

Lowen decided it was easier to swim to the shore on his back and put the instrument under the front of his T-shirt. They were soon on the beach, being greeted enthusiastically by Paddy. Imogen put on her dry jeans and T-shirt and Lowen squeezed some of the water out of his.

'Here, take this,' said Lowen, handing the instrument to Imogen. 'Be careful with it and put it under my bed. I'm going up to Rame Head to get my bike.'

When Imogen and Lowen started heading in different directions Paddy looked confused and woofed at Lowen.

'It's OK Paddy,' said Imogen. 'He'll be home soon. Come on, boy.'

On her way back, Imogen was thinking about the night and what they had to do. She felt glad this was a shared task and smiled to herself at the thought of how close she and Lowen had become.

When she reached their house, she froze. The kitchen light was on. She rested her bike against the wall and made a sign to Paddy to keep quiet. There didn't seem to be anyone in the kitchen, nor could she hear voices. Taking her trainers off, she took a towel off the washing-line to wrap round Lowen's instrument and slowly turned the handle to the back door. Paddy pressed his nose at the gap as Imogen slowly opened the door into the kitchen. She breathed a sigh of relief when she stepped into the kitchen and no-one was was there. Paddy went straight to his water bowl, taking thirsty mouthfuls and splashing the kitchen floor. Imogen walked stealthily from the kitchen into the darkened hall that led to the stairs. Paddy, having cleared his water bowl, followed Imogen and together they took the stairs at a careful pace. Reaching the landing, Imogen stopped. She could hear her dad saying,

'Paddy's not in the kitchen.'

78

'Oh, really? I was asleep. He's probably in with one of the children.'

'I'll just go and check.'

'OK. If you must. But please don't wake either of them.'

That was Imogen's cue to get into her room and bed as quickly as possible. She left her clothes on and pulled the duvet up round her neck. Paddy didn't need instructions, he leapt on the bed and curled into a ball, placing one foot over his nose. Within less than a minute the handle of her bedroom door was turning. On seeing Imogen seemingly fast asleep and Paddy's doleful eyes looking up at him, her dad smiled and quietly closed the door. Imogen waited until she heard her parents' door close, before getting up and changing into her pyjamas. She didn't want to risk taking Lowen's instrument to his room, so after giving it a careful inspection, she placed it under her bed. She reached for her mobile phone and sent Lowen a text, 'Mum and Dad are awake — all cool but be quiet. Btw your strings in my room.'

CHAPTER 23

Lowen arrived back 45 minutes after Imogen. He had picked up her text message so had thought up a story, in case he got caught. He was glad to get out of his wet clothes, which he bundled under his bed. He was soon asleep.

'Lowen. Up. It's 10 o'clock,' said Kim, knocking on his bedroom door. Lowen reluctantly emerged from the warmth of his duvet, and shuffled sleepily into the bathroom before heading for the kitchen. To his surprise he found Imogen was up and was buttering toast.

'Want some?' she said to Lowen, offering up a plate with four slices.

'Yeah. Thanks.'

Kim and Heath looked at each other and smiled.

'Well, you two, what are you up to today? Imogen, are you seeing Katy?'

'Erm. Thought I'd take Im to the Aquarium. You wanted to go didn't you Im?'

'Yes. Great, that's cool. Thanks Lo.'

'Oh, OK. That's lovely. Isn't it?' Kim said, looking hard at Heath.

'Yes. Surprising, but good you two are finally getting on.'

Imogen just smiled. Lowen greedily stuffed toast in his mouth and took another piece with him as he left the kitchen.

'You coming?' he said, leaving the kitchen door open.

'OK. Give me five mins to finish my toast.'

'What's got into your brother?' said Heath, looking from Imogen to Kim.

'Nothing. He just promised to take me, that's all. Better go before he changes his mind.'

'Well you stay with him. I don't want you wandering off or going out on that kayak for a while. Give me a kiss before you go,' said Kim, taking Imogen's hand.

Imogen raced up the stairs to her room. Lowen was there waiting for her.

'Where is it?' he said.

Imogen pointed under her bed and Lowen retrieved his precious instrument. Unwrapping it from the towel, he inspected it to make sure it wasn't damaged, gave the strings a light strum and put it in his guitar case.

'OK. Let's go. Have you heard anything from your dolphin yet?'

'No, nothing,' replied Imogen. 'What's the idea of going to the Aquarium?'

'I'm not sure yet, only I know someone who works there and he looks after the giant octopus they have in the tank. It's just a thought, but he might help.'

'We can't just tell anyone!' protested Imogen.

'Shush. Keep your voice down. Let's talk on the way.'

Lowen hid his instrument in his room, and they both picked up their bikes and headed for Cremyll to take the ferry over to Plymouth. They each had tickets for the Aquarium from an earlier student visit that year, so neither had to pay anything to get in.

'We don't have to tell him anything at this stage, Im. Let's just find out what we can about their octopus and how they caught it.'

Imogen agreed, and they walked down past the information boards, fish tanks and sharks until they reached the massive tank holding the giant octopus. Imogen always loved visiting the Aquarium, but this time she was on a mission and was fizzing with excitement. She stood transfixed, peering hard into the tank.

'I can't see it,' Imogen said. 'I've only ever seen it once, it's always hiding.'

'Yeah, well the one that attacked me wasn't shy. Wait here and I'll go and find Phoenix.'

Phoenix was in his first year, studying to become a marine biologist and he was a big enthusiast when it came to the giant Pacific Octopus.

'It's really intelligent. Can open jars, solve puzzles and is a bit of an escape artist. Watch, she'll show herself soon, she knows I'm the one

81

who usually feeds her, and it's near feeding time. Look, there she is.'

'I can't see her,' said Imogen.

'Nor me. Hang on, that's an eye.'

'Yes. Look closely. She can change colour to merge in with the rocks. Here she comes. Watch this.'

Phoenix took from his pocket a screw-top jar with a small crab inside it, opened the feeding hole in the tank and dropped it in. Within seconds the giant octopus had unscrewed the jar, eaten the crab and placed the jar on a rock near the opening for Phoenix to retrieve.

'Wow! That was awesome,' said Lowen.

Imogen was mesmerised by it. The octopus seemed to be looking from Phoenix to Lowen, and then straight at her. She nearly fell over when the octopus made her jump by tapping impatiently on the glass.

'It's OK,' said Phoenix. 'She's just hungry. She knows exactly what time I feed her. These Cephalopods are amazing, but they can get very grumpy when they're hungry. The female will often eat a mate if he doesn't move quickly enough.'

'So you don't ever have two together in the same tank then?' asked Lowen.

'No way. Besides, we only have the one and she's enough of a handful. They are known to escape from their tank at night when no-one's around and eat fish in another tank and return, looking innocent.' They all laughed at the thought of this mischievous clever octopus, which was now looking at the tank opposite with beautiful tropical fish, as if it understood what Phoenix was saying.

By the time Imogen and Lowen left the Aquarium, they had learnt a lot about Giant Pacific Octopus, but Lowen had to ditch his idea of somehow catching and putting it in the same tank.

'It was a good idea, but we'll just have to think of something else,' said Imogen as they climbed on their bikes. 'Unless,' she continued thoughtfully. 'What if we swapped them?'

'Well that's stupid. It's going to be tough enough dealing with one

giant octopus, two is suicide!'

'Not if we find a way for it to escape on its own. Phoenix said they are always escaping. One in Canada went down a pipe and got out into the ocean through a drain.'

'When did you suddenly get so brainy? That's not a bad idea, Im.'

They cycled back to the ferry and bought ice-creams from the nearby cafe. On the ferry they were both in deep thought. Imogen was concentrating, trying to get a message to Nihplod, but she got nothing back.

'I don't get it. Nihplod said he'd speak to me today,' Imogen said as they carried their bikes off the ferry onto the beach.

'Perhaps they're busy fighting that manic octopus. Let's hope they kill it, so we don't have to try and catch the thing.'

'It's not the octopus's fault. It's been taken over by the Grey Force. Hang on. It's Nihplod,' said Imogen, standing still with a frown of concentration.

'What's he saying. Is my mermaid with him?'

Imogen ignored Lowen and just stopped for a few minutes in thought-conversation with Nihplod. She finished with a nod of her head, as if she understood and then looked at Lowen and sighed.

'What?' asked Lowen impatiently. 'Come on Im, what did he say?'

'I've just got to get this right,' said Imogen, then continued slowly. 'Nihplod told me, we have to meet them at sunset tomorrow by the rocks at Rame Head and you're to bring your silver strings and anything we can think of to help trick the octopus into letting us catch it.'

'No way! How we going to catch that thing and find somewhere to put it by tomorrow? Anyhow, it must weigh a ton, it's not what we have on our plate on holiday in Spain!' Imogen agreed, but didn't want to let Lowen know and just said, 'We'll think of something. We have to.'

'Trick it? What does he mean by trick it? Get back to that dolphin and ask!'

'I don't know. I'll ask him later.'

They decided to go home and get towels and something to eat, then go to Whitsand Bay for a swim and talk. Kim had made a quiche, and fruit pie, they cut themselves a slice of each and left the house without a word. When they reached the long sandy beach, Imogen was the first to go in. The sea was calm and just right for swimming. As the water took her body weight, she floated on her back for a while, deep in thought. If she had been chosen by the Knowledge, then she had to come up with a plan. She concentrated hard on thought and spoke to Nihplod.

'We need some help. I just don't know how we can catch that huge octopus, or what you mean by trick it.'

'You will need another human — you will know who to trust. Think about what you have learnt today. We will bring the octopus to the rocks tomorrow when the sun meets the sea.'

'Lowen!' called Imogen as she swam to shore. 'Just spoken to Nihplod.'

Lowen was much further out than Imogen, but heard her call. 'OK,' he said and turned to swim back.

Imogen had dried herself off with the towel when Lowen joined her, flicking water over her.

'So what did he say? Hope you told him it's impossible.'

'Have you still got that Rubik's cube?'

'What?' said Lowen, in an irritated voice.

'Nihplod said to think about what we learnt today. That octopus gave the jar its full attention.'

'Yeah, for a split second.'

'Phoenix told us, they like doing puzzles. It took you weeks to figure out the Rubik's, and that was with help. I think that's sort of what Nihplod meant by tricking it. He also said we need to get someone else to help us.'

'Yeah. Well he's right there. The Hulk would be good.' Lowen thought for a moment and laughed. 'That's not bad Im. Rubik's cube, maybe you've got something.'

They both fell into laughter, and then sat in quiet thought, while

84

eating the quiche and pie. It was difficult for them to think of who would believe them, let alone who to trust. It was Imogen who broke the silence.

'It's got to be Dave or Phoenix. Dave has a boat and knows about fish and Phoenix is an octopus expert.'

'Yeah,' said Lowen. 'But I don't fancy telling either of them, and Phoenix won't like swapping his giant octopus for that psycho one. It's not going to happen Im... it's impossible. Tell your dolphin.'

'We've got to try. What about your mermaid? That thing might kill her if we don't catch it.'

'Shut up!,' said Lowen. 'Let's go and see Dave. But you can tell him.'

CHAPTER 24

When they arrived at Kingsand quay, they found Dave mending one of his crab pots.

'Hi Dave. You got a minute?' asked Lowen as he rested his bike against a stone wall. 'Just that Im's got something to ask you.' Imogen prodded Lowen with her elbow while smiling benignly at Dave.

'You two look like you're up to something. Something no good, it looks to me. OK, come and sit on the bench.'

'You've got to promise you won't tell,' said Imogen as she sat next to Dave, not wanting to be face on, with the half-truth she was about to tell.

'You know I want to be a marine biologist, right?'

'Well, no, I didn't, but go on,' said Dave looking intrigued.

'As a project, I need to catch this big fish and to study it for a few days, then let it go. Lowen is going to help, he's sort of involved with the project. He, no I wondered... erm... can we borrow your boat and a really big fishing net?'

Dave turned to look at Imogen, who was struggling to stop herself holding her breath and was pulling funny faces in the process. Lowen thought Imogen might crack, so interjected to give her time to get herself and her story together.

'We only need to borrow the boat tonight, more late afternoon really, and will keep to the coastline, honest. No further than the Head.'

'Let me get this straight. You want me to let you two borrow my boat and fishing nets tonight to catch a big fish for a project. And I've got to keep it secret?'

'Yes,' they said in unison.

'No way. We've only just had Sea Rescue out for you,' he said patting Imogen's shoulder. 'Besides, there's no big fish in these waters.'

It took them both some time persuading Dave. Eventually he agreed, but only if he went with them and drove the boat. He was more curious

than anything, to find out what they were up to, and chuckled to himself after they had left. Dave had been pretty mischievous himself in his youth and admired their spirit. He was trying to think what big fish they were talking about. Imogen had first said a Wolf Fish that she had seen by the rocks, but quickly changed her story when Dave said they only live around the Japanese coast. He thought perhaps she meant a conger eel and hoped not. A 20 foot long giant conger eel had been caught not so long ago and they're not easy to catch. But Dave was so curious to find out what it was, he promised to have his boat and nets ready for 6pm.

CHAPTER 25

Dave took a call from Kim around 5pm. She was checking that Imogen and Lowen were going fishing with him. Dave laughed heartily, causing Kim to hold the phone away from her ear.

'Yes. No worries. I'll have them back by 8pm, latest. Just a bit of fishing to help with a project, apparently.'

Dave left the dinghy on the shore, for them to row out to his boat. He had started the engine when they boarded, and was a bit surprised to see Lowen had turned up with his guitar case and Imogen was holding a Rubik's cube and metal puzzle.

'You won't be catching any fish with that,' he said laughingly. 'Right. As instructed, there's the net, nothing in these seas bigger than that. Just hope it's not a conger eel you've seen. They've got teeth, but nothing I can't handle.' Imogen laughed nervously and gave Lowen a hard look. He was trying not to laugh and nodded to Imogen to say something.

'It might be,' she said. 'It looked really big.'

They had agreed not to tell Dave about Nihplod and the mermaid, thinking it was best for Dave to see for himself and they would act surprised, pretending they hadn't seen either before. Imogen sent Nihplod a thought message to let him know so he and the mermaid would make it look as though they didn't know them. As they got close to the rocks at Rame Head, Dave slowed the engine and Imogen and Lowen scanned the sea looking for a fin or any sign of them. The sun hung low in the sky and would soon be setting, casting hot colours across the sea and sky. Then Imogen spotted something as the gulls parted and dived in the sky. It was the albatross.

'What the heck? Will you look at that,' said Dave. 'Never in my life... that's massive. We don't get albatross around here.'

'That's so cool,' said Lowen, and Imogen managed an unimpressive 'Wow!' while keeping a more watchful eye on the sea. Suddenly, the giant

88

octopus struck, lashing at the boat and pulling the side with another two arms in an attempt to capsize it.

'Whooa... what!' shouted Dave with a quiver of fear in his voice. 'Is this your marine project? Quick! Imogen, hand me that gutting knife by your feet.'

'Where's Nihplod?' said Imogen, as she looked round wildly for the knife. 'Lowen, start playing!' But Lowen had frozen, remembering his previous encounter with the octopus on the rocks, and hoping the mermaid was all right. The boat shook as if caught in a raging storm. Imogen handed the gutting knife to Dave and, just as he was about to stab an arm of the octopus, in a flash it snatched the knife out of his hand and threw it in the sea. The octopus pulled itself up partly into the boat and grabbed Dave round his neck with another arm. He was starting to go red in the face with the pressure on his windpipe. Without thinking, Imogen threw the Rubik's Cube at the octopus. To her surprise it snatched it in mid-air, still not letting go of Dave, but its curiosity was enough to loosen its grip. While the octopus studied the Rubik's Cube, Dave managed to pull its arm off him and the octopus partly slipped back into the sea, now using four of its arms to rapidly twist the cube. Coughing and spluttering, Dave tried to re-start the engine.

'Noo!' shouted Imogen. 'We can't go.'

'Are you kidding! This thing's psychotic. We've got to get out of here fast!'

Lowen, on seeing the mermaid on a nearby rock, snapped out of his fearful state and began to play the enchanted instrument: just in time, as the octopus had at that moment completed all six colours of the Rubik's Cube and had tossed it aside. It was about to focus its attention back on the boat and Dave, when it too spotted the mermaid on the rock. Dave, while attempting to restart the engine, looked to see what had distracted the octopus. He couldn't believe what he was seeing. He was trying to remember if he had drunk any cider, or whether this was all a dream.

'What have you kids got me into?'

When the dolphin appeared next to the boat and raised its head for a pat from Imogen, Dave's mouth fell open in disbelief. The octopus was torn between continuing its attack on Dave or going for the mermaid. It was surprised to see the mermaid, as it had left her for dead in their last battle. Nihplod was talking to Imogen in their thought language, and explained they had managed to hide the guardian of the Knowledge Well and that they had been in a violent battle with the octopus.

'The music will soon take effect. We must work quickly.'

Imogen understood, and pulled at the fishing net, giving one corner of it to Nihplod, who dragged it partly over the edge of the boat with his beak. On seeing Nihplod with the fishing net, the mermaid gracefully slid off the rock and swam towards the boat. Lowen's music was beginning to work its trance on the octopus, despite its efforts to ignore it. Its head started to sway with each silver-stringed chord, and one arm waved as if conducting an orchestra. Lowen stopped playing for a second to greet the mermaid as she swam up alongside the boat.

'Hola,' said Lowen, giving her one of his winning grins.

'No! Don't stop playing,' said Imogen urgently. 'You can chat to your mermaid when this thing is secure in the net.'

Lowen got the point when he saw the octopus was beginning to break the trance and its beady eyes had latched on to him. Dave was looking in bewilderment, from Imogen with the dolphin to Lowen and the mermaid. For a moment he had forgotten about the giant octopus until he saw what they were trying to do. Imogen, the dolphin and mermaid were dragging the net over the octopus's head. He too grabbed up one end of the net to help. It wasn't an easy task as now two of its arms were waving in mid air, conducting the invisible orchestra.

'I'm not sure this net's big enough,' said Dave. 'We really need a trawler net. Anyhow, what do we do next? Don Juan here can't sit playing to this thing all night.' Dave couldn't really believe what was happening and was sure he would wake up in his bed at home, soon. 'Don't suppose you bought another Rubik's Cube with you, Im?'

'No, but I've got a metal puzzle,' she said throwing it to the octopus's waving arms.

With its brain capacity being spread between its head and all eight arms, the octopus could think independently and it snatched the puzzle. Although still fully in a trance, the two waving arms dropped just enough for them to drag the net over the rest of its arms, while it worked on the puzzle. The dolphin and mermaid brought their ends of the net together and passed them to Imogen and Dave. Bringing the rope through the ends of the net, Dave soon had the octopus caught firmly in the robust fishing net.

'Yeah! We did it,' said Imogen beaming round at Lowen and Dave. 'Is there enough rope to tie it onto a rock?'

'I think so. Then can we get out of here? I don't know what to tell your mum. And what's going to happen when he stops playing?'

Imogen was only half listening to Dave, she was in conversation with Nihplod and asking the very same question.

'We'll have to go home. Lowen can't stay here playing, it's so clever it won't take it long to find the rope under the rock and untie it.'

Nihplod gave a dolphin chuckle. 'The mermaid will put an enchantment on the rope's knot and as soon as the Grey Force's spell wears off, she will release the giant octopus. It will be glad to get back to its home in the Pacific Ocean.'

'Will the sea lion, guardian of the Well be alright?'

Nihplod assured Imogen that the guardian of the Knowledge Well would soon recover and be capable once again to take up its place to stop the Grey Force closing off the Well forever. Nihplod continued.

'It is important that you help us rid our seas of death-snot. This is killing and stupefying many species in the oceans. My people of Nettogrof will not survive and in turn, nor will your people. The world will be left to the Grey Force of ignorance, conflict and destruction.'

Imogen had tears in her eyes and hugged Nihplod.

'I'll try. Can't believe how stupid I used to be about plastic.'

'Hey, Imogen,' called Dave. 'Stop hugging that dolphin. We've got to go.'

Dave had managed to re-start the engine, he was about to move off when the mermaid leaned over the boat beckoning him to her. Lowen looked on with envy as she gently kissed Dave's forehead. Dave blushed, and said thank you. The noise of the boat's engine sounded gruff against this touching scene. As they headed off, the mermaid blew a kiss to Lowen, and Nihplod gave Imogen a tail-fin wave. Keeping his eyes on the mermaid, Lowen stopped playing and sighed.

'She's awesome,' he said dreamily.

Imogen looked to see what the octopus was doing. The trance still seemed to be holding and she saw the mermaid touch the knotted rope before disappearing beneath the waves. Lowen and Imogen looked nervously at each other, then at Dave, who was whistling a country and western tune.

'You alright?' asked Lowen.

'Yes. You kids OK? Happy you've got your marine project sample, Im?' he said nodding at a medium sized catfish on the deck.

Imogen and Lowen were both surprised and bewildered by the appearance of the catfish.

'Erm, yes. Thanks Dave,' she replied while silently mouthing, 'What?' to Lowen. They both started giggling.

'What's so funny?'

'Nothing,' they replied in unison.

They were soon back in Kingsand bay and Dave brought his fishing boat alongside the waiting dinghy.

'There you go. You two hop in first and I'll put your catfish in a bucket with sea water. Don't know why you brought your guitar, Lowen? Could 'ave at least given us a sea-shanty tune.'

Imogen and Lowen looked quizzically at each other as they climbed into the dinghy and picked up the oars.

'Here yer go,' said Dave, handing the bucket to Imogen, before joining

them in the dinghy. 'There, look at that,' he continued, while tapping his watch. 'Eight o'clock on the dot.'

On reaching the bay, they helped Dave drag the boat up onto the beach, thanked him and said goodbye.

'What do you think?' said Imogen, spluttering while trying to hold back laughter.

'It must have been my mermaid kiss. Erased part of his memory and conjured up that catfish.'

They were both still laughing when they arrived home to the welcoming smell of fish-pie. Kim cast a disapproving eye over the catfish and told Imogen to be in bed by nine-fifteen.

CHAPTER 26

The event with the octopus had brought Lowen and Imogen closer and they discussed ways they could help Nihplod and the mermaid with their battle against the Grey Force. Lowen listened attentively to Imogen telling him about Nettogrof.

'Do you think my mermaid is connected to your dolphin and Netter whatever?'

'It's Nettogrof,' said Imogen, correcting him. 'And yes, Nihplod told me it's all connected. Everything in the oceans, plastics and the Grey Force and all of us.'

Lowen was beginning to share Imogen's interest in marine life, and together they went back to see Phoenix and the Giant Pacific Octopus at the Aquarium.

'Do you think your octopus can work out a Rubik's Cube?' Imogen asked, handing one to Phoenix.

'I don't know, we can try if you like.'

Phoenix went round to the feeding hole and dropped it into the tank. At first the octopus seemed uninterested, after picking it up and discovering it wasn't food. Then when they turned their backs to the tank in conversation, the octopus picked it up again. When Lowen turned to look back at the tank, he saw the octopus studying the cube, bringing it close to its face with one arm, and using two others to turn and twist the colours round.

'Well! Will you look at that. It's trying to work it out. Yes, nearly there... and done.' Phoenix talked excitedly about this new discovery and thanked Imogen for bringing the Rubik's Cube.

'This is another level of intelligence. There was no food involved as a reward, this was pure curiosity and intellectual challenge.'

'They can all do it then,' said Lowen. Then, noticing Phoenix's quizzical look added, 'I mean it's amazing, and I guess others like this

octopus could be equally clever.'

When Lowen and Imogen left the Aquarium they were both deep in thought. Neither had ever considered that the sea was full of so many intelligent species, and other worlds that connect to theirs. The sea had always been a place for fun, for swimming and kayaking, which they'd assumed, if they ever thought about it, was owned and governed by humans.

'Funny thing, my mermaid and your dolphin have opened my eyes to another world. None of my mates would believe any of it.'

'I've looked it up,' said Imogen. 'Land is only 30 percent of the world – the rest is sea. Think I'll be a marine biologist.'

'Yeah. Well, if that crazy octopus gets its way, there won't be anything left to study.'

'It's not the octopus's fault,' said Imogen in its defence.

When they were back on the Peninsula, they pushed their bicycles over the stones to the sand and ebbing tide. There, they cycled slowly in tandem following the ripples in the sand for a while, before resting to stare out to sea.

'We must go to Rame Head tomorrow, Im. Need to check the giant octopus is still in the net.'

'Yes, but can you get Dad's binoculars? I don't fancy getting too close to it. I can't remember how long it is before it gets back to being normal. I'll check.'

'When you do, will you ask your dolphin if I can come with you to Nettogrof next time?' Imogen considered Lowen's request. It wasn't so long ago that she would have been too possessive to share something so special with anyone, and especially not with her brother.

'Yes. You can come. I don't know when though.'

Gazing out to sea, Imogen thought about her time on Nettogrof. It seemed so much had happened, and so much time had passed, since she was there. Remembering the weird trees, Etarip and the girl, whom she longed to make a friend, she sent a thought-message to Nihplod.

The following day Imogen and Lowen cycled up to Rame Head. Lowen had taken the binoculars from the bookshelf and called out, 'Just borrowing your bins dad,' before heading out of the front door. Imogen had not heard back from Nihplod and she was feeling a bit anxious as they started to climb part-way down the Head.

'It's no good Im. I still can't see from here. We'll need to get closer.'

'Let me look,' said Imogen, taking the binoculars from Lowen. 'Isn't that the rope knot?'

'Yes. I could see that, but not the net or if it's still caught in it. We'll have to take our kayaks round to get nearer.'

'I don't want to,' said Imogen. 'I think we should wait until I hear from Nihplod. Anyway he'll know if it's managed to escape or not.'

'You're scared,' Lowen said, slightly mockingly.

'Yes. Aren't you?'

Lowen thought about it, 'Yes.' They both laughed and agreed to wait for two days, hoping that Nihplod would get back to Imogen.

'Your mermaid will be alright,' said Imogen, reassuringly.

It was three days before Nihplod got a thought-message back to Imogen.

'Do not worry, the giant octopus is still caught in the net. By the next moon the spell of the Grey Force will loose its hold and the guardian of the Well of Knowledge has almost recovered.'

'Shall we let it out then?'

'No,' came the reply. 'A swordfish will cut it loose, but you are needed to collect the net from the sea.'

Imogen ended by asking, if, once the guardian sea-lion was back guarding the Well, could she go back to Nettogrof and bring Lowen? Nihplod agreed and added,

'There is someone on Nettogrof who is part of your history.'

Before Imogen could ask what he meant, she lost thought connection with Nihplod.

'That's so annoying!' she said to Lowen, when she relayed the

96

telepathic conversation with Nihplod.

'That's cool. Wonder if my mermaid will take me.'

The day after the new moon, when it was only a thin curved slice in the sky and the sea was as calm as a rock pool, Imogen and Lowen headed off in their kayaks, toward the rocks at the bottom of Rame Head. They were getting close and Lowen was just ahead of Imogen, when he stopped paddling.

'What? Why have you stopped?'

Imogen didn't need an answer, she soon saw why. The net was empty and, to her horror, she saw an arm of the giant octopus. Then it raised its head up from the sea.

'Keep still Im,' whispered Lowen. 'Think it's cool or it would have killed us by now.' Imogen had reverted back to her old habit of holding her breath and spluttered air from her lungs before whispering back.

'Why hasn't it gone?'

As if in answer to her question, the octopus looked straight at her, then at Lowen and as fast as a swift in flight, made a dash towards them. With one arm it threw the Rubik's Cube at Lowen and with another, the metal puzzle at Imogen. On seeing they had both caught their respective puzzles, it sank into the sea and sped away. They were both so stunned, neither moved or spoke, the only sound was the gentle lapping of the sea against the rocks. Lowen was first to break the silence.

'What was that about?'

'Getting us to take our rubbish home,' replied Imogen. Laughing so much at her own joke, she nearly fell off her kayak. Their laughter filled the air and the seagulls cawed back in unison. After gathering up the fishing net, Lowen dragged it onto his kayak and they paddled back to Kingsand harbour. There, they put the net on Dave's dinghy, picked up their bicycles and pedaled home. They were still spilling short bursts of laughter when they came through the back door into the kitchen. Heath was there making up a sandwich to take into his study. He eyed them suspiciously.

'Feel like sharing the joke?' he said, looking first at Lowen, then at Imogen, whose laughter now had turned into a full blown giggling spasm.

'You wouldn't get it Dad,' replied Lowen as he walked past into the hall, followed closely by Imogen and Paddy at their heels.

CHAPTER 27

Dave had come back from a night's fishing to find one of his nets left in his dinghy. He relayed this event, along with other fishermen's tales, in the pub when Heath and Kim were there having a pint before Sunday lunch.

'Damnedest thing,' said Dave. 'It went missing weeks ago and then there it was, in my dinghy. No-one's 'fessed up, and damned if I can think who'd want to borrow a blooming great net like that.'

'That's nothing,' said another fisherman, with certainty that his story would top Dave's. 'I was out fishing just off the French coast when bits of old fishing net and tangled line were thrown up from the sea onto the deck of my boat. First I thought it was a diver messing about, but no, no diving boat or diver in sight, and I was out there three hours or more.'

'Reckon you had too much cider on board,' teased another fisherman, 'bit like Carl's story of the Mermaid of Zennor. Convinced he heard her singing on a night's fishing on the west coast last week.'

'When did you say you found your net?' asked Heath.

'Tuesday. Why? Wasn't you, was it Heath?' They both laughed heartily and others at the bar joined in. Heath turned to Kim and said quietly.

'I think I know who did though.' Heath told Kim about Lowen and Imogen arriving home sharing a private joke the same day Dave's net turned up. They agreed not to confront them, but to keep more of an eye on what they were up to.

Over the next few weeks Imogen had been recruiting all her friends to help with the beach cleans and Lowen had amazed everyone at the B-Bar and other music venues with his silver stringed instrument and his new songs in Spanish.

'That's an awesome riff, Lo,' said Jack. 'So cool. Don't know how you find time to practise to get that good, with exams.'

'This little beauty helps,' said Lowen, tapping the sound box.

'When did you learn Spanish lyrics?' asked another friend.

'Picked it up from online tutorial.'

'You know,' said a geeky looking boy at one of the gigs. 'It's really cool you singing in Spanish. I learnt at Uni about a band of Spanish musicians that were shipwrecked off our coast back in the 11th Century. That story would make a cool intro to your gig.'

'Yeah. I'm sure I knew that. Yeah, that's an idea,' said Lowen while wondering if that was his mermaid's connection. She's ancient then, he thought, but mermaids must be immortal, right?

'The lyrics. What's it about?' It was then that Lowen realised he didn't know and that he really needed to learn Spanish.

Heath and Kim were pleased, but feeling a little suspicious of their children's sudden change in attitudes. Imogen had surprised Kim with her uncharacteristic view on plastics — now always preferring glass bottles, and had even taken to picking up any plastic she saw discarded and filling up their recycling boxes.

'What's got into her?' asked Heath. 'She's started lecturing me and even insisted I change my toothpaste.'

'Admitted, this is a sudden conversion, good thing though. It's Lowen who's bothering me. He's been acting very strangely lately — more secretively than usual. Plus, not complaining about taking Imogen out with him. And have you seen that flashy instrument he keeps under his bed?'

'I heard him playing it in his room. Wonderful sound. Said he bought it in a bric-a-brac shop in Plymouth.'

'Well, I've never seen anything like it. And did you know he has asked to do Spanish as an option?'

Imogen had been so dedicated to her campaign against plastics and learning about marine life, she had almost forgotten about Nettogrof. It was while on a beach clean at Whitsand Bay that she received a thought-message from Nihplod.

'Can you and Lowen come to Nettogrof on the second sunrise?'

'Wow! Yes,' replied Imogen. 'That's Saturday, we're not at school and Mum and Dad will be busy decorating.'

When Lowen was cycling back from a jamming session at Maker Heights, Imogen was waiting for him at the end of their lane. She was now really excited about the thought of going back to Nettogrof and was hopping from one foot to the other, with Paddy jumping up at her, joining in the spirit of things.

'What's up, Im?' Lowen asked, getting off his bike to walk with her. You look like you've won an Oscar or you're in need of the loo.'

'Very funny. I've heard from Nihplod. We're going to Nettogrof on Saturday.'

'Brilliant! Can't wait to see those weird trees you've been on about, and to get to see my mermaid.'

'Nihplod didn't mention her. I think it may be another dolphin.'

Lowen was disappointed, but still hopeful that he would get to see her. Imogen woke at 5am and was too excited to get more sleep. She opened her curtains to look for the albatross. She had come to associate it with Nihplod and her ocean travels. It was still dark, and the only birds she could see were a few seagulls and a magpie. Paddy's hearing was almost as sharp as a bat. From his bed in the kitchen, he had taken the stairs with great bounds, thumped open Imogen's bedroom door and nearly knocked her over with an enthusiastic nudge.

'Stop it Paddy! Shush, you'll wake everyone.'

To Paddy's delight, Imogen got back into bed and allowed him to snuggle up by her feet. It was Lowen who was up first and had gone into the kitchen to make tea and toast. With a mug of tea in one hand, he gave Imogen's bedroom door a knock with the other. He was surprised to be greeted by a low woof from Paddy.

'What's Paddy doing here? Come on, get up Im, it's 7.30. You said we have to be at the rocks for 8.30 ish. Here's tea and I've made toast.'

Imogen groaned from interrupted sleep and Paddy leapt off her bed and overtook Lowen on the stairs, in his haste to reach his food bowl in the kitchen. Kim was next to get up. She was usually the first up every morning and couldn't quite believe her eyes when she walked into the kitchen to see Lowen dressed and tucking into toast. Then Imogen walked in carrying half a mug of tea and snatched up a slice of toast.

'Well, this is a first. Have you both got up early to help us with the decorating?' Kim asked mockingly.

'Err. No. We're going out on our kayaks and then to the Aquarium. A marine project. See you later,' said Lowen while still eating toast as he left the kitchen.

'Yes. See you later Mum.' Imogen took extra toast with her as she followed her brother.

This time, at Imogen's suggestion, they were both prepared for the ocean. Under their jeans and T-shirts they had on their wetsuits. They cycled down to the quay, bundled their clothes into a linen bag and gave it to the cafe owner to look after for them. Lowen helped Imogen take her kayak off the hook and they launched into the bay, paddling proficiently and swiftly towards Rame Head rocks.

CHAPTER 28

When they arrived there was no sign of Nihplod and Imogen looked round nervously to check the giant octopus had not returned. The sun was out and the sea was sprinkled with flickering lights like chips of glass, making it difficult to scan to the horizon.

'No sign of your dolphin. I was really hoping my mermaid may have turned up on the rocks to surprise me.'

'There. Look. There they are,' shouted Imogen, pointing at two fins turning into leaping dolphins, heading towards them.

'Cool. Let's drag our kayaks up onto the rocks.'

'No need to, Nihplod will do his magic trick.'

Nihplod and the other dolphin were soon parallel to them, with heads raised for a greeting. After patting Nihplod and a minute of thought conversation, Imogen slid off her kayak into the sea and held onto Nihplod. He sank slightly to make it easier for her to climb on his back.

'Come on Lo. Your dolphin is called Gaia.'

Lowen was in the water in a blink, throwing one leg over Gaia as if riding in a rodeo.

'Be careful, it's not a horse,' said Imogen, feeling protective and slightly possessive of the dolphins.

Before they dived into the sea, two bubbles rose from the dolphin's blowholes: one fell over the kayaks, and the other split to fall over Imogen and Lowen. The kayaks shimmered, then seemed to dissolve into the air. With astonishing speed they were soon in warmer waters and they rose to the surface. Neither were prepared for what happened next. Within a dolphin length from Lowen a giant triangular flat fish sprang out of the water, rising above his head and belly flopped with a deafening crash, giving Lowen a sea shower.

'Woo. What was that?' he shouted, tightening his hold round Gaia. Imogen was laughing so much she nearly fell off Nihplod. When another sprang from the sea, so close it made her jump and fall in. Nihplod chuckled as he helped her back on with his beak.

'They won't hurt you,' he said in thought.

'I know. I've read about them and watched a video. They're mobula rays.' Imogen could tell by Nihplod's silence he was impressed and she felt pleased with herself. Then another ray sprang up, and another, turning somersaults: it was like a sea of giant popcorn, popping up and flying through the air, some two metres high. The dolphins stayed still for them to watch the extraordinary fish-dance until the sea smoothed and the last ray belly-flopped. Then they were gone.

'That was awesome,' said Lowen.

Imogen was still dazzled by the spectacular sight. Being that close was an incredible experience, one she would remember all her life. Nihplod and Gaia had decided to take them the scenic route, they introduced Imogen and Lowen to a family of orcas, named Killer Whales by Spanish seamen for their collective fishing technique. Gaia swam alongside one adult male so Lowen could feel the power of these majestic sea giants. Swimming next to its full nine metres length, Lowen was close to tears with admiration and a sense of privilege that he could stretch out and touch it. He hadn't quite got the hang of telepathy, so he exclaimed, 'Thanks, woo's and awesome,' in his air bubble while patting the dolphin to emphasise his pleasure. The army of lobsters marching across the seabed behind the bravest, with its claws held high, ready for combat, left Imogen with a fit of giggles, until they rose to see that familiar mist. Nihplod and Gaia slowed their speed to almost stationary as they met side-by-side in conversation.

'That's heavy duty fog,' said Lowen, turning to Imogen.

'It's magical, created by the dolphins to protect Nettogrof.'

'Yeah? I believe you.'

'It's true,' said Imogen indignantly.

'No. I do believe you, Im. I can believe anything now. Bit disappointed not to see my mermaid though.'

'Still time for her to show. Anyway, wait 'til you see the castle.' As if prompted, Nihplod and Gaia swam into the dense mist. Although they swam next to each other, neither Imogen nor Lowen could see beyond their own nose.

'This is weird, Im.'

'Yes, I felt really scared the first time.'

'Why are we whispering?'

Imogen didn't answer, she was thinking of Nihplod, wondering whether she would see him on the island as a boy again. Nihplod picked up on Imogen's thoughts and said, 'Yes.' As they emerged from the mist, the sun bouncing off the sand, it was so dazzling it took a while for them to focus. Then Lowen saw Nettogrof for the first time.

'Wow! Im. It's so vivid and that weird looking castle. Looks like a Disney set.'

'Told you.'

Nihplod and Gaia stopped swimming a few metres from the shore.

'This is where we get off,' said Imogen. Then in thought language to Nihplod, 'See you soon.'

CHAPTER 29

Lowen gave Gaia a hug and pat before swimming off towards the shore. He turned to look for Imogen, who was close behind. She was trying out a new swimming mode, that Nihplod had said was faster and used less energy. They were soon on the glistening sands and feeling the sun warm through their wetsuits. Two trees stood like sentries each side of the shingle path as if to welcome them. Lowen stood still, trying to take it all in. He looked down at his feet, which felt warm in the soft white sands, then looking up towards the castle, he had a sudden burst of energy and sprang into a sprint up the shingle path. Imogen laughed at his enthusiasm and called,

'Wait for me... Nooo, don't grab that tree!'

Too late. The tree whipped its branch back out of Lowen's hand and lassoed his feet, causing him to fall hard on his bottom. When Imogen caught up with him, he was dazed and surprised to be getting an obvious telling off - the tree was wagging one of its branches, within centimetres of his nose.

'Told you about the trees. How would you like someone grabbing a finger and trying to break it off?'

'But it's only a tree,' said Lowen, getting to his feet and backing away from it. 'Anything else I need to look out for? What about that stuff growing round the castle, does it bite?'

'Don't be silly. Just the trees, they are weird and have a bit of attitude.'

Imogen talked excitedly about the castle and banqueting table as they walked together up the shingle path. Passing a field of bright yellow flowers and trees with fruits, some looked like lemons and others had dark purple knobbly things the size of tangerines. As they approached the castle they heard voices and then a group of six people of different ages walked into view. They were all carrying musical instruments and talking excitedly. Lowen couldn't understand a thing, but Imogen could just about make out some of what they said.

'They're saying something about fish, sea-plants and a goat. I can't get the rest, they're talking so fast.'

'Watch out!' said Lowen, grabbing Imogen's arm and pulling her to one side. 'They nearly walked into us. Are we really invisible?'

'Yes. I keep telling you.'

'Hey, Im. Look at that girl, she looks like a dark brown version of you.' Imogen looked hard at the girl as they walked past. She recognised her from her last visit. It was the girl she smiled at and who was singing to the dead fish under the tree.

'No way. She's pretty.'

'Yeah, don't know about that, but she could be your twin. Come on, I'm starving. Let's go banqueting.'

They both laughed and walked through the courtyard to the banqueting hall. As they entered, Imogen was immediately struck by how much less food and drink there was on the table compared to her last visit. She hadn't noticed the open ovens before, where a boy was dishing out something steaming into a carved bowl with a ladle that looked like a large hollow pod.

'Shall we check out the hot food?' said Lowen, stuffing a round yellow fruit into his mouth. When they got closer to the ovens, Imogen was more interested in how they worked than trying the contents. Two sheets of what looked like glass hung over the ovens and were catching the sun's bright rays. Rainbow colours sprinkled just above the pots as the moisture from the steam met the sun rays.

'That's beautiful,' whispered Imogen.

'Tastes good too,' said Lowen lifting the small bowl to his mouth. 'Bit like a very tasty vegetable stew mash with something sweet.' After taking another mouthful he offered the bowl to Imogen. 'Here, try some.' Imogen finished what was left in the bowl and then they both studied the ovens.

'Amazing. There's no electricity, only the heat from the sun, intensified by these plates that looks like glass.'

Imogen agreed and added,

'They use the sun big time. When I was here before, I saw them dig up vegetables from a shallow pit that had been baked by the sun. I tried one, it was a bit knobbly and funny looking but it tasted better than roast potatoes.'

A goat came sauntering into the great hall, looked at them and bleated. It walked towards them and was within a metre when it stood still, looked straight at them and bleated again.

'It can see us,' said Imogen in a whisper. 'What do you think it wants?'

It became obvious, when it started to walk out of the hall and turned its head round to look at them and gave a very loud bleat.

'Come on then, let's follow it.'

They followed the goat out of the banqueting hall into the courtyard, passing a small group who were discussing something that seemed serious. Round the side of the castle, up a few stone steps they arrived at an open circle surrounded by small shrubs and olive trees. In the middle of the circle was a small dead fish covered partly by seaweed. The goat stopped and gave another little bleat, as if to say, there it is. Neither of them understood the significance or what they were supposed to do.

'What's this about?' asked Lowen, as if Imogen would have the answer.

'How should I know?' she replied with a shrug.

They were about to head back to the banqueting hall when they heard singing and a group of musicians walked into the circle.

'Wow. That's an awesome riff. Wish I had my mermaid ukulele instrument.'

The musicians formed a circle round the fish and seaweed while they played and moved slowly, first round one way, then the other.

'That girl was singing this one to a dead fish before,' said Imogen as they both swayed and tapped their feet to the beat.

'She's the one that looks like you,' said Lowen pointing to the girl who seemed to be looking in their direction.

Then, before Imogen had time to comment, another sound came into play. A familiar sound of silver strings. They both watched mesmerised as a dark-haired boy in woven shorts joined the circle, and moved the tune seamlessly into another song.

'That's my instrument,' said Lowen, with a mixture of surprise and indignation. 'How did he get that? It's mine!' Lowen was about to move in to grab it when Imogen held him back.

'Don't. That's Nihplod,' she said smiling and giving him a shy wave. 'He looks older, but it's him.'

'Nihplod,' said Lowen. 'What, your dolphin? No way.'

The girl sang solo, a song Lowen recognised. The words were slightly different but some were definitely Spanish, like he had heard the mermaid sing. They both listened quietly to the enchanting song they both associated with the song of the sea. When she came to the end of the song, the others picked up another melody and sang quietly, almost in a whisper, gradually raising their voices to a triumphant chorus. Nihplod took the girl's hand and walked over to Imogen and Lowen.

'This is Sage,' said Nihplod introducing her first to Imogen, her look-a-like, then to Lowen. 'You all have a special connection. Come. We should talk and celebrate together.' Imogen was overwhelmed and couldn't take her eyes off the girl, who she realised did look like her. Lowen was less impressed with the girl: he couldn't take his eyes off what he considered to be his silver strings.

'I thought it was special,' he said sulkily. 'Suppose every mermaid and dolphin boy has one?'

Nihplod laughed and put his arm round Lowen's shoulder while handing him the silver stringed instrument.

'No. There is only one and this is yours.'

'But how? I hid it under my bed.'

'I keep telling you Nihplod has magic powers! You're being boring. Let's find out about the girl and what's going on.'

Lowen carefully inspected the instrument and gave the silver strings a strum.

'Yeah. Cool. It is mine,' he said beaming at Nihplod and then turning to the girl with outstretched hand. 'Pleased to meet you.'

The girl patted his hand and they all laughed. They walked back towards the castle and settled beyond the courtyard by a small group of trees. Nihplod sat cross-legged and they joined him. Imogen was the first to speak, turning to the girl, Sage,

'Can you see me? Do you understand what I'm saying?' She spoke slowly while gesturing, pointing to herself, then to the girl and waving her arms as if conducting an invisible orchestra. The girl smiled and then looked quizzically at Nihplod.

'She can see you now, but only has some thought-language skills,' said Nihplod. 'I have given you powers to understand Nettogrofian and your histories are in her songs. They have been passed on through generations.'

'That's cool,' said Lowen as he strummed a cord on his silver strings.

Sage said, 'This song is for you.'

She picked up her flute and began to play. It was a beautiful, haunting tune that rose up to the sky, and the trees swayed, without a breeze, to the melody. She waved her hand in a gesture to Lowen to accompany her. Lowen soon picked up the riff and when he could play on his own, she started to sing... 🎼♪♫♪

The song she sang was about a brother and sister who were twins and both accomplished musicians. They left their shores in Spain and went to sea, filling their ship with music to take to other lands. A storm rose and their ship went off course, splintering its hull on the rocks. The girl was crushed by the waves and was drowning. Then, like magic, a dolphin appeared in the stormy seas and carried her off to an enchanted island of peace. Where the sun was warm and the trees were friends and connected the people to the earth and sky. The girl had a small hole in her happiness, as her twin brother was lost to her. Here, the song ended on a hopeful note, that one day he would find his way to Nettogrof. When

she stopped singing, both Imogen and Lowen had tears in their eyes and Imogen flung herself at Sage and gave her a hug.

'As much as you're annoying, I'd hate never to see you again,' said Lowen, giving Imogen a pat on her back.

'Me too.' Then turning to Nihplod whose smile sparkled with his eyes, she said. 'Are we related then? How?'

Lowen turned to look hard at Nihplod, waiting for his answer. First Nihplod said something to the girl, that neither Lowen nor Imogen could hear. The girl squealed with delight. She first hugged Imogen, then Lowen, kissing the palm of their hands and holding them to her face.

'Our blood is of the same,' she said, with one arm round each of them. 'We are descendants of the twins and you have found your way to Nettogrof.'

Imogen was so overwhelmed by this revelation, her legs went wobbly and she plopped down on the ground. Lowen took time to process what had been said and looked quizzically at the girl, who smiled broadly back at him.

'This is true,' said Nihplod. 'The ship sunk on the rocks near you, in Cornwall. This happened many, many moons ago when our seas were free of death snot and before some people travelled the seas to make slaves. You have descended from the twin brother and Sage is a descendant from the woman.'

'Woo... that's awesome,' was all Lowen could think to say as he gently touched the girl's face. Then, realising the connection, he continued. 'My mermaid! My mermaid must have been on that same ship. She's a musician and she told me, they came from Spain. Don't suppose, we're related?'

'Noo,' said Nihplod and Imogen in unison and laughed. Then, Imogen who had been deep in thought suddenly sprang to her feet with an urgency.

'We have to help Nettogrof grow seaweed that's not contaminated with plastics, and create safe pools in the sea where small fish can feed.'

'Woo.. hold up there little sis. Good idea, but I'm still getting used to the idea that I'm part Spanish. It's awesome!'

Imogen laughed. 'Yes, Spanish,' she said, thoughtfully touching her own face. 'Mum said we're all a bit of something else and Nihplod told me we're all made up of particles of the universe.' Nihplod turned to Imogen, 'It would be good if you could help the sea-gardens. As you saw in the banqueting hall, they only have food from the land. But for now let's enjoy your union with Sage.' Sage held her flute out to Imogen, 'This is for you,' she said.

'Thank you,' said Imogen giving her a hug. Then turning to Lowen, Sage first blew a note on something concealed in her hand before giving him a small flute made from a large dried seed pod. Lowen smiled and thanked her, then blew a couple of notes on the pod. He was surprised how good it sounded. Sage produced another flute and they all sat down together and played. Lowen worked hard on his thought-language skills and between them, with some translations from Nihplod, they talked about their different lives. Sage was fascinated by mobile phones and Imogen asked Nihplod if she could one day come to visit them or even live on the Peninsula.

'Perhaps, one day. But your world is very different to life here on Nettogrof so it would be difficult for her to stay long.'

Imogen understood how Sage could find living in Cornwall with cars and technology unnerving. She tried to imagine living on Nettogrof and as much as she enjoyed visiting, she could never live there. They talked and laughed for what seemed like hours, then Lowen reminded Imogen, they should be heading home.

'You're right,' she agreed. 'First, Nihplod. We need you to go and get some kelp with roots, that we can plant under rocks and get the rock pools started in the sea.' Nihplod nodded.

'Cool,' said Lowen. 'While you're gone, we'll start work on making the rock pools. Not too far out, so the islanders can easily harvest the kelp.'

'Let's do it,' said Imogen excitedly. 'Come on, let's go.'

112

Nihplod was ready to run down the shingle path to the sea. He gave Imogen a broad smile and said he would be back soon.

'The rock pools with the kelp can also act as a nursery for the fish,' Imogen called after him and then turning to Sage said first in words, then in thought. 'Don't know if you understood about the non-polluted seaweed, but it would be good if you came to help.'

Sage nodded and smiled broadly, 'Yes and I can get Bee and Thor to also help. They may not understand what we are doing and you will be invisible to them, so try not to bump into them.'

Imogen and Lowen laughed. Nihplod had disappeared out of sight and they went on ahead of Sage before she took another path, saying she would come to join them on the beach.

'Wow Im, this is pretty cool, finding a distant relative. I wonder if Sage and her brother's line is on mum or dad's side. She looks so like you.'

Imogen and Lowen had reached the beach when they saw a dolphin leap in the distance.

'That was quick,' said Lowen. 'Do you reckon that Nihplod is back with some kelp already? Come on, we need to get some rocks.'

'What? Wait, Lo. I'm getting an urgent message from Nihplod. Something's happened.'

CHAPTER 30

Lowen stood still looking intently at Imogen and mouthed silently at her. 'What's up?'

Imogen didn't answer. She ran into the sea and swam out to Nihplod, leaving Lowen wondering whether to follow her or wait. 'Im! What's going on?' Imogen had reached Nihplod and saw Lowen was about to swim to them.

'No. wait there. I'll be back. Gaia is on her way.'

Lowen heard voices behind him and he turned to see Sage smiling at him. She was with another girl and a boy who looked around 15 years old. Sage said in thought 'Remember they can't see you.' Lowen found it hard to concentrate on thought-language while looking from Sage to Imogen, who seemed to be listening to Nihplod with a look of concern: and then she gasped.

'Sorry, Sage,' Lowen said, turning to face her, and pointing at Imogen and the dolphin. 'Have to go. I'll be back in a bit. Get your friends to heave some big rocks down into the sea to create large pools.'

Lowen swam quickly out to Imogen and Nihplod.

'What's going on, Im?'

'There's a raging battle. The Grey Force has somehow turned all the sea creatures against each other, even those that were friends and helped each other.'

'Why?'

'To cause chaos so they can rule the oceans and seal off the Knowledge Well forever. Plastics have made the sea creatures and seabirds weak. It's getting dangerous. We have to go soon. Gaia is on her way.'

Nihplod was nodding and nudged Lowen with his beak. Lowen took the kelp from him.

'Thanks,' he said. 'Can't believe you managed to get this with a

marine war going on.'

'Isn't he amazing? But even Nihplod is worried. We have to get going, Lo.'

'Yeah. I hope the giant octopus is on our side,' he said, as they both swam back to the shore to see Sage and her friends rolling rocks into the sea.

Imogen and Lowen helped them create the rock pools and secured the roots of the kelp under the rocks. Sage's friends did not seem to notice rocks seemingly moving into position on their own. They all worked quickly and well together as they joined Sage in song.

'There's not much of it now,' said Imogen to Sage. 'But it's a prolific grower and will spread quickly.' She broke a small piece off for Sage to taste.

'It's good', she said with the hint of a tear showing in the corner of her eye. Her friends followed her lead and with some hesitation, broke off a small piece to try. They both nodded and smiled with approval, before bursting into song.

'They do a lot of singing here,' said Lowen, laughing. Come on Im, we better go. There's Gaia now with Nihplod.'

Imogen gave Sage a big hug. 'Goodbye,' she said. 'I've never had a distant cousin before. One day you must come to visit us in Cornwall.'

Lowen stepped forward and hugged Sage. 'Yes, it's really cool. You must come to see us.'

Her friends just saw Sage's arms outstretched, so they also held their arms out towards the sea to thank it for bringing the new sea vegetable to them. Lowen and Imogen turned and waved before diving into the sea to join Nihplod and Gaia.

CHAPTER 31

Lowen climbed onto Gaia and when Imogen reached Nihplod, she looked back at Nettogrof and Sage, who was on the shore waving farewell before walking back up the shingle path with her friends. Nihplod blew a bubble over Imogen and her flute, before making a dive into the sea.

'We must go with speed if we are to return you and your brother safely to Cornwall,' said Nihplod in thought-language. 'The battle is raging and the Grey Force has told a pod of orcas that you and your brother killed one of their young by tying fishing rope to its tail. They are looking for you.'

'What! But we didn't. Why say that?' Imogen said.

'Because the Grey Force is afraid you will help to rid the oceans of plastics.'

Imogen looked at Lowen who seemed to be oblivious to their situation and enjoying his ride on Gaia. She had to talk to herself to avoid holding her breath. They were soon through the mist and dived deep into the ocean. It felt like they were travelling at an incredible speed. Everything looked different from before. It was darker and felt electric, like before a storm. Fish and sea creatures were whizzing around in different directions as though they were caught in a whirlwind. An eel that looked like a thin black dragon came alongside of them. Its white beady eyes, in its small red head with a mouth full of jagged teeth, made Imogen scream, when its black body twisted and came within a nose-length of her face.

'It's alright,' assured Nihplod. 'She's just frightened. She won't hurt you.'

Then they came upon a frightening scene of blacktip reef sharks fighting each other. It was like a frenzy of twisting tails and gnashing teeth, biting chunks out of each other and blood clouding the water. Imogen could see Lowen on Gaia just ahead, and they had to move quickly away

from a shark that was about to attack them. Nihplod dived deeper into the ocean to avoid conflict. They sped past octopus, eels and transparent light fish, many species that normally lived quite peaceful lives on coral reefs or isolated in the depths of the oceans. Nihplod and Gaia moved swiftly through the water until they came to seas that felt calmer. Here they surfaced and swam alongside each other for a while to discuss a strategy. Imogen and Lowen looked at each other.

'You OK Im? That was a bit scary. Like underwater world war.'

'I'll be glad when we get home,' she said, trying to hold back tears.

'Don't worry Im. We'll be home soon. Gaia said we're not far now.'

Then they both felt the tension coming from Nihplod and Gaia, who had stopped swimming and were as still as hawks on the wind. Imogen and Lowen looked up and saw what looked like a hundred black and white giant faces of orcas rise out of the sea. The water poured off them as they rose up revealing their massive bodies and giant tail fins that started to beat the water, creating waves. Fear swept over Imogen, and Lowen sank down closer to Gaia as if trying to hide.

'Can't Nihplod make us invisible?' he whispered.

'That wouldn't help. They can sense us.'

Huge waves began to form from the beating of the orcas tail fins, turning the gentle ripples into storm-high waves that came at them like an avalanche.

'Hold on tight,' said Nihplod. 'I have spoken to one of the elders and I am hoping she will give time to reflect on what I have said.'

Lowen was already gripping Gaia with both arms and legs, as they rode the waves, like champion surfers. A massive wave crashed down over Imogen and Nihplod and she nearly lost her hold.

'Why are they doing this?' asked Imogen.

'They want us to give you up to them. We have said no, so they are trying to shake you off.'

This was true, but what Nihplod had left out, was that if they didn't give up Imogen and Lowen, that they would kill them too. Then it suddenly stopped. The orcas were still and the waves slowly lessened in height.

'I need to communicate with the elders on my own,' said Nihplod. 'Don't be afraid. Hold on to Gaia and I will be back soon.' Imogen realised she had been holding her breath and let the air out as she slowly climbed off Nihplod.

'What you doing?' said Lowen in a concerned voice.

'It's OK. Nihplod needs to talk to them.'

'Talk to them! Hasn't he got a better plan than that?'

Imogen felt insecure letting go of Nihplod and slipping in to the sea, that seemed endless, surrounded by giant hostile orcas. When she held on to Gaia, the fear fell away and once again she felt that protective bubble around her. It seemed like an hour had passed and Nihplod was still head to head with one of the orcas. It looked like the other elders had heard Nihplod and had let go of their hostilities, but one had yet to be convinced. Nihplod looked so small next to these massive shining black and white orcas.

'He's brave,' said Lowen. 'They could crush him with a flip of a tail. It looks like his talk is working though, Im.'

'Yes. Look. Here he comes.'

Nihplod swam back to them leaving the orcas watching him. When Imogen climbed back on to Nihplod, she was expecting the orcas to swim away, but they didn't move.

'Do they believe we didn't kill their calf?' she asked.

'Yes, but they are still angry with humans for the death snot and fishing ropes. I have convinced them you are young humans who want to help. They will let us pass now.'

One by one they lowered their giant heads back in to the sea, and moved to make a break in their circle for us to swim through. It was a chilling experience, as Nihplod and Gaia swam side by side slowly, with respect, to pass these giants of the sea. One raised its black and white, massive head as they passed. It was just enough to catch a glimpse of its beady eye, with its deep look of sorrow.

Neither Imogen nor Lowen said a word. They kept their heads lowered and even Lowen was holding his breath. It was probably less than a minute, but it seemed as though time was suspended as they moved in slow motion past these giants of the sea. When they had enough sea behind them and saw the orcas submerge and go in the opposite direction, Lowen was the first to speak.

'Woo, Im. That was close. I'll be glad to get home.'

'Me too,' said Imogen. 'Nihplod said most of the wars are being fought in oceans away from our coast so we should be OK.'

Then Nihplod and Gaia both nose-dived and they raced through the water at amazing speed — Imogen realised they had broken the time barrier, and had come back into their time zone. The sea felt colder than before. They were just off the coast of Cornwall and in the distance, they could see that familiar rugged coastline as they drew closer to Rame Head with its little chapel ruin on top.

'Look, Im. We're home. Can't see my kayak though.'

'You will,' she said and, as if by command, there, by the rocks was a shimmering on the water which gradually became a clearer form — their kayaks and paddles waiting for them. Lowen looked over to the rocks at Rame Head and for a moment he thought he saw her, the mermaid, but it was only a seal. Lowen sighed and dreamily patted Gaia's head.

'That was awesome,' he said. 'We'll be on the case of plastics and pollution. If you see my mermaid, say Hi.'

Lowen climbed off Gaia and smiled as his silver stringed instrument shimmered into view on top of his kayak.

'Come on, Im. We better get home.'

Imogen was deep in conversation with Nihplod.

'Thank you. It was brilliant meeting our distant cousin,' said Imogen, while giving Nihplod a hug. 'What will happen with the wars. Will the Grey Force win?'

'No. Not if we have help from you and other young humans. Together we can win. Some of the more intelligent who live in the oceans, that have managed to avoid eating plastics, and are not stupefied, are calling meetings of ocean species. The giant octopus is now free from the Grey Force. It is collecting broken plastic fishing rope, that we get tangled up in, and throwing it back onto the boats. With the help of the mermaids and octopus, many are starting to see they have been fed untruths, by the Grey Force. Sadly, it has taken many lives and some wars are still raging, but there is light in this darkness, and we thank you for your help.'

Imogen felt tears sting her eyes as she gave Nihplod a final farewell hug.

'I'll miss you,' she said, as she left Nihplod to join Lowen.

Lowen gave Imogen a tearful smile as he steadied her kayak, for her to climb on to.

'They'll be okay, Im. I know it. And we've got work to do,' he said, while giving Imogen an affectionate arm rub.

A breeze, from nowhere, blew the smell of seaweed and spots of salty water over their faces, as if to welcome them home.

Before paddling their kayaks back to Kingsand harbour, they watched Nihplod and Gaia as they leapt and dived their way out to sea.

Something that may interest you

The fictional Spanish mermaid who Lowen meets on the rocks at Rame Head, is based on folklore about a 16th century Galleon from Spain carrying merchandise and a band of musicians that was shipwrecked off the coast of Cornwall.

■ The chimpanzee that Imogen sees helping the islanders pick fruit from high branches is based on the bonobo. Bonobos are less aggressive than chimpanzees and are considered kind and altruistic.

■ The fictional dolphin called Nihplod, is based on the bottlenose dolphin, that many of you may have seen swimming off the coast of Cornwall. Dolphins are known for their intelligence, their friendliness to humans, their use of echolation (sonic sound) and their ability to swim to great depths. Dolphins are known to fish together with humans and recently protected surfers under threat.

■ Giant Pacific Octopus has three hearts and nine brains, one brain in each of its eight arms. It's known for its intelligence, ability to open jars and solve puzzles, and can change colour for camouflage.

■ Wandering Albatross, from the Diomedeidae family, has the longest wingspan of any living bird, 3.5 metres, and can live up to 50 years.

■ Giant Mobula Rays can leap up to two metres out of the water, then bellyflop, making an incredible boom. Scientists are still undecided on the reason why.

■ Orcas, named Killer Whales by ancient fishermen because of the way they worked together to catch food, are in fact the largest member of the dolphin family. They can grow up to 9.5 metres in length.

■ Pacific Ocean garbage patch is where plastics and other debris has been caught in the rotating ocean's currents, known as a gyre. There are five ocean gyres. The garbage patch in the Indian Ocean has more microscopic plastic particles.

■ Seabirds, dolphins, whales and octopus are among sea-life suffering and dying from plastic pollution and ghost fishing nets.

Foetal A

Because of the suffering that your enemy will inflict on you during the siege, you

will eat the fruit of the womb, the flesh of the sons and daughters the Lord your

God has given you. Even the most gentle and sensitive man among you will have no

compassion on his own brother or the wife that he loves or his surviving children,

and he will not give to one of them any of the flesh of his children that he is eating.

It will be all that he has left because of the suffering your enemy will inflict on you

during the siege of your cities. The most gentle and sensitive woman among you- so

sensitive and gentle that she would not venture to touch the ground with the sole

of her foot will begrudge the husband she loves and her own son or daughter the

afterbirth from her womb and the children she bears. For she intends to eat them

secretly during the siege and in the distress that your enemy will inflict on you in

your cities.

Deuteronomy 28:53-57

1

Foetal Attraction

All characters and events in the Inspector Crime Files of

Inspector Blaise novels are fictitious and any

resemblance to real persons, living or dead is purely

coincidental.

2

Foetal Attraction

Special thanks to all the officers at Strabane Police

Station for their kind assistance.

Foetal Attraction

Blaise slumped lazily behind the wheel of the black Renault Espace, a gift left to him by his sister, Julia when she had immigrated to Canada to continue with her career in nursing. He luxuriated in the blissful tranquillity of what was a genuinely unusual Saturday off from the often-thankless task of policing the streets of Northern Ireland, streets that could change unexpectedly and become dangerously volatile. Now, enjoying a moment of stilled calmness, a certain surge of excited adoration seeped through his veins, an excitement only befitting that of a love-struck teenager, his eyes stared lovingly at his young lover. A smile curved his mouth as he watched Cathy O'Hare emerge from the supermarket on the opposite side of the road, a road narrowed by numerous cars parked on either side and apparently ignored by the somewhat lethargic traffic wardens.

Like a swan amongst scavenging vultures, Cathy O'Hare's radiant beauty shone as she gracefully glided through the throng of busying shoppers. Hands gripped at the plastic carrier bags filled with the ingredients for the romantic meal that she had promised him. The shoulder-length dark auburn hair fluttered in the cool spring breeze as she stepped in between two parked cars intending to cross the road. The cheerfully replied smile turned to that of sudden annoyance as the heavens opened unexpectedly and the rain battered down without mercy. There, as Cathy stepped out onto the road, that unseen irritating Gremlin of Chaos showed its impishness and the carrier bags in Cathy's hands burst spilling the contents onto the rain-lashed tarmac. Only for the embarrassed stress on her face, Blaise would have burst out into a fit of laughter. Then as he made to rush to the assistance of his young lover, he stared in shocked fear at the sudden appearance of a white transit van that sped towards the crouching Cathy, travelling in the wrong direction. In that terrifying moment, Blaise fought to release the seatbelt, his limbs lead-like with panic as he tried to warn her, fearing that he would see her mown down. Inside Blaise screamed with anxious fear but there was no sound and the fear intensified as he imagined that he was about to witness Cathy's death.

Yet again, the horror of Blaise's recurring nightmares returned without mercy to torture and torment within his dream-state. In semi-awakened panic-stricken fear, Blaise sat upright in bed his naked flesh completely coated with beads of cold sweat, his pulse racing in rhythm with his pounding heart. The omnipresent sickening nightmare had returned without welcome, the same nightmare that had tortured him nightly and had been the reason why he shied away from any form of relationship for fear of something terrible happening that would destroy his happiness. He had hoped that by falling in love with Cathy and having conquered his drinking that the nightmares would end and permit him a loving relationship.

The blackened clouds exposed an almost perfectly orbed moon that seeped unhindered through the slatted window blinds. With an almost secreted sensuality, the nightly glow coated the naked shoulders of the blissfully slumbering Cathy as she lay face down on the bed, unaware of her lovers surrender to the torment. In the stilled calmness, the beads of tormented sweat turned icy cold on his naked body as he sipped a coffee on the sofa. A quiet anxiousness began massaging his mind as he sat in the solemnity of silent solitude. Was there perhaps some great divine plan written out stating that he was supposed to lead his life alone and without love? A quiet sadness echoed within as Blaise turned back the pages of his private history, hurting upon recalling all the long lonely nights of not having someone special in his life, to enjoy that sense of belonging that he now enthusiastically treasured with young Cathy O'Hare.

The lethargic awakening of Cathy ushered all thoughts back into the recesses of his mind as she snuggled up to him on the sofa, her soft fingertips caressed Blaise's chest and she knew from the cold beads of sweat that he had had yet another nightmare.

'Did you have another nightmare, baby?'

'Eh no__ it__ you kept me awake with your loud farting and you were stinking too you dirty sod. What on earth have you been eating?'

'You cheeky sod,' Cathy laughed, playfully slapping her hand on his chest. 'My God, you can certainly sweat, Blaise. I hate it when you have these terrible nightmares.'

'It's ok babe, you go back to bed, I'm grand here with my coffee.'

'Why don't you come with me, maybe I can help you forget those nightmares.'

'Babe__ I'm__ tired. Besides, I'm going to work in two hours.'

Cathy pulled the duvet from the bed and covered Blaise on the sofa before wrapping her nakedness in a short satin robe, keenly preparing a fresh pot of coffee.

'Eh, listen Blaise__ I've been thinking about going back to do light duties.'

'How can you go back to work?' Blaise gasped surprised, twisting around on the sofa to stare towards the kitchen. 'Your leg's not healed properly yet. And don't give me any bull; I've seen you limping with the pain at times, Cathy.'

'I need to get back, Blaise. I'll go bloody mad if I stay cooped up in here much longer,' Cathy called out from the kitchen.

'Just take it easy for another few weeks, babe. See how you feel in a month or so.'

'Well_ there is one way of keeping me from going back to work,' Cathy smiled, making her way from the kitchen, carrying two coffee mugs and a certain sparkle in her eyes. 'I've been thinking__ it would be lovely to__'

'Jesus__ are you thinking what I'm thinking you're thinking?' Blaise laughed.

'I hope so. I'd really love you to get me pregnant, Blaise.'

'Christ Almighty__ we__ are you serious, Cathy? I mean, we aren't even married yet, not that that matters of course, but__ Jesus, a baby.'

'I've been thinking about it ever since I moved in with you, Blaise,' Cathy beamed with excitement as she snuggled under the duvet.

'I can just see the Big Crooks face__ he'd have my dangly bits hanging in his office.'

'Oh don't be so dramatic, Blaise. Uncle Andy's not that bad really. Besides, I think he and Aunt Violet would love to see me pregnant. I mean, especially if we were married. God, the look on your face_ have I surprised you, Ben?'

7

Foetal Attraction

'Wait a minute,' Blaise grinned. 'We seem to have gone from you going back to work to us getting married and having a kid. And, by the way_ was that a proposal?'

'Well, I suppose it was. I mean, I couldn't wait for you to get down on one knee, could I? Besides, you really aren't getting any younger.'

'You cheeky tart,' Blaise laughed, wrapping his arm around Cathy's shoulders. 'Jesus__ I eh__ never thought about marriage.'

'Oh, I see. I suppose you're just using me for sex and doing your cleaning__ I thought you loved me?'

'Of course I love you, stupid. I just never thought that you and I would__ well, me being almost twenty years your senior like.'

'Jesus, you're only forty eight, Blaise. Just think of all the guys at the office and at those functions, they'd be so envious of you having such a sexy babe on your arm.'

'Jesus__ marriage, bloody amazing,' Blaise sighed thoughtfully. 'I mean, Jesus.'

'I would really love for us to get married and have a kid,' Cathy smiled warmly.

'So, you truly want to get married and start a family?' Blaise asked, still not believing that Cathy desired to be his wife. He never imagined that he would one day be married and the thought of having a child with Cathy thrilled Blaise immensely. He stared up at the large framed photograph of his late father that hung over the fireplace, thinking quietly how proud his father would have been to see him settled and to be married with children. Then, for a split second, he imagined that something would go wrong and he would find himself alone.

'I love the idea of us getting married, Cathy. I mean, what about your career?'

'God Almighty, would having a child mean the end of my career? There is such a thing as child-minders you know,' Cathy enthused, placing her coffee mug on the side table. 'Now, when an amazingly sexy and young woman asks you to marry her, you are supposed to take her into your arms and carry her over to the bed where you then make mad passionate love to her,' Cathy continued, straddling Blaise under the duvet, her mouth then playfully kissing over his face. 'Come on__ we can start this family right now. Take me to bed.'

The mixture of the unexpected marriage proposal and being tired from the nightmare that had cruelly ruined his sleep caused such turmoil within Blaise's mind resulting in a rather unwelcome halt to Cathy's lustful intentions.

'Damn, this has__ I mean, this has never happened before,' Blaise sighed, as he lay on his back on the bed immensely disappointed.

'Don't worry about it babe. I suppose it happens to a lot of guys your age,' Cathy tried to make light of the situation.

Blaise sighed as he leaned back against the headboard, desperate to light a cigarette, but he felt determined not to surrender to the craving. He felt contented that he had stopped drinking, no more drink-fuelled partying and sleeping with strange women. No more would he turn up at work half-drunk and weary, which pleased his superiors. No more would he be wondering where he had spent the night, or with whom. Again, Blaise heaved a lingering heavy sigh, a tranquil thankfulness that he had fallen in love with Cathy and now, after a few months together, were now contemplating marriage and starting a family. Blaise's mind then began to flood with concern, the same concern that caused him to experience such tormenting nightmares. Then, quietly, he questioned his commitment to Cathy, thinking then that perhaps he was tempting fate and was perhaps sentencing the relationship to a kind of disaster, perhaps he was even bringing into effect the possibility of something terrible happening to Cathy. Blaise closed his eyes then sighed annoyed, chasing the thoughts from his mind.

Cathy exhaled a painful groan, which she tried to stifle as she rolled over onto her side keenly snuggling into Blaise. The hunger for his attentions returning as again she attempted to arouse him, which seemed to work, only the ringing of the telephone thwarted her intentions as Blaise immediately reached to answer it.

Blaise paid no attention to Cathy's pleas to ignore it, sighing heavily then as Blaise held the receiver to his ear. DS Jack Phillips' voice sounded urgent on the other end of the telephone as Blaise listened with dutiful interest, informing Blaise of the discovery of a body.

'You certainly pick your moments, Jack,' Blaise sighed, touching a hand softly over Cathy's stomach in an attempt to appease her. 'Right ok, come and pick me up, I'll be ready shortly. Oh, by the way, Jack. You are now officially in Cathy's bad books, and that's definite.'

'It's ok, baby,' Cathy sighed half-heartedly, touching a hand over his naked back as he dropped his feet to the floor. 'I know the job will always come first.'

Foetal Attraction

'Sorry babes, we'll talk when I get back home this evening. Maybe I'll be more ready for you later, then you'll be sorry, you'll need a rubber ring when you need to sit down.'

'I think my plan for getting pregnant is going to prove that bit more difficult,' Cathy grinned as she rose out of the bed. 'I've never thought of the job as being a contraceptive before.'

'True enough babes. Would you do a quick coffee?'

'Do you want me to do you a quick something to eat?' Cathy smiled making towards the kitchen naked then slapped both hands on her buttocks. 'You're missing this big boy.'

'Keep it warm for me for later. No, don't bother with anything to eat babes.'

'Did Jack say anything about this body?'

'He bloody better not have.'

'I don't mean mine, you silly sod.'

'I was joking woman. No, he just said that someone discovered the body of a young girl on a building site this morning. Apparently it was you dear Uncle who told Jack to phone me,' Blaise continued as he fumbled with the knot in his tie. 'Are you wearing that tie with the navy suit__ are you really?'

'Apparently not,' Blaise sighed, hurriedly slipping the tie off and held out several for Cathy to choose for him.

'The pale blue one will be nice with the shirt. You men just can't colour co-ordinate at all can you?'

Foetal Attraction

'Christ, this is it then, you'll be dressing me from now on,' Blaise smiled.

'Absolutely, and by the way my darling__ I'm a woman determined to have a baby and just to let you know the job won't stop that from happening, do you hear me?'

'No problem babes, I'll inform the Chief Super.'

Cathy stood naked and directly opposite Blaise adjusting his tie, teasingly touching her inner thigh up and down his leg. 'See, my leg feels fine.' Christ, I've just had a thought. The Big Crook and I will be related if we do get married. I could call him Uncle Andy.'

'Now that I would love to see,' Cathy laughed. Besides, Uncle Andy and Aunt Violet treat me like their own daughter. You really couldn't ask for better parents.'

'Did they not have any kids of their own? I don't think in all the years I've known him that I've ever asked him about kids.'

'To be honest, and don't you bloody repeat this. I think it's Andy's fault.'

'I could believe that, you know what they say about the Scots, they won't part with anything,' Blaise joked, gripping his hands onto Cathy's waist.

'You're absolutely terrible Inspector Blaise, now let me go you big horny sod and I'll pour that coffee for you.'

'Don't you bloody tell the Big Crook what I said by the way? Oh you wee beauty,' Blaise gasped aloud finding a packet of cigarettes in the jacket pocket, his mind a sudden surge of question as he thought about lighting one.

'Don't you dare, I hope you're not thinking about lighting that Blaise? You know what smoking does to your sperm count.'

'Who's counting them, I just like to give you the lot,' Blaise said, sipping his coffee.

'Right, there's Jack, get out and__' Cathy unexpectedly snatched the cigarette packet from Blaise's hand, crushing them as she threw them into the bin. 'Now go do your job.'

Foetal Attraction

2

Blaise stood on the driveway of his home, taking a long deep breath of the cold air, quietly cursing at the telephone call that had disturbed his time with Cathy and of the unexpected marriage proposal. An icy, bone-chilling wind swept eagerly across the expanse of open countryside, bringing with it a deeply despised fine rain, the kind that looked harmful enough but could soak right through to your very soul. There, in that stilled moment, Blaise cursed DS Jack Phillips for having disturbed him and Cathy. Thoughts then began to seep quietly into his mind, pleasant, welcome thoughts of his murdered colleague and dear friend, DS Charlie Brown. A certain sensation of guilt and anger aggravated him then as he blamed himself for his friend's murder, convinced that he could have prevented Charlie's death if only he had paid more attention to what he had been going through. A gentle smile then touched Blaise's lips upon reflecting on how Charlie would have reacted to the news that he and Cathy were now planning to be married, knowing that he would be so happy for them both.

The cold rain tapped against his face like a multitude of tiny drumming fingers chasing away all thoughts as the discovery of a woman's body awakened the detective within. Then, with growing eagerness, Blaise pulled open the passenger door and slumped into the seat.

'Right Charlie__ shit__ I mean, Jack.'

'No worries, I bloody do that myself at times Blaise.'

'It just takes a bit of getting used to.'

'That's for sure, it's bloody still hard to believe that Charlie's__'

14

Foetal Attraction

'It sure is, Jack. He was my colleague for nearly ten years or so.'

'Aye, anyway, I'm sorry for getting you out of bed so early Blaise.'

'That's ok, I had to get up, the phone was ringing,' Blaise joked, breathing a deep sigh.

'Are you finding it hard to give up the smokes?'

'Bloody right I am, I think I've ate my weight in bloody mints,' Blaise groaned.

'So, how come you're so bloody cheerful this early in the morning?' Jack Phillips exclaimed, steering the car along the narrow country road, the rain similar to that of a crystal-beaded curtain as the windscreen wipers swished from side to side almost aggressively. 'So eh, how's thing with Cathy__ is her leg any better?'

'She's dying to get back to work, but I told her to rest it for a few more weeks. She still gets pains and twinges in her calf. I mean, even her physiotherapist has told her to rest it,' Blaise continued, cursing then as he threw two mints into his mouth. 'So, bring me up to speed on this body, Jack.'

'Apparently some old tramp discovered the corpse. Young Will Chambers took the call, and then the sod called me. I was just about to__ anyway, somehow the Big Crook got wind of the discovery and he phoned me to call you.'

'I don't think that man ever bloody sleeps. Maybe he's some kind of demon and just flies about all night looking for crime,' Blaise suggested jokingly.

15

Foetal Attraction

Jack Phillips steered the car from the Derry Road and down into the Canal Basin, where there are several small buildings in the process of construction. A large, free car park stood opposite to the premises that were under construction and to the right of the car park there were locked premises used for market traders on a Friday.

'Right, so maybe our traveller friends have left a shop-lifter for us,' Blaise joked, scanning his eyes before him as Jack parked the car.

'They have really demolished these buildings here,' Jack Phillips stated. 'I just hope to God that they aren't building any more pubs, the town's got enough of them.'

'Sure half of the bars are closing down, it's this damn recession.'

'True, I mean, you'd think that if there was ever going to be a pub that would make money then it would definitely be in Strabane, they're nearly all alcoholics Blaise.'

'These big supermarkets are the cause, they can sell drink really cheap, that's why most of them drink in the house now. It doesn't help the domestic violence, right enough.'

'It's not as bad as it used to be though.'

'Christ, is that the Forensics team here already?' Blaise exclaimed thrusting himself out of the car. 'They're definitely keen this morning.'

Blaise watched the navy-suited Forensics officers busy themselves around the scene of the incident. Special lighting illuminated the immediate area and a large white tent covered the section in which the body lay. Blaise studied the surroundings noticing the lack of houses and immediately wondered why the victim had been in such an abandoned part of the town, although there was also the possibility that the murder took place there.

'Oh Jesus Christ, this place is a bloody swamp,' Blaise complained, noticing his shoes sink into the muddy ground.

Upon entering the tent, Blaise recognised the large rounded buttocks that stuck up in the air and stretched the material of the thick tweed trousers.

'I know that big rump there,' Blaise grinned, crouching then beside the pathologist. 'Doc, how are you?'

'Ah, my dear Blaise, how on earth are you? The burly man replied with a cheerfulness befitting that in his similarity to a bearded Santa Clause. 'What took you so long, I received the call over two hours ago, couldn't you leave that pretty little woman of yours?'

'Two hours ago!' Blaise groaned, staring directly at his colleague, who just replied with a shrug of his shoulders. 'Anyhow, what do we have, Doc?'

'A body, my dear Blaise__ and a dead one at that,' Doctor McElroy replied with a smile that burst through his well-groomed greyish beard.

'No disrespect but it looks more like an alien, Doc,' Blaise stared inquisitively. As he crouched over, Blaise noted that the body hair appeared completely shaved off. His eyes then focused upon the wound across the victim's abdomen, and gave all the indications of the victim having received some type of surgery. The mystery was why the victim was lying there dead.

Foetal Attraction

'This is a strange one for you my dear friend,' the Doctor smiled then groaned as he leaned closer to the victim. 'Look here, Blaise. 'The fingertips have been completely severed. I'd hazard a guess that the killer made this somewhat crude attempt to conceal the identity of the poor soul__ damn futile if you ask me.'

'What's all that scaring on the stomach, Doc?' Blaise questioned with interest. 'Has she been for an operation do you think?'

'It would appear so, but that will come to light later on my table Blaise, as you know.'

'Maybe she has done a runner from one of the hospitals?'

'Look here, Blaise,' Doctor McElroy said, pointing the tip of his silver pen around the abdominal area. 'Judging by the tinting of the flesh around this area here it would indicate that our victim has been dead for approximately three to four days.'

'I suppose you will give me a more precise time once you get the bacon slicer out, eh? Blaise said thoughtfully. 'What about this surgery then__ surely to God she wouldn't have had her fingertips removed if she was in hospital__ I mean, why would she have them cut off?'

'Maybe she was terrible nail-biter,' Jack Phillips jokingly added. 'It looks like it was well done though, the stitching I mean.'

'Do you think she has been in hospital, Doc?'

'Damned thing is Blaise,' Doc McElroy sighed forlornly pointing to the victim's mouth. 'All of the teeth have been removed also__ damned strange. But, as you so eloquently put it my dear Blaise, once I get the bacon slicer out hopefully then we shall discover more of this poor soul's unfortunate end. This, I'm afraid is man at his best.'

'I eh, she's naked, is there no sign of a hospital gown or anything?' Blaise enquired thoughtfully as he glanced around the enclosure, glancing at Jack Phillips then fixed his gaze upon the female Forensics officer who appeared from outside.

'No belongings what-so-ever have been discovered as yet, Inspector,' the woman replied, immediately kneeling beside the Pathologist to aid him in the process of taking and storing samples from the lifeless victim.

'I'm certain that toxicology will tell us a bit more Inspector,' Doc McElroy smiled, kneeling upright as he grunted with the effort. Blaise stared in silent question at the female officer, who appeared at first to ignore him.

'I expect that you will be interested to learn just why someone has taken these extreme measures to conceal the identity of the victim Inspector?' The female officer added.

'Eh, that amongst other things, miss eh__? Blaise smiled, touching the tip of his thumb back and forth over his chin as he expected the female officer to introduce herself. 'Do you have a name or do we need to guess?'

'Is it important to you Inspector?' The female officer smiled.

'Well, not if you wish to keep it a secret. Is that a Southern accent by the way?'

'Sure and begorra tis sir,' the female officer joked. 'I do be from the South tis a true fact, begorra.'

Foetal Attraction

'Right, help me to my feet Jacinta,' Doc McElroy groaned painfully, reaching out one large, thick-fingered hand for assistance.

'Ah so it's Jacinta,' Blaise smiled, cursing himself then for flirting as he found it habitual. Right, I'll take a look outside Doc,' Blaise continued, feeling a sort of guilt rise within, after all, it had only been an hour since Cathy had proposed to him.

'You just can't help yourself, can you?' Jack Phillips grinned, following Blaise outside.

'Inspector, over here,' called out one of the Forensics officers, busily taking plaster casts of a vast array of footprints. Look, I've found several footprints here, deep ones that lead over to the body, but the returning prints seem lighter, if you get me?'

'I do indeed, Ronnie,' Blaise said. 'It looks like our victim has been carried in here then?'

'I've also taken some casts of tyre tracks too, it looks as though the killer has unloaded the victim from the car, which was parked about here, see the difference in depths of the tyre tracks, Inspector?'

'Very good, Ronnie, don't suppose you could tell me the make of the car?'

'Well, bit unclear as yet, but I'll let you know once I get back to the lab and run it through my computer. I'll not confuse you with the details of how it works,' he joked.

'Oh nice,' Blaise sighed, thankful to have found two extra strong mints in the pocket of his thick jacket. 'I wish to God I'd never decided to give up smoking.'

'Me too,' Jack Phillips laughed. 'I've got to listen to him all day, Ronnie.'

'It's not easy, once they have got you hooked you're in trouble,' The Forensics officer said.

'Right then, let's get on, chat to you later Ronnie,' Blaise shouted as he walked away, ignoring the mud that spattered up around his ankles. 'Who discovered the victim, Jack?'

'It was some old tramp__ apparently he's been sleeping rough in one of the partially built buildings. He stumbled across the victim whilst he was searching about for whatever.'

'And where is this knight of the road?'

'He's at the station, uniform took him in, and they said they'd take him to the canteen.'

'Christ, if the poor sod survives that then hopefully he'll give us a statement,' Blaise laughed, crunching into the mints in his mouth that did little to quell the craving for nicotine. 'You just never know Jack__ it could be possible that he saw the killer.

Uniform are doing the rounds, checking for any possible witnesses and all that.'

'I just don't get this, Jack,' Blaise said thoughtfully, stroking his chin with his thumb. 'I mean, what in God's name happened to that poor soul in there?

'Maybe some lunatic has found a medical website and they're trying out experiments or something, maybe even practising to be a surgeon, in their own whacky mind I mean.'

21

Foetal Attraction

'Maybe she was an illegal and got caught with her hands in the till so they decide to make an example, Jack.'

'Could be, I wouldn't be surprised right enough, not with the way this world is going.'

'What__ maybe she was a drugs courier, maybe that's why she was cut up__ I just can't think why she is in such a terrible mess.'

'The thing is Blaise; it could just be some lunatic who likes to do a bit off cutting and dismembering.'

Blaise stood in momentary silent thought, his mind pondering quizzically on why someone had carried out such an evil and savage murder on the young woman. He questioned the suggested idea that the victim had been a drugs courier, but pondered then on the question that if that was the case, then, would the dealers have taken the time to stitch the victim up again, and would they even bother to try to hide the identity of the woman.

'I think we'll take another look at the body Jack. Are uniform searching for any sign of the victim's clothing?'

'They're searching as we speak,' Jack Phillips replied eagerly following Blaise into the illuminated tent. 'The poor soul doesn't look that old either.'

'Right Doc,' Blaise sighed.

'Ah, Blaise,' Doc McElroy muttered thoughtfully, pointing the tip of his pen to the victim's right ankle. 'There seems to be a little tattoo of sorts here.'

'It looks rather dainty,' Jack Phillips smiled.

Foetal Attraction

'Right, let's have a look then,' Blaise said immediately crouching beside the pathologist. 'It looks like a small red heart__ there's a black rose passing through it.'

'I've seen one like that before somewhere,' Jack Phillips said thoughtfully. 'Maybe it has some kind of meaning, I'll make a quick sketch and then get the photographer.'

'It looks like you'll be visiting the tattoo artists, Jack. Oh, did you tell uniform to stop any workers from entering the site, and tell whoever is in charge that this site is closed down until further notice.'

'I already did that and got a right ear full too.'

'I hope you gave him shit, this is a murder scene. By the way, did you make the arrangements for setting up an incident room here, Jack?'

'I called the station earlier, it'll be sorted.'

'Christ, this is unreal,' Blaise sighed aloud. 'Why in God's name would somebody want to cut this poor woman up like this__ what's the reason I wonder?'

'It's just so bizarre,' Jack Phillips sighed. 'Here's a thought, Blaise. What if this poor sod went to some sleazy back-street plastic surgeon for some work and it messed up, or she died on the table and the surgeon went a bits nuts here to hide her identity?'

'It's a thought, Jack. I mean, anything's possible,' Blaise mused. 'But a plastic surgeon__ in Strabane, hardly likely, Jack.'

'I suppose so, not many wealthy people about in this town.'

Foetal Attraction

'I hardly imagine that there is some back-street plastic surgeon operating in this town,' the pathologist added. 'I rather assume that you boys would know of it if that where the case.'

'Maybe this is his first patient, it could be that he has just started up,' Jack Phillips said.

'I expect that this case will cause you many a sleepless night my dear Inspector,' groaned the colossal, tweed-suited man as he rose with great effort to his feet. 'It's a damned strange one, but I suppose it's what we can expect in these mad times. It's so disconcerting that in this era of all the wonderfully modernised technological advances that mankind, has, in some strange way reverted backwards to a more barbaric lifestyle.'

'True enough, Doc, nobody seems to give a damn anymore__ everybody's obsessed with wanting, the more we get the more we want,' Blaise sighed forlornly. 'Anyway, if, as you presume, Doc, she has had surgery of some kind, why is she here, and why was she in hospital, if she was, that is?'

'Well, hopefully once I get this poor wretch onto my table and investigate inside, then perhaps I shall be in a position to enlighten you my dear Inspector.'

'What in God's name went on here?' Blaise sighed heavily. 'Just what happened after she left the hospital, presuming that she was in hospital that is__ and if she was, did she leave on her own accord or was she perhaps abducted__ why__ what the hell is going on here?'

Just as Blaise pondered with Jack Phillips and the pathologist, there was an excited shout from one of the uniformed officers, who burst into the tent with eager enthusiasm as he held a black bin liner. 'Sir__ I've found the victim's clothes.'

Foetal Attraction

'Calm down, they just might not be the victim's clothes, constable,' Jack Phillips said.

'Excellent work constable__ well done,' Blaise groaned with a look of annoyance on his face. 'Maybe you could try that wee bit harder to contaminate the evidence, eh? Christ Almighty, were you asleep during your training constable.'

'Jesus Billy, you should have left the bag where it was,' Jack Phillips sighed with a shake of his head. 'Well done anyway, I appreciate it's your first day. So, where did you discover this bag then, Billy?'

'It was over amongst the pile of rubble,' the young officer replied. Sorry, I wasn't thinking Sir,' he apologised, directing his gaze towards Blaise.

'It's ok Billy, CID are well used to uniform not thinking,' Blaise joked, searching the pockets of his wax jacket for a pair of latex gloves, which he always found awkward to pull on. 'How the hell do you get yours on so damn quick, Jack? I imagine that you're a dab hand with those condoms.'

'Never use them Blaise__ can't seem to find ones big enough.'

'That's because you're not supposed to pull them on over your head,' Blaise laughed, crouching then to delve carefully into the bin liner. 'Here's a sort of chocolate-coloured denim jacket. It feels slightly damp too,' Blaise continued, his thumb touching against a pin that was stuck through the lapel. 'Looks like our victim wore a brooch or badge of some kind; it just may have been pulled off during a struggle with her attacker. No signs of any blood though.' Blaise then removed a pair of cream coloured trousers from the bag that gave off a musty odour. He held the waist stretching it to its fullest on realising that the trousers had an elasticated waistband. 'Now then Jack, do you think that perhaps our victim has recently giving birth? These look like maternity trousers.'

'Could be, that would explain the scarring on the stomach, a back-street caesarean perhaps?'

'Good God, that just could be the answer gentlemen,' the pathologist grunted. 'It does have the appearance of a medically trained person, but, I'm not certain.'

Blaise removed a white satin, long-sleeved blouse then a white lace bra, each item carefully placed into individual evidence bags. 'Now then, there's no sign of any briefs.'

'Could be the killer kept them, a sick trophy if you know what I mean?' Jack Phillips said, handing the sealed evidence bags to one of the Forensics officers. 'Maybe she didn't wear any briefs, Blaise, you never know?'

'What, like a hooker who only uses her briefs to keep her ankles warm you mean,' Blaise smiled, spilling out the contents of the handbag onto a clear plastic sheet. He ignored the brown leather purse as he slowly touched his gloved fingertips through the feminine clutter, noting that amidst the cosmetics and lipsticks that there was a cigarette lighter but no cigarettes.

'At least we don't need to worry about nicotine on her fingertips.'

'Jesus Jack,' Blaise grinned, continuing to scan his eyes inquisitively through the now opened purse in his hands. He allowed the few coins and one ten pound note to fall out onto the sheet, then, as he removed all the cards, Blaise smiled upon discovering a driving license. 'Well, now we know who our victim is,' showing the licence to his colleague.

'Alice O'Leary__ that address is in Ballylaw, I think I know those wee rented cottages, Blaise,' Jack Phillips said. 'You wouldn't think that that was the same person lying there would you?'

'She is only young too; it's such a bloody shame. Another young life destroyed,' Blaise sighed heavily with anger, his mind reflecting over the countless lives wasted by the senseless violence of sectarianism, terrorist atrocities and of course, the psychopaths that lurked in and around the area.

Foetal Attraction

3

Leaving behind the suburban congestion of concrete and tarmac, Jack Phillips steered the car cautiously as he negotiated the narrowed twists and turns of the uphill roads, the dull, overhead clouds slowly gave way to a bright, pale sky that gave the pretence of a summer's day, but, in reality, it was icy cold. The car passed by the sedate rural area of Artigarvan, lush green fields lined the journey until they arrived at the few secluded rented cottages in the Ballylaw area. Both men immediately laughing as they stared at a hideously lime-green Lada estate car that looked as though it hadn't been driven in years and had surrendered to the growth of rust, it's grotesque appearance doing nothing for the reputation of the owner.

'You'd definitely need to wear a disguise if you drove that thing, eh?' Blaise laughed emerging from the unmarked police car. 'I mean, can you imagine__' Blaise's remarks cut short by the appearance of a young man standing in the widely opened front door. He looked rather bemused, as he stood dressed in loose-fitting grey sweatshirt and baggy combat trousers, headphones loose around his neck giving the impression that he didn't have a care in the world as he stood idly scratching at the mass of uncombed hair.

'Can I help you guys, like?'

'If that's your Lada then it's you who needs the help,' Jack Phillips joked.
'Eh__ what__ can I help you guys like, who are you looking for?'

'Do you__ is this number fourteen?' Blaise questioned, searching his jacket pockets for the driving license of Alice O'Leary. 'Do you live here, sir?'

'Aye and aye, what's it to you like?'

Foetal Attraction

'Detective Inspector Blaise, Strabane Police, and this is DS Phillips. Do you know a Miss Alice O'Leary, sir?'

'I do, aye, what's the problem like?' the young man gasped with awakened alarm, staring at the detectives bewildered and anxiously concerned. 'What eh__ where is she__ is there something wrong like?'

'I think we should go inside sir, we need to talk to you now,' Jack Phillips calmly said, stepping forwards, giving the young man no choice but to step backwards into the hallway permitting the detectives to enter. 'Why don't you take a seat, sir?'

'Can you tell me who you are, sir, and your connection to Alice O'Leary?' Blaise said.

'Aye, John__ Patterson__ it's John Patterson. Alice is__ well, we live together like.'

'Well, I'm afraid that we have some bad news, sir,' Blaise sighed as he sat on an armchair that had seen better days. 'We discovered a body this morning and we believe it to be that of Alice O'Leary.'

'Oh__ shit__ no__ please, don't let__ please no, not my Alice,' the young man gasped with shocked disbelief, his eyes wide as he stared at Blaise.

'I'm sorry, sir, but we need to ask you to identify the body. Jack, make a coffee for Mr Patterson,' Blaise said, giving his colleague the opportunity to look around.

'I can't believe this like__ are__ you sure it's my Alice__ maybe you've made a mistake.'

Foetal Attraction

'Well, I hope so, but honestly I don't think so, sir,' Blaise sighed, watching the young man battle within to hold back his tears. 'When did you see her last?'

'Eh, this is Saturday. Tuesday it was, aye, that's right. Alice said that she was going to visit her mother for a few days like, just to rest, her mother said she would buy her some stuff like.'

'Tuesday you say, hadn't you phoned her or anything?'

'I don't have a mobile phone or a landline, I'm not working and, as you can see, I'm pretty shitting poor like.'

'So eh, where does Alice's mother live?'

'She lives out in Donegal somewhere, I'm not sure where exactly like.'

'Right ok, so eh, do you know what Alice was wearing the last time that you saw her?'

'Oh aye, she looked real nice so she did like. Eh, Alice was wearing a brown velvet type jacket with her new creamy coloured trousers. Oh, and she wore a white blouse.'

'Now, I understand this is difficult for you, sir,' Blaise continued, recognising that the young man was now starting to tremble. 'Can you remember if Alice was wearing a brooch of any kind, maybe a badge?'

'I'm not sure___ I can't honestly remember, sorry. Are you sure it's my Alice?'

'Well the indications are that is Alice O'Leary,' Jack Phillips said.

Foetal Attraction

'Well, to be honest, the clothing that you have just described match's those that were discovered in a plastic bag close to her__ where we discovered Alice.'

'I don't get you here like,' the young man gasped confused. 'You say you found her clothes in a bag__ I mean, was she__ naked like__ did somebody__ rape her?'

'Did Alice have any distinguishing marks, a tattoo perhaps?'

Aye, she did, Alice had little tattoo of a heart and it had a black rose going through it like.'

'We're not certain yet as to any sexual activity, sir. We will need you to formally identify the body I'm afraid.' Blaise continued, taking the coffee mug handed to him by Jack Phillips, who shook his head slightly to tell Blaise that he could find nothing relevant.

'This is unreal__ I mean, I can't believe__ who would want to__ kill my Alice?' The young man continued in his subdued grief, continually glancing at the door as if hoping that at any moment Alice O'Leary would just appear as if it was all a big mistake and nothing had happened.

'Had your partner been in hospital recently, sir, perhaps a minor operation__ or perhaps she had intended to visit a clinic or health centre?'

'Was she attending anti-natal perhaps?' Jack Phillips added.

'Hospital, no, well, only for those check-ups like, you know, the ones that pregnant woman are always going for. Why__ was it something to do with the baby like?'

Foetal Attraction

'Baby,' Blaise gasped, almost spitting the coffee from his mouth with surprise. 'What baby, do you mean that Alice was pregnant?'

'Some bloody cop you are, couldn't you see the big bloody bump like__ Jesus?'

'Eh, to be honest, I never really noticed, sir,' Blaise lied, recalling the large scar across the victim's stomach. 'Are you positive that she was pregnant, sir?'

'We didn't really get a good look at the__ at Miss O'Leary, sir,' Jack Phillips lied, looking as bemused as Blaise looked.

'Of course I'm bloody sure__ Christ, we had been trying for a kid for ages. Alice was over the bloody moon that she was having a kid like.'

'Right, I see,' Blaise sighed.

'Eh, maybe if this woman that you found wasn't pregnant then it isn't Alice__ maybe__ what if this woman stole Alice's purse?'

'That's why it's imperative that you make a positive identification for us, sir.'

'Right__ ok, so where do I need to go to do this like?'

'The body will be at a place called Forster Green in Belfast, sir. I can arrange for a car to take you there.'

'Eh, Doc McElroy said the mortuary is full out there,' Jack Phillips said quietly. 'The Doc said that he would be carrying out the post mortem at Altnagelvin Hospital in Londonderry.'

32

Foetal Attraction

Blaise sat silent as he sipped his coffee, his eyes closely studying the mannerisms and facial expressions, quietly pondering on the possibility of Alice O'Leary having discovered that the unborn baby had some form of mental defect and that perhaps she had planned to abort it and something went wrong. He also thought that just maybe Alice O'Leary had visited a back-street abortionist and the operation had tragically went wrong, that the person then callously dumped Alice's body after attempting to remove all traces of her identity.

Blaise continued to stare at the young man, telling himself that there was no point in telling him that time was a great healer. What words could he possibly utter to console or comfort anyone in that particular time of sorrowed grief__ was there any point in trying? Perhaps, Blaise contemplated quietly, that this poor inconsolable wretch beside him now saw no future for himself and would, at some point, be found floating face-down in the River Foyle. In that moment of mind-questioning sympathy, Blaise suddenly wondered just how he would react or feel if anything were to happen to Cathy.

'You eh__ you said that your partner was pregnant, how did you feel about that, sir__ I mean, were you happy about it__ did you look forward to being a father?'

'Why would somebody want to hurt Alice, Inspector? She never had a bad thing to say about anyone like, she was so sweet and wouldn't harm a fly,' the young man sobbed with a sudden flood of heartbroken tears as he clasped both trembling hands to his face, completely ignoring Blaise's question.

'Were you both happy with the situation,' Blaise questioned again. 'I mean, did you or your partner have any problems with her having a baby?'

Foetal Attraction

'Problems__ no, the only problem was that I wasn't working like. We were both happy about the baby. I mean, we would've managed, everybody does.'

'Was your partner employed, sir?'

'Partner__ her fucking name's Alice__ it's Alice,' the young man screeched angrily. I can't believe that__ Alice is__'

'Where did eh__ Alice work__ did she have a job, sir?'

'She eh__'

'Look, don't worry, it's sod all to do with us, we don't care if it was on the quiet,' Blaise said sympathetically. 'If Alice worked whilst claiming Social Security it's nothing to do with us and we won't say.'

'Well, she did do a wee job; she helped in a friends shop on The Melmount Road, only a few days a week like__ the wee shop at the corner near to that factory.'

'I know the one you mean,' Jack Phillips sighed. 'It's another factory that has closed and added to the jobless figures.'

'I know the shop that you mean, sir. You said that Alice was going to visit her mother, did she often stay away for several days?' Blaise questioned.

'Look, I'm sorry for lying__ I don't know why I said it, but, the truth is, Alice and I had a stupid argument and she went to live with her sister.'

'What was the argument about?'

34

Foetal Attraction

'The bloody usual__ money__ it was always money like.'

What is the sister's name__ where does she live, sir?' Jack Phillips asked, scribbling into his notepad.

'It's Geraldine__ she lives in the house just next the shop where Alice worked. It's Geraldine Winters. She doesn't like me much because I'm unemployed.'

'You said that you and Alice had a fight, sir,' Jack Phillips probed, now standing at lace-curtained window, sniffing at the pungent aroma from the curtain, a stale tobacco odour combined with what resembled that of a damp dog. 'This fight, was it a heated argument, or did it turn into something a bit more confrontational?'

'I think what my colleague is asking is, did you hit your partner, sir?'

'What__ no, I wouldn't hit Alice__ never. I wouldn't harm a hair on her head, I love her,' the young man said defensively, rubbing his wetted, reddened eyes with his palms. 'We__ just argued for a bit, Alice stormed out then said that she was going to her sisters for a while.'

Jack Phillips' eyes then noticed four deep indentations in the dark-beige coloured carpet, as he glanced away from the window, indentations made by legs of some kind, possibly from that of a heavy coffee table or dresser. His inquisitive nature pulsated then with awakened question, pondering enthusiastically on the very idea that perhaps, in that very same spot there had been a wooden chest. Could it be possible that this assumed chest would have been large enough to store a body__ perhaps the body of Alice O'Leary?

35

Foetal Attraction

'Are we missing something here, sir' Jack Phillips questioned, scribbling again into his notebook, pointing to the spot at the nearby wall. 'Have you recently got rid of a piece of furniture?'

'What__ how do you know that? It was an old Welsh dresser; it was rotten with that woodworm so I dumped it at the bottom of the garden.

'So eh, you said that you and Alice were happy about her being pregnant, is it possible that maybe she was only pretending to want it. I mean, did she say anything about the financial stress that it would cause you both?'

'What__ don't be fucking__ what are you asking stupid questions like this for? Jesus, my poor Alice is. What the fuck has this got to do with Alice being murdered like?'

'It's just routine, sir,' Blaise said. 'You'd be surprised at the questions we are required to ask.'

'Some can sound truly senseless at times,' Jack Phillips sighed casually.

Blaise sat quietly pondering, unconsciously rubbing the tip of his thumb from side to side across his chin, his thoughts then focusing on the possibility that perhaps the victim had secretly intended to have an abortion. Perhaps if that were the case then Alice O'Leary had attended an illegal abortionist and perhaps the operation had gone tragically wrong. Blaise reflected silently on the large wound over the victim's abdomen and that the pathologist had said that he thought the work was that of a professional. A certain sense of confidence filled Blaise then as he imagined that the post mortem on the victim would clarify certain matters and would, perhaps, give him a clearer path to investigate. 'Here, would you like a cigarette?' Jack Phillips offered the young man, giving one then to the grateful Blaise.

'How eh__ did Alice get to her sister's house__ surely to God you didn't take her in that__ car outside?' Blaise probed.

'Are you joking__ that piece of shit is knackered. No, Alice called for a taxi on her mobile whilst she stood outside. At first, I thought she was going to ask for a lift from the guy in a van that was parked on the road, but he just drove away when I went outside.'

'I see, what kind of van, can you describe it, sir?' Jack Phillips probed.

'It was just a van like__ dark red or was it green? I didn't pay that much attention, there's always some kind of van driving up and down that bloody road.'

'Do you think that maybe this van followed Alice in the taxi?' Blaise asked.

'I couldn't really tell you, I'm not even sure that Alice took a taxi, I just went into the kitchen and had a few beers like.'

'What did you do after you had a few beers?' Blaise continued.

'Nothing__ I just crashed on the sofa like.'

'Is it possible that Alice could have returned to the house while you were sleeping__ maybe you both had another argument?'

'Maybe you don't remember her returning,' Jack Phillips added suggestively as he stood directly facing the young man. 'Perhaps you both had another argument and things got out of hand__ maybe you didn't mean to give her a slap or two?'

Foetal Attraction

'Fuck off__ are you arseholes trying to say that I__ killed Alice?

'Clam down there, sir__ you seem to have a bit of a temper.'
Blaise said calmly.

'We are just asking questions here, sir,' Jack Phillips added.' I
mean, it's not unknown for someone to lose control after they've
had a few beers.'

The young man sighed deeply as he slumped onto the sofa, eyes
darting back and forth between the two detectives; nervously biting
on his nails upon recognising that from the suggestive questioning
he was a now a suspect.

'Those three scratch marks on your right hand__ they look fresh
and sore__ how did you come by those then, sir?' Blaise questioned
with growing interest.

'It was eh__ I've got two Dobermans in the shed. I was eh__
feeding them and they got a bit boisterous like.'

'I see,' Blaise said, looking up at his colleague, who scribbled into
his notebook. 'I hope that you had a Tetanus shot, we wouldn't
want you getting lock-jaw and being unable to answer any further
questions that we may have.'

Blaise took a deep thoughtful breath, his eyes staring directly at
the young man. 'Now, this may sound like a stupid question, but,
did Alice wear underwear. You see, the reason I'm asking is that
we didn't find any briefs with her belongings?'

'What do you want to know about her knickers for__ Jesus Christ?
This is getting bloody ridiculous. Why are you so interested in
Alice's knickers? '

Foetal Attraction

'Just answer the bloody question and stop your mouthing,' Jack Phillips shouted, much to the surprise of Blaise. 'This is a murder investigation and we need to ask all sorts of questions, so cut out all the shit and answer the Inspector.'

'Aye__ ok__ aye, Alice wore knickers, what woman doesn't?'

'What about house keys, sir, did Alice have any when she left the house?'

'No, we only have the one set__ we lost the other key some months ago like. We couldn't really afford to have another key cut, not that I'm ever out much anyhow like.'

'Right then, I'll arrange for a car to take you into Londonderry to identify Alice's body,' Blaise said rising from the chair to make towards the front door. 'Where are these dogs of yours, sir? I like Dobermans__ they're intelligent and very obedient.'

'They're locked up in the shed; they keep running onto the road, I am scared they'd be run over with the nutters that speed up and down that bloody road.'

'Oh, by the way,' Blaise said thoughtfully. 'Can you describe the shoes Alice wore when she left, we never found those either.'

'Christ, I couldn't honestly tell you, sorry. What man really pays attention to his what his woman wears__ unless he needs too that is?'

'Right, if you can think of anything, you can reach me on this number,' Blaise said, handing his card to the young man.

Foetal Attraction

'Eh, I don't suppose you could lend me a few smokes could you? I'm bloody skint until I get my Social money.'

'Sure,' Blaise said searching the pockets of his jacket, remembering that he didn't have any cigarettes. Jack Phillips was then stunned when Blaise took a ten-pound note from his wallet and handed it to the grateful young man, knowing only too well what it felt like to crave a cigarette, after all, he had just learned of the death of his partner and unborn child.

'So, as well as giving up the drink and chasing after every woman that you see, you have become charitable__ very commendable,' Jack Phillips grinned, sitting behind the steering wheel of the car. 'Do you think he's our man, Blaise?'

'Not sure, Jack, but we'll soon find out. Now, I think we'll go visit this sister, see what she can tell us.'

'What about a nice cuppa first, Blaise__ maybe we'll get something to eat too?'

'Good idea, Jack, some sod disturbed me this morning and I didn't get the chance to have breakfast.'

Foetal Attraction

Blaise and Jack Phillips arrived at the house on the Melmount
Road, both met almost immediately by a rather corpulent, flush-
faced woman, who stood at her front door with thick arms folded
across a voluptuous chest. Narrowed eyes stared questioningly as
Blaise held out his warrant card and introduced himself and Jack
Phillips.

'Are you Mrs Geraldine Winters?'

'I bloody better be or my husband's being sleeping with the wrong
woman all these years,' the woman grinned cheerfully. 'What do
you want with me__ it's not my husband is it__ oh God, please
don't tell me that__ sweet Jesus in Heaven he's not__ he hasn't__
been hurt at work or something has he?'

'Do you mind if come in, Mrs Winters?' Blaise said, stepping one
foot up onto the step, feeling slightly dwarfed by the woman before
him. 'We just need to ask you a few questions regarding your sister,
Alice.'

'My sister__ why__ is Alice ok?' The woman gasped, clasping a
chubby-fingered hand to her gaping mouth with anxious concern.
'Oh sweet Mother of Christ__' As if recognising the seriousness of
the situation the woman backed into the hallway, eyes staring like
emerald orbs as she allowed the two detectives to enter.

Blaise and his colleague followed the flustered woman into the
brightly decorated sitting room that gave host to a variety of large-
leafed, spreading houseplants. Both men watched then as the
rotund, panting woman sank heavily onto the cream-coloured
leather sofa. Fraught with anxious concern, she twisted and
stretched short, chubby fingers adorned with gold and diamond

rings each squeezed tightly onto every finger as though refusing to ever to move.

'I'm afraid that I have some bad news for you, Mrs Winters,' Blaise sighed.

'Oh God__ please__ no, please don't say what I think you're going to say,' the woman panted breathlessly, almost as though she were ready to collapse.

'I'm truly sorry, you see, your sister's body was discovered earlier this morning,' Blaise explained with soulful sympathy. Blaise detested this part of the job, and absolutely hated to be the bearer of such bad news, especially when it involved a murder case and which constantly left him feeling hopelessly useless when it came to consoling the relatives, knowing that no amount of words would ever be adequate.

'We have strong reason to believe that your sister was murdered, Mrs Winters,' Blaise said softly, wishing then that he had called the station to request a female officer to console the woman. 'I appreciate how you must be feeling, but I need to ask you a few questions, is that ok, Mrs Winters?'

'Oh my God! How__ what happened__ poor Alice,' the woman sobbed into her hands. 'This is just terrible. How could this happen__ how?' She sighed through streaming tears, reddened, puffed eyes staring searchingly between the two detectives. 'Poor Alice__ she__ was having a wee baby too. What__ about the baby, is it?'

'I'm so sorry,' Blaise comforted by touching a hand softly over the woman's shoulders. 'According to your sister's partner__ John

42

Foetal Attraction

Patterson__ Alice had come to stay with you for a few days__ would that be correct, Mrs Winters?'

'Yes__ that's right inspector__ she__ Alice had had another row with that bloody idiot,' Geraldine Winters continued, the crumpled handkerchief muffling sniffs and snorts as she tried to regain her composure.

'That would have been on__ what day, Mrs Winters?'

'It was Tuesday, yes that's right. Alice was crying, I think that wee shit had hit her. I wanted to go and wring his bloody neck but Alice wouldn't allow me. She is so bloody protective of that useless__ sorry__ Inspector, what were you going to say there?'

'Was there any bruising or marks on Alice__ did she say if her partner had hit her?' Blaise continued with his soft questioning.

'I don't think so__ no, she was really upset though, and I'm bloody certain that wee shit did hit her. Oh, poor Alice__ I just can't believe this. That skinny wee rat was always hitting her.'

'Why didn't she leave him? I just can't understand why women stay with these guys who continually beat them__ it bloody beats me,' Jack Phillips said, returning to the sitting room after having prepared a pot of coffee. 'I mean, I honestly don't accept all this rubbish about loving their partner even though he kicks the living daylights out of them.'

'That's true enough, it's strange though,' Blaise sighed.

'I just knew that useless junkie would go too far one day.'

'Here you are, I made some coffee,' Jack Phillips smiled.

Foetal Attraction

'By that statement, I think you assume that Mr Patterson murdered Alice,' Blaise continued to question with calm voice. 'Do you think that he would kill Alice?'

'Was your sister happy with the knowledge that she was pregnant, Mrs Winters?' Jack Phillips said. 'Do you think that she may have been concerned as to the financial stress of bringing a child into this world?'

'Alice was as happy as a pig in shit__ it meant the world to her. I think poor Alice was under the impression that it would encourage that useless sod to look for a job. Though I bloody doubt that idiot could hold down a decent job.'

'So eh, can I take it then that you and Mr Patterson didn't get along?'

'Christ no, do you know how you feel when you suddenly realise that you've just stepped in dog-shit, Inspector? Well, that's how I feel every time I see him. My husband, Paddy didn't like him either. He just pretended to like him, for Alice's sake.'

'Right, I know what you mean,' Blaise laughed. 'This husband of yours, where is he?'

'Paddy's in England somewhere, he's a truck driver. He should be home tomorrow. Oh God, he'll be devastated about this.'

'You used to be a nurse, Mrs Winters is that right?' Jack Phillips asked. 'I remember you coming to my house.'

'Oh yes, I thought I knew you from somewhere,' Geraldine Winters smiled, her eyes almost sparkling with the liquid crystal tears. 'It was your wee daughter, wasn't it?'

'That's right, you helped her after she was diagnosed with her kidneys, and you helped her with dialysis and all that.'

'Yes, how is she now?'

'Jasmine's fine, well, she's handling life a lot better now after her transplant.'

Almost telepathically, Blaise stared at Jack Phillips, both sensing that both were thinking on the same question. Could it just be possible that, with Geraldine Winters having some medical knowledge, then, it just could be possible that she was carrying out illegal abortions? Was it possible that Geraldine Winters had tried to abort her sister's unborn baby and something had gone wrong?

'You eh, you said that Mr Patterson used drugs, is that correct?' Jack Phillips asked.

'Is this Mr Patterson prone to violence__ did he beat your sister regularly?' Blaise questioned, scribbling into his notebook as an unwanted sudden craving for a cigarette gnawed annoyingly at him.

Geraldine Winters never replied to the question put to her, but simply nodded in the affirmative, snorting into her crumpled handkerchief. Liquid lined eyes staring direct at Blaise as her chubby fingers gripped strongly onto his hand, softly requesting to see her sister's body.

'Where did you__ find poor Alice, Inspector__ was she at home? I wish now to God that I didn't let her go back home to that useless junkie sod.'

'Well all I can tell you for now, Mrs Winters is, that Alice's body was discovered earlier this morning in a building site on the Derry

Road. You said there that you shouldn't have let Alice return home, I thought that you said she was staying with you?'

'She was__ well, Alice took my cat into the vet, that was Tuesday, late afternoon not long after she arrived.'

'I presume we're talking about the vet in Strabane and not somewhere in England or Scotland. I mean, that was Tuesday and this is now Saturday__ weren't you a bit concerned when Alice didn't return here?' Blaise questioned.

'I just thought that Alice had went back to him, she was like that__ one minute she hates him, the next she can't live without him. I knew she'd bring the cat back to me.'

'Didn't you try to call her? I understand that you bought a mobile phone for Alice.'

'I did try, several times in fact, but I knew that she hardly kept it switched on. She was forever going on about how mobile phones caused brain tumours and all that nonsense. I mean, if we listened to everything that we were told then__ '

'I know exactly what you mean, Mrs Winters,' Blaise sighed.

'This is just__ I can't believe that poor Alice is__ oh Alice,' the woman gasped aloud, bursting into a flood of sorrowed tears again, her rounded face covered by trembling hands.

'I'm sorry about this, Mrs Winters__ I think we'll have a wee break. Jack, would you pour the coffee mate, please?'

'You've made a full pot too, thanks,' Mrs Winters sniffed, reaching then to pour out the coffee into the three mugs.

Foetal Attraction

'You don't mind if I have a cigarette do you, Mrs Winters,' Jack Phillips said, dropping a cigarette onto Blaise's lap. 'Damn, I forgot you were trying to stay off them, sorry Blaise.'

Blaise held onto the cigarette as though it were made of gold, and there was no way he was giving it back. The sensation of the cigarette tip between his lips filled him then with an overwhelming calmness, eagerly sucking in the toxins as Jack Phillips held out the lighter, just as he had done at John Patterson's house.

'God, that makes me feel slightly dizzy,' Blaise grinned. It is bloody good though__ real nice.'

'Alice and that idiot were always arguing about money,' Geraldine Winters snarled with an awakened anger. Alice told me that they were arguing because that idiot wanted money for drink,' she continued, taking a long deep breath to calm her growing rage. Alice said that she walked out on him because he punched her.'

Blaise scribbled into his notebook again, cursing at his weakness for giving into his craving, but took immense pleasure from the nicotine that swirled around inside him.

'Christ Blaise,' Jack Phillips grinned. 'You look white, are you feeling a bit on the dizzy side? You're smoking it too fast man. '

'I am a bit, Jack, but I don't care,' Blaise smiled, stubbing the finished cigarette out into the ashtray on the small table at his side.

'Would you say that Mr Patterson was the violent type, Mrs Winters? I mean, when we questioned him earlier he seemed rather placid.'

'Bloody flaccid more like if you ask me, Inspector.'

Foetal Attraction

'Do you remember if Alice had any bruises on her body, maybe a cut lip, just something to substantiate that her partner had hit her?'

'No__ that evil wee shit had punched her stomach__ can you bloody believe that__ imagine doing something as terrible as that, Inspector.'

'Why would he do that, surely he wouldn't want to put the baby's life at risk?'

'That bloody idiot called Alice all sorts of horrible names__ she told me that he was shouting like a madman at her. Christ Almighty, he even said that the baby wasn't his and the sod even accused her of having an affair.'

'I see,' Blaise said thoughtfully, slowly building up a picture of John Patterson in his mind. He began then to ponder if he was on the verge of gathering enough evidence to arrest John Patterson on suspicion of murder. I really need to ask this, Mrs Winters. Was your sister, to your knowledge, seeing anyone else? I mean, what made Alice's partner accuse her of having an affair__ would your sister do that sort of thing?'

It was all bloody rubbish, Alice wouldn't do that, she wasn't the type, Inspector. For some crazy bloody reason, she actually loved the wee shit, she really did. I mean, she told me that he had said if he found out that she was seeing someone else then he would rip the baby from her womb with his bare hands.'

Those spoken words made Blaise sit upright, his mind a torrent of question. 'Did Mr Patterson ever tell Alice that he wanted her to have an abortion__ could he have perhaps forced her into having the baby aborted?'

Foetal Attraction

Quite unexpectedly, the woman pulled her corpulent frame up from the sofa and made immediately towards the kitchen, passing Jack Phillips, who had just made a pot of coffee. 'Right, enough of this, I want to see my sister now, Inspector,' she said commandingly, removing a red coat from the walk-in cupboard. The stress and trauma of the situation caused the woman to pant with exhilarated breathlessness.

Of course, Blaise didn't relish the idea of Geraldine Winters arriving to view the victim at the same as John Patterson, fearing that several of his officers would perhaps be harmed by the powerful, rotund woman if they had had to stop her from strangling Alice's partner.

Blaise informed Geraldine Winters that she could identify her sister's body at Altnagelvin Hospital in Londonderry and that an officer would arrive to accompany her.

'By the way, is your cat here, Mrs Winters?'

'Oh my good God, I__ just assumed that Sox was with Alice and she'd bring it home. Where is the wee soul then?' The woman muttered with concerned thought, her reddened eyes staring then at silver-framed photograph on the display cabinet. 'There, that's my baby there, Inspector,' she continued with the look of a proud mother.

'Very nice,' Blaise smiled with secreted disinterest. 'I think that we need to chat with Mr Patterson again, Jack.'

'It looks like he's taking us for mugs, Blaise,' Jack Phillips replied with a subdued anger.

'I think so, Jack.'

49

'Yes, well, if he's not all stupid with those drugs then he'll be messing about with that bloody stupid van of his__ it's a heap of scrap. He asked my Paddy to help him sort it up, but Paddy said it was a waste of time.'

'Does he own a van, Mrs Winters?'

'Yes, he keeps it out of sight at the back of the house__ he doesn't have it taxed or insured that's why he hides it. I mean, he filled Alice's head with all sorts of rubbish, she is so__ was so gullible, the silly thing.'

'Mr Patterson never mentioned a van when we spoke to him earlier. I think we need to have a good serious chat with him this time, Jack.'

'Right, well, thanks for everything Mr Winters__ no doubt we'll be in touch.' Jack Phillips smiled, hurriedly following Blaise to the car.

Foetal Attraction

5

A plain-clothed WPC that Blaise had requested arrived just as the two detectives planned to leave Geraldine Winters alone. It was Elizabeth Harris, a cheerful, live for the day type of woman, who was in her mid-thirties and not that unfamiliar with Blaise. She had been a sergeant until a colleague complained of religious discrimination and subsequently demoted to constable. Although the allegation proved inconclusive, the hierarchy had been well aware of the illicit relationship between Blaise and the then married officer and, of course, steps needed to be taken.

'Hello Liz,' Blaise smiled, quietly musing on how attractive and feminine she looked in her chocolate brown trouser suit that matched with a neatly fitted beige blouse. A cascade of silky jet hair framed a thin, gently tanned face and her ocean-blue eyes sparkled in the instant reflection of the semi-drunken weekends that they had stolen together.

'Hi Blaise,' WPC Harris beamed. 'I'm here to escort a Mrs Winters to ID the body of her sister, is that right?' Her voice spoke softer than usual as she deliberately positioned herself directly opposite Blaise, and stood dangerously close.

'Listen Liz, try to make sure that there's nobody else there, I want to avoid a confrontation with the victim's partner, a Mr John Patterson,' Blaise explained, his mind demanding that he ignore the sensation of growing thoughts that began to surge within. 'So, how are you?'

'Oh just the usual, Blaise,' WPC Harris replied with a forced forlorn sigh, inside desperately desiring for Blaise to just take her into his arms and give her a huge hug. The loneliness of the past

51

eighteen months had been unbearable during her secret battle with the shameful guilt of her unfaithfulness and for destroying her marriage.

'I know it's been hard for you this past while, Liz. It's all my fault.'

'It's done now, Blaise. No point in the both of us feeling bad,' WPC Harris continued an undeniable guilt in her captivating eyes that gave certain invite to Blaise to call on her.

'Look, if things were different, Liz. I know how it feels on those lonely nights, things will get better though,' Blaise smiled, touching a comforting hand up and down her arm, wishing then that he hadn't for that innocently intended touch had stirred him.

'Jesus Blaise. I honestly wish that we hadn't__ it was__ is Mrs Winters ready?'

'She is, she's in the kitchen, Jack will get her for you, won't you Jack?'

'I wish you would've requested somebody else, Blaise. God, I've been doing my bloody best to avoid you.'

'Sorry Liz, your name just popped into my mind.'

'Well, anyhow, I here you have set up home with Cathy O'Hare, isn't she a bit young for you?'

'I suppose, it just sort of crept up me, I never thought that we would__'

'I'll go see if Mrs Winter's is ready,' Jack Phillips sighed with a hint of disapproval.

Foetal Attraction

'Look, you don't need to explain, Blaise. Anyway, try not to request me again, it's only that I can't bloody stop these feelings inside me whenever I see you, you sod.'

The conversation between the two halted instantly by the re-appearance of Jack Phillips, his narrowed eyes angrily darting between his two colleagues. 'Mrs Winters will be out shortly, she's just taking a phone call, it's from her loving, faithful husband,' he said with a note of cynicism, aware of the sexual chemistry between Blaise and WPC Harris.

'Right that's fine and I get it, Detective Sergeant,' WPC Harris sighed.

Jack Phillips stood with his hands in his trouser pockets, desperate to control the embittered anger that boiled within as his mind reflected with concern for his ex-colleague, Bobby Harris, who had been the husband of WPC Harris. As the affair between Blaise and WPC Harris became public knowledge, DS Bobby Harris made a forced request for an immediate transfer, much to the despair of their superiors.

'Right, Jack,' Blaise groaned sitting in the passenger seat of the unmarked police car. 'I think we'll have another word with this Patterson guy, eh?'

'I was just wondering how Bobby was getting on in Antrim,' Jack Phillips said wryly. Bobby liked it here in Strabane__ bloody shame he was forced to leave though.'

'I know what you're getting at here, Jack. Liz and I never meant for things to go as far as they did__ it was stupid drunken lust, Christ, it's just one of those things that happen,' Blaise growled, trying somehow to defend his past actions with WPC Harris.

Foetal Attraction

'Besides, their marriage was on the skids long before I got involved__ everybody knew how bad it was. Jesus, Bobby can't say anything, he was doing the dirt on Liz for years.'

Jack Phillips never replied, thinking it best not to say anymore for fear of the conversation boiling over and things being said that shouldn't be said. Jack Phillips could not rid himself of the angered desire to punch Blaise in the mouth, just as DS Bobby Harris had done on discovering of his wife's affair with Blaise. The promised threat by Bobby Harris of having his revenge still rang loudly in the ears of Jack Phillips as he concentrated on steering the car towards their destination.

'Have you heard anything from Bobby__ you know what he's like Blaise? He did promise that one day he would get you back.'

'I'll cross that bridge when I come to it, Jack. Meanwhile, let's try to keep our minds on this case__ after all, we've got a killer to catch.

'Right, so do you think that this Patterson guy maybe killed his partner?'

'Maybe he did Jack__ it's just possible that he and the victim were having a big row and that he somehow accidentally killed her. Anyway, I'm interested in this van that he is supposed to own, the one Mrs Winters mentioned.'

'Right enough, Blaise. Although I never saw it when we were there__ it just could be that he used this van to transport Alice O'Leary's body to dump it.'

'I don't think that he would've cut and stitched her stomach though, I definitely don't think he's had any medical training.'

Foetal Attraction

'Could be that he done it to throw us off the scent. Although, I have to admit that when I first saw the victim I thought it was a bloody alien of some kind. I've never seen anything so hideous in my bloody life.'

'It was a bit weird though, Jack.'

'That Mrs Winters said that Patterson threatened to cut the baby out of the victim's womb, do you think maybe he could have? I mean, who knows what was in his mind, especially if he was high on whatever drugs he uses.'

'He's been lying to us anyway, Jack. He told us that he would never hit Alice, yet the sister tells us he beat her regularly,' Blaise continued, searching his pockets for some mints to fend off the nicotine craving that haunted him. 'I just can't see him as the killer though.'

'Well, hopefully we'll find out a bit more from the pathologist soon, Blaise.'

'This crazy world never ceases to amaze me, Jack. All the technology and progress and we still need to deal with all the blood-thirsty barbaric mentality of people,' Blaise sighed, quietly cursing his luck for not having any mints.

'Well, here we are again,' Jack Phillips said, steering the car onto the roughly gravelled driveway of John Patterson's cottage.

Blaise sat upright in the passenger seat almost immediately, staring directly ahead through the windscreen. An awakened interest widened his eyes upon sighting John Patterson at the far end of the over-grown, mistreated garden. With watchful, silent gaze, Blaise pondered on just why he appeared to be digging

55

between two dense, spreading bushes. The young man completely oblivious to the inquisitive detectives parked in the driveway, both aware of the inquisitive, yet docile Dobermans.

With cautious, hesitant forwards steps, Blaise and Jack Phillips kept their eyes trained on the two dogs as they lethargically allowed the strangers to pass unhindered, dark eyes watching with disinterest, perhaps waiting to receive a gentle pat on the head or to receive a large piece of meat. Their owner, still unaware of the detectives as the earphones covering his ears pulsated with music, and he casually danced and swayed whilst he dug into the ground, until Blaise touched a hand on his shoulder.

'Holy shit__ you gave me a bloody fright there,' the young man gasped. 'I never heard you,' he continued, thrusting the spade hard into the upturned soil and rested his hand on the handle.

Blaise stared thoughtfully at the young man then at the spade. 'Doing a bit of gardening, Mr Patterson__ I hope you haven't buried something like a cat perhaps?' 'Jack Phillips said.

'Now why would I be burying a cat? I've just cleaned up all the dog-shit; two big dogs can leave some amount of crap lying about.'

'You looked rather happy there,' Blaise smiled. 'Digging and dancing to music__ I mean, you'd think gardening would be last thing on your mind, sir.'

'Maybe he's just happier living on his own__ is that it?' Jack Phillips said, glancing at Blaise. 'You won't mind if I have a look at what you buried here?'

'Go ahead, if that's what you want,' the young man replied, surrendering the spade to Jack Phillips.

Foetal Attraction

'We were having an interesting chat with your partner's sister,' Blaise stated trying to provoke a reaction. 'Mrs Winters informs me that your partner was taking a sick cat to the vet__ that was Tuesday afternoon. I don't suppose that Alice had returned here, did she?'

'Now, why the hell would Alice bring a cat here?' The young man laughed, looking rather puzzled by the question. 'There's two dogs there, I don't think a cat would like to be here, do you? Anyhow, what makes you__ hey, are you saying that you think Alice came back here with a cat and__ I killed her like, is that it?'

'Now calm down, Mr Patterson,' Blaise said with the threat of a growl, his eyes staring direct at the young man, who appeared to be growing angrier. 'We're only trying to trace your partner's last movements, you don't mind that do you?'

'Definitely no sign of a cat,' Jack Phillips said, holding up the bag of dog dirt. 'You know, the statement that you gave us earlier resembles this bag, Mr Patterson.'

'Eh, what do you mean like?'

'What you told us earlier was all crap,' Jack Phillips continued.

'What we are trying here is to establish why your partner was murdered, Mr Patterson,' Blaise said through gritted teeth as his anger grew.

'Look, let's calm down here,' Jack Phillips said, recognising the threat of anger from his colleague, hoping to avoid any confrontation or sudden violent outburst from him, to which Blaise was rather accustomed. 'No point in getting mouthy with us, sir, we're just trying to catch your partner's killer.'

Foetal Attraction

'I'm just saying that you guys seem more interested in some stupid cat than who murdered my Alice,' the young man complained, searching eagerly through the pockets of his loose-fitting khaki trousers, finding a half-smoked hand rolled cigarette that appeared half-smoked. 'You wouldn't mind if I finished my wee spliff eh?'

'Do you smoke that crap a lot then?' Blaise quizzed.

'It's for medical reasons__ I suffer from inverted vertigo.'

'Inverted vertigo__ what's that?' Jack Phillips asked looking puzzled.

'I get frightened when I'm not high,' the young man grinned impishly.

'Very witty, Mr Patterson,' Blaise groaned. 'Maybe you'll not be that fucking smart if my colleague here goes for a wee walk,' Blaise continued, seizing the young man by the throat. 'I'm in no mood for any more of your crap.'

'Jesus,' Jack Phillips gasped with alarm, gripping at Blaise's arm. 'I think that you better start telling us exactly what went on between you and your partner, Mr Patterson.'

Blaise felt a hint of guilt at losing his temper, breaking the promise that he had made to himself, and to the memory of his late father. He wanted to be more like his father, to be the respected police officer that his father had been. More importantly, Blaise could not afford to have any more complaints made against him, as that would play directly into the hands of the hierarchy, who wanted nothing more than to put a definite end to his career, even though Blaise had made many arrests.

58

Foetal Attraction

'You told us earlier that you had never hit Alice, yet we learned different from Mrs Winters. You see, she informed me that Alice came to her on several occasion all tearful and bruised, bruised because you had beaten the poor girl,' Blaise said aggressively, stepping closer to the young man again. 'I bloody detest men that hit their women__ I take immense pleasure from beating the crap out of these so-called hardmen who can only hit women.'

'I__ never hit her, never. Well, maybe once when we were out of our heads on drink like, that's the truth. Honest to fuck, I would never hurt Alice, and especially now that she is__ well, was pregnant,' the young man ranted, his eyes then unexpectedly flooding with grieving tears as he stood with the look of a lost child.

'Right, so tell me again how you got those scratches on your hand, Mr Patterson,' Blaise said sternly, forcefully seizing the young man's wrist to lift up his hand. 'How did you get them__ where you struggling with your partner before you killed her?'

Jack Phillips watched cautiously as Blaise continued to shout aggressively at the young man. His hand fiercely shaking John Patterson's wrist, then, in a moment of angered rage, Blaise gripped the young man by the throat vigorously throttling him. 'Did you kill her__ did you murder Alice O'Leary. Admit it you bastard, you cut her up, didn't you?'

'Blaise, for God's sake man, control yourself,' Jack Phillips shouted, rushing to the aid of the frightened young man, who sank to his knees gasping and choking for breath.

'Damn, sorry, Jack,' Blaise apologised with a deep guilt-ridden sigh. In that moment of concerned thought, Blaise twisted round to

59

stare at the two Dobermans, thankful then that they remained unconcerned and docile.

'Here, take a bloody cigarette man,' Jack Phillips said angrily. 'I'll take Mr Patterson here inside while you calm down. Christ Almighty.'

Jack Phillips calmly led the gasping young man into the house, pouring him a glass of water. 'I'm sorry about that, my colleague's under a lot of stress at the moment. Have you been to the hospital to make a formal ID yet?'

'Christ__ I couldn't__ bloody breath,' the young man panted and coughed, gripping both hands onto the edge of the worktop, head bowed with anxious, guilty sorrow. 'I know you'll probably think that I'm a coward, but I couldn't go. I couldn't stand the thought of seeing my Alice just lying there.'

'I can understand that my friend,' Jack Phillips replied in a friendly tone, leaning his shoulder against the door frame of the kitchen, watching as the young man began washing three mugs for tea. His hands trembled slightly and Jack Phillips pondered on the idea that he was genuinely frightened of seeing his partner in the chapel of rest, or was he afraid of the questioning by Blaise. Then, in that very moment, Jack Phillips realised that John Patterson hadn't once shown any remorse or grief at the loss of his unborn child. Was it possible that he had discovered Alice was having an affair and carried out his alleged threat?

'You know, I've witnessed quite a few murders, some really horrendous ones too. Of course, I've been involved in a few murders too where the husband or partner had been arguing and, in the heat of the moment things just got out of hand and the partner ended up dead, accidently of course,' he continued, focusing his eyes on the young man's face, hoping for some kind of reaction or guilt. 'I mean, we all know and understand that people react differently in these situations, they've accidentally killed the one that they love__ they panic and do all sorts of crazy things or even hide the body.'

'Aye, very good__ very fucking clever,' the young man grinned unexpectedly. 'All this pals act__ pure shit. You__ do you honestly fucking think that__ fuck it, forget it,' the young man groaned loudly, though continued casually pouring out three mugs of tea.

At that particular moment, Blaise entered the kitchen purposefully, his eyes staring directly at John Patterson as he accepted the mug of tea from him. 'I see you have a van parked at the back of the house?'

'Eh, aye, I'm trying to save to get it taxed and insured like.'

'I'm not interested in that, what I'm interested in is why you failed to mention it to us earlier. I mean, when I asked you how Alice managed to travel to her sister's house on the Melmount Road, you never said that you took her in the van.'

'I never mentioned it because I thought it didn't matter.'

'I mean, that was all crap about the taxi, wasn't it? You drove Alice to her sister's, and don't give me any bullshit about not driving it because it's not taxed, half the bloody town do it.'

'Alice wouldn't let me drive her, I offered, but she told me that__.'

'More lies, eh,' Jack Phillips groaned loudly.

Foetal Attraction

'You'll not mind then if I have Forensics take a look at it?' Blaise continued, sipping his tea as he lit another of Jack Phillips' cigarettes.

'Look, honest to God, lads, I never killed Alice, we were planning to get married__ once I found a decent job like. You know yourself how hard it is to find work. Honestly, I wouldn't kill anybody.'

'I can appreciate that,' Jack Phillips said. 'So what kind of work do you do? You don't look the labourer type to me.'

'Actually I was at Queens__ I was studying computer science, but I dropped out for a while, which I regret now.'

Blaise placed his mug down on the table, having firstly to move a pile of old magazines and newspapers. 'If you're so short of money, how can you buy all these papers?'

'To be honest, I take them from reception room like in the dentists or doctors.'

'Mrs Winters said that you suspected Alice of having an affair, and you had said that the baby wasn't yours__ you could maybe elaborate on that for me?'

'Could it be that Alice was perhaps planning to leave you for this alleged other man, maybe that's why you killed her, is that it, Mr Patterson?' Jack Phillips added to Blaise's question.

'No, that's absolute shit!' John Patterson defended angrily. 'I didn't fucking kill Alice, get that into your thick fucking heads. That Geraldine has filled your heads with shite, she's such an evil bastard, she's never liked me, the fat whore.'

Foetal Attraction

'Now, calm down, Patterson, you apparently told Alice that if you found out that the baby wasn't yours then you would kill it yourself__ did you say that, Mr Patterson?'

'No bloody way__ well, I might have said it, but it's rubbish, it was the drink. You know how it is like?'

'Not really__ I would never threaten to kill an unborn child, not even when I was drunk,' Blaise said, again warning the young man to curb his anger and sit down, which he did immediately, remembering of Blaise's throttling rage.

'I just wondered sometimes about Alice, she would stay out late at times saying that she was with friends. I mean, we used to enjoy really good sex together, then, it was as if these past few months she hated me like.'

'So that's why you imagined that she was having an affair__ do you have any knowledge of who it may have been, any names for us to check out?'

'Sorry no, but I bet you that fat evil sister knows. In fact, it wouldn't bloody surprise me if she had set Alice up with someone,' the young man sighed heavily, trying to hold back the threat of tears.

'Right, I think we'll leave it there for the time being, Mr Patterson,' Blaise said In a more friendlier tone. 'I'll have the Forensics team take a look at your van, so don't touch it for now. It will help in ruling you out of our investigation.'

'Here's my card,' Jack Phillips said. 'If you can think of anything that may help us give me a call on that number, Mr Patterson.'

Foetal Attraction

'I think we'll call it a day, Jack. Go home and enjoy your Saturday with the family and I'll see you in the morning.'

'Oh good, now I'll have to do the damn gardening.'

Foetal Attraction

6

The following morning was pleasantly bright and sun-kissed although cold, but the clean, fresh chill awakened the brain and lungs creating that sense of well-being. September, it seemed, never failed in its coming to bring a strange concoction of weathers, especially to the shores of Northern Ireland. It appears that, in this small country on God's good earth, is the only place that you could experience the four seasons in one day. Cold white snow to greet you in the morning, a torrent of heavy rain later to wash it all away then a cold fresh chill until evening when you could enjoy that touch of sunshine.

By mid-morning, the azure sky with its lazily drifting clouds had become a blanket of heavy, dense greyness. A bitter wind accompanied a substantial crystal curtain of merciless rain that battered down annoyingly against the office window, as though desperately trying to irritate Blaise, who found himself deeply engrossed in the freshly received report from the pathologist's office. So intense was his inquisitive reading that the black sweetened coffee in the polystyrene cup had cooled considerably without even a taste.

'Good God Almighty! Now I understand why the victim had all those stitches across her stomach,' Blaise exclaimed with startled disbelief. 'This is bloody unreal.'

'Now you've intrigued me, Blaise,' Jack Phillips yawned slightly, dragging his eyes away from the Financial Times, a newspaper that could have been written in hieroglyphics as far as Blaise was concerned, his philosophy being, that if a newspaper didn't contain sports news and a variety of scantily clad women then it wasn't worth reading.

Foetal Attraction

'Listen to this Jack. According to the pathologist__ Hey, do you recall the victim was supposed to be pregnant?'

'That's right, what is it, Blaise?'

'Well, according to the pathologist here the victim had her entire uterus removed.'

'Dear God, why would anyone want to do something like that,' Jack Phillips gasped, now ignoring the half-eaten jam doughnut. 'So, what are you thinking, some kind of nutty professor?'

'It just could be, Jack,' Blaise sighed, stretching his arms behind his head as he reclined thoughtfully behind his desk. 'The bloody question is, why would someone want to remove the victim's uterus__ why kill the unborn child__ and where in hell is it?'

'Maybe this nutcase, whoever he is, is using the foetus for some kind of medical experiments. It's the only bloody plausible explanation I can think of, Blaise.'

'I'm getting a horrible feeling that this isn't going to be the only one, Jack. Christ, it will create widespread fear amongst all pregnant women if this gets out.'

'So I take it then that we can rule out this Patterson guy then?' Jack Phillips continued, now resting his buttocks on the edge of his desk. 'Who the hell would carry out such a barbaric action__ this has to be the work of a medically trained professional__ a surgeon perhaps doing some kind of experiment or possibly dissecting the body of the child for whatever reason,' Jack Phillips suggested, arms folded across his chest as he shook his head in disgust. 'It could just be that some doctor type is up to something weird.'

Foetal Attraction

'It's definitely somebody with medical knowledge that's for sure. What did that Patterson guy say he was studying?'

'It was computer science, he dropped out he said, Blaise.'

'Right ok, we'll leave him then. Christ, the report here states that the body had been drained completely of blood, probably to stop leaving a messy trail, eh Jack?'

'Or it could be another attempt to conceal the identity of the victim. What about the Forensics report, is it here yet?'

'It's here Jack. Listen, tell young Will Chambers to get in touch with the General Medical Council, find out if there has been any doctors or the likes struck off for any kind of illegal practices and so on.'

Right, will do__ I don't think he'll be in till noon though, I'll leave a note for him.'

'Oh, tell him to inform the boss man or whoever he talks to what we have discovered here, maybe they would be able to shed some light on it.'

'I'll have a word with some of my informants too. Is there anything in the Forensics report, Blaise?'

'I don't know about interesting, Jack. There were traces of dog hairs found both on the victim's clothing and in the plastic bag. There were also traces of cat hairs too, and apparently the body was wiped clean with medical spirits.'

'Dog hairs you say?' Jack Phillips asked.

Foetal Attraction

'Apparently two types of dog, a Red Setter and a Golden Labrador. The cat hair belonged to a Siamese cat, and please, no pussy jokes, Jack.'

'Maybe the hairs were already in the bag prior to the clothing being put in it?'

'I'm aware of that Jack, I'm a detective too you know,' Blaise grinned. 'It just could be that whoever carried out this murder is doing experiments with animals too.'

'You just could be right there,' Jack Phillips replied, allowing a smile as he watched Blaise unconsciously stroke the tip of his thumb from side to side over his chin as he sat deep in thought. 'Maybe our killer is an animal lover and he carried out the evil deed at home, or in his garage, something like that.'

'So, you're assuming that it's a man then, Jack?'

'No, not really__ I mean, I can't see a woman being responsible, not with moving the body and all that, unless she had help that is.'

'It's definitely somebody with a medical background that's for sure,' Blaise sighed heavily with pulsating thought. 'Get young Will onto this Medical Council as soon as possible.'

'Well, it is Sunday, Blaise. I'll call him to go now just in case there's someone there.'

'We'll need to come up with something pretty sharpish, Jack.'

'I'll take a wander and see if any of my informants know anything.'

Foetal Attraction

'Touts, Jack, call them touts,' Blaise laughed with a shake of his head, elbows resting on the desk as he continued to search his inquisitive eyes over every word in the typed reports. He continually grunted and groaned as he wrestled with the nicotine craving, his hand searching through the pockets of his jacket for mints but found none, but discovered a piece of crumpled paper, which he then tried to straighten out on top of the Forensics report, staring at the handwritten phone number. He suddenly remembered that he had met a psychic woman whilst he was in the shop in Ballymagorry and that woman had unexpectedly mentioned his late father. That brief encounter had awakened a spark of interest within him, but with all that had transpired, he had completely forgotten about the psychic woman, whom he thought to be genuine. Thoughts of the investigation faded temporarily as Blaise then mused on paying the woman a visit, perhaps he thought, she would even be able to help him solve the case. A sense of child-like excitement filled him then as he pondered over his relationship with Cathy O'Hare and the unexpected marriage proposal that she had sprung on him.

A lingering thoughtful sigh left his mouth then as Blaise imagined that his murdered colleague and good friend, DS Charlie Brown would certainly have approved of his relationship. Then, the possibility that the elderly psychic woman could truly communicate with the souls of the departed quietly excited him, musing then on how wonderful it would be to talk with his parents.

'Go on man, give her a call, what have you got to lose,' echoed the encouraging voice of his conscience. 'If you don't call her then you'll never know for certain.'

Before he realised, Blaise dialled the telephone number, and with an uncharacteristic nervousness in his voice, he introduced himself

Foetal Attraction

immediately to the voice on the other end of the telephone, continually ranting without pausing for breath as he explained how he had met the woman and of what she had said to him. The calm, pleasant voice soon put Blaise at ease and an inner warmth calmed him as he then arranged to visit the woman.

Blaise slumped back in his chair, recalling some time ago that his sister, Julia had been a strong believer of Spiritualism and that there was life after death. She believed that death was only the end of a short journey for the eternal soul and an experience of some kind for the Spiritual growth and development of each soul. Julia had also told him one time that a spiritualist medium had foretold of her going to live in a distant land and that was where she would meet her life-long partner. That strong-held belief had been the foundation that had helped her cope with the death of both parents and had given her the inner strength to help Blaise through his embittered, drunken years.

'Well, what are you looking so pleased about?' The bold, familiar voice of the DCI echoed in the stilled air. 'You look as though you've just won the lotto,' the colossal Glaswegian continued, his broad shoulders filling the space between the door frame of the office door.

'Eh, I was just checking to see if Cathy was ok, boss,' Blaise lied sitting forward in his chair, feeling that uncontrollable sensation of a scolded schoolboy confronted by the headmaster. 'I just like to keep a wee check on Cathy.'

'Is that right, and tell me, how is she, Ben.'

'She's fine, her leg's still a bit weak but she's grand.'

'Did you talk to Cathy on the landline there?'

'Aye, I did, why do you ask that, boss?'

Blaise stared up at the towering DCI recognising a glint in his eye as he almost smiled.

'It just a bit strange, I mean, the thing is, Ben, I've been talking with Cathy upstairs in my office only minutes ago.'

'What__ why is she here?' Blaise gasped with embarrassment.'

'I can always tell when I'm being bullshitted, Ben,' the DCI sighed with a superior look, resting one buttock on the edge of Jack Phillips' desk.

Blaise sat back in his chair again, shaking his head slightly with amusement at the DCI's ability that never failed to catch anyone out when he suspected them of lying, one of the unquestionable attributes that had made him a truly efficient and respected police officer.

'Young Cathy did pop in to have a wee word earlier.'

'What about, if you don't mind me asking boss?' Blaise asked curiously, for a moment then imagining that perhaps Cathy had come to inform her uncle of their proposed marriage. 'Did she eh__ '

'Ask about returning to duty? She did request that, Ben. What do you think?'

'About what, boss?' Blaise asked, momentarily lost in thought at the prospect of visiting the elderly psychic woman in Ballymagorry.

'I'm asking what you think about Cathy coming back to work, you dunderhead.'

Foetal Attraction

'Dunderheed, what the hell does that mean?'

'It's an old Scottish word we use for idiots like you, Ben. It's a half-wit.'

'Jesus, that's a good one boss,' Blaise laughed. 'A dunderheed, I like that word.'

'Ben, if you don't give me your views on Cathy coming back to work I'll shove my hand up your arse and pull out your tonsils, I swear to God.'

'I don't have any I __'

'Don't you bloody dare finish that sentence, Ben,' the towering Glaswegian groaned. 'Right__ enough of the kidology here, we're short on manpower, so what do you say?'

'Kidology, is that another Scottish word, boss?'

'Ben, tell me what you think right now or I swear to God.'

'To be honest, boss, I really don't think that Cathy should return, not just yet. Her leg is still painful at times, don't let her kid you, I've seen her stumble a few times.'

'Are you sure that's the real reason, Ben? I mean__ maybe you've got used to going home now and having your meals ready for you__ somebody to cuddle up to.'

'Well, I have to admit it has been nice, boss. Honestly though, Cathy's still needs a bit more time, she'd only be putting herself at risk. Christ, you would be responsible if anything happened to her, and I don't mean by those stiff-arses upstairs, I mean your wife.'

72

Foetal Attraction

'Christ, I never thought about that, Violet would bloody kill me if anything happened to Cathy again.

'Maybe another month or so would do her the world of good boss.'

The DCI left with the decision not to allow Cathy to return to work, leaving Blaise alone to concentrate on the murder investigation.

'Right Alice, tell me what happened to you,' Blaise sighed aloud, as his eyes again studied the Forensics report. 'What happened to you after you left your sister's house and where did you go__ who did you meet?' Blaise continued, making a mental note to visit Geraldine Winters again to enquire as to the name of her vet that Alice took the cat to for treatment.

'Come on man, think, what in the hell has been going on here__ why were you killed and why remove the uterus__ what could the killer be doing with the uterus? I must make some enquiries to the other stations see if there are any similar cases around the country.'

A multitude of pondering, desperate question flooded and pulsated within, deep searching questions that begged for answers, questions such as; did Alice O'Leary keep the alleged appointment with the veterinarians__ could she have met the killer there__ was she singled out or was it just a random murder by some crazy killer. Blaise continued to ponder on the possibility that it was almost certainly the work of a doctor of sorts and was perhaps carrying out strange medical experiments, or perhaps it was just a deranged psychopath. Blaise made another note to have the asylums checked out for any possible escapees. Blaise then suddenly pondered on another question. 'Why, after severing the victim's fingertips and removing the body hair and teeth then draining the body of blood, why didn't the killer sever the toes, if it were a probable attempt to remove sources of DNA?

Just as Blaise was thinking about going to look for a cigarette from one of the uniformed officers, the telephone rang. It was DC Will Chambers, and just as Blaise picked up the receiver, the DCI popped back into the office, perching himself on the desk of Jack Phillips, which creaked threateningly under the weight.

'Hello, yes Will, what did you find out__ anything?'

DC Will Chambers explained that he was fortunate enough to find someone at the General Medical Council buildings and that they were extremely helpful when he called. He informed Blaise that he found out the name of a surgeon suspended by the medical council in 1998 for unethical practices.

'Unethical practices, what does that entail, Will? Never mind, pay this doctor a wee visit see what you can find out and if it's worth me interviewing them, let me what you hear.'

'So, anything concrete on the investigation, Ben?' The DCI asked casually.

'Nothing as yet, boss, but were looking into a few leads and Jack is doing the rounds with his touts. Young Will Chambers thinks he's on to something, he found out that some doctor or other had been struck off for unethical practices, whatever the hell means.'

'He was probably touching up wee girls or something. Anyhow, I'm going to take Violet for her Sunday dinner, so, let me know if you come up with anything__ tell me tomorrow.'

Foetal Attraction

Blaise watched the DCI leave, then stretched his hands to the back of his head reclining back lazily as he drifted off to sleep.

Foetal Attraction

Mary-Jo Delaney held a gentle hand against a swollen, rounded stomach that pushed out proudly against the soft material of her towelling bathrobe. Her face showed a beaming radiance of unmistakable motherhood as she left her husband to the front door, turning her head to receive a kiss goodbye on the cheek, a kiss intended for her lips. She never replied to the somewhat disheartened husband who told her that he loved her and couldn't wait for the birth of their first child. Her dark ebony eyes stared back silent, almost looking as though filled with contempt, arms folded across her chest as she watched her husband walk down to the end of the tarmac driveway to his car. He turned back to her, shaking his head with questioning bewilderment. 'Jesus, Mary-Jo, what's wrong with you, you've been bloody acting so weird ever since you fell pregnant. Don't you want to have kids?' The concerned husband complained with loud discontentment, arms outstretched in anticipation of some kind of reaction from his wife. 'What is it, what's wrong with you, Mary-Jo?'

'Oh just go to bloody work.'

'See, you can't even bring yourself to say my bloody name. Have I done something wrong? I've given you everything you've asked for.'

With a lingering heavy sigh, Mary-Jo stepped back into the hallway, standing with the door slightly open as she watched her husband leave, noticing that there appeared to be someone sitting in a van parked directly across the street. But just as she was about to close the door, her husband returned and threw his arms around her, holding her with a gentle firmness in a desperate hope of receiving even a hint of affection from his wife.

Foetal Attraction

'Look babe, things will be better once you've had the wee cub, you'll see,' the husband said, his attempt to kiss his wife spurned immediately.

'Just bloody sod off to work, Mick,' she said with a supressed growl, her hand pushing her husband out through the door again, and once again, she glanced at the parked van, hoping that the occupant hadn't witnessed the early morning row.

'I'm fucking serious Mary-Jo, you better start getting your act together,' her husband complained as he stood on the step. 'When I get home tonight we'll have a serious talk.'

'Right ok, whatever,' Mary-Jo replied sarcastically, glancing over her shoulder as the telephone rang unexpectedly. She watched her husband drive off then used her heel to close the door as she rushed to answer the telephone, wondering who could be calling her so early, on answering, she groaned as the caller hung up and there was no number to call back. Then, noticing that the front door wasn't closed fully, she made to close it but the dog in the back garden barking wildly drew her attention. On investigating why the dog barked so aggressively, she found nothing to justify the two-year-old collie acting up, as it stood with a long length of chain fastened to the kennel. She searched her eyes once more over the back garden from the window, calling to the dog to be quiet. Her mind playfully imaging her child playing and laughing with the dog, then, she listened to kitchen radio as she filled the electric kettle cursing quietly at the telephone ringing again, but once more, the caller hung up.

'Bloody weirdo's, at this time in the morning too. I mean, what bloody pleasure do these idiots get from calling people up then hanging up,' she mumbled loudly.

Foetal Attraction

Seated now at the kitchen table, Mary-Jo sipped a coffee, her eyes fixed on the colourful Donegal china photo frame of her marriage. She and her husband looked so happy five years ago, and they were happy, until the night that she met Johnny Mulgrew. Mary-Jo had been on a night out with friends and whilst drinking and dancing the night away, she found herself falling for the barman and a lengthy, exciting affair began.

Mary-Jo sipped the coffee that she hoped would waken her, quietly struggling with her conscience for she had a decision to make and soon. She sat anxiously considering leaving her husband to begin a new life with her lover, but she pondered over what she was about to throw away, especially the family and friends that would perhaps shun her. Of course, at that moment, Mary-Jo began to question on whether she could truly trust Johnny Mulgrew, would he remain the kind, considerate man that she had met, would she find that she missed her husband and would probably end up regretting everything and being alone.

With her mind anxiously deliberating her future, Mary-Jo made her way upstairs to take a shower, but first she wanted to finish her coffee. Her eyes stared at the secret photograph of her lover that she concealed in her handbag, quietly reliving their stolen moments together, moments that had seen her feel so alive and human. Sat on the edge of the unmade bed, a gentle smile curved her un-glossed lips as she began to muse of her proposed new life with her lover that she felt was growing stronger. He had shown such emotional joy when she had told him of the baby and that it was his. The very idea of living this new life filled Mary-Jo with a sense of excited wonderment as she kissed the photograph with decisive decision, telling herself that she would leave her husband that very day. With immense enthusiasm, she pulled a large suitcase from underneath the bed, and began to fill it with her clothes and belongings.

78

Foetal Attraction

Suddenly and quite unexpectedly, she became aware of someone standing behind her in the bedroom.

'Jesus___ how did you___?' Mary-Jo gasped with startled alarm, her eyes wide as she stared at the skulking figure, who wore a long, khaki coloured Parka coat with the hood pulled right up, almost concealing his face. With fearful panic, she tried to escape from the bedroom and gasped upon recognising him. 'John, what the hell are you doing here?'

As Mary-Jo attempted to leave, the intruder landed a swift unexpected punch to her mouth causing her to fall backwards to the floor dazed and bewildered from the savage blow. She tried to plead with her attacker as he roughly bound her wrists with sticky tape then dragged her bodily up onto the bed face down. She begged him to be careful as she was pregnant, but the man continued to grunt as he then bound her ankles together, placing a blindfold tightly around her eyes. Again, Mary-Jo attempted to speak, but he pressed her bloodied face hard down into the pillow as he told her to be quiet.

'Why___ John___ why are you___ doing___ this?'

The bedroom filled with uncertain fear and bewildered terror as Mary-Jo lay trembling on the bed, not a sound disturbed the nothingness as she waited on whatever was going to happen next. Waiting on her attacker saying something or at least telling her why he was acting in such a terrifying and violent way, so frightened that she wet the bed. The intruder remained silent as he stood by the bed staring down at her, a silence that was as frightening as was the attack itself. Then, the moment that she dreaded happened, she began to sob as he pulled the hem of her robe right up around her waist, his gloved hand touching over her buttocks as he leaned his face close, then, he began to kiss the soft exposed flesh as he slid the briefs down slightly.

Mary-Jo forced her bloodied face up from the pillow, gasping for breath as she pleaded with her attacker not to harm the baby, but he continued kissing her body, pressing his face down hard onto her buttocks.

'Please__ stop this__ John__ please,' she sobbed fearing what she expected would happen.

'Shut up, just shut up,' the man growled, roughly turning her onto her back, his eyes staring at the exposed nakedness, which he then kissed lustfully, and Mary-Jo sobbed harder as she pleaded louder, hearing the attacker undo his trousers. The telephone rang and the attacker then hurriedly fastened his trousers, and ripped Mary-Jo's briefs from her, forcing them into her mouth before rushing downstairs and outside. He quickly reversed the dark green van up the driveway leaving the back doors open as he hurried inside. Mary-Jo still sobbed with fear and uncertainty as he untied her hands and quickly removed the bathrobe leaving her in just a short satin nightdress. The attacker punched her again forcefully, which completely stunned Mary-Jo and she lay dazed and bewildered. He quickly tied her wrists again then lifted her up into his arms and carried her downstairs to the waiting van, wrapping her in the duvet and covered her with large sheet to conceal her, throwing several pieces of wood and empty cardboard boxes around and on top of her before hurriedly driving off.

Foetal Attraction

Blaise sat thoughtful for a few silenced moments luxuriating in the stilled, solitary nothingness around him. His eyes drifted lazily over the cream-coloured office walls and, for the very first time noticed that under the plastic wall clock hung a sign. NO SMOKING. Those very words, in red, sent a resurgence of nicotine cravings that instantly annoyed him, causing him to search every cluttered drawer of his desk, only finding a packet of mints. As he crunched aggressively on the mouthful of mints, his eyes wandered over the walls again casually staring at the framed photographs of colleagues past and present. Photographs once easily noticeable but now half-hidden by the accumulated piled documents and well-read newspapers that formed untidy columns that had inadvertently gathered on the tops of the filing cabinets. A slight sense of guilt and shame quietly filled him then as he stared at the nicotine-stained window blind, a fresh champagne colour when newly fitted some months previous.

With arms stretched behind his head, Blaise reclined in his chair deep in thought as he mulled over the information that DC Will Chambers received via a friend in London and had told Blaise over the telephone, and he had scribbled it down onto his notepad.

The information from the General Medical Council read that there was a female surgeon in Northern Ireland suspended from the medical register for unethical practices, but they refused to divulge fully the actual reasons. The female surgeon, a Polish woman, disappeared in 1998. A Miss Jana Zaleski is in her late forties. She had been summoned to appear before a committee to answer the allegations against her, but failed to attend and hasn't been seen since. All her employment files had disappeared from the hospital in Omagh where she worked. A photograph and details were to follow by fax. Will stated that he was going to visit the woman at the address, which was a secluded farmhouse on the outskirts of Donemana, and that he would report to Blaise if he discovered anything substantial.

Blaise filled with a subdued hope that the doctor would turn out to be the killer and that he would then discover the reason behind the murder of Alice O'Leary and her unborn child. Of course, Blaise wanted to know if this woman was involved in some type of medical experiment, but whatever it was, it did not and could not possibly justify the murder of an innocent young woman and her unborn child.

That pondering moment, that very instance where Blaise quietly felt a certain hopefulness of catching the killer, was disturbed in a suddenness of noisy interruption as Jack Phillips thrust open the office door with his buttocks, hands filled with two polystyrene cups of tea.

'Christ Blaise,' he groaned, sounding exhausted. 'I've been all around the bloody town talking to shopkeepers and just about anybody in the street, I even collared a few of my informants__ nothing, not a damn thing. I mean, can you believe it, in this town?' Jack Phillips sighed as he slumped into his chair.

Blaise stared in startled bewilderment, for in that moment, it was not Jack Phillips sitting before him, and a chilling sensation thrust up his spine as his shocked, widened eyes saw his late friend and colleague, DS Charlie Brown.

The uttered words of Jack Phillips disturbed the vibration and chased away the pleasant memory and mind-vision that had sent a surge of warm happiness through him.

Foetal Attraction

'I said I've brought you a cup of tea, Blaise. Are you ok; you look as though you've seen a ghost or something?' Jack Phillips smiled as he placed the polystyrene cup down on the desk. 'You're a bit pale there, are you ok?'

'Christ, sorry Jack, I was miles away,' Blaise sighed, pushing the guilt of his murdered friend to the back of his mind, his eyes staring down at the cup. 'So, what did I do to you to deserve this canteen concoction of strange liquid?' Blaise smiled, seeing through the weak tea to the bottom of the cup. 'So, what were you saying when you came in there?'

'I was just saying that I have been questioning just about everybody in the town about the murder of Alice O'Leary.' His face contorted with a look of disgust as he removed the lid from the polystyrene cup. 'I was talking to a few of the neighbours and some shoppers in the sister's shop. Not one bloody person claims to have seen anything suspicious on Friday or Saturday. I mean, you'd think that somebody noticed something.'

'Young Will called me earlier, Jack.'

'Why did he call you that?' Jack Phillips joked, closing the lid of the cup again refusing to attempt to taste the liquid.

'You're very witty today, Jack. What happened, did the wife finally get over her headaches?' Blaise retorted, tasting a sip of the tea, his face resembling that of a squashed soggy sponge. 'That has to be the worst attempt at tea yet, I think we should arrest the canteen staff for impersonating cooks.'

'What did Will have to say__ did he find out anything interesting, Blaise? I'm actually surprised that he found anything out, given that it's Sunday.'

Foetal Attraction

'As a matter of fact he did, he has a friend who works at the GMC in London. Apparently there was a surgeon reported for some kind of naughtiness or other and it appears that she failed to attend a hearing and she has disappeared.'

'Where is Will now?'

'Apparently this surgeon is a Polish woman and hasn't been seen since she was supposed to appear at a hearing in 1998. Will is checking out the last known address.'

'That sounds promising; at least it's a positive lead, a suspect that sounds plausible, given that the victim has supposedly been cut up with medical expertise.'

'I hope Will does find her and brings her in for questioning, Jack. I'd bloody love to hear the whys and what for's.'

'What about the Forensics report, anything in that?'

'No, not really__ but there is one thing though bothering me, Jack.' Blaise sighed, flipping open the report, lit a cigarette that his colleague passed to him then pointed to the sign under the wall clock amusingly. 'Why did our killer go to all the trouble of severing the fingertips and the teeth, draining her blood?'

'It's probably to hinder us in identifying the victim, Blaise, you know that.'

'I know, but the Doc thinks that the killer is almost certainly medically trained, and we have this surgeon missing. I mean, surely a surgeon would know that it a waste of time; they would know that Forensics would do all the DNA stuff__ anyway. This is just bloody too crazy for words. I mean, why did the killer not remove the toes then after going to these lengths__ do you know what I mean, Jack?'

'I see what you're getting at, Blaise,' Jack Phillips said thoughtfully, rising from his chair to cross over to the window, then, just as he had always done, dropped the cigarette end onto the lower roof under the window. 'What about thinking along the lines of a ritual type of killing?'

'Fuck me, do you mean like Devil worshipping and all that shit, Jack?'

'I know it sounds stupid, but it could be, that's all I'm saying. There could be a group of crazies who think they are Satin's servants__ something like that. A secret sect if you like, although I haven't heard anything.'

'Well you wouldn't would you, not if they're secret,' Blaise grinned. 'Anyway, if you want to think along those lines of Devil worshipping and all that, maybe you should start questioning the canteen staff.'

'I just hope they don't start serving spotted dick then, God knows what it would consist of__ or who from,' Jack Phillips smiled, slumping back into his chair. 'What were you pointing at the clock for by the way?'

'I was pointing to the bloody sign under it, Jack__ NO SMOKING.'

'Christ, is that the first time you've noticed it? Some detective you are.'

'Seriously though, I've never noticed it, Jack.'

Foetal Attraction

'Anyway, what do we know about this Polish woman other than she's a psycho doctor__ any record of her?'

'Not a thing on her, Jack. She could be back in Poland, or possibly over the water on the mainland working under a new name.'

'If we get a photograph of her we can check with the immigration people, we can check if she took a flight back home or whatever.

'Right, since it's all quiet, I'm going to grab a wee bit of shut-eye in the back room, give me a shout if anything crops up, Jack.'

Foetal Attraction

DC Will Chambers steered the unmarked police car from the main road in Donemana, feeling each wheel bump and splash into every conceivable pothole on the narrowed path. The engine stilled and silent as it halted at the wooden gated entrance of 305 Ash-Pine Manor. The young detective made his way from the car on foot along the gravelled driveway towards the two-storey, salmon-pink coloured house. The boarded up windows and doors gave the impression that the dwelling was abandoned and, from viewing the surrounding overgrown lawns and uncared for hedgerows, he knew that the occupants had long since vacated the premises.

 DC Will Chambers kicked his foot idly against clumps of weeds that poked up through the loose-gravelled driveway, his eyes scanning inquisitively over every boarded window. Around at the rear of the house, he became quietly interested in one of the window boards that appeared loose. He gripped the loosened board at the corner, having then to thrust backwards as the board screeched and cracked noisily, surrendering to the partially rusted fixings then crashed to the ground. With keen inquisitive eyes, Will Chambers stretched up on his tiptoes immediately noticing that the glass pane had been broken and all of the surrounding sharp edges of glass removed, perhaps by squatters he mused.

 After removing his recently new suit jacket in the car and fetching a torch, the young detective scrambled up onto the broad window ledge, the sound of glass crunching under foot echoed in the dark musty kitchen as he cautiously clambered inside. With narrowed eyes adjusting to the semi-darkness, he sprayed the illuminated torch over the eerie emptiness, his feet crunching and cracking over glass particles on the tiled floor. A cold, dank chill soaked through his shirt causing him to wish that he had kept his jacket on, cursing then on remembering that he had left his mobile phone in the jacket pocket. In a suddenness of questioning uncertain nervousness, he spun round spraying the torch beam searchingly over the floor upon hearing what sounded like a hurried movement, eyes wide as he scanned the area. An icy shiver tingled up his spine then, the very hairs on the back of his neck strained upon glimpsing a huge rat that scurried across the floor and jumped into one of the kitchen cupboards that was open.

The ambience inside the daylight-starved property hung heavy with a putrid stench, but there, in that unpleasant air, the young detective could smell what appeared to be the fresh pungent odour of cigarette smoke. The young detective moved further into the kitchen, cautious and watchful as the torch beam illuminated the immediate area of the spacious hallway slowly opening the kitchen door. There, in the hallway, Will Chambers noticed a half-smoked cigarette on the floor, on closer inspection the cigarette appeared as though squashed by a foot, the extinguished tip almost fresh as he held it reluctantly to his nose. His mind questioned then on the possibility of squatters living in the premises, although he remained cautiously aware that his life could be in danger.

Will Chambers shone the torch quickly up the wooden stairs then pointed it straight at the closed door to his right. With gentle pressure, his fingers pushed open the door standing in readiness as he threw the beam over the spacious empty room, his eyes fixing with interest on a small clutter of food packets that littered the marble fireplace. On the wooden floor lay crumpled, grubby blankets, sure sign that someone had, or was using the property. The torch beam then focused on an array of cigarette ends casually discarded into the open fire, and closer inspection, the burnt embers told him that the fire had been in use. A faint, yet unmistakable aroma of sweaty feet lay heavy in the air causing an uncertainty within the young detective as he nervously pondered on the possibility that the intruder could still be on the premises.

The adrenaline began to surge through his concerned body upon realising that he would be unable to call for back up as he had left his phone in his jacket. With a forced deep breath, he tried to ignore all the mind-thrusts of hidden dangers that could possibly lurk within each of the rooms, his mind over-active with all sorts of frightening happenings. Another few deep breaths and he forced himself to calm down; the torch gripped tightly in his sweaty palm as he then climbed the darkened staircase, one foot at a time, slow and cautious. He wished right there that he hadn't watched all those horror movies in recent months as an array of mind-visions played with his conscience, teasing him with strange ideas of ghostly happenings and demons suddenly appearing ready to kill him, the creaking of every floorboard and the pungent aroma not helping to calm his racing nerves.

'Come on, Will, bloody grow up and stop being so stupid,' his mind thundered upon reaching the top landing. A slight grin warmed his face as he thought of the ridicule that he would have received from his colleagues if they had been with him, wishing then that they were there. The stilled, uncertain atmosphere suddenly changed to that of immediate surprised fear, the adrenaline pumping through his veins like wild, untamed rapids upon hearing a muffled voice followed by anxiously hurried footsteps coming from the bedroom at the far end of the landing.

The confidence in his police training drew Will Chambers towards the bedroom where he had heard the sounds, the torch gripped firmly in readiness. 'POLICE!' He shouted. 'Come out__ come out where I can see you,' he shouted again with a boldness wrapped in anxious nervousness. 'You better come out now.'

Foetal Attraction

The young detective raised his left hand pushing open the bedroom door with great force, the torch spraying its beam into the room, eyes searching anxiously but seeing nothing and his shoulders drooped with relief. 'I definitely thought I heard something,' Will Chambers sighed aloud. 'I really must stop watching these stupid horror movies,' he continued, entering the bedroom to take a final check then stood silent on the landing.

In a suddenness of absolute surprise and unexpectedness, Will Chambers gasped aloud as the bedroom door to his right thrust open and two shadowed figures rushed him as they shouted aggressively. Overwhelmed and effortlessly overpowered by the two men who immediately began savagely beating him, punching and kicking at his face and body like wild animals.

The unexpected horrendous attack lasted only moments, such was the ferocity and savagery and the young detective sprawled in bloodied agony on the floor, unable to defend himself as the two attackers tied his hands. Like an old carpet, the attackers dragged the dazed Will Chambers by the ankles down the stairs then threw him into the corner of the sitting room, an angered voice warning him to stay silent.

'What the fuck are we going to do with this arsehole? I'll bet he's told his mates where he is__ they'll be looking for him soon.'

'Shut up you big pussy, just get the bags and we'll fuck off out of here.'

'Where are we going to go now__ what if the cops are outside?'

'Look, just shut the fuck up and let me think.'

'What about him?'

Foetal Attraction

Will Chambers lay on the cold concrete floor, his entire body throbbing and pulsating with agonising pains, his wrists numbed from being tied too tightly and he slowly rolled onto his side, groaning from the severe pains, which he knew were broken ribs. Alone and uncertain as to his own safety, the fear growing as he then assumed that he would be killed by his attackers. He groaned quietly as he then attempted to sit up against the wall, planning to escape somehow as he wrestled in the darkness with his bindings, the terrible pains surging and pulsating fiercely through his badly beaten body, he then tried to stand up.

'Thinking of leaving us?' Laughed one of the men, shinning the torch directly into Will Chambers' face, his clenched fist crashed then with such force against his bloodied, swollen face, a knee thrust heavily into his stomach sending the young detective sprawling in agony to the floor again. The blood that seeped into his mouth muffled the agonising groans as both men again savagely kicked into his limp body, as he lay helpless on the floor.

'That's enough, I don't think he'll be going anywhere for a while.'

Following the brutally vicious attack, the violent vibrations in the atmosphere calmed and only the panting painful groans of the young detective echoed within the damp, cold walls of the house. Now alone in the darkness as his attackers left the room, Will Chambers desperately feared that his captors would certainly kill him, and realised that there was no possibility of escape due to the weakness and severity of pains in his body. He tried to keep focused whilst struggling to breath, which felt agonising as his ribs were broken and his bloodied, swollen face felt numbed and painful and found it extremely difficult to see as his eyes swelled and blood covered his face. Then a terrifying fear filled him, words that would perhaps be the last he heard on earth.

Foetal Attraction

'You get those bags and I'll take care of that nosey fucker in there.'

Foetal Attraction

The overhead florescent light hummed quietly in the background as Blaise and Jack Phillips continued to study the Forensics report and the report from the pathologist's office. Both reports gave nothing to go on except for the fact that a medically trained professional appeared the most likely to have killed the victim, but the reason for the removal of the uterus remained a mystery.

'I hope that young Will is having more luck than us, eh Jack?'

'Let's hope that this Polish woman turns out to be the killer, I'd love to interview her and find out just what she's up to.'

A loud repetitive knocking on the office door disturbed the two detectives, both then turned to stare at Dave Jackson, the desk sergeant. He was a tall man with sloped shoulders and rather thin face. The years of drinking Irish whiskey rewarded with a reddish, veined nose. 'There was a phone call from some guy reporting that his wife is missing. I just thought that you guys might be interested since he says that she's pregnant.'

'Maybe she's just headed off somewhere, could be she's had a craving for pizza and hedgehog or something crazy like that,' Jack Phillips grinned. 'You know what pregnant women are like; their hormones are all over the place.'

'The guy that phoned sounded really upset, he said he thinks his wife's been kidnapped or something.'

'What makes him think that for Christ's sake?' Blaise laughed.

'He said the bedroom was a mess and that there was a lot of blood on the bed.'

Foetal Attraction

'Jesus, did it not occur to the man to check with the hospital first, maybe his wife has went into labour or something.'

'He said he had called the hospital but she wasn't admitted. I sent a car around to check it out just in case, Blaise,' the uniformed sergeant said. 'I think you guys should go check it out, the husband sounded really upset.'

'Oh well, if you think we should go, Dave,' Jack Phillips grinned, lifting his rain jacket from the hanger on the back of the office door. 'Do we have an address or do we have to guess, Dave?'

'Oh right,' the desk sergeant grinned, looking at the report log. 'It's Brookvale, that's the wee site just off the Melmount Road there.'

'Yip, I know the place,' Blaise said, pulling on his wax jacket after looking at the office window to see the torrent of rain. 'I just hope to God this isn't what I'm thinking, Jack.'

'Let's bloody hope not, Blaise. All we need is some nutter abducting pregnant women and killing them.'

'If it is there's no doubt some politicians will blame us for not doing enough, then if we do throw cops all over the place, they bloody blame us for being too heavy handed.'

'True, it's the only bloody job where we are in a no win situation. Anyhow, let's hope this isn't the second victim,' Jack Phillips sighed.

'If DC Chambers calls in, Dave, tell him to ring my mobile.'

'Will do, Blaise,' the sergeant laughed. 'Get it, Will do?'

Foetal Attraction

'You need to get out more, Dave,' Blaise groaned. 'Will's been a while, eh?'

Blaise and Jack Phillips drove the short distance to the given address, where a small crowd of onlookers stood opposite to the house, all excitedly talking amongst themselves, keenly giving their views as to what had occurred. Every neighbour then watched Blaise then as he ducked under the blue and white tape that cordoned off the premises, his eyes searching around him. Jack Phillips crouched on the driveway upon noticing a crumpled piece of paper, discovering that it was a photograph of two people. He removed the gloves from his pocket and carefully picked up the discarded photograph, un-crumpling it to stare at the smiling faces, then placed it into a small evidence bag before putting it into his pocket.

The frantically anxious husband, his eyes reddened with tears and anger immediately met Blaise at the front door, thick, strong fingers gripped Blaise's arm eagerly ushering him upstairs. 'Upstairs__ I'll show you, the bloody duvet is missing too,' the man ranted nervously in his anxious concern.

'Look, I understand this is difficult for you sir, but please try to calm down,' Blaise said, following the husband upstairs. 'Look, John,' Blaise called to the uniformed officer at the front door. Try not to let everybody in and out__ it's a possible crime scene.'

'Look, in here,' the husband said close to tears again.

'I'm Inspector Blaise by the way, and you are?'

'I'm Michael, everybody calls me Mick. My bloody wife is missing__ she's always home when I finish work. She's been kidnapped.'

Foetal Attraction

'Right, so shall we start at the beginning here sir. What makes you think that your wife has been abducted?'

'Look at the place man, it's a mess.'

'Right, let's forget the bedroom for now, let's go downstairs and you can start from the beginning,' Blaise said, noticing his colleague enter as he led Mick Delaney downstairs to the sitting room. 'This is DS Phillips.'

'Right good, very good__ now can we please try to find my wife.'

'We'll do everything that we can sir, that you can depend on,' Blaise said calmly. 'Now, talk to me sir.'

The husband sank onto the brown leather sofa, sitting then on the edge as the anger and frustration surged through him, fists clenched tightly on his knees. He then began to explain that he arrived home at five thirty, thinking it unusual that there was no sign of his wife; she should have been at home preparing the evening meal. The husband continued to say that he thought then that his wife was perhaps having a sleep, but on checking discovered that the bedroom was a mess, a suitcase lay on the floor with clothes lying all over and that there was blood on the pillow.

'Did you call the hospital__ perhaps she had a little accident?' Blaise questioned.

'I thought that myself, so I phoned the hospital but they said she wasn't there. I mean, the bloody duvet is missing and I found one of her house slippers on the stairs, the other was in the bedroom.'

'And I suppose you picked the slipper up from the stairs sir?'

Foetal Attraction

'Eh, I did, sorry.'

'What about friends or family, did you call them to check if your wife was perhaps there?'

'Sure I did, nobody has seen her__ where is she Inspector__ where could she be?'

Blaise followed the husband upstairs, his eyes continually scanning for any possible clues to the woman's disappearance. The husband entered the bedroom first immediately pointing out the blood stained pillow. 'Look at that, something terrible has happened to Mary-Jo. I'll kill the bastard who took her, I promise you that, and I don't give a fuck if you arrest me.'

'Look, we understand your anger sir,' Jack Philips said trying to calm the man. 'I understand that your wife is pregnant, is that correct sir?'

'She's five months__ it's our first. If anything happens to either of them, as God is my judge, I'll rip the fuckers head off.'

'Calm down sir, we don't know for certain that your wife is in any danger. Was eh, was your wife happy enough sir__ I mean, how was she when you last spoke to her?'

'Mary-Jo was grand__ well__ she was happy most of the time.'

'No problems between you then?' Blaise questioned as he studied the pillow, noticing that the bed sheet was particularly crumpled and that there appeared to be a stain of some kind on it. 'Was your wife happy about the baby__ how did you feel about it, any problems? I understand that having a child, especially the first can cause a bit of a panic, financially too. '

'Of course she was happy, we both were. Look, cut all the shit and go and look for my wife.'

'Before we can do that sir, first we need to gather the facts, just try to bear with us, please,' Blaise said.

'Is there any possibility that your wife was maybe seeing someone else?' Jack Phillips questioned bluntly, much to the surprise of Blaise. 'I only ask in the likely event that perhaps your wife has left you for somebody else. Sorry if that sounds a bit blunt.'

'Oh, and I suppose that she decided to just take the fucking duvet instead of her clothes, Jesus, what a stupid bloody question,' the husband groaned rising to his feet angrily.

'You see, there is the question of the suitcase here, it looks as if your wife was packing some clothing into it,' Blaise said, positioning himself between the husband and Jack Phillips. 'Can you think of any reason why your wife would be packing some of her clothes?'

The husband sat down again, rubbing his hands back and forth over his head, fighting back the tears. 'I don't know__ maybe she__ I don't bloody have a clue.'

'What was your wife wearing the last time you saw her, sir__ when was the last time?'

'This morning, I went to work about half seven. Eh, I can't remember what she was wearing. I think it was her pale-green bathrobe.'

Jack Phillips said nothing but noticed the mentioned bathrobe lying untidily in the corner of the bedroom, nodding in the direction of the robe for Blaise to notice it. Then, in a moment of thought, Jack Phillips made his way downstairs into the sitting room, removing the photograph that he had placed in the small, clear evidence bag. He noticed then that the smiling woman was the same woman in the framed photographs that adorned the shelving on the display unit. Jack Phillips then stared at the man in the photograph, the arms of Mary-Jo Delaney tightly around his neck. Was this man a secret lover or perhaps a family member, Jack Phillips quietly pondered, thinking that it looked more like a lover. Then, just as he was about to place the photograph back into his pocket, he stared at the man again, his mind an explosion of question as he tried to think where he had seen him before. No matter how hard he tried, he could not place him, the familiarity plaguing his mind. 'I bloody know you, now where have I seen you before. Come on, think, Jack. Where have we met or where do I know you from.'

The arrival of the CSI team disturbed Jack Phillips, who quickly replaced the photograph back into his pocket, but his mind continued to ponder on the familiarity of the man in the photograph with Mary-Jo Delaney. Then, a sudden idea flickered within as he wondered if it was just possible that the husband had discovered that his wife was about to leave him for this man and he had perhaps killed her. As he continued to muse over the idea, Jack Phillips searched his inquisitive eyes around the sitting room, noticing then that behind the large sofa, was a duvet minus a cover. Immediately he thought of the missing duvet from the bedroom and began to inspect closely for any possible signs of bloodstains. He left the duvet on top of the sofa and made a quick search into the kitchen checking in the washing machine for any sign of the duvet cover, but it was empty, as was the washing basket.
'Jesus, no washing to be done, now that does seem strange,' he smiled quietly to himself.

Foetal Attraction

Jack Phillips made his way through the throng of busying CSI officers, ignoring the disapproving glares and groans of complaint as he then climbed the stairs. The question of the photograph played constantly with his mind, pondering then if he should bring it to the attention of the husband, perhaps then, if he was guilty of killing his wife, he just could breakdown and confess.

'Christ, if only life was that simple,' he sighed on entering the bedroom.

'What was that, Jack?' Blaise questioned, glancing at his colleague over his shoulder. 'Did you say something?'

'No, I was just thinking out loud,' Jack Phillips replied, training his eyes on the husband, who was sat on a chair, his eyes were red and puffed but tearless and Jack Phillips wondered if the man was genuinely upset for his missing wife or was just a good actor.

'Are you__ I need to ask, Mr Delaney,' Jack said. 'Are you absolutely certain in your own mind that your wife wasn't involved with another man?'

'No, definitely not__ why would she, we were happy together,' Mr Delaney shouted angrily. 'What are you saying here? We were fucking happy, no problems, nothing.'

Blaise stared at the angered husband recognising a look of subdued guilt on his face. 'Did you have an argument with your wife before you left for work this morning? I'm just thinking that maybe she has left to teach you a lesson or something, you know what women can be like at times.'

'Bullshit, Mary-Jo wouldn't do something as stupid as that. Shit, what are you trying to say_ that I'm a wife-beater__ is that it?'

Foetal Attraction

'Try to remain calm, sir,' Blaise said. 'I understand how you feel.'

'We're just trying to get a clear picture of events and establish the facts,' Jack Phillips added, deciding not to mention the photograph until he had spoken to Blaise about it first.

'When you left for work this morning, did you notice anything out of the ordinary, maybe someone hanging about or a strange car?' Blaise probed again. 'There doesn't appear to be any sign of forced entry, although, there are signs of a possible struggle. Would there be anyone with a grudge against you or your wife?'

'Christ, I don't think so__ Mary-Jo gets on with everybody. I don't know anybody that doesn't like her.'

'What about you, sir__ maybe somebody you've upset?'

'Nobody I can think of. I mean, why the fuck would anybody want to kidnap my wife, it's not like I'm made of money__ I don't have two pennies to rub together.'

'The world's full of weird people,' Jack Phillips added.

'Eh, where does your wife work, Mr Delaney?' Blaise questioned. 'Does she work?'

'Eh, she did, she worked part-time in the Adult Training clinic in town_ she helped those unfortunate people with disabilities. She bloody loved that job and the people. I mean, she actually went to work in the morning signing.'

'Do you know if she had any problems with anybody there, did she ever mention anyone in particular, maybe someone that was paying her too much attention?'

Foetal Attraction

'What__ like one of those handicapped ones trying it on with her you mean? No, Mary-Jo would've handled that of carry on. Wait, I do remember that she mentioned one guy. I think he used to bring her flowers and sometimes chocolates__ always keen to do things for her. She used to joke that I had a rival.'

'I see, was this person a patient at the clinic__ did she ever say if things maybe got out of hand, anything like that?'

'I don't think so, it was a while ago right enough. I think he left the place.'

'I don't suppose you would have a name for this eh__ guy?'

'No, she sorted it out. Look, what's all this crap about, get out there and find my wife.'

'We'll do that once we have something to go on, sir. We don't have a magic wand that tells us where to look for somebody,' Blaise stated with an authoritative voice, quietly irritated by the husband's attitude, although understood his concerns.

'I eh, noticed a duvet downstairs,' Jack Phillips said. 'Why would there be a duvet hidden behind the sofa sir?'

Mick Delaney breathed a heavy sigh as he pushed both hands into his trouser pockets and leaned back against the bedroom wall. 'I was sleeping on the sofa. I was trying to__ it's been bloody nearly two months since we've made love. I mean, I'm only human like. I tried but Mary-Jo went off her head, so I just started sleeping on the sofa.'

'We've all been there at one stage, sir,' Jack Phillips sighed with a distant memory of many nights on the sofa during his wife's pregnancy. 'Is that what happened, you had an argument this morning about sex?'

'No, she wasn't moody about that. She's been a bit distant these past months__ you know what pregnant women can be like?'

'Did you hit her, maybe a wee slap__ accidentally of course? I know how it feels when you get frustrated,' Blaise said thoughtfully. 'Is that the reason for the blood on the pillow, you slapped her and maybe gave her a bloody nose?'

'Catch yourself on, I never hit her,' the husband protested.

'I notice the suitcase, maybe she was going to leave you because you hit her?'

'I can understand if you did give you're a wife slap,' Jack Phillips added. I know I've wanted to give my wife a slap at times, they just have that way about them,' he lied, pretending to make light of hitting his wife, hopping that the husband would confess.

'I'd never hit my wife__ never,' Mr Delaney gasped, his eyes almost bulging with anger as he stared at both detectives.

'Does your wife have any brothers,' Jack Phillips asked, thinking of the photograph in his jacket pocket?'

'No she's an only child.

'Right well, I think we'll leave it at that for now, Mr Delaney,' Blaise said thoughtfully. 'Does your wife have any distinguishing marks, scars or the likes?'

'Perhaps she has a birthmark or maybe even tattoos of some kind?' Jack Phillips added.

Foetal Attraction

'Eh, she does have a wee scar on her left cheekbone; she got that falling one night when she was out with friends. Christ, I'd never seen her so drunk__ it was her thirtieth birthday.'

'Any other identifying marks, sir?'

'She has a wee red rose tattooed on her right shoulder and a Celtic chain design thing around her left ankle. She had them done as a teenager.'

'I don't think it will be long before the CSI people are finished. Try not worry, I'm sure your wife will turn up with a good reason,' Blaise said, slightly angered by the fact that he couldn't find any mints in his pockets to quell the growing nicotine craving.

'We'll do our best to trace your wife, Mr Delaney,' Jack Phillips added, patting a comforting hand on the husband's shoulder.

Blaise made his way downstairs, closely followed by his colleague, and then checked his mobile phone for calls. 'Where the hell is Will got to, he's bound to be finished interviewing that woman by now?'

'The wee sod's probably at home tucking into his mother's Sunday roast,' Jack Phillips grinned. 'I'm looking forward to my dinner too, I'm ravenous.'

'Give me one of your cigarettes Jack,' Blaise sighed. 'Get uniform to do the usual around the neighbours and we'll check out the special needs place tomorrow when it opens.'

'I'll drop you at the station and I'll see you in the morning then, Blaise.'

Foetal Attraction

Blaise pushed open the door to the incident room, the humming drone of the overhead fluorescent light echoed in the stilled emptiness. Like a multitude of tormenting tapping fingernails, the fierce rain splattered against the window as the untamed wind howled hauntingly like the unseen banshee. The blanket of blackened, dense cloud fought bravely to shield the awakening day of nature's light.

  In that moment of thoughtful solitude, Blaise chewed angrily on several mints as his sorrowful eyes fixed upon the photograph of Alice O'Leary that was pinned to the white board. A radiant, cheerful face stared back with lively, orbed eyes, eyes that were now lifeless. A sudden unwanted mind-vision of the young woman's murdered body flashed sickeningly before him, the sadistic cruelty that had caused her death too hideous to contemplate. Then, an instinctive fear filled Blaise as he gazed thoughtfully at the photograph of Mary-Jo Delaney, a silent, hopeful prayer echoed in his mind as he pondered on the possibility that she would meet the same barbaric end as Alice O'Leary.

  With buttocks resting on the edge of the desk, the soulful pondering of Blaise then disturbed by the unexpected early appearance of DS Jack Phillips.

  'Jesus, you're early this morning, Blaise__ couldn't you sleep either?'

  'This damn case is annoying me already, Jack. I just can't fathom out why somebody would cut out that poor souls uterus. I mean, what in God's name would possess another human being to carry out such a barbaric act? I just don't understand it.'

Foetal Attraction

'I wish I could answer that one, Blaise, I really do,' Jack Phillips sighed forlornly. 'Oh, by the way, before I forget__ here, have a look at this.'

'What is it, Jack?'

'It's a photograph that I found lying on the driveway of the Delaney house.'

'Did you not give it to Forensics?'

'They can have it later. Look at the man in the picture__ I'm bloody positive that I know him from somewhere.'

'I can't say that he rings any bells with me, Jack.'

'Do you think that they look close?'

'Like lovers you mean?'

'Could be, they just could be, Blaise. I'm thinking here that maybe our Mrs Delaney is having some naughty fun with this guy here__ and just maybe the kid she's carrying is his and not the husband's.'

'Right, I see where you're coming from here, Jack. Are you thinking along the lines that she could have just run off with him?'

'There was a suitcase on the floor and some clothes scattered about though.'

'Maybe the happy couple had a wee row in the morning and she decided that she would just bugger off. On the other hand, perhaps the hubby found out about the affair and had it out with her? Or maybe the happy hubby has taken his dear wife for a drive and dumped her body somewhere.'

106

Foetal Attraction

'So you're thinking that Mr Delaney has perhaps murdered his wife, Jack?'

'I'm just throwing in some possibilities, Blaise, all ifs and maybes for now.'

'Show that photo to the team, maybe one of them will recognise your man.'

The arrival of DC's Gemma Galbraith and Charlie McKean awakened both Blaise and Jack Phillips from their sombre ponderings. DC's Jim Whyte and Bill Johnson arriving then, all sat on the grey plastic chairs, stretching, yawning and going through the usual motions of trying to adjust to the new day.

'Right people, let's start with our newest member here,' Blaise said with a clap of his hands to wake everyone up. 'What do we have on the murder of Alice O'Leary__ Charlie, have you anything for us?'

'Eh, sorry boss, nothing__ everybody that I spoke to came up blank, although they wanted to know details about the murder.'

'Ok, so as you're our most junior officer, part of your job in CID is to go to the canteen and to try your best to convince them to make a half-decent pot of coffee.'

'That's it Charlie boy, go and fetch the coffee,' DC Jim Whyte joked.

'Right smart arse what can you tell us about the murder?' Blaise quizzed in hopefulness, resting his buttocks on the edge of his desk with arms folded and sucked intensely on yet another mint s 'Talk to me Jimmy boy. Tell me you know where the killer is.'

'Wish I could. I chatted with the neighbours, boss,' DC Jim Whyte said, his expression serious. 'Nobody saw anything out of ordinary on the day in question. Several of the neighbours that knew Geraldine Winters said that they never saw the sister or didn't know that she was staying with her.'

'So then, what you're saying is that nobody saw Alice O'Leary at her sister's house or on the Melmount Road__ nobody at all?' Blaise groaned with disappointment.

'Eh, why was the victim at her sister's__ I thought she lived somewhere in the Ballylaw area?' DC Gemma Galbraith quizzed, searching into her handbag.

'Don't bother looking for your notebook, Gemma,' Blaise sighed.

'I'm not I'm looking for my sweeteners for the coffee, boss.'

'Right, come on, concentrate here people,' Blaise continued. Alice O'Leary was allegedly staying with her sister following an argument with her partner, Mr John Patterson. Now, apparently Alice O'Leary had intended to take her sister's cat to the vet__ this is when we can presume that she met her killer. The sister, Geraldine Winters, states that she never saw Alice again after she left the house with the cat on the Tuesday afternoon, thinking that she had returned home to her partner to make up.'

'Did she keep the appointment with the vet, boss?' DC Jim Whyte quizzed.

'No, uniform apparently questioned the receptionist,' DC Gemma Galbraith answered, tapping the end of the tube to shake out two sweeteners, which she held in her hand. 'God, this Charlie boy won't last long if he is this slow getting coffee's.'

'So, what about this cat then, was it found with the body of the victim?' DC Bill Johnson asked. 'Did the sister not wonder where it was?'

'You're not listening__ I said that the sister thought Alice had returned home to her partner. Anyway, apparently the couple were always falling out.'

'If we've ruled out the partner, boss, are there any other suspects that we should know about?' DC Jim Whyte questioned, impatiently watching the door for the return of Charlie McKean with the coffee.

'The thing is people, we really don't have anything. Will Chambers though has been in contact with GMC in London and he's following up a lead__ some Polish woman, a surgeon. We have to wait though until his mummy wakes him up and he gets in to tell us about it.'

'I hear there's another woman who has been reported as missing, boss?' DC Bill Johnson enquired thoughtfully.

'Jack and I were discussing that when you lot were still in your beds,' Blaise groaned. 'All the signs are that this woman has been abducted. Jack here found a photograph of the woman with a mystery man. Pass it around Jack.'

'Christ, now there's a bloody face I didn't think I'd see for a while,' DC Bill Johnson gasped, the oldest of the detectives and the longest serving officer in the station. He touched a hand lightly over his well-groomed silver hair as he stared at the photograph in his hand, stroking the thin matching beard thoughtfully. 'That's Johnny Mulgrew__ you must remember him, Blaise? He killed that wee girl back in the mid-eighties.'

'Jesus, that's right, Bill__ we won't go over that again. 'I'm bloody glad that you decided to remain a DC, you'd be a bloody loss if you took promotion and went to another station,' Blaise smiled. 'You're our own wee memory man, aren't you Bill?'

'I'd rather stay an ordinary DC any day and do real police work, Blaise.'

Blaise held the photograph in his hand and stared at it. 'No wonder I didn't recognise the bastard,' his voice sounding deep with anger. 'He used to have thick curly hair and a stupid moustache,' he continued, stroking the tip of his thumb back and forth over his chin, much to the amusement of his colleagues.

'So, who is this Mulgrew, I take it he's not that well liked?' DC Galbraith questioned.

'The dirty evil sod ran over the top of a wee girl on the back roads of Artigarvan, he was drunk so he left the poor wee soul to die,' Blaise growled at the memory.

'So what's the connection with this guy and the missing woman?' DC Galbraith asked. 'What's this woman's name?'

'The missing woman is Mary-Jo Delaney__ it would appear that she is having extra martial naughties with this Johnny Mulgrew. She is pregnant too, but there is every possibility that she has absconded with this rat.' DS Jack Phillips said suggestively.

'Right, so now we have the rats name, you run a computer check on him, Gemma,' Blaise smiled with an amusing wink. 'You're pretty good with the computer.'

'Teachers bloody pet,' DC Jim Whyte joked.

Foetal Attraction

'Gemma, once you find an address for this Mulgrew, Jack and I will pay him a wee visit. Bill, you take young Charlie with you and talk with the locals near the Derry Road, see if maybe anybody saw anything out of the ordinary Friday night or Saturday morning. Christ, somebody must have seen Alice O'Leary's body being dumped in that site. Maybe you could also have another talk to the neighbours on the Melmount Road.'

''Eh, by out of the ordinary, you don't mean like a job application, do you?' Bill Johnson joked, scribbling into his notebook.

'Very good, Bill,' Blaise smiled. Right, Jim, you and Gemma have another word with Mr Delaney, I don't think that he's telling us the full story.'

'Should we mention the possibility that his wife was perhaps involved with another man?' DC Jim Whyte asked.

'No keep that under your hat for now, Jim. We might just be able to use it if we need to get heavy with him,' Blaise said thoughtfully.

The mood lightened as everyone simultaneously applauded at the appearance of DC Charlie McKean, pushing his back against the office door as he carried a plastic tray with the coffees in slightly unsteady polystyrene cups.

'Christ, you didn't need to rush, Charlie,' Blaise joked.

'I'll go get the address of this Mulgrew guy for you, Blaise,' DC Galbraith said, taking one of the coffees with her from the tray. 'I'll only be a few minutes.'

'Now, do you see that gents, that's what you call decisive professionalism,' Blaise smiled, taking a coffee.

'So eh, what about this lead that Will's been following up, Blaise?' DC Bill Johnson asked thoughtfully. 'Have you anything on that for us?'

'Well, apparently there was a Polish doctor, a surgeon, and she was reported for doing some kind of strange thing with the organs of some cadavers.'

'What__ like experiments and so forth you mean?' DC Johnson asked.

'God only knows, Bill. Anyway, this woman failed to attend a tribunal and hasn't been seen or heard of since,' Blaise continued.

'So, do you think that there's a possible connection?' DC Whyte asked.

'There just could be, Jim. The pathologist said that the wound on the victim's stomach area was definitely carried out by someone with a medical background.'

'You said that this Delaney woman is pregnant too,' DC Johnson quizzed. 'Are you perhaps going on the premise that she could be our next victim?'

'Maybe this mad Polish surgeon is killing pregnant women just to carry out experiments on them or with the child?' DC Whyte said thoughtfully.

'Grotesque as it may seem people, it just could be, but I hope to God not,' Blaise sighed.

'Here we go,' DC Galbraith beamed on returning to the office. 'There's that address of Johnny Mulgrew. He served eight years for death of young girl, a hit and run on the back roads of Artigarvan. He was then re-arrested for an armed robbery and was released in 1997 and has had a clean record since,' DC Galbraith continued, grinning as she playfully curtsied to the teasing of her colleagues.

'Good work Gemma,' Blaise praised again, reading over the report. 'Right, Jack, we'll go visit this__ Mr Mulgrew. According to this report he's married with two kids.'

'I just hope that if he has absconded with Mrs Delaney that her husband finds out where he lives,' DS Jack Phillips smiled at the thought.

'Right people, so we all know what we have to do, obtain as much info as possible. Now, off we go,' Blaise said forcefully, hurriedly ushering the team outside. Then, he tried several times to contact DC Will Chambers on the mobile phone, a slight concern in his mind as he failed to reach his young colleague.

'Maybe young Will is huffing because he didn't get any information for you, Blaise,' DC Jack Phillips joked, following Blaise from the incident room.

'Oh by the way, did you get anything from the old tramp that found the body of Alice O'Leary, boss?' DC Whyte asked, popping his head in through the door.

'Unfortunately the poor old sod died of a heart attack when he was tucking into some food the canteen staff made for him.'

'I bloody knew that stuff would kill somebody someday,' DC Whyte laughed.

Foetal Attraction

Blaise and Jack Phillips arrived in the Ballycolman Estate, eyes eagerly searching the given address of Johnny Mulgrew. Blaise mused quietly that it was a pleasant difference not to require armed backup now that the country languished in a type of peacefulness. With the main threat now stood down, a faction remained to carry out certain punishment beatings and a variety of other illegal misdeeds on both sides of the so-called religious divide. A peace now established throughout the country, yet, with that, a new problem arose. For it appeared that the youth culture in particular had now taken up the carrying of knives, as in most of the cities on the mainland.

Blaise stared over the wooden fence into the shamefully neglected garden, his eyes flitting over the collection of discarded children's toys, toddler's bicycles and a bright yellow plastic pedal car along with several assorted children's prams, all littering the garden. Blaise pushed through the gate and paused thoughtfully on the footpath, his mind suddenly exploded with playful thought, the moment threw up joyful mind-visions of himself married to Cathy O'Hare and of him running and playing with his own child.

'Blaise__ are you ok__ Blaise?' Jack Phillips questioned, removing the cigarette packet from his pocket. 'Are you having a craving, here, do you want one?'

'Eh__ what? Yes go on sod it,' Blaise sighed surrendering to his desire to quit smoking, but quietly remained hopeful of giving up completely one day. 'It's so bloody ridiculous how something so obviously dangerous can make you feel so good inside. I mean, it's only a paper tube filled with toxins and we bloody crave it so much,' Blaise continued to rant as he stared at the cigarette.

Foetal Attraction

'True, it's a bit like being trapped on a desert island with a nymphomaniac who has every sexual disease under the sun,' Jack Phillips quipped.

Both detectives turned immediately as the front door to the house opened, a woman stood staring back at them with narrowed, reddened eyes, her face almost skeletal with a pallor complexion.

'What do you two want? If you're looking for that bastard he's not here.'

'I take it you are Mrs Mulgrew?' Blaise smiled sarcastically, noticing with quiet pity the woman's unkempt appearance, as she stood unsteady on her feet, looking rather half-drunk. The loose-fitting red sweater and tracksuit bottoms hid a somewhat bony figure and her bleached blonde hair hung in a ponytail halfway down her back. A small child, a girl wearing only a white vest that was soaked down the front from constantly salivating as she sucked on a pacifier whilst tiny arms clung around the mother's leg nervously and bright-orbed eyes stared up silent.

'We need to speak urgently to your husband, Mrs Mulgrew,' Blaise said as he held up his warrant card. 'I'm DI Blaise and this is DS Phillips.

'Well, you better come in then,' the woman invited, groaning noisily as she stooped to lift the child up into her arms, almost stumbling.

Blaise followed the woman into the sitting room, suggesting immediately that she sat down as she stumbled a second time. 'It's a wee bit early to be drinking don't you think, especially when you've got a child there,' he continued, feeling somewhat of a hypocrite himself for the years that he had indulged.

Foetal Attraction

'I wasn't drinking this morning, Inspector,' the woman explained, seating the child beside her on the sofa. 'Some of the girls came round last night just to cheer me up. Don't worry about my daughter, my mother looked after her last night. You might think I'm scum but I can look after my child well enough.'

'Oh I can see that,' Blaise smiled. 'All I need to know is the whereabouts of your husband, it is important that we speak to him.'

'I don't know and don't bloody care,' the woman groaned, fighting back her tears. 'That bastard's not been home in three days, and to be honest, I hope to God he never comes home.'

'I take it then that you have had a row?' Jack Phillips said casually looking around.

'I'm bloody sick to death of him he's always out drinking and screwing about with his mate.'

'Who is this friend, Mrs Mulgrew?' Blaise questioned, seating himself next to the woman, playfully waving his fingers at the child. 'Do you know this friend?'

'Aye I do.'

'Well__ what's his name woman?' Blaise grinned.

'Oh right, it's Tommy Kelly. That sod is always with him. I mean, Holy Christ, ever since he got out of jail he's hardly been home. He bloody promised me that he'd look for work but he's always drinking with that Kelly sod.'

'If eh__ how old is your wee girl there?' Jack Phillips questioned. 'She looks like a wee angel.'

Foetal Attraction

'I know what you're thinking,' the woman smiled then groaned shamefully. 'You're wondering how I've got a two year old when my husband was in prison for years.'

'It did cross my mind, Mrs Mulgrew.'

'Well, it was a bloody night of drunken madness. I was out of my head on the gin and feeling really lonely__ I ended up sleeping with Johnny's brother. He doesn't know it was his brother though, and don't you sods tell him either.'

'Yes well, I think we've all had nights like that at some point in our lives,' Blaise grinned thoughtfully.

'So eh, what does your husband say about you having someone else's child?' Jack Phillips asked as he smiled at the silent child seated next to her mother.

'Oh that sod's head is too fucked up to even care.'

'How do you mean his head's messed up?' Blaise questioned with interest.

'He's been going through hell ever since poor wee Sinead, God be good to her.'

'That's right, I remember something about that,' Blaise said, as though terrible thoughts exploded within. 'Remind me what happened again, Mrs Mulgrew, if you can talk about it.'

The woman groaned as she leaned forwards to sit the child on the carpeted floor, handing her a small teddy bear to play with. Then, as her eyes glazed, she lit a cigarette from the partially crushed packet and stared towards the ceiling in quiet thought.

Foetal Attraction

'Ever since__ Johnny found poor wee Sinead__ Jesus, I've never heard a man scream or cry like Johnny did that night__ it was horrible.'

'Ah, that's right,' Blaise said sympathetically. Your husband found your baby dead.'

'Johnny was drunk__ we had a party that night. Johnny heard wee Sinead crying and went up to settle her down,' the woman continued, smoking vigorously on her cigarette as her mind relived the horror, a horror that could only be stilled by excessive drinking and consuming sleeping pills.

'So eh, what exactly happened, Mrs Mulgrew?' Jack Phillips asked.

'Johnny couldn't settle the wee soul so he took her into our bed. She always fell asleep like that. Johnny fell asleep too. He__ must've__ rolled over on top of the wee soul and__ smothered her,' the woman continued bravely through a gentle stream of crystal tears.

'Jesus, that must have been terrible,' Blaise sighed. 'It's just something parents do without thinking. I mean, you don't really give things like that a thought, do you?'

'Johnny went crazy after that. He couldn't bear to even look at another kid after that.'

'What a terrible thing to carry about with you,' Jack Phillips sighed, offering then to make the woman a cup of coffee.

'No__ wait, I'll make it. You'll probably go on then about the state of my bloody kitchen.'

Foetal Attraction

'Let Jack make it,' Blaise said, telling the woman to remain seated for fear of her tripping over the child on the floor. 'I seem to remember that your husband was arrested on a number of occasions, mainly drunk and disorderly.'

'God, Johnny blamed himself, he just couldn't stop crying and started drinking more and more. He cursed God every day after that for taking his wee angel away.'

'Understandable, I'd probably do the same,' Blaise sympathised.

'Jesus,' the woman laughed. 'I remember him telling the priest one day that he was going to turn bloody protestant.'

'I can't honestly say how much that must've affected him or what he was going through,' Blaise sighed, only able to imagine how the guilt ate at Johnny Mulgrew.

'To be honest, I really hope that big sod doesn't come back home,' Mrs Mulgrew complained. 'I just want to get on with my life. I want to find myself a wee job and start living again. That's why some of my friends were round last night; they're trying to convince me to divorce the useless sod.'

'When your husband isn't home for days, do you know where he goes or who he stays with?' Blaise continued.

'What wee whore he's sleeping with you mean?' The woman growled. 'I asked him once before what he does__ that got me three bloody days in hospital so it did.'

'I see__ you eh, you said that your husband wanted to get back at God for what happened__ what did he mean by that?'

Foetal Attraction

'It was nothing__ he was just mouthing with the drink and drugs, although one night he did scare me. He went on about killing all the kids in the town.'

'Really, why would he say something like that?'

'It was just crap, he said he would kill all the children then God would know what it felt like. He said he wanted God to hurt the same as him like.'

'I see, do you think that he would harm any of the children?'

'Christ no, he might be a real bastard but he would never harm a wee child,' Mrs Mulgrew said confidently lighting another cigarette.

Jack Phillips returned from the kitchen with three coffees, handing one to the woman then another to Blaise, eagerly lighting a cigarette, which Blaise smoked keenly.

'Why are you looking for Johnny__ what's he done this time?'

'We just need to eliminate him from our enquiries,' Blaise said, enjoying his cigarette.

'Would you know if your husband was perhaps seeing another woman?' Jack Phillips questioned casually, sipping his coffee as he stood with shoulder against the wall.

'Christ, that's nice way of saying screwing around Mr Phillips' Mrs Mulgrew laughed sarcastically.

'I mean, do you think he was seeing anyone in particular__ someone special, so to speak.'

Foetal Attraction

Mrs Mulgrew sipped timidly at her coffee, the air filled with cigarette smoke as she stared thoughtful, eyes hiding a life of sorrow. 'Why are you asking if Johnny was seeing another woman__ what's going on here like?'

'It's nothing to get alarmed about,' Blaise smiled, pondering then telling the woman that he suspected her husband of having an affair with the missing woman, Mary-Jo Delaney.

'Do you know where your husband would be now, Mrs Mulgrew?' Jack Phillips enquired, his eyes watching the child on the floor grab onto her mother's leg as she tried to stand up.

'If he's anywhere he'll be with that bloody Tommy Kelly__ probably out of his head with drugs and lying with some dirty wee whore.'

'Would you happen to have an address for this Kelly?' Jack Phillips asked.

'Sion Mills, somewhere near that wee corner shop, that's all I know.'

This Tommy Kelly, he served a few years with your husband for armed robbery, didn't he?' Blaise questioned thoughtfully.

'Do you think maybe they're planning something together, Blaise?' Jack Phillips questioned as he finished his coffee.'

'Well, if they are, I hope to God your lot catch them and put them away for good,' Mrs Mulgrew groaned, the look on her face showing an immense hatred towards her wayward husband, who had apparently abandoned his wife and child and seemingly had no thought as to their welfare.

Foetal Attraction

'Right then, we'll not disturb you any longer,' Blaise said rising from the sofa, handing the empty coffee mug to the woman. 'I think you should talk with a solicitor if you're serious about a divorce.'

'You'd be better off without that idiot if you ask me,' Jack Phillips added.

'Look, try to get yourself sobered up, Mrs Mulgrew, for your own sake and the child's too,' Blaise said touching the woman's arm. You wouldn't want anyone reporting you to the Social Services.'

'Aye, you're right Inspector__ don't worry though, I don't normally drink during the day, honest to God.

Blaise and Jack Phillips headed immediately towards the small village of Sion Mills, both hopeful that they would find Mary-Jo Delaney with Johnny Mulgrew in the house of Tommy Kelly. Blaise though, quietly mulled over what Mrs Mulgrew had said earlier, that her husband wanted to get back at God for the death of his child. The hint of possibility flickered in Blaise's mind that perhaps Johnny Mulgrew had killed Alice O'Leary, but knew that he didn't possess the skills to have removed the unborn child and stitched the abdomen. Of course, the question remained as to Mary-Jo Delaney and her relationship with Johnny Mulgrew.

'I just hope this Mulgrew is crashed out with the drink, I don't fancy having to wrestle with him if he gets angry__ he's a real animal,' Jack Phillips sighed with concern.

'You're getting too old for this job if you're letting idiots like that worry you Jack,' Blaise joked, quietly agreeing with his colleague. 'You know, with what Mrs Mulgrew said, it just could be that her husband is the killer__ or helping the killer.'

'So are you thinking that perhaps he has kidnapped the Delaney woman for the killer?'

'Maybe he is kidnapping pregnant women for this missing doctor. Which bloody reminds me, Jack,' Blaise continued. 'Give that young Will a call again, see where the hell he is.'

'Still no answer__ I swear to God, if that wee shit is lying cosy with his girlfriend I'll bloody give her his danglies to wear as earrings,' Jack Phillips complained, again trying to call their colleague, but to no avail. 'Why in the hell is he not answering his phone__ are you sure it's the right number, Blaise?'

'Of course it's the right number, Jack. Maybe the wee shit is down with something. Did you try his home number?'

'I don't have it on my mobile__ I'll try when we get back to the station.'

'There's the wee shop, maybe somebody in there knows where this Kelly lives,' Blaise said, lighting a cigarette.

'Thanks, where's mine?'

'You can have one once you've been into the shop Jack,' Blaise grinned cheekily. A worrying concern then flooded into Blaise's mind as he tried to think why his young colleague had failed to report in.

Jack Phillips slid into the seat one hand on the steering wheel as he handed Blaise a bar of chocolate. 'The woman in the shop said that Tommy Kelly lives in that house right over there. You can munch on that and hopefully it will stop you going on about trying to stop smoking.'

Foetal Attraction

'Good detective work,' Blaise smiled. 'I'll have this once we've spoken with our friend. Here, do you want a smoke first Jack?'

'The thing is, the woman in there told me that Tommy Kelly has been in hospital this last three weeks following a serious car crash, apparently he's in a bad way.'

'I see, let's hope he doesn't die,' Blaise said sarcastically. Right, we'll sit here a while see if there's anybody in the house before we knock the door eh.'

'You just want to eat your chocolate, you're like a big bloody kid,' Jack Phillips laughed, training his eyes on the house opposite.

'Tell you what though, Jack. It's a damn shame that that linen mill has closed down after these years. 150 years of history lost.'

'My father worked as a supervisor in there for years.'

'Right, I'll give Will another try and you take a look see if there's anyone home.'

Blaise then watched with light amusement as his colleague nervously negotiated the on-rushing traffic that passed either side of the road. A growing concern for the safety of Will Chambers filled Blaise's mind then on receiving no answer from his mobile phone. Blaise then immediately called the station ordering the duty sergeant to send a patrol car to Will's house. A moment of jollity then returned as Blaise watched his colleague clamber over the five foot high locked gate, making his way to the rear of the house when there was no answer at the front door. On the other hand, they had possibly seen Jack approach and were ignoring him. Perhaps they were hiding as they tried to keep secret the fact they had kidnapped Mary-Jo Delaney.

Foetal Attraction

Then, just as Jack Phillips disappeared from view, Blaise burst into a fit of laughter as his colleague came running towards the gate hurriedly followed by a barking dog.

'Jesus H Christ,' Jack Phillips panted anxiously, slumping into the driver's seat. 'Why did that bloody dog not bark before I climbed over the gate?'

'Your face was a bloody picture Jack,' Blaise laughed. 'I thought for minute that your backside was getting bit there.'

'So did I__ did you see the bloody teeth on it?'

'So, was there anyone at home?'

'If you weren't my superior I swear to God,' Jack Phillips grinned, raising a clenched fist.

As the car journeyed towards the Adult Training Centre in Strabane, Blaise took a call from the duty sergeant, who informed him that he had received word from the patrol car. The officer had spoken to the mother of Will Chambers and she had said that she hadn't seen her son in several days, assuming that he had been staying with his girlfriend. The duty sergeant further explained that the girlfriend hadn't seen him either and was now concerned as he hadn't called her either.

'This is starting to worry me, Jack. Where the hell can he be for God's sake?'

'Was he okay__ I mean, was he having any problems?'

'Not that I'm aware of, Jack. He loves the move up to CID.'

'What about his personal life, any probs with his mother or girlfriend?'

'I don't think so, Jack. How could he complain, he was getting good home cooked meals and all that from his mother, and, of course, plenty of sex, from the wife he tells me.'

'You'll never change, Blaise,' Jack Phillips laughed. 'Life to you consists of good food and sex with no ties.'

'That used to be my priorities, Jack__ used to be. Life with Cathy is pretty good,' Blaise smiled, pondering on telling his colleague of Cathy's marriage proposal, but knew he couldn't as Cathy wanted to tell her uncle first.

Jack Phillips steered the car into the Day-Care Centre for Adults with learning disabilities then Blaise led the way into the reception, immediately met by a cheerful young woman.

'DI Blaise, Strabane Police. I'd like to speak to whoever is in charge.'

'Oh, that would Mrs Duffy, I'll get her for you Inspector,' the young woman smiled, using the telephone on the reception desk.

'Yes gentlemen, can I help you?' A large-framed woman smiled as she appeared from a side office and made towards the two detectives. 'How can I help?'

'I'm Inspector Blaise, this is DS Phillips. I'm looking for some information on one of your employees, a Mrs Mary-Jo Delaney.'

'Please, come into the office. Would you like a coffee?'

'No thanks__ eh__?' Blaise smiled entering the office first.

'Oh sorry, I'm Siobhan Duffy, the manager here. Now then, what can I do for you?' The woman smiled sinking into the high-backed leather chair behind a desk that gave host to an array of small framed photographs of patients past.

'Right, was Mrs Delaney employed here on a full-time basis?' Blaise began his questioning.

'No, Mary-Jo works part-time, she is a great help here and the patients, so to speak, adore her.'

'So she got on well with everyone then?'

'Absolutely Inspector, we're all just one big happy family. You see, we hold weekly meetings here, it lets everyone involved air their grievances or views on matters relating to the running of the centre.'

'That sounds like a good idea,' Blaise smiled. 'We should try that, Jack.'

'I can see the DCI approving that, God,' Jack Phillips sighed.

'Was there ever any problem involving any of the patients and Mrs Delaney?'

'God no, she's well liked here as I say. She's been missed terribly though since she took time off.'

'Mrs Delaney is only a few months pregnant, isn't it a bit soon to take maternity leave?'

'It wasn't maternity leave, Inspector. No, she just needed a bit of time off_ personal problems, so to speak.'

Foetal Attraction

'What__ like marital problems you mean?' Blaise continued.

'Well, some weeks ago, Mary-Jo did confide in me. She really wasn't her usual jovial self. We had a little chat__ the poor thing was close to tears.'

'Really__ what was that about then, Mrs Duffy?'

'Oh__ she made me promise not to tell anyone. I really shouldn't say, Inspector.'

'Well I think you had better tell me,' Blaise said commandingly. 'I must warn you, Mrs Dufy, if you know of anything that will aid in our inquiries you must tell me.'

'God__ well, some weeks ago, Mary-Jo told me that she was going through some marital problems, though she didn't say exactly what. You see, she had had an affair and got herself pregnant to the man. She just couldn't believe that she fell pregnant after only sleeping with him once.'

'How could she be sure that the baby wasn't her husband's__ did the husband know of the affair and the pregnancy?'

'I couldn't say, Inspector, Mary-Jo took her leave soon after talking with me.'

'Right, do you know if the husband ever hit Mary-Jo, maybe when they argued?'

'Well, to be honest, that Mickey Delaney has always been a bad sort.'

'I take it then that you know him?'

'We attended the same school, he was a bully then and I'd say still is. My husband drinks in the same bar and he tells me that Mickey Delaney is terribly aggressive and violent.'

'Would you know a Johnny Mulgrew__ did Mary-Jo ever mention him?'

'No sorry, I can't say that I do. Please tell me what this is all about, Inspector.'

'Well, I suppose this being Strabane, it will be all the gossip soon enough,' Blaise grinned. 'Mr Delaney reported his wife missing several days ago.'

'Oh my God!' The woman gasped with immense alarm.

'I honestly don't think that there's cause for concern, Mrs Duffy. I imagine that all the stress and with all that's been happening around her, that she has probably went off somewhere for a few days__ at least we hope that to be the case.'

'We'd be grateful if you don't go broadcasting this, Mrs Duffy,' Jack Phillips said.

'Well, you've been really helpful, Mrs Duffy,' Blaise said rising to his feet.

'Please, let me know if you find her, Inspector.'

Blaise stood outside leaning his arm on the roof of the car as he pondered over the possibility that Mickey Delaney had discovered his wife's affair and of the unplanned pregnancy. Perhaps he had confronted his wife about the affair and things became heated, just perhaps he had given her one punch too many.

Foetal Attraction

'What now, Blaise?' Jack Phillips asked opening his cigarette packet. 'Do you want to go to the house that young Will was supposed to be visiting?'

'I'm not doing too well at giving up these bloody smokes, eh Jack? No, I think we'll just go back to the station and have a wee think.'

Foetal Attraction

Amidst the chaotic clutter of stacked files, discarded reports and well-read newspapers, the fax machine purred quietly as it produced several pages out onto its tray. There, for the inquisitive eyes of Blaise, lay the details and a photograph of Dr Jana Madzia Zaleskia, courtesy of the General Medical Council in London. A footnote, boldly typed, made certain apology for having previously issued DC Chambers with an address that was a temporary residence used by the woman in question. The newly supplied address was that of the parent's home, and in addition to the offered apology, it stated that the photograph was out of date by 12 years.

Blaise sat with eager interest at his desk, stapling the corners of the gathered pages together as he made comment to Jack Phillips that he had forgotten all about the fax machine, not that he had ever really used it. With keen eyes, he then studied the first typed page, noting the bold typed apology as he crunched into several mints.

'There's a photograph of the woman that we need to speak to, Jack.'

'What woman is that?' Jack Phillips muttered, slightly aggrieved that his reading of the newspaper had been disturbed, which he dropped unceremoniously into the waste bin, an absolute first in the act of good housekeeping within the office. 'Who is she, Blaise?'

'Dr Jana Madzia Zaleski__ the Polish surgeon that disappeared ten years ago or so.'

'Oh right__ is she the same woman that young Will is supposed to be making enquiries about?'

'It's an old photograph apparently, Jack.'

Foetal Attraction

'I see. Polish you say__ I suppose if she had been a dancer she'd be a real pole dancer?'

'Jesus Jack__ that was pretty pathetic, stick to being a copper.'

'Sorry, it sounded a lot funnier in my head__ honest,' Jack Phillips sighed, sitting one buttock on the corner of Blaise's desk, almost toppling over a small pile of ignored internal memos that had grown over a period of time.

'So eh, where are we now then, Blaise?'

'Apparently, poor Will received a temporary address that this woman was using whilst working at the hospital in Omagh.'

'It's probably a friend's house__ or a lover's house perhaps?'

'It could be, Jack. There's no mention of a partner or husband in the notes. I expect Will shall give us all the details__ whenever the wee sod returns to the station.'

'Maybe he's been kidnapped by a group of sex-starved amazons and they're using him as their plaything.'

'In that case then, he won't be long. Anyway, I have the address here for this woman's parents__ Sycamore Lodge in Ballymagorry.'

'Sure I doubt if she'll be there, she hasn't been seen in over twelve years, Blaise.'

'We'll soon find out,' Blaise continued.

'So, have you any more thoughts on this Mary-Jo Delaney then, Blaise?' Jack Phillips questioned, hurrying his stride to keep up with his eager colleague as they made their way to the station car park. 'Have you given her much thought?'

'To be honest, Jack,' Blaise sighed thoughtfully, searching his jacket pockets for the packet of mints before slumping into the passenger seat of the unmarked police car. 'I'm a bit in two minds about our Mrs Delaney.'

'How so, what are you thinking then?'

'Well, the notion that she has ran off with this Johnny Mulgrew just isn't ringing any bells with me, Jack.'

'Do you think that perhaps she's been kidnapped too by the person that killed Alice O'Leary__ giving that she is pregnant also?'

'That just could be the case, Jack. I mean, what woman in her right mind would leave without taking her war paints? Besides, she'd have taken some clothes at least__ she wouldn't bugger off with just the duvet_ that was the only thing missing apparently.'

'That true enough, so what are we thinking now?'

'I'm wondering what this doctor woman has been doing these past years, Jack.'

'Could be she just gave up medicine and now runs a wee pub or something.'

'Or it just could be that she is operating a discreet clinic somewhere__ maybe carrying out illegal abortions and the likes?'

'Right, so you're thinking that she has maybe carried out an abortion on Alice O'Leary and it went wrong?'

Foetal Attraction

'It's a possibility, Jack.'

'So why go to all the bother of cutting off fingertips, removing teeth and so on. I mean, surely this doctor would know that we would still trace the DNA of the victim.'

'God knows, Jack. Maybe she has an accomplice and he did the removals before dumping the body.'

The unmarked police car slowed to a snail's pace upon reaching its destination. Jack Phillips remained silent as he steered the car from the main road onto the steep path that led up to the house on the hill.

'I wonder why they called this place Sycamore Lodge.' Blaise said sarcastically, staring either side of the path lined with sycamore trees.

'The grass could be doing with a good cut,' Jack Phillips said, closing the driver's door as he then stood on the gravelled driveway. 'There's plenty of ground to this place, eh? My Christine would be in her glory living in a place like this.'

Blaise ignored his colleague's comments as he interested himself on the windows of the house, looking for any sign that someone was at home. He noted that the Victorian lace curtains looked dull and greyish on each of the upstairs windows and wondered then if anyone still resided there. Then, recalling the discovery of dog hairs on the victim's clothing, Blaise looked for any sign of a dog, hoping to spot a Golden Labrador or Red Setter. A sigh of disappointment echoed in the air at the lack of barking.

'You'd think that a place this big would have a dog running about, eh.'

Foetal Attraction

'Thank God they don't,' Jack Phillips said, following Blaise up the entrance stairs. The two officers then stood in front of a large white door that gave host to an unhindered covering of wind-strewn dust, an irritation of growing impatience surged through Blaise as he kept his finger pressed against the doorbell.

'It's definitely ringing__ I can hear it,' Jack Phillips muttered, leaning his head close to the door. 'Maybe she's down in the basement sharpening her tools.'

'Or maybe she's operating on Mary-Jo Delaney,' Blaise joked.

'I'll take a wee wander around to the back.'

'Hold on, Jack, someone's coming.'

The two detectives stood with pensive anticipation as the door slowly opened, exposing a frail elderly man, who slowly touched a trembling, skeletal-like hand over his pallor face as dark-ringed sunken eyes stared with silent question at the unexpected guests.

'Hello__ Inspector Blaise__ Strabane CID,' Blaise stated loud and slow. 'This is my colleague DS Phillips. We need to speak with Dr Zaleski__ is she here, sir?'

The thin elderly man remained silent in his questioning gaze, his gaunt features and rather skeletal frame giving the impression that he was almost ready to make that wondrous heavenly journey.

'Dr Jana Zaleski__ is she at home, sir?' Blaise again questioned as he stepped closer to the man who looked rather bewildered. 'Do you speak English__ can you understand me, sir? Jesus, I think the old guy is either deaf or can't bloody understand English,' Blaise again repeated himself. 'Can you understand me, sir?'

Foetal Attraction

With slightly mumbled, yet inaudible reply, the elderly man turned his back with lethargic motion then began to shuffle unsteadily along the length of spacious hallway. Blaise and Jack Phillips took that as invitation to enter so followed the man into the semi-darkened sitting room that begged silently for the dedicated attentions of a housekeeper with an abundance of enthusiastic energy.

'Christ, don't tell me that we'll need to call in an interpreter,' Jack Phillips sighed.

'Do you understand English, sir__ can you understand what I'm asking you?' Blaise questioned again, this time with more deliberate clarity.

'Yes__ English__ I understand,' the elderly man finally replied, his muttered sentence seeming forced through a feeble breathless voice. 'English__ I can understand__ yes.'

'Good, now we're getting somewhere,' Blaise sighed with a smile, noticing the difficulty that the elderly man appeared to experience with his breathing. 'Where is Dr Jana Zaleski__ we need to speak with her urgently, sir?'

The elderly man mumbled inaudibly again, his frail frame trembling uncontrollably as he made slow, steady steps towards the armchair that appeared to have been in use for many years. Blaise stepped closely behind him; just to be there should he fall or stumble. He helped the man to sit on the chair, watching then as slender, twisted fingers reached with apparent great effort towards the ebony-framed photograph that sat on the side table.

'Oh__ my poor__ Jana,' the man sighed soulfully, pointing to the photograph.

Foetal Attraction

'Christ, how old was that photograph the GMC sent us, Jack, this is a photograph of a grave, for God's sake,' Blaise groaned.

'Is that the grave of Dr Zaleski, sir?' Jack Phillips asked, staring at the photograph then.

'When did your daughter die, sir?' Blaise questioned, disappointed that his lead was fruitless. 'Did your daughter pass recently?'

The elderly man clutched the photograph to his chest, his dark sunken eyes filling with tears as he mumbled quietly. 'Oh my poor sweet Jana, I'm sorry.'

'Jesus Blaise, the man's near to tears,' Jack Phillips groaned, lunging forwards immediately then as the weeping man began to struggle for a breath, seizing the inhaler from amidst the assorted medication on the table. 'I think we should call him an ambulance, Blaise.'

'I think he'll be ok. Are you feeling better now, sir?' Blaise asked as the man who nodded in reply, still clutching feeble hands onto the inhaler.

'When did your daughter pass away, sir?'

'Blaise__ Christ sake, the woman's dead, let's just leave it,' Jack Phillips sighed forcefully, suggesting then that they left the man to rest with his memories. 'Have you eaten today, sir? I'll make you a drop of tea.'

'You're a proper Florence Nightingale aren't you, Jack,' Blaise whispered with amusement, but felt the same sympathy for the poorly man. His eyes then watching as the man sunk deeper into the armchair, the framed photograph clutched to his chest as eyes stared soulful, reliving a treasured private memory.

'Come on, let's leave the poor old soul to sleep,' Jack Phillips suggested, taking a crumpled blanket from the sofa to cover the man as he slept.

'That looks like our woman there, Jack,' Blaise said noticing the two photographs that hung on the wall opposite as they made to leave. 'The two women there must both be doctors judging by the white coats.'

'Right enough, Blaise. That one on the right must be the mother.'

'I wonder what was in these frames,' Blaise sighed, stooping to pick up several smaller frames from the floor, two with broken glass.

'Well, I think we can forget about our theory of the doctor here performing illegal abortions or the likes, eh Blaise.'

I suppose so, Jack. I was hoping that this doctor would be our killer, damn gut instinct wrong again,' Blaise groaned, placing the frames onto a side table. 'I think then that we'll concentrate on this Johnny Mulgrew, but for now, we'll grab some lunch.'

14

The following morning, Blaise rushed towards the police station, he had uncharacteristically overslept and his mind still pulsated with all the exciting ideas and mostly one-sided deliberations with Cathy O'Hare. The young woman had kept Blaise wakened most of the night with over-excited wedding plans and an eagerness to set a date. Although Blaise found the prospect exciting marrying Cathy and one day starting a family, his mind was lost to the investigation of Alice O'Leary's murder and to the strange disappearance of Mary Jo-Delaney, hoping that she would not be murder victim number two.

'Are there any messages for me, Pete?' Blaise asked the duty sergeant at the desk. 'What about that bloody Will Chambers, anything?'

'Afraid not, Inspector, there's nothing at all for you. Is young DC Chambers sick or what?'

'He bloody will be when I get hold of him. Where's the DCI?'

'He's having a briefing regarding some drugs raid planned for Springhill Park. Apparently there's a tip-off about some guns being there too.'

'Right, you know where I'll be if that Will calls in,' Blaise groaned as he made his way upstairs to his office, halting halfway as his mind exploded with thoughts of Johnny Mulgrew actually being the killer. He pondered seriously on the idea that after the death of his daughter and of the undeniable guilt that must be tormenting the man that he was now so lost within that he was murdering pregnant women. However, what of the apparent stitching on the victim's stomach.

Foetal Attraction

'Jack,' Blaise said loudly thrusting himself into the office with awakened urgency. 'Hey, about this Johnny Mulgrew guy.'

'Jesus, Blaise,' Jack Phillips gasped with surprise. 'You gave me a fright there. Yes, what about Mulgrew?'

'I'm ready to bet my salary on this Mulgrew being our killer,' Blaise said with immense enthusiasm as he eagerly searched his desk for the report on Mary Jo-Delaney. 'Didn't the husband and Mulgrew work as a hospital porters some years back?'

'Are you thinking that maybe there's a link between the doctor and this Mulgrew__ or even the husband, sure the doctor is dead__ when did she die by the way?'

'I've been thinking about too, Jack. The old guy never said either.'

'No he didn't.'

'Remember the two photographs of the women in the house, what if we just jumped to conclusions, what if both the mother and daughter had the same Christian name and it's the mother who is dead, not the daughter?'

'So do you really think this Mulgrew is connected then?'

'It just could be that he was supplying the doctor with bodies for some kind of experiments or whatever.'

'I'm not sure, Blaise, I think we're barking up the wrong tree. Sure, we don't even know for certain that this Delaney woman has been abducted. And how did Mick Delaney or Mulgrew get a job in the hospital with the records they have?'

'God knows, Jack,' Blaise sighed aloud in a moment of thought.

140

Foetal Attraction

'I'm almost positive that Mulgrew has abducted her and is keeping her at that house, besides, it would suit him to know that pregnant women were suffering after what his wife had told us.'

'Do you think that he would actually harm pregnant women just to get back at God for the death of his daughter__ what would he hope to achieve?'

'Who knows what's going on in his mind, Jack? His wife told us that he's lost the plot, his mind's all messed up. Christ, maybe I'm just clutching at straws.'

'I don't know, Blaise. Sure, if as you say, this doctor woman isn't dead and the grave in the photograph was the mother, well, it does put her back in the frame, no pun intended. I mean, she may not even be involved at all.'

'So you reckon it could be another mad doctor type, Jack? The pathologist did say that someone with medical knowledge had removed the uterus from our victim.'

'Right, so where does this Mulgrew fit in?'

'God knows, Jack__ God bloody knows,' Blaise sighed thoughtfully, searching through his pockets for some mints to calm the craving for nicotine. 'I'm still convinced that he is involved in some capacity or other.'

'You reckon he's carrying out these abductions of pregnant women for this mad doctor__ like Burke and Hare the grave robbers used to do? Only these poor souls weren't dead or buried.'

'I take it that that was the DVD you watched last night, Jack?'

'Aye, it was pretty good too.'

'I think we should have another word with that old guy again, assuming he hasn't dropped dead. I think he might just be holding out on us about his daughter, he knows where she is I'll bet.'

'I'll ask Bill to check the name with immigration, Blaise.'

Sergeant Jim Black of Traffic Division called Blaise on the mobile phone, informing him that he discovered DC Chambers' car partially burnt out in a caravan park in Newtownstewart on the B46 road. There was no sign of the young detective and his jacket lay undamaged in the backseat of the car.

'What was young Will doing out in that neck of the woods?' Jack Phillips questioned as the unmarked car then sped towards Newtownstewart. 'Was he having any problems?'

'Christ, we all have problems, Jack.'

'I meant with his mother or his wife.'

'I don't think so, Jack.

'You don't think that maybe he's topped himself, if he was getting things a bit tight, financially I mean.'

'Christ no, at least, I bloody hope not, Jack. That's all we'd need right now. Damn, give me one of your bloody cigarettes.'

'Light me one too, Blaise.'

'You don't think that Will was depressed do you, I mean, we would have noticed surely to God.'

'That's just the thing, Blaise. Nobody really gave him any credit, I mean; most of the lads usually just took the piss.'

Blaise lowered the window, his eyes thoughtful as he watched the stream of cigarette smoke surge upwards and out into the air. 'We'll have a look at this car then I suppose we'll need to talk to Will's mother.'

The dark green Mondeo pulled to a halt at the caravan park in Newtownstewart, a police patrol car and Land Rover were already at the scene when Blaise and Jack Phillips arrived. The sight of DC Will Chambers' partially burnt out car filled Blaise with uncertain fear as he worried then on what had become of his young colleague. Questions began flooding into his racing mind, could it be possible that some faction of the paramilitaries had abducted and murdered the young detective, or, as previously discussed, he had simply lost some secreted battle with depression and had committed suicide.

Sergeant Jack Black stood beside the burnt out car holding the jacket of Will Chambers, which he showed to Blaise on his approach. 'This is your friend's jacket, his wallet and mobile are in the pockets.'

Blaise immediately checked the contents of the wallet to ensure that it belonged to his young colleague, and everything appeared to be intact with no money missing.

'Was the Fire Service out, Sergeant?'

'No, the old man over there said that the car just burnt itself out at the front. Apparently he managed to put out the last of the flames with a hose attached to that water main over there.'

'Is that the old guy over by that caravan?' Blaise said, fixing his eyes on the elderly man who stood waiting at his caravan. 'Did he say if he saw who set the car on fire?'

'Eh no, he said that he noticed the reflection of the flames on the caravan window and came out to see what was happening. He never saw anyone he told me, Inspector.'

'Have you called the forensics boys, Sergeant?'

'I was in the process of doing that when you arrived. The back of the car is untouched by the flames lucky enough. What's the craic here, Inspector__ has your mate disappeared?'

'It's looking like that, it's DC Will Chambers. He was uniform he just made CID last year.'

'I think I remember the name. Do you think he's had a breakdown or something?'

'Not sure what the hell is going on. Make sure your boys keep an eye out for him eh, Sergeant,' Blaise sighed, scanning his eyes across the stretching fields and woodlands, pondering with subdued anxiousness that his assumed troubled colleague could be wandering aimlessly.

Blaise held onto the wallet and mobile phone as he slowly made towards the caravan where the elderly man was waiting and watching. 'Hello, sir, Inspector Blaise, Strabane Police,' he introduced himself, sounding friendly as he entered the caravan on invite, immediately accepting a cup of tea.

'I understand you were the first to see the car burning, sir? And I'm told you tried to put the fire out, well done to you. Though, to be honest, you should have left it for the Fire Service.'

Foetal Attraction

'I was surely first. I was just resting on top of the bed when I noticed the flames flickering on the window there.'

'Did you see anyone at the car?'

'Not a soul, I just rushed over to the hose and tried to put it out.'

'It was brave of you, sir, you could've been injured,' Blaise praised, sipping the tea that tasted truly palatable, strong and sweet, just like his sister, Julia had made for him. 'Are you certain that you didn't see anyone at all, even close by?'

'No, honestly son, I never saw a soul. Was the car stolen?'

'It belongs to a colleague. Now, could you give me your name?'

'It's Eamon O'Neill.'

'You're absolutely positive that you never saw anyone__ you never saw the car drive in?'

'Sorry nothing.'

'Is there anyone else in these caravans this time of year?'

'Well, there's Mr and Mrs McKeown, they're an old couple. They sold their house and live here all year round.'

'That sounds the perfect way to live,' Blaise smiled, enjoying the tea. 'Is there anyone else living here?'

'There's another couple just at the top there. They are as bloody odd as hell, here for a while then away for a while. They would hardly break breath to you. Anyhow, would you like more tea_ I've nice wee fresh scones there if you want one?'

Foetal Attraction

'Eh, no thanks, I'd better get on.'

Jack Phillips knocked on the door abruptly informing Blaise that he had discovered one set of footprints in the mud leading from the car to what appeared to be tyre tracks.

'It just could be that Will took a lift from someone in a waiting car, Blaise. Or there were two men.'

'Right, that's great, Mr O'Neill, thanks. The uniform boys will probably be around later to take a statement.'

'Right then, no problem, Inspector I'll be here all day.'

Blaise and Jack Phillips began to return to the burnt out car, both watching then as a white transit van arrived, several white-suited forensics officers spilling out then and began immediately to survey the scene.

'When you said the footprints led to tyre tracks, do you think that maybe Will could have called his girlfriend for a lift?'

'Or it just could be that he's been kidnapped, who knows?'

'True enough, Jack. I think we should pay young Will's mother a visit, see if she can maybe enlighten us as to what in the hell's going on with her wee son. Then we'll chat to this girlfriend.'

Mrs Betty Chambers positioned her tall, poker-like body in the space left by the opened door, her rigid stance and gaunt features epitomising that of the stereotypical stern headmistress. The unexpected appearance of Blaise and Jack Phillips stirred a worrying concern within the woman, a thin-fingered hand clasped to narrowed, glossed lips as she filled with bewildered panic, almost as if recognising that her son had met with some kind of terrible accident. Widened eyes then stared with questioning gaze through thick-rimmed glasses as she focused on her callers.

'Hello there, Mrs Chambers,' Blaise smiled. 'Do you remember me__ Inspector Blaise?'

'Of course I remember you, Inspector. What is it__ has something happened to my little Will?'

Blaise fought desperately with himself not to laugh, thinking how glad he was that his young colleague wasn't Willie. He just knew that the woman's question wouldn't have sounded so serious otherwise, such was Blaise's jocular mind.

'Has__ Will had an accident, Inspector?' The woman quizzed again with anxious concern, inviting her callers inside. 'That's why you are here, isn't it?'

'Calm yourself, Mrs Chambers,' Blaise smiled, touching a comforting hand on the woman's bony shoulder. 'Your wee boy is fine__ it's just that, well; he hasn't been in touch for a while.'

'What!' The woman exclaimed with surprise. 'That isn't like him at all; he often tells me how important it is that he keeps constant contact with the police station.'

Foetal Attraction

'I was just passing and thought I'd pop in. Has he been poorly?'

'Tea__ I'll make a nice a pot of tea. Please, sit down,' The woman muttered with an energetic state of worried concern, her slender, rigid body almost quivering with the anticipation and dread that every mother sensed when her child perhaps collided with danger.

'Please__ don't be getting upset, Mrs Chambers,' Blaise again comforted, recognising the woman's bewildered state of mind. 'Will can be a bit__ well; you know yourself what he can be like. Whenever he is fed up he just disappears for a wee while, doesn't he?'

'Here, you sit down and talk to Blaise and I'll make the tea,' Jack Phillips said suggestively. 'You just rest and I'll do the necessaries, Betty.'

'Oh, yes that's fine, thanks Jack.'

'I hope you have some of that homemade soda bread.'

Blaise sat back on the sofa beside the flustered woman, smiling as he tried again to calm her racing nerves as slender hands trembled in fear of hearing some bad news concerning her son.

'How has he been this past while, Betty__ do you know if he's having any problems?'

'I think that that silly girl has turned his head,' Mrs Chambers said with a stern growl, almost vicious as she breathed through gritted teeth. 'She makes him stay with her at times you know. She's so devious, giving him a few drinks so that he can't drive home.'

'Don't you like her then, Betty?'

Foetal Attraction

'Oh she's nice enough don't get me wrong, Inspector. She's trying to convince Will to get her pregnant, she's so desperate to marry him, to have him all to herself. I don't think the girl has done a day's work in her life.'

'Did it ever occur to you that they both just could be genuinely in love, Betty? Maybe young Will is keen to marry her.'

'Oh no, my Will wouldn't go off and leave me, not with my weak heart and my terrible arthritis. I wouldn't be able to cope on my own, Inspector,' the woman complained, her breathing then becoming forced and heavy as she touched a hand to her chest.

'I didn't know you had__ you always looked so healthy to me,' Blaise stated recognising the pretence. Recalling then when Will Chambers had told him of his mother faking every conceivable ailment under the sun whenever he had mentioned moving in with his girlfriend. 'Would you say that Will was perhaps a bit depressed? I mean, sometimes he looked as though his mind wasn't on the job. I know he loved being in CID, but at times you'd get the impression that he didn't care about anything.'

Mrs Chambers sat upright, her faked aching heart forgotten as she sat wringing her hands tightly. 'It's that girl__ Will hasn't been the same since she got her claws into him, always on the phone wanting him to call her__ like a bitch on heat. All the others were the same, doing their best to take Will away from me.'

Blaise realised then just why his young colleague had acted in the way that he had, it was his mother causing all the frustrating problems, faking ailments and pretending that she desperately relied on her son and was the cause of all the past breakups in his relationships. Blaise felt a certain anger rise within, he wanted so

149

Foetal Attraction

much to slap the woman before him, to waken her to her senses and stop her from acting in such a tyrannical manner and to support her son in whatever direction he decided to go.

'When exactly did you last see or talk to Will, Mrs Chambers?'

'Goodness now let me think, Inspector. 'Oh yes, it was two days ago__ no, three it was. Oh dear, I'm not sure, it must be the medication.'

'Perhaps you're taking too much, Mrs Chambers,' Blaise said, knowing that most of the woman's medication was for nothing, the ailments were all in her head.

'Right, here we are,' Jack Phillips said cheerfully, returning to the sitting room with the tea tray. 'Have we discovered where our young Will could be then?'

Blaise exhaled a subdued, discounted sigh, raising his eyebrows as he took the teacup from his colleague. 'I think that perhaps young Will has just taken himself off for a few days to think things over, Jack. Maybe he is just trying to make a few decisions on his own.'

'You know, it sounds to me as though you are trying to keep young Will at home with you, Betty,' Jack Phillips joined the conversation bluntly, causing the woman to cast a cold, silent stare in his direction. 'I mean, Will's a grown man now__ he has a life to lead, Betty.'

Mrs Chambers removed her spectacles, inhaling a slow breath then of thoughtful pondering as she rubbed a knuckle against her eyes, as though fighting back the tears of unwanted realisation. 'It's just that I'm afraid to be on my own since Will's father died. There are a lot of terrible people out there.'

Foetal Attraction

'Jesus__ isn't that what everyone wants, Betty? I mean, you'll have the house all to yourself and you can do as you please,' Jack Phillips smiled. 'You could even get yourself one those toy boys.'

'Why don't you ask Will and his girlfriend to move in with you? I mean, they are planning an engagement. If they marry and have kids then you would be with the grandchildren every day, wouldn't that be nice?' Blaise said.

'You won't know until you ask, Betty. It could just work out perfectly for all concerned,' Jack Phillips added.

'Anyhow, that aside,' Blaise sighed. 'Would you have any ideas where young Will would go__ does he have any particular place that he likes to go for a bit of peace?'

'Not that I know of, Inspector. Do you think that perhaps something has happened to him? I wouldn't be able to live with myself if anything happens to him.'

'Eh, I can't recall the girlfriend's name, what it is again?' Blaise sighed thoughtful, remaining secretly concerned.

'It's Imelda__ Imelda O'Kane. She lives in one those rented flats in the town__ on the Main Street.'

'Right well, I think we'll go have a word with her,' Blaise said, rising then to his feet after finishing the tea in his cup. 'If you hear from Will, please tell him to call me immediately, Betty.'

'I certainly shall dear__ the minute he does.'

'Well, thanks for the tea, Betty,' Jack Phillips smiled opening the front door to lead the way outside.

Foetal Attraction

'Where the hell could he be, Jack?' Blaise groaned with a mixture of worry and anger as he slumped into the passenger seat of the car, smiling at the woman as they began to reverse out of the driveway. 'What if the wee sod has just decided to head off somewhere__ to start a new life?'

'Jesus, that's a bit dramatic,' Jack Phillips laughed, the possibility then toying with his mind. 'He wouldn't just up and leave__ what about his job. No, I can't see young Will disappearing without a word to his mother__ or his girlfriend.'

'It's just not right, Jack. Something just isn't right here; I'm bloody starting to think that something has happened to him.'

'When you say something, do you think he's possibly been kidnapped or something like that?'

'It just could be, Jack. I mean, we did find his car burnt out.'

'True, especially when his wallet and phone were still in his jacket,' Jack Phillips found himself forced to agree. 'It just could be somebody that he has arrested in the past.'

'We'll check any prisoners that he has arrested and have been released recently when we return to the station.'

'Late home tonight again then,' Jack Phillips sighed. 'You'll definitely not be popular with the wife again, Blaise.'

'Christine will forgive you when she sees the overtime pay.'

'I suppose, that's the best way of getting around an angry woman isn't it, Blaise? Just give her some money to spend.' Jack Phillips laughed.

Foetal Attraction

Blaise made his way towards the red-bricked rented flats opposite the small car park whilst Jack Phillips remained in the car. He deliberated within his agitated mind over the inexplicable disappearance of his young colleague, pondering then if perhaps there was any possible connection to the murder of Alice O'Leary, and the assumed abduction of Mary-Jo Delaney. Of course, Blaise wondered then if perhaps his young colleague had made contact with the killer during his investigation into the whereabouts of the missing Dr Jana Zaleski. Blaise questioned then on where Will Chambers could be captive, and, was he still alive.

There was no answer at the door to the flat and just as Blaise made his way back to the car, the phone in his pocket rang. Sergeant Black informed him then that his presence was required due to the discovery of a body. In that very moment, Blaise experienced a terrible fear that perhaps the body was that of his young colleague, but strangely thankful then when the caller informed him that the body was that of a young female.

16

Blaise allowed his eyes to marvel over the fresh open countryside as the unmarked police car steered a cautious course along the narrow, tree-lined path that separated acres of grassy fields. He felt angered that the serene picturesque splendour of nature had been horrendously sullied by the gruesome discovery of a body. To happen across a body on Mother Nature's wondrous garden seemed somehow acceptable should it be a tiny bird, hedgehog or even that of a badger. However, to discover a human body lying lifeless amidst the flora and fauna was particularly more harrowing and showed fully the extent of man's savage and barbaric nature.

Blaise carefully stepped into the muddied ditch his eyes studying the lifeless body of the young woman that sprawled before him. His stomach wretched at the sickening sight as he stared down at the bloodied stumps where toes had once been, fingertips also severed and all body hair shaved, just as that of the body of Alice O'Leary

'Jesus Christ, Blaise,' Jack Phillips sighed with shocked disgust, crouching at the very edge of the leaf-strewn path. 'That definitely looks like victim number two.'

'Yip, it's the same M.O. all right, Jack,' Blaise groaned, touching his fingertips onto the cold flesh of the victim's chin, noticing also that the teeth had been removed.

'Christ Almighty.'

'Judging by these tattoo's it looks like we have found Mary-Jo Delaney,' Blaise continued as he scanned his eyes over the sodden, bloodied duvet that lay crumpled close by. I was bloody hopeful that we would find her alive. This is ridiculous, Jack. We need to find this crazy sod before he kills anymore.'

Foetal Attraction

'I think now we can start looking for a serial killer__ what do you say, Blaise? Are we going to find a string of young pregnant women murdered now?'

'It's bloody looking that way, Jack.'

'Maybe we should look into that address of the missing doctor that young Will was checking out__ what do you say, Blaise?'

'That just might be a good idea, Jack. I wonder if this Johnny Mulgrew has anything to do with this,' Blaise continued, his eyes transfixed on the staring lifeless eyes of the victim, as if pleading with him to catch her killer.

'I don't think that the Big Crook is going to enjoy hearing this. Christ, if the press get wind that some psychopath is murdering pregnant women there'll be some bloody panic,' Jack Phillips stated, noticing then several blood droplets on several leaves. 'It looks like the poor soul has been dumped here, it's pretty deserted.

Blaise clambered up the ditch, staring direct at the uniformed constable who reached out a hand of support. 'Who found the victim here?'

'It was an elderly couple, Inspector,' replied one of the officers, removing a notebook from his pocket. 'It was an elderly couple out walking their dog, Inspector. Apparently the dog had jumped into the ditch and pulled at the duvet revealing the body underneath.'

'When was this exactly?'

'Eh, a couple of hours ago__ it was approximately 11:30 am, Inspector. The call was taken by WPC Harris; she was on the desk at the time.'

Foetal Attraction

'Has the pathologist been called?'

'Yes the Sarge called them. Oh, the nightshift boys sighted that Johnny Mulgrew that you were looking for, Inspector.'

'Did they arrest him?'

'Afraid not__ the sod disappeared before the officers could get to him. He was in a pub and escaped through a fire exit.'

'Oh well, just keep looking for him__ I want him more than I want your sister.'

'That'll be the day,' the uniformed officer laughed. 'If you touch my sister I'll have to forget that you're an Inspector.'

'What have you got there?' Jack Phillips asked.

'It's the victim's wedding ring, Jack. I'll show it to the husband to get him to confirm it's his wife's before we get him to identify the body.'

'Christ, I can imagine how he'll feel__ not only has the poor sod lost his wife but he's lost the unborn child too,' Jack Phillips groaned with quiet anger.

'Did eh__ did we mention the photograph to the husband, Jack. The one you found with his wife and Johnny Mulgrew?'

'Jesus, you can't be thinking of showing it to him now? That will certainly push him right over the edge, Blaise.'

'Second thoughts, we better not. I just wonder if maybe the husband knows this Mulgrew character. It just could be that they are all friends.'

156

Foetal Attraction

'Did I not mention his name to the husband, Blaise?'

'I can't remember, Jack. I've got an idea.'

'Oh God help me.'

'No, listen, when we are chatting to him, you pretend to call the station and just mention Mulgrew's name loudly so that the husband overhears the name and he just may say something.'

'Do you think that this Mulgrew is involved then, Blaise?'

'God knows, Jack. I'm just trying to come up with something positive, something to kick start our investigation on the right bloody road.'

'What about this Polish woman then? The doctor I mean, do you fancy taking a drive out to the address?' Jack Phillips questioned thoughtfully, still sickened by the senseless murder of another young pregnant woman. 'That's if this woman is alive, we're not even certain if that grave in the photograph at the old man's house was that of his late wife or the daughter.'

Blaise threw his eyes around the scene, not much to see, dense trees ran either side of the narrow footpath. The locals would remember a peacefully beautiful scenic walk at any other time, but not now, the sickening sense of man's evil hung heavy in the cool afternoon air.

'Just where is this evil sod carrying out his evil deeds, Jack?'

'It just could be at that address young Will was looking into to. Maybe he confronted the killer, or maybe Will is now one of his victim's too.'

Foetal Attraction

'Right, we're just wasting our time here, Jack. It's pretty obvious that the body's been dumped here, but from where, Jack__ where is this damn madman or woman doing the dirty deed__ where?'

Blaise and Jack Phillips headed slowly back towards the car, suddenly, Blaise stopped and gave a thoughtful stare as he stroked his chin with the tip of his thumb. Then, resting both hands on the bonnet of the car, his head hung low as he breathed a heavy sigh.

'What if we're looking at this all wrong, Jack? Pregnant women attend some kind of clinic, don't they?'

'Antenatal clinics they're called, Blaise. Why__ what are you thinking, what's on your mind?'

'What if there is somebody at this clinic who's picking out individual women__ maybe looking for a certain type of woman, young? Maybe it's somebody with some kind of a sexual motive__ a twisted perversion, as well as them removing the uterus for whatever bloody sordid reason.'

'There wasn't any sign of sexual activity on the first victim,' Jack Phillips replied with questioning stare. 'The pathologist would have found signs of sexual activity, penetration and so on.'

'What are we not seeing, Jack? There has to be a bloody particular reason for these killings__ but what__ what are we missing?'

'There has to be a doctor or surgeon involved somewhere, Blaise. Christ, perhaps there's several doctor's secretly carrying out experiments of some kind.'

'Let's get away from here,' Blaise sighed deeply, stuffing his mouth with mints as he slumped into the passenger seat.

Foetal Attraction

'Where are we headed for then, Blaise?'

'We better go talk to the husband first, Jack. I bloody hate being the bearer of bad news.'

'It's not a nice part of the job at all.'

'We'll go see the husband first then take a run out to that address that Will was checking into to, Jack.'

'So what about this antenatal clinic idea of yours then, do you honestly think that perhaps there is someone singling out individual women for this crazy doctor?'

'I'm just thinking about it, Jack. It is another plausible avenue that we could explore I suppose,' Blaise sighed as he continued to crunch into the mouthful of mints with thoughtful annoyance. 'I just can't get this bloody Johnny Mulgrew out of my mind__ I just know that he is involved somehow.'

'Right, so getting away from all this for a moment,' Jack Phillips thoughtfully sighed. 'How are you and young Cathy getting on__ I mean is it serious?'

'Absolutely__ I've honestly never felt as happy, Jack. I'm so bloody glad that I've managed to stay off the drink, well, most of the time. I mean, my life was going nowhere.'

'That's true__ not to mention close to losing to your job.'

'I know I behaved like an asshole, Jack. Look, I know that you hate me for that stupid carry on with Lizzie Harris and her husband putting in for a transfer.'

'It was pretty terrible, Blaise,' Jack Phillips replied with an angered glance. 'You were the bloody talk of the station__ the Big Crook covered your arse many a time. Christ Almighty, you went through almost half of the female officers there and those bloody parties you had at your place.'

'I was a bit of an idiot right enough, Jack. But hey, all that crap is behind me now. I'm really looking forward to__ well, I just want to settle down with Cathy and do my job.'

'Do you think that you'll both get married? Cathy is a really nice girl, a heart of gold.'

'It would be nice, Jack. We'll just have to wait and see.'

'It would be nice to see you finally settled. Listen, I want you to know that I'm trying to forget the stuff between us over Bobby Harris. He was a really good friend__ you doing the dirty with his wife just messed his head right up.'

'I know that, Jack. Christ it was a stupid drunken moment, though it did help her in a way, it stopped her getting too depressed.'

'She was really down, I suppose it did help, I'll give you that. It's best all forgotten now. Though I will say that you better watch your back, you know what Bobby's like.'

The unmarked police car pulled into the driveway of the Delaney household, Blaise telling his colleague to remain in the car as he then made towards the house. Blaise was then confronted by a rather concerned looking woman as she stood holding open the front door.

'Hello, Inspector__ have__ you found Mary-Jo. Please say yes, please, Mick's really upset.'

Foetal Attraction

'Is Mr Delaney at home then?'

'He's in the sitting room. I'm Mick's sister by the way,' the woman said, appearing as if she were ready to explode with grief.

'Look, do me a favour, stick the kettle on or pour your brother a good drink,' Blaise said quietly, touching the woman's arm.

'Oh my God!' She gasped, covering her gaping mouth with a trembling, shocked hand. 'Is__ she dead?'

Blaise made his way into the sitting room removing the wedding ring from his pocket, his eyes fixing directly on Mick Delaney, who stood wide-eyed with anxious anticipation and a large of vodka in his slightly trembling hand.

'I eh__ I'm afraid that I have some bad news, sir,' Blaise began, showing the wedding ring to the distraught man. 'Is this your wife's ring, sir?'

'Where did you__ shit__ is Mary-Jo__ is she__?'

'I'm really very sorry. Your wife's body was discovered on a quiet back road near to Ballymagorry, Mr Delaney,' Blaise continued, feeling his pulse race with the detestation of having to break such bad news. 'I've made arrangements for a car to take you to make a positive identification, sir.'

Mick Delaney didn't hear the comforting words of his tearful sister as he slumped heavily onto the sofa, gulping down a large mouthful of his drink.'

'Maybe you'd be better with a cup of tea, sir,' Blaise said knowing that the man would ignore his suggestion.

161

Foetal Attraction

'I'm sorry to ask at this time, sir, but would you know if anyone had a grievance against your wife?'

'A what__ why the fuck would__?'

'Mickey, calm down now,' the sister said boldly. 'The Inspector's only asking, it's his job, he doesn't know what a lovely girl Mary-Jo is.'

'Did eh__ did you find Mary-Jo's other ring; it was her late mother's__ she'd never take it off?'

'That was the only the ring we found, sir. Could you give me a description of this ring?'

'It was a lovely eternity ring, Inspector,' the sister replied. 'It was silver with red rubies and a thin gold band in the middle.'

'I'm afraid that that was the only ring on the __ on Mary-Jo, we'll keep a look out for it though.'

'I bloody knew that Mary-Jo had been kidnapped, didn't I say. I fucking knew it,' Mick Delaney sobbed loudly, swallowing the remnants of his glass allowing it then to fall onto the floor. 'Why__ what bloody reason would some fuck-wit have for kidnapping my Mary-Jo?

'I'm truly, sir.' Blaise again expressed his sincere condolences. 'I can assure you that we'll do our best to catch your wife's killer.'

'Well I'm telling you,' Mick Delaney growled through gritted teeth, eyes bulging with rage. 'You better pray that you do catch this bastard before I do.'

'I understand how you must feel, Mr Delaney, but you must let the law deal with this. You'll only end up in prison.'

'Do you honestly think that I give a fuck__ I'll kill the bastard with my bare hands,' Mick Delaney continued, fists tightly clenched as the sorrowed rage thundered within.

'Calm down, Mickey,' the sister again tried to comfort, sitting then beside her brother on the sofa, tear-soaked eyes staring up at Blaise. 'Do__ you__ know who killed poor Mary-Jo, Inspector?'

'Not at the moment I'm afraid, but I can assure you both that we'll do all in our power to catch him.'

'Well, I'll see you out, Inspector, and thanks for everything,' the sister tried to smile through her tears, leading Blaise to the front door.

'Eh, just between you and I, Miss,' Blaise whispered as he leaned close to the woman. 'I understand that there was a bit friction between Mrs Delaney and her husband. Would you know if Mrs Delaney was perhaps involved in a secret relationship with someone, if you get me?'

'God, look, give me your number and I'll call you tomorrow.'

Blaise handed his calling card to the whispering woman then headed back to the car, hopeful that the sister would later shed some light on the assumed relationship with Johnny Mulgrew.

'That poor sod in there is ready to explode, Jack,' Blaise sighed as he slumped into the passenger seat, throwing mints into his mouth, spitting them immediately. 'Stuff this give me one of your cigarettes, Jack. I'm really starting to get pissed off with this crap about stopping smoking.'

Foetal Attraction

'So, Victoria Bridge then is it, Blaise?'

'Yes, Ash-Pine Manor, Jack. Blaise recalled from memory, luxuriating blissfully in the sensation of nicotine that flooded his body. '305 Ash-Pine Manor it is, Jack.'

'Hopefully this will be the place where this mad doctor is carrying out the dirty deeds, Blaise.'

'Let's hope so,' Blaise sighed, allowing the cigarette smoke to leisurely escape from his mouth. 'Let's just hope also that we find young Will there too, or signs that has been there.'

'I just hope to God that we do catch this evil sod there.'

'Me too, Jack__ me too.'

Foetal Attraction

Blaise slumped wearily in the passenger seat arms folded across his chest as he stared ahead into the evening's darkening sky, almost gunmetal blue in colour. His mind pulsated with an unwanted debate as he considered the prospect of discovering that his young colleague had already met a murderous end. The very notion played mercilessly with his mind that the body of DC Will Chambers could be buried somewhere, perhaps even in the grounds of the house that he was about to visit. On that very assumption, Blaise filled with trepidation at the thought of being the one to inform his mother of the tragic news, knowing only too well of her undeniable love for her only son, not to mention the drastic effect that Will Chambers' murder would have on everyone at the police station.

Blaise filled with an angered frustration as his tormenting mind raged at the thought of not having any concrete evidence or definite suspects to connect with the gruesome murders of Alice O'Leary and Mary-Jo Delaney. The only connection between the women was that they were both young and pregnant, and, as the pathologist had stated following the post mortem on Alice O'Leary, someone with skilful medical knowledge had removed the uterus, leaving Blaise to question on the horrific reasons as to who would carry out such a barbaric act and why.

All pondering thoughts and deliberations subsided quietly as the car pulled into the unlit driveway of 305 Ash-Pine Manor, the illuminated headlights spreading across the front of the building like a false moonlight.

'The bloody place is all boarded up. Are you sure this is the right address, Jack?' Blaise complained with an explosion of disappointment.

Foetal Attraction

'Of course it's the right address. I noticed the sign on the gatepost. 305 Ash-Pine Manor__ that was address wasn't it?'

Surprised anger and frustration pulled Blaise from the car, his hand gripping the torch that he had taken from the glove box and sprayed it across each boarded up window. The icy night air had stretched a thin blanket of sparkling frost over the expanse of uncared for lawns as Blaise walked to the side of the abandoned house then around to the rear, his eyes puzzled and angry as they followed the torch beam.

'Did that wee shit not even call to let you know that the place was deserted?' Jack Phillips questioned as he followed behind.

'No__ sure he never got back to me, Jack. I was bloody certain that someone would be here__ I was almost positive that we'd find young Will here too.'

'Where in the hell could he have bloody gone, Blaise?' There must be something seriously wrong__ I mean, he wouldn't just vanish like this.'

'I'm beginning to think that poor Will has met with a terrible end. I can't put my finger on it, it's a gut feeling, Jack. There's definitely something not right here,' Blaise continued, scanning inquisitive eyes around the immediate area, drawing the torch beam over the ground at his feet desperate to find something, anything that would tell him that Will Chambers had visited the house.

'What about this other address__ Sycamore Lodge, what if the GMC people contacted Will with an amended address?'

'Back to this Polish woman, Jack,' Blaise sighed shining the torch onto his wristwatch. 'Maybe we'll take a wee run out there.'

'It's not that late, Blaise. Maybe we'll be lucky and bump into this woman, assuming that she isn't dead.'

'Let's go then, we can stop off at this girlfriend's house, he may just be there with her. Christ, what a couple of dumplings we are, Jack. We hardly know anything about this girl.'

'True enough, though Will never spoke about her, besides, he's not been with us that long to share his intimate secrets,' Jack Phillips smiled, steering the car around the perimeter of the abandoned house then out onto the road towards Strabane.

'Listen, we'll take a look at this Sycamore Lodge first, then on the way back we'll have a wee chat with this girl of Will's__ Imelda wasn't it, Jack?'

'Yes, that sounds good to me, I'm ready to put the feet up,' Jack Phillips yawned. 'Oh, by the way, you never answered me when I asked you about your new life with young Cathy. Do you find it strange coming home at night to someone waiting for you?'

'To be honest, Jack, it was weird at first. I mean, you have to pick your moments when you want to belch or even fart,' Blaise laughed, and in that one solitary moment, all the stress and pressure of the murder investigation eased. 'Have you ever watched any of those programmes about psychics and all that, Jack?'

'I've seen a few, why?'

'Do you believe that these psychic people can actually talk to the dead, so to speak?'

'Christ Almighty, what's Cathy been putting in your food, Blaise__ I mean, you turning all religious on me now, are you?'

Foetal Attraction

'No, it's just that__ well, I met this wee elderly woman a while ago in a shop in Ballymagorry.'

'Are you going to tell me that she was a ghost or something?'

'No, listen, she came up to me and said things about my old man. Christ, she mentioned the nickname that I used for him, Jack.

'Maybe she knew him, everybody knew your father,' Jack Phillips sighed, giving his colleague a questioning stare.

'She gave me her phone number if I wanted to talk.'

'Don't get me wrong, Blaise. I'm not saying that it's rubbish, I suppose there has to be something after we bite the dust. I mean, take the brain for instance, it's far too complex and complicated for it to exist for only say__ eighty years or so and then just nothing.'

'So is this why you're trying to stop smoking__ did this psychic woman say that you had to stop?'

'No, I just want to__ slow down man, there's the bloody turn.'

'I know that, Jesus,' Jack Phillips sighed, cautiously steering the car up the steep hill from the main road.

'The bloody place is in complete darkness, Jack. Let's hope that the old man hasn't been taken into hospital_ or dropped dead.'

'Maybe our crazy doctor woman is out picking her next victim, or maybe there's several doctors scouring the streets for pregnant women.'

'Don't be so bloody melodramatic,' Blaise grinned. 'Let's just take a wee look and see if there's anyone at home.'

Foetal Attraction

'Supposing this doctor is dead__ I mean, there were a few photographs of the younger woman with a young boy, he looked a bit deformed, if you get me.'

'That's right, Jack. I forgot about that.'

'Of course, assuming that the young doctor is dead, where is the older one, the mother?'

'Christ, we'll need to clarify which one is dead, Jack. I mean, assuming that the daughter is dead, surely, she would be buried beside the mother, and there would be two graves in the photo maybe. The old guy never said we just bloody assumed it was the daughter.'

'Right enough, Blaise. There's definitely something weird about this one. What about all those photo frames without photos?'

'Maybe the old guy has fallen out with the entire family.'

'We definitely need to talk to him again, get a clearer picture.'

'We'll get back to the station once we've had a chat with this Imelda, hopefully she'll know where Will has got to. You can do a check see if we have anything on this son of the mysterious doctor.'

'Back to the station__ I thought we were going home?'

'Right, okay, first thing in the morning then grumpy arse,' Blaise groaned humorously. 'I bloody forgot__ Betty Chambers gave me the number of this Imelda, I'll give her a call she if she's at home.'

'Honest to God, you're getting worse, Blaise.'

169

'Right good morning people,' Blaise bellowed with an energetic boldness on entering the incident room, which unfortunately caused Jack Phillips to spill a drop of coffee onto his pale blue tie. 'it's a lovely fresh morning so let's get our bloody heads together and catch this killer.'

There was an air of stilled tension within the incident room as the detectives seated themselves around one table, notebooks at the ready. The large white board on the wall showed the gruesome injuries inflicted upon the two victims, eyes staring from each face as though silently pleading with every detective to catch their killer. The questions still requiring answered, who is or are these evil life-takers. What are the motives for such barbaric killings and where are they?

DC Bill Johnson scratched fingertips idly through thinning silver hair then stroked his small, well-groomed beard. 'Eh, young Charlie and I visited some of the neighbours on the Woodend Road close to where Alice O'Leary's body was discovered,' he began, glancing quickly at his notepad. 'Nobody saw anything suspicious though there was one guy__ he was out walking his dog on the morning in question. He told me that he remembered seeing a dark coloured van parked close to the entrance of the building site.'

'I don't suppose that he saw the driver or noticed the registration?'

'Sorry, boss, no luck there I'm afraid. He said that his eyesight is playing him up and needs new glasses. He couldn't make out the reg or properly see the colour of the van, given that it wasn't quite light that morning.'

'Oh well, keep visiting the neighbours there lads,' Blaise sighed.

Jim and I have a witness living near to the Delaney house that recalls seeing a dark coloured van parked opposite to the house the morning Mrs Delaney disappeared,' DC Gemma Galbraith added. 'The woman said she didn't really pay much attention to the van at the time, but she thinks that it was dark green in colour. She didn't see the driver unfortunately.'

'Jack, check that forensics report, I think they took moulds of some tyre tracks, see if they could identify the model of van.'

'That's right so they did, I'll look into that, Blaise.'

'So, now we know that we're looking for a dark coloured van, possibly dark green__ at least that's something people. It's just a pity that nobody has seen this driver,' Blaise sighed thoughtfully.

'What about showing pictures of different types of vans to these witnesses, it just might jog their memories, boss,' DC Jim Whyte suggested.

'Good idea, you take care of that then, Jim,' Blaise smiled, his moment of thought interrupted when a uniformed officer entered the room informing Blaise that there was a woman in the reception area she had requested to speak with him urgently.

'It sounds like the Child Support Agency has finally caught up with you, Blaise,' DC Bill Johnson joked.

'Now, do you want me to tell everyone about your wee incident with that transvestite in Donemana,' Blaise said as he left the room, which filled with jocular comments and cheering and louder shouts of denial from DC Bill Johnson.

'Who is it__ did she give a name, Harry?'

Foetal Attraction

Mickey Delaney's sister, Janice sat twisting her hands with nervous concern as she waited anxiously in the reception. She didn't like the thought of being inside the police station for fear that someone would recognise her leave and that would certainly cause some suspicion with her neighbours, particularly as there was a punishment beating handed out to one the neighbours the evening before. She was one of the few on the nationalist/republican side who had decided to put aside all long-held grievances and differences and to accept the newly formed Police Service of Northern Ireland, though her late father would have probably disowned her.

Blaise stared at the woman dressed in navy tracksuit, a somewhat habitual dress code taken up by half of the females in Strabane. She had tied up her thick jet-black hair with a blue ribbon allowing full view of her thin face that showed a quiet attractiveness enhanced by a hint of make-up.

'Eh__ can I help you, Miss__? Blaise quizzed, trying to recall if he had met the woman.

'You said I should give you a call if I wanted to tell you anything,' the woman said timidly, changing her gaze between the floor and Blaise. 'You don't remember me, do you, Inspector? I'm Mickey Delaney's sister__ Janice.'

'Jesus, that's right, imagine me forgetting a pretty face,' Blaise smiled, leading the woman into a nearby interview room, offering her something to drink.

'You asked me at Mickey's house if I thought that Mary-Jo was maybe seeing somebody else. How did you know that, by the way?'

'Well, I'm a bit of a detective,' Blaise joked. 'No, seriously, we found a crumpled photograph outside on the path__ it was Mary-Jo and she had her arms around a man we know as Johnny Mulgrew. Would you happen to know this man, Janice?'

'Oh I know that sod all right, Inspector,' the woman replied with supressed anger in her quiet voice. 'I knew him at school, he was a horrible evil bas__ sorry, and he was really bad. Always acting the big hardman like, he carried a knife at school and threatened people with it. He was just a big bully.

'Did he ever use the knife on anyone?'

'I'm not sure, he bloody threatened to cut my boobs off one day when I witnessed him beat another boy and take his money. He used to do that to a lot of younger boys, he would make them hand over their money saying that it was for the IRA.'

'Was he involved with the IRA?'

'Was he hell, they wouldn't have a wee shit like that?'

'No, they only recruit nice people,' Blaise smiled sarcastically.

'Look, I'm not here get into an argument about the rights and wrongs of being in the IRA, Inspector,' the woman said with an unexpected bold confidence. 'Sorry, that's my father coming out in me, God rest his soul.'

'So, back to this Mulgrew__ what can you tell me about him?'

'Mary-Jo and Mickey were going through a really bad spell. Mickey started drinking real heavy with his workmates and gambling too. Mary-Jo tried to talk to him about it, that's when he started to hit her about the place.'

Foetal Attraction

'So why did she not leave him, I can't understand women who stay with their partners when they beat them.'

'It's called love, Inspector__ being a man you wouldn't understand, it's like, well__ never mind.'

'Right, so how did Mary-Jo get mixed up with this Mulgrew__ does she like the muscular aggressive type?'

Janice Delaney slumped back in the grey plastic chair, her green eyes widening slightly as she bit on her inner bottom lip. 'I'd rather we were sitting in a pub somewhere __ I hate police stations.'

'Me too on both counts.'

'Well, if you like you can take me for a drink later,'

'Now then, you're putting me in an awkward position here, Janice. I'm spoken for, otherwise I definitely would.'

'Oh well, you can't blame me for trying,' Janice smiled impishly. 'For a Peeler you're not bad looking.'

'Police officers are human too, Janice.'

'I'm only joking.'

'Right, let's get back to your sister-in-law and this Mulgrew, you're embarrassing me now,' Blaise playfully joked, trying to help ease the woman's nervousness.

'I suppose_ if we must. Anyway, as I was telling you, Mary-Jo was at her wits end with all the crap from Mickey. Honestly, she was suicidal. I think in a way it was lucky that she met Johnny. Although, I did try to warn her what he was like, that he was a bad shit,' the woman continued, leaning her elbows on top of the table as she relaxed more.

'Had they been seeing each other long?'

'Christ, Mary-Jo told me that she had only been seeing him a few months when she bloody fell pregnant to him. Jesus, imagine that evil fucker having a wee brat.'

'How did Mary-Jo feel about that?'

'She wasn't happy about it at the start, but then she told me that she was going to leave Mickey. She said that Johnny wanted her to divorce Mickey and to go live with him.'

'Did Mary-Jo tell her husband that she planned to leave him?'

'Jesus no__ she was shit scared of him. She knew Mickey had a terrible temper. To tell the truth, I don't think Mulgrew wanted Mary-Jo, not after she fell pregnant.'

'So you reckon that Johnny Mulgrew didn't want the child then,' Blaise said, watching the woman's slender fingers tapping nervously on the table. 'Do you smoke__ would you like one?'

'No thanks, I just want to get out of here. Listen don't tell Mickey that I was here,' the woman said as though pleading. 'Maybe that bloody Johnny Mulgrew killed Mary-Jo; I wouldn't bloody put it past the evil big shit, Inspector.'

'Eh, did Mary-Jo know that Mulgrew was married?'

Aye she knew surely, I just think that Mary-Jo was so desperate to get away from Mickey. I think she actually convinced herself that he would leave his wife for her. She was just so gullible.'

175

Foetal Attraction

'I don't imagine that it was a nice situation to be in, especially if your brother was beating his wife,' Blaise continued, closing his notepad that he had scribbled into. 'Well thanks a lot for coming in to explain things, Janice.'

'Oh it was my pleasure,' the woman smiled flirtatiously, fixing her sparkling eyes on Blaise as she slowly rose to her feet. 'It's a pity that you're with somebody; I think that you and I could have some good fun together.'

'I'm sure you're right, but I doubt if I'd be able to keep up,' Blaise smiled, leading Janice Delaney back into the reception area again. 'Well thanks again.'

Blaise watched her as she made towards the red armoured door then brushed past her to push the heavy door open for her.

'Thanks, you're a gentleman,' she smiled, touching a hand against his chest. 'If you change your mind, give me a call Inspector,' she continued, scribbling her mobile number onto the manila folder.

'Right, I'll keep that in mind__ you never know.

Blaise made his way upstairs to the incident room, answering a call on his mobile. It was Cathy O'Hare and she informed him that she had found an abandoned puppy and intended to keep it, then, almost in the same breath, questioned Blaise if he had decided on a definite date for the wedding.

'Well, as it's your day, sweetheart, you name the day. Just as long as there's no football on that day,' Blaise joked, his mind too busy with the murder investigation to concentrate on any wedding plans, hanging up the phone then as his colleagues all sat staring at him as though desiring to make some kind of jocular remark.

Foetal Attraction

With nothing further to discuss at that particular moment, Blaise told his colleagues to continue probing for answers and any possible clues, suggesting then to Jim Whyte that he ran some background checks on Mickey Delaney, his sister and Johnny Mulgrew. 'See if there's anything fresh on them, Jim.'

Blaise and Jack Phillips made then into the town to question the elderly woman that had told Jim Whyte and Gemma Galbraith that she had saw a dark green van parked outside of the Delaney home on the Melmount Road. Then, the nicotine craving exploded within Blaise finding that the woman wasn't at home, so surrendering weakly yet again, Blaise made his way into the nearby shop to purchase a packet of cigarettes.

'Jesus now, isn't that just terrible, Mary-Jo Delaney being kidnapped and all. She's such a lovely girl too,' the female shop assistant remarked casually.

'Yes, terrible,' Blaise smiled. 'Do you know her then?'

'Just to talk to really, whenever she would pop into the shop.'

'I don't suppose you saw anything suspicious or out of place on the morning that Mrs Delaney disappeared, did you?'

'Oh are you the police?' The woman gasped with surprise, as though shocked to be in conversation with a police officer.

'Inspector Blaise__ I'm investigating into the disappearance of Mrs Delaney. So if there's anything that you can tell me I'd really appreciate it. Perhaps you noticed someone hanging about.'

'Now, when you mention it, there was this weirdo in the shop that morning. It was early, we had just opened.'

Foetal Attraction

'You said we__ was there someone with you then?'

'Yes, Mary was here too. She's my supervisor so to speak, she just comes to help me open up and sort the papers.'

'What about this man you say came into the shop, why do you say he was a weirdo__ in what way?'

'I know you shouldn't really talk about people like that, but he honestly looked creepy. He was wearing a balaclava and had the hood of his jacket pulled right up. To be honest, I was frightened; I thought he was going to rob the shop.'

'Did you get a look at his face__ Mrs eh__?'

'It's Bernadette__ McConnell. I live two doors from the shop here. I couldn't get a look at his face, he had that balaclava thing on. He was wearing a long green coat__ jeans, yes really dirt jeans. That's all I can remember, Inspector.'

'That's fine,' Blaise continued, scribbling into his notebook. 'I don't suppose you noticed if he was driving a car or maybe a van?'

'Eh, yes__ he was driving a van. God, what colour was it now. Oh yes, it was dark green I think. He was parked right outside opposite to Mary-Jo's house.'

'Is that right, did he buy anything in the shop?'

'No, the miserable sod just looked at the magazines on the top shelf. You know the ones. Oh, and kept glancing out the window.'

Blaise moved towards the window checking to see if he could see the Delaney house from that spot. 'I think that maybe this guy was keeping a watch on house. Did he perhaps mention Mary-Jo?'

178

'No, he just looked at those dirty magazines for a little while, then he left rather hurriedly after glancing out of the window. Oh wait,' the woman gasped remembering. 'He did buy something, I remember now, because he just stared down at the floor as he handed me the money.'

'What did he buy__ can you remember?'

'It was a roll of brown tape.'

'I see,' Blaise said thoughtfully, trying to recall if either of the two victims had been bound by brown tape. 'I see you have CCTV, is it working?'

'Yes, it's always working.'

'Excellent, I'll need to take it. The one for the morning that Mrs Delaney disappeared.'

'I'll fetch it for you, Inspector. Oh, don't forget to pay me for those cigarettes.'

Blaise tucked the CCTV tape under his arm as he left the shop, eagerly tearing off the cellophane from the cigarette packet, dodging the on-coming traffic. Then, with the cigarette in his mouth, he puffed away with an exhilarated pleasure drawing the smoke deep into his grateful lungs. 'Why am I bloody even trying to stop this lovely habit, I must be completely crazy.'

Blaise explained just what occurred to Jack Phillips, who was waiting in the car, suggesting then that they returned immediately to the incident room to view the tape.

'Christ Almighty, you actually bought a packet of cigarettes.'

Foetal Attraction

Blaise heard the heavy footsteps in the corridor heralding the approach of DCI Andrew Cruickshank. Those footsteps were not those of the usual long, somewhat lethargic strides, but were those of urgency. The DCI hardly ever visited anyone, like a great God, if he desired to speak to you then he summoned you to him, and his command required urgent, unhindered haste no matter what. As the footsteps drew closer, not only Blaise, but Jack Phillips too felt somewhat like naughty schoolboys in the wake of being handed out some great punishment.

The slightly opened office door sprung wide and the towering, broad-shouldered man thrust his colossal frame before the two pensive detectives. Questioning eyes drifted quickly between Blaise and Jack Phillips, his face expressionless as usual. The DCI unbuttoned his dark grey jacket before sitting one buttock on the edge of Jack Phillips' desk, large, thick-fingered hands clasped over a thigh best described as a tree trunk.

'So, gentlemen, how are things progressing?' The deep, strong Glaswegian voice echoed. 'Have you pulled anyone for these bloody murders yet?'

'We're following up on several leads, boss,' Blaise replied, secretly pondering on how he would react to the news that he and Cathy were planning to marry, thinking then that perhaps those large, vice-like hands would soon be twisting around his neck. Blaise swallowed a lump of nervousness that unexpectedly formed in his throat, having to cough to clear it. 'I'm still having serious concerns over DC Will Chambers, boss.'

'Still not heard from him yet? He better have a good excuse.'

Foetal Attraction

'The thing is, nobody has seen or heard from him in days, not even his mother or girlfriend.'

'I think that there is something serious here,' Jack Phillips added.

'By serious, do you mean something has happened to him, maybe kidnapped or murdered possibly?'

'Well, he was supposed to be checking the address of a suspect,' Jack Philliips said.

'Has he not been in contact at all then__ do you think he has tried to arrest this suspect and has himself been held captive, or worse?'

'That thought has crossed our minds, boss. Jack and I were just discussing coming to talk to you about that. Maybe we should send some uniforms out to the house and give it a thorough going over?'

'Christ Almighty, Ben__ have you not been bloody out to check yourself?'

'Sure we were out, it was late and the entire place was all boarded up. Perhaps there's another way in, but we didn't see it.'

'Right, I'll organise that with the Chief Super, you just carry on with what you were doing and I'll sort this out. Where is this place then?'

'305 Ash-Pine Manor, that's in Victoria Bridge, boss.'

'Right, are there any other problems before I go?'

'Oh eh,' Blaise said almost in a whisper. 'Cathy told me to invite you and your good lady wife to dinner. She said she'll phone you with all the arrangements.'

Foetal Attraction

'Lovely, no problem,' the DCI replied, not even a look of delight at the invite. 'How are you both getting on, I hope you're behaving, Ben.'

'We're getting on the best, I'm so glad that we met. Cathy's done me the world of good.'

'That's good, let's hope that it stays that way, Ben. How is Cathy's leg coming on? The Mrs was out with her the other day__ she told me that Cathy is still limping a bit.'

'It will take time, boss. She's doing all the exercises and it's a lot better than it was.'

'That's good__ tell her not to rush it.'

'You know yourself, boss, she's so determined to get back.'

The towering man made towards the door, turned and stared directly at Jack Phillips. 'Did I not tell you before about smoking in the office, Jack? The bloody place is stinking. Ben, you're the senior officer, put a stop to it.'

'I've warned him about that dirty habit, boss.'

'Right, well, see that you both stop it, the cleaning staff are complaining. The offices aren't that long decorated.'

Blaise stood behind his desk hands resting on hips as he stared in disbelief at his colleague. 'How the hell does he do it, Jack? He seems to know everything that goes on. I'm almost convinced he is God, or his brother.'

'It wouldn't surprise me in the least,' Jack Phillips laughed. 'That's why I wouldn't like to be you if anything happens between you and Cathy. Christ, can you imagine having that big mad Jock after you, especially if you've upset his wee niece.'

'That's true enough, Jack,' the DCI bellowed from outside the office as he stood talking with another officer.

'See what I mean,' Blaise grinned quietly.

WPC Judith Carlyle entered the office with a gentle smile, a manila folder in her hand, which she handed to Blaise. 'Hello, Inspector, here's the report from forensics on that Mary-Jo woman.'

'Oh right, thanks, Judith. How have you been?'

'I'm fine. Good to hear that you have settled down, the rest of girls can relax now,' the young officer joked before leaving.

'Right now,' Blaise said aloud as he read the report. 'There were several particles of a synthetic material discovered under the victim's top lip__ possibly similar to that found on hooded jackets.'

'Didn't the woman in the shop say that the guy she saw in the shop that morning was wearing a hooded jacket?'

'Yes, she did, Jack. There were also small traces of sawdust on the victim and several hairs belonging to a rabbit, cat hairs too. Oh yes, there was a small particle of green paint discovered on the flesh of the victim__ according to forensics the paint is consistent with Transit vans manufactured 1998-99.'

'It looks like we need to be looking for that dark green van that was seen opposite the victims house,' Jack Phillips said.

'Christ, it says here that the victim was killed by a Ketamine injection, overdosed, possibly after the uterus had been removed.'

Foetal Attraction

'That's used as an anaesthetic by vets, and for humans too, I think.'

'According to the pathologist the victim's heart stopped due to the amount of Ketamine injected. Christ, it says here that there were traces of semen discovered and signs of penetration were evident. Unfortunately no match found on our database.'

'Christ, you're reading both reports at the one time, Blaise. Watch you don't miss something.'

'Right, is everyone gathered in the incident room, Jack?'

'They're all waiting with eager anticipation,' Jack Phillips joked, lifting his coffee after discarding the newspaper into the bin.

Blaise burst through the door of the incident room, closely followed by Jack Phillips. He gave every officer a quick glance as he sat on the edge of the desk, gripping both manila folders.

'Okay my wee cherubs, does anyone have anything new pertaining to the investigations in hand__ anybody__ no?'

Jack Phillips pinned several more photographs onto the white board, pointing out that they were now looking for a dark green transit van with the driver wearing a long army-type coat with fur edged hood.

'Now then, we have two victims both in their late twenties- early thirties, pregnant and the foetus has been removed on both occasions. The pathologist states that these operations almost certainly involve someone with medical expertise__ possibly a doctor or surgeon. The removal of fingertips and teeth etc. could be to slow down our identifying the victims.'

'This driver has been seen several times close to both murder scenes,' Jack Phillips added. 'It's bloody imperative that we keep a good eye out for this guy, he just could be the one carrying out the abductions for this crazed lunatic.'

'Do we not have a positive ID on this van driver__ has nobody actually seen what he looks like?' DC Gemma Galbraith questioned, glancing at the white board.

'Jack and I will study some CCTV footage we have acquired. I know this sounds bloody crazy, but ask about__ see if anyone knows or has heard of some cult or religious groups new in town.'

'What, like maybe they're carrying out some kind of ritual killing, things like that, you mean, Blaise?' DC Bill Johnson questioned.

'Go back to all those you have questioned, maybe someone will have remembered something. Check again with everyone about this bloody van, see if anyone remembers the registration number, or having seen this mysterious driver,' Blaise groaned impatiently. 'Now come on people, we've got next to bloody nothing so far on this case.'

'Right then, off you go brave officers of the law, go investigate,' Jack Phillips joked, holding open the office door.

'We'll have a look at this CCTV footage__ switch that damn machine on, Jack.'

'I'd offer you a smoke but if the Big Crook caught us he'd go ballistic,' Jack Phillips laughed. 'Bloody cleaners complaining, they should just do their jobs and be bloody grateful that we are messy sods, otherwise we wouldn't need them.'

185

Foetal Attraction

'Aye, safer just sucking these bloody mints,' Blaise groaned, his eyes fixed on the screen. 'The picture isn't that clear is it, Jack? Stop__ rewind it back a bit__ there, look he's facing the woman.'

'But the shop assistant said that he mostly stared at the floor, besides he wore some kind of balaclava that covered most of his face, Blaise.'

'Maybe he's a real ugly sod. There, stop it there, Jack. If we get a copy of that screen shot maybe forensics could enhance it.'

'Why, what's the point, he has the back of his head to the camera.'

'Look, the woman is wearing glasses and there's a chance that with the light there we just might be lucky enough to get a reflection of his face on the glasses, Jack__ if it's clear enough.'

'You're a bloody smart arse,' Jack Phillips grinned. 'That's a bloody clever one, Blaise.'

'That's why I'm an Inspector, Jack,' Blaise joked. 'Give that tape to forensics and tell them of my idea about the shop keeper's glasses.'

'Right will do. So what are you planning on now, Blaise?'

'Lunch, Jack__ I need something warm and satisfying inside me.'

'Good bloody job we're not in a gay bar when you said that.'

Blaise and Jack Phillips sat in a bar in Strabane ordering lunch, Blaise sipping at a glass of white lemonade whilst Jack enjoyed a half pint of lager.

'So do you honestly think by coming in here we'll possibly see this Johnny Mulgrew?'

'I've heard that this is his local, so hopefully, Jack.'

'According to his wife he will probably be with his friend getting out of his head on drugs. I don't think we'll see him.'

'Try to be more positive you old sod,' Blaise grinned.

'Hey, look, isn't that our reporter friend at the bar?'

'The Bloody Ferret, so it is, Jack,' Blaise sighed, watching then as the thin, unkempt man began to approach.

'Well, if it isn't my old friend, Inspector Blaise.'

'I've never been your friend, now sod off we don't want your offensive appearance spoiling our food,' Blaise growled. 'Here, on second thoughts you horrible wee shit, take a seat.'

The thin man rubbed at the greying stubble on his rather pointed chin, showing brownish teeth as he smiled eagerly upon lifting the menu, asking the two detectives what they had ordered.

'Put that down you half-wit, it isn't an invitation to dine with us. I want some information from you.'

'Oh right, did you say you'd buy me a large Irish?'

Foetal Attraction

'Think back to 1998,' Blaise said.

'Oh, I see you're back on the drink again, Blaise.'

'It's lemonade you clown.'

'Have you got any juicy news for me then? You were always good for a bit of news when you were a drunk, Blaise.'

'If you ever call me that again you wee rat I'll take you away somewhere and drown you in your own piss. Now shut the fuck up and listen to me.'

'Here's your large Irish,' Jack Phillips groaned returning from the bar to hand the grinning man his drink.

'Right, think back to 1998. Do you recall a Polish woman, a surgeon at the hospital in Omagh?'

'Eh, vaguely now_ pure nectar that was__ did you say another?'

'Jack, if you don't mind mate.'

'I always think that when you taste whiskey like that then surely God himself must be an Irishman.'

'Well enjoy it it's your last,' Jack Phillips said.

'Enough of the shit__ do you remember this woman?'

'Apparently now this doctor was rumoured to have carried out an abortion on a young girl. I think she was only 15. It was without the consent of the hospital. It was only a rumour now.'

'I see,' Blaise said thoughtfully.

Foetal Attraction

'Nothing ever came of it, well, not that I heard anyhow. This doctor was supposed to appear before a tribunal but she buggered off and hasn't been heard of since.'

'Her mother was a surgeon too, wasn't she?'

'Eh, she was, well respected too. She worked in Altnagelvin in Derry. I think now that she packed it all in to go work with the poor in Africa, the stupid sod,' the reporter continued.

'Well each to their own,' Blaise sighed.

'The bloody woman went missing in some river and her body was never found.

'What about this daughter, she went under the same name as the mother, didn't she__ Jana Zaleski?'

'The daughter was newsworthy. Now apparently the father disowned her because she fell pregnant to some local politician. She fell out with her father and left home to live with this guy, who I don't know.'

'Don't bullshit you horrible shit, you know.'

'No seriously, nobody knew. Anyhow, this Zaleski woman left home to live with this person. But guess what? He's bloody married and wanted nothing to do with her.'

'Didn't she try to cause a stink or anything?'

'No, she just hit the bottle__ and me when I tried to talk about it with her. The bloody woman just went crazy on the drink and bloody violent too. I eh, if I remember right, the brother came over from Poland to sort her out.'

Foetal Attraction

'Where is this brother now, do you know where he lives?'

'He went straight back to Poland once he made his sister stop drinking.'

'You said she was pregnant, what happened to the child?'

'Ah, at last,' Jack Phillips groaned to the apologetic waitress. 'I've waited that bloody long for my lunch I've forgotten what I had ordered.'

'To be honest, Blaise, I lost interest in her__ I really can't tell you anything about the child, who knows, maybe it died at birth.'

'How come you know so much about this family?' Jack Phillips added, pushing a forkful of fish into his mouth.

'I wrote a piece about the mother and daughter for a woman's magazine one time.'

'Right well, you can sod off now,' Blaise said forcefully.

'Hey, why are you asking me about this woman__ has something come up about her, maybe I could help?'

'You could help the environment by going home and taking a good shower, then, if you like, you could kill yourself.'

'Oh Inspector Blaise, I thought we were friends.'

'Are you still here?' Jack Phillips glared.

'Look, here take this have a drink and then sod off,' Blaise groaned passing the man a ten pound note. I don't want to see you in two seconds, now I'm warning you.'

Foetal Attraction

'Do you think that maybe this doctor went to Poland and returned under a different name, Jack?'

'That just could be the case, maybe we should visit all the hospitals and check for any Polish women?

'Maybe we should have another word with the disgruntled father, tell him we know more than he thinks, just maybe he will tell us what's going on and where this bloody daughter is.'

'Bloody phone, I should have switched it off,' Blaise complained then as he removed the mobile from his jacket pocket.

'Inspector, you better get out here,' said the voice on the end of the phone, sounding extremely urgent. 'We're at this 305 Ash-Pine Manor and the shitting bad news is that we've bloody found young Will Chambers__ he__ he's been shot.'

'Christ Almighty, we'll be there shortly,' Blaise gasped with shocked surprise, staring wide-eyed at his colleague.

'What__ what's happened, have you won the Lotto?'

'Come on, Jack. It's young Will, he's been found shot at that bloody address we checked,' his voice whispered but urgent.

'I don't bloody believe it, Blaise,' Jack Phillips gasped, almost choking on his fish, rising then to follow his colleague hurriedly, both forgetting to pay for their lunch.

'Christ Almighty, Jack. Why the hell didn't we search that bloody place__ we should have checked it out properly?'

'It was all boarded up sure, how the hell were we to know, Blaise.'

Foetal Attraction

Immense anger and tension hung heavy in the uncertain air as Blaise and Jack Phillips arrived at 305 Ash-Pine Manor, parking the car between the abundance of cars already attending the scene. Blaise immediately ushered into the now opened house by DC Bill Johnson.

'Blaise, you better get in there and take a look at young Will before the forensics boys get here.'

'Christ, Bill. Is he dead right enough?'

'Definitely, the poor sod's had two put in his head.'

'Jesus, he's been tied up and beaten half to death by the looks of it,' Blaise sighed as he crouched close to his young colleague's body. 'Whoever it was really gave him a kicking.'

'Look, Blaise, over there at the fireplace. It looks like there has been somebody hiding out in here for a while, there's plenty of food wrappers and the floor is covered with cigarette butts.'

'Whoever it was must be hiding for a good reason, especially if they're armed,' Blaise groaned, scanning his eyes around the sitting room now lit by the un-boarded windows.

'I'll look into any possible armed robberies,' DC Bill Johnson said. 'We should hopefully get plenty of prints and I'm sure we'll get DNA from those cigarette butts and food wrappers.'

'There's two types of cigarette there, Bill. Hand rolled and filtered indicating the possibility of two or three people. That looks like blankets over too. Hopefully the forensics will get plenty in here.'

'I'll point it all out, though they won't need me telling them.'

192

Foetal Attraction

'I can't bloody believe this,' Blaise sighed, gently stroking a hand over the head of his murdered young colleague. 'He must have disturbed whoever was here__ any sign of a struggle outside?'

'Don't know, Blaise, haven't looked.'

'Well go and fucking look__ Jesus Christ, you're supposed to be a bloody detective__ Christ Almighty. The rest of you stop standing about with your thumbs up your arses,' Blaise continued to rant in his rage, knelling beside the lifeless Will Chambers, resting one hand on his chest as if comforting him in some quiet way.

'Blaise, try to keep it calm,' Jack Phillips said as he crouched close to him. 'The guys are just as shocked as you are.'

'Aye, right, it's just that they__ this is__ Why the hell did he not call for back up before he entered the bloody house?'

'But the entire place was boarded up when we checked, wasn't it?'

'Right enough, Jack. Maybe he was outside and these fuckers jumped him and held him captive inside after beating the shit out of him. That means then that they took Will's car and dumped it in Newtownstewart.'

The forensics team arrived and demanded that everyone leave the scene, all officers then wearing their navy boiler suits and gloves as they began to unload the collection of gadgets and lighting.

'Oh Blaise,' one of the forensics officers called out as he approached. 'Eh, Tommy said to tell you that the CCTV footage you gave him was hopeless, the images were too blurred when enhanced. He tried all sorts of ways but the more he tried the worse it got. He sends his apologises.'

193

Foetal Attraction

'Right thanks, Dermot. That's that then eh, Jack?'

'Oh well it was worth a try,' Jack Phillips sighed, leading Blaise from the room. 'Jesus, we'll need to inform poor Betty.'

'Bloody hell, I honestly don't think that I could, not right now, Jack. That poor woman will have a heart attack for real this time.'

'I'll ask Gemma to inform her, shall I?'

'Good idea, Jack. We'll head back to the office and try to fathom out what the hell's going on.'

Foetal Attraction

21

DCI Andrew Cruickshank burst into the office resembling that of a grizzly bear with haemorrhoids, causing Blaise and Jack Phillips to gasp with startled surprise at his unexpected arrival.

'Jesus H Christ Almighty__ What the hell has happened to DC Will Chambers?'

'Eh, aye__ Jack and I were at lunch when I got the call, boss. It looks like poor Will probably didn't know about whoever was in the house.'

'Surprised them, you mean__ why did he go into the house without calling for back up first?'

'We found his car burnt out in Newtownstewart, boss,' Jack Phillips added. 'Will's jacket was in the car so we assume that he took his jacket off before entering the premises, of course, leaving his mobile phone in the jacket pocket.'

'So what's story, what happened, Ben?'

'Well__ it looks like whoever was hiding in the house overpowered young Will and gave him a real battering. He was lying with his hands and ankles tied and__ shot in the head.'

'Dia-fucking-bolical. Whoever it was I want their heads on a plate, Ben__ and bloody sharpish too. Christ, I'll need to tell the Chief Super, he's in a meeting with some politician.'

'More bloody cut-backs I suppose,' Blaise sighed.

'Why was DC Chambers at that house in the first place, Ben? I hope it was part of an investigation and not house hunting.'

Foetal Attraction

'DC Chambers was following up on a suspect. The address supplied came from the GMC in London. This Polish doctor apparently rented it. According to the pathologist, our victims were worked on by someone with immense medical knowledge.'

'You can't think that this Polish woman beat the shit of DC Chambers then murdered him__ or is it a separate incident?'

'Well, that's what Jack and I were about to look into, boss. It just could be possible that whoever was hiding in the house is helping this crazy doctor woman. The thing is, this woman disappeared almost twelve years ago and hasn't been seen since.'

'Could be using an alias__ have you a photograph of her?'

'It's over twelve years old apparently. The other thing is, she was supposed to have a child but there's nothing on birth records, nothing at all.'

'Yes, according to the woman's father, she had a bastard imbecilic son. Maybe he meant that the son is retarded or something,' Jack Phillips said. We spoke to the old man, but to be honest, he doesn't look long for this world.'

'So where the hell is this bloody woman?'

'God alone knows, boss. We think that maybe the old guy knows more than he let on when we visited him.'

'We're also looking for a Johnny Mulgrew in connection with the murder of Mary-Jo Delaney,' Jack Phillips stated.

'Johnny Mulgrew__ would that be the same Mulgrew, armed robbery, GBH, and just about everything illegal you can think of?'

Foetal Attraction

'The very same, a real gentleman,' Jack Phillips continued.

'Right, three bodies, Ben__ any certain suspects or are you still running around guessing?'

'Fuck sake, boss, cut me some slack here. Look, do you know how hard it is policing those streets out there, not a bloody sod would piss on you if you were on fire.'

'I've done my bit on those streets, Ben. Christ, if you think that's bad you should try being a cop in Hong Kong.'

'Aye well, I think that you more than anybody should know what we are up against here.'

'Look, it's been a pretty emotional day. Why don't you and Jack head home and get a fresh start in the morning, the rest of the team I'm sure will bring you up to speed.'

'I think we should just work on and get this sorted out.'

'Ben, you're too uptight, I know you. Look, go home and get a good rest, tell Cathy to massage your head or something, you need to unwind and think straight.'

'Right, okay then. I don't think Jack will argue with you there.'

'I wouldn't bloody argue with the boss anytime,' Jack Phillips laughed, slumped behind his desk.

'Right, you two get home now and we'll talk in the morning.'

Foetal Attraction

Blaise thought it strange that he was going home early evening, his mind pondered over surprising Cathy with a nice bottle of wine and some chocolates. He pushed all thoughts of the day to the back of his mind, yet still hurt at his young colleague's murder. Blaise crept quietly into the hallway and stripped naked, with the wine in one hand and handcuffs in the other, he burst into the sitting room.

'Right you dirty bitch, get your knickers off and__'

Blaise stood shocked, unable to speak as Cathy and the minister stared back at him.

'Oh__ eh__ sorry,' Blaise apologised, hurrying towards the door.

'Oh don't leave on my account,' the female minister laughed, Cathy unable to speak as she burst into hysterical laughter also.

'Well, I think that you will have a wonderfully happy life together, Cathy. I think it best that I call back to finalise the arrangements.'

'Oh God, yes, that would be a good idea, Reverend. Oh, and don't worry, I won't let him live this down__ ever.'

'I'm sure you won't, Cathy. Right then, you can come out now, Inspector.'

Blaise re-appeared dressed in his bathrobe and still clutching the wine bottle and feeling embarrassed. 'What the hell was the minister doing here?'

'I invited her round to discuss our possible wedding plans and__'

'Why are you hesitant, Cathy, you're frightening me here?'

Foetal Attraction

'The minister was here to talk with me. I mentioned to her a few days ago that I was thinking about changing my religion.'

'Why__ I mean, why would you want to do that?'

'I don't really know, it's just that__ well, I would like to try something different so to speak.'

'I don't get you, babe. Well, I understand that maybe your missing something in your life. I mean, that's fine, but I think all of this religion thing is crazy anyhow.'

'I thought you believed in God?'

'I do, I can pray to him in my bed I don't need church. Look, in my opinion, what causes more trouble than anything in this country?'

'Well, I suppose religion,' Cathy replied, taking the wine from Blaise and made towards the kitchen.

'I'm talking about being Protestant or Catholic, they hate each other but half of the bigots attend church or chapel. It's pretty hypocritical don't you think. I mean, look at other countries__ they have Holy wars. Two words totally in contradiction to one another. I mean, how can you have a Holy war?'

'Look, I was just saying that__'

'Babe, all I'm saying is that the world would be a better place if we were all Christian and left it at that. Well, the Western world that is.'

'I haven't heard you rant on like that before, is anything wrong?'

'Well, actually there is, babe,' Blaise sighed slumping onto the sofa, the filled wine glass in his hand.

'Judging by your face it's something serious.'

'We bloody found young Will Chambers shot, the poor wee sod had been beaten senseless and then shot in the head.'

'Oh Jesus,' Cathy sighed with shocked surprise, comforting Blaise on the sofa. 'Are you still investigating those two murders?'

'What's that noise from the bedroom?' Blaise quizzed.

'Oh eh, I was going to tell you about that,' Cathy smiled eyes sparkling full of excitement. 'I was in town and there was this guy selling puppies,' Cathy continued as she hurried to the bedroom, returning with a puppy in her arms.

'Jesus, you bought a dog_ I thought you said you found a pup?'

'Yes, the guy said that if he couldn't sell them then they would have to put down. Besides, I really like King Charles Spaniels.'

'You sweet gullible lunatic,' Blaise grinned.

'Why__ what do you mean?'

'That wee Spaniel you have there is a bloody Saint Bernard woman. That wee thing there will grow to be a monster.'

'Jesus__ I know, the vet told me when I took it in for a check-up. I felt like a right fool, Ben.'

'I've told you not to call me that you tart,' Blaise grinned as he took the pup onto his lap. 'Have you got a name wee dog?'

Foetal Attraction

'I called him Ben, after a really lovely guy that I know.'

'Very nice, I'm honoured to have a dog named after me.'

'I never said that it was you, big head. Anyway, I can't believe that Will Chambers is dead__ that's so unreal.'

'It sure is, he's only been here a about fourteen months too.'

'So, apart from that, what's bugging you about this murder investigation__ I take it there's no witnesses coming forward?'

'It's not that, Cathy, it's just__ well, we're trying to trace this bloody Polish woman.'

Quite unexpectedly, there was a loud knocking on the front door, and when Cathy opened it, Blaise sighed heavily upon hearing the unmistakable loud voice of DCI Andrew Cruickshank.

'Uncle Andy__ Aunt Violet,' Cathy greeted cheerfully, inviting her guests to enter.

'Ah, there's my Inspector in his usual pose,' the DCI said almost smiling. 'I've brought Violet for that dinner you promised.'

'What? Cathy gasped, looking anxiously flustered.

'I__ said that Cathy would ring you about arrangements. I never said tonight,' Blaise sighed, handing the pup to Cathy as he excused himself to change clothes.

'Look, don't panic, my mistake,' the DCI said. 'I'll ring for a takeaway__ Chinese ok with everyone.'

'Fine with me, boss,' Blaise said, now dressed in sweatshirt and tracksuit bottoms. 'Are the ladies ok with Chinese?'

'Great,' Cathy smiled. 'I'll sort out some plates.'

'I'll give you a hand,' Violet Cruickshank said, following Cathy to the kitchen.

'So, how's the head, Ben__ you more calm now?'

'Well, discovering that Will was killed was a bit of a shocker.'

'Bloody right it was, Ben. Our Lords and Masters upstairs are making noises. Any new evidence on the murders of these two women__ please say yes, Ben.'

'Bits and pieces, boss. It's this damn Polish doctor, she's getting on my tits. We can't seem to trace her and apparently she had a child but there are no birth records or anything.'

'Maybe she gave birth in Poland?'

'But immigration would have a record of her and the kid coming into the country__ there's bloody sod all.'

'Maybe the child died at birth or soon after?'

'Anyway, we have CCTV footage of some guy witnessed hanging about at both murder scenes. He was wearing a balaclava and a hood; unfortunately, there's no clear picture of him. We think that he's driving a dark green van.'

'Right, pull every van with that description, Ben. Get Traffic onto it, it will give them something to do.'

'I've already done that, boss. I'm certain that this van and driver is carrying out the abductions, the van was definitely witnessed outside of Mary-Jo Delaney's home at the time of her disappearance.'

'Right, ok__ you forget about Will's murder I'll assign a new squad to that one, if I can, you just concentrate on the case you're with now,' the DCI sighed, leaning back on the sofa. 'So, the other thing I want to ask you, Ben.'

'Aye, I'm still off the drink and behaving.'

'That's good, but that's not what I want to know. How is Cathy's leg, is she any better?'

'She seems to be__ I haven't really seen her limp or wince these past few days to be honest.'

'That's good, because the suits were asking me about her absence, the inconsiderate shits.'

'Andrew, mind your language please dear,' Violet Cruickshank smiled, causing Blaise to grin as he had never before heard the DCI being told off__ by anyone.

'So are you considering asking Cathy to return to duty?'

'Aye, but only if she's up to it, light duties for a while though.'

'That will cheer her up, boss.'

'Does she need cheering up, Ben?'

'You know what I mean, boss.'

'Right, foods on the table guys,' Cathy said.

'Well, do you want to tell Cathy the good news, Ben or shall I?'

'What good news? Cathy beamed excitedly. 'What news?'

'You tell her, boss.'

'Right, well I think you should get back to work, but only if you're up to it mind, and don't bull__ don't lie.'

'Oh I'm ready, thanks Uncle Andy. Oh, we have a bit of news too,' Cathy smiled reaching out her hand to Blaise.

'You better not be pregnant you're__'

'Be quiet Andrew.'

'Well, Ben and I are engaged to be married. Well, not really engaged but we are planning to marry, aren't we baby?'

'Definitely, we sure are sweetheart.'

'Well congratulations to the both of you. Isn't that wonderful news Andrew?'

'Wonderful.'

'I know that you are pleased boss, aren't you, eh?' Blaise questioned with a smile.

'I couldn't be happier.'

'Uncle Andy doesn't do smiles, isn't that right, Uncle Andy?'

'Now, I'm still your DCI, so shut up. Look, great news, congrats to the both of you. That means that you need to try extra hard to make my wee lassie happy.'

23

'Good morning, Jack, how are you my friend?' Blaise grinned as he entered the office cheerfully.

'What the hell__ right, what have you done with the real Blaise?' Jack Phillips smiled, noticing a certain sense of wellbeing in his colleague.

'I'm just feeling good, Jack,' Blaise said smiling. 'Right, the DCI wants us to forget about investigating Will's murder; he's assigning it to somebody else.'

'Christ, I thought he would__'

'Let me finish, Jack. We will look into it, but discreetly.'

'Dangerous, Blaise__ bloody dangerous, but I'm with you.'

The telephone rang and the pathologist said that he was compiling a detailed report to send to Blaise but wanted to give a brief explanation on the murder of DC Will Chambers. The pathologist explained that the savage beating that Will received prior to being shot in the head caused immense internal bleeding and was the probable cause of death. Most of Will's ribs were broken, and his spleen severely ruptured and his left femur was broken, not to mention his face and head received several hard blows with a blunt object.

'Holy Christ, doc, they certainly meant it, eh?'

'The interesting thing is, Inspector. Your young colleague certainly had strong jaws for we discovered a fingertip in his bloodied mouth.'

Foetal Attraction

'Did they cut off his finger, doc?'

'No not at all, on the contrary, Inspector. You see, your young friend has bitten the fingertip off of his attacker.'

'Jesus__ does that mean that you__?'

'Carried out a DNA analysis, you're going to ask, yes. Not only that Inspector, we have an absolute positive match. So, for a nice bottle of Cognac I can supply you with a name.'

'Doc, I'll bloody send you over a crate of the stuff. Give me the name you big beautiful man.'

Jack Phillips stared across at his colleague, hands outstretched.

'Paddy Flynn__ I seem to know that fucker. Thanks doc, send over your report soon as, and no worries, I'll get you that Cognac.'

'So what was that all about, Blaise?' Jack Phillips enquired.

'That was the pathologist, Jack. He was giving me the info on Will. He said that Will bit off the fingertip of one of his attackers, our good friend, Paddy Flynn.'

'Christ, is he not dead yet,' Jack Phillips sighed thoughtfully. 'That bloody man is a compulsive armed robber and a damn slippery sod too.'

'Well, he won't get away with this one, Jack. When he murdered Will he left behind incriminating evidence and he definitely will go down for it this time.'

'Shouldn't you inform the investigating team that are supposed to be doing Will's murder?'

Foetal Attraction

'Eh, I'll send them a note,' Blaise smiled.

'Right so all that aside, Blaise. Are you going to tell me why you're so bloody happy this morning?'

'Well, my old friend__ the thing is, Cathy and I are planning to get married.'

'Congratulations, bloody good on you, Blaise.'

'Right, let's go see this Paddy Flynn and tell him that we found his missing fingertip,' Blaise said enthusiastically.

'Hopefully the sod will be dying with a hangover and in severe pain,' Jack Phillips groaned as he pushed himself up from the chair.

'Shit, do we have an up to date address for this scumbag, Jack?'

'Tell you what, Blaise. You get two coffees and I'll look him up on the database thing.'

'You're a cheeky sod, Jack. Two sugars is it?'

'Jesus, that was bloody quick,' Jack Phillips gasped as Blaise returned to the office within two minutes.

'I bumped into WPC Trudie Conway on the stairs__ lucky enough she was carrying two coffees so I confiscated them.'

'Anyway, the file on Paddy Flynn is coming up shortly. Didn't he used to live in Sion Mills, Blaise?'

'He did that, maybe he still does. Here's your coffee, it looks dark and feels warm so it should be ok. I think the last time I arrested Flynn he was living in Sion Mills.'

Foetal Attraction

'Ah, here we go,' Jack Phillips smiled. 'Yip, he's still living in Parkside Gardens. I know that house too well. I've been to arrest him there myself on quite a few occasions.'

'Well, what are you waiting for, Jack?' Blaise groaned impatiently. 'Bring your coffee if you must.'

'Christ, I can't wait to see this scumbags face when we collar him,' Jack Phillips grinned. 'He will be livid, especially now that he will go down for a long time the murdering bastard.'

'I bet his poor wife will probably thank us too, eh Jack.'

'Without a doubt, he has given her a terrible life. He's put her in hospital more times than I care to remember.'

Such was their haste and eagerness to arrest the murderer of their colleague, Blaise and Jack Phillips arrived in the sleepy hamlet of Sion Mills in under five minutes. Both detectives then stood at the door of Paddy Flynn, scanning their eyes up and down the tranquil street before banging on the door aggressively.

The trembling nervous wreck of Mrs Flynn stood sleepy eyed at the door, staring with surprise at Jack Phillips without muttering a single word upon recognising the man that arrested her husband numerous times and had given months of happy living.

'Hello, Brenda, do you remember me?'

'Jack Phillips___ I suppose you're looking for that useless bastard of a husband, well he's not here. I haven't seen the rat in three days. I mean, Jesus Christ, my weans are hungry like and he's out gallivanting with his mates and probably lying with some wee whore.'

Foetal Attraction

'Are you sure he's not here, Brenda, you wouldn't be hiding him now would you?'

'Hide that bastard, no. I want him out my life for bloody good.'

'Right, well you won't mind if we come in to take a look then,' Blaise said boldly, brushing passed the woman.

'Aye, look if you want, but don't you wake the weans, I'm warning you.'

'Would you happen to know where he might be then, Brenda?' Jack Phillips said softly, removing the cigarettes from his pocket, which he offered to the grateful woman.

'Thanks Jack, for a Peeler you're ok, honest, there's not many like you in this country.'

'Well there would be if people showed more respect to the police, Brenda. Here, take this and get the kids something decent to eat,' Jack Phillips said, handing the woman a twenty pound note.

'Sweet Jesus, you're a bloody diamond, Jack, thanks,' the woman smiled, tucking the blonde hair back behind her ear. 'You know,' she smiled quietly. 'If you want you can come back later.'

'Now, you know that I'm happily married, Brenda.'

'Right,' Blaise interrupted with a sigh. 'No sign of him here. Do you know where we could find your husband, Mrs Flynn?'

'He's more than likely with that Jimmy Kelly. I don't know where he lives, honest. But I hope to God that whatever it is you're looking for him for gets him locked up for a while, long enough for me to divorce the rat.'

Foetal Attraction

'Well you can rest assured that he will be going away for a long time, he murdered a police officer,' Blaise growled.

'Holy Sweet Mother of God!'

'Jesus, don't cry, Brenda,' Jack Phillips comforted. 'I thought you wanted rid of him.'

'I do, this is tears of bloody happiness,' the woman tried to laugh. 'Finally I'll be rid of that horrible bastard.'

'Right, very touching,' Blaise groaned. 'Let's go Jack.'

Blaise slumped into the passenger seat with a disappointed groan, his hands eagerly searching pockets. 'Shit, no mints, give me one of your fags, Jack.'

'Eh, I don't have any.'

'What! Well you better stop at that shop down the road there and get some then.'

'Have you ever tried actually buying a packet yourself, Blaise?'

'Now, detective sergeant__ what would your dear wife say if you arrive home and tell her that you've been demoted and your being transferred ? I bought a packet the other by the way.'

'Christ, I'd save some money then,' Jack Phillips grinned. 'These cigarettes aren't cheap you know.'

'Jesus, you're turning into a right miserable sod,' Blaise joked, handing his colleague a five-pound note.

'When the hell did you last buy a packet of twenty, Blaise?'

'Here, there's another five. Now hurry up and let's get back to the station and find this Jimmy Kelly's address, he's bound to have previous. And don't you bloody dare mention to Cathy that I'm smoking or she'll do something unsavoury to me.'

'That Brenda Flynn is going to be one happy woman when we collar her hubby,' Jack Phillips said, parking the car outside of the shop. 'She can look tasty when she is all done up too.'

'I bet, I heard her offering you back later you crafty old sod.'

'Jesus__ I wouldn't, I couldn't do that to my wife, Blaise.'

'I'm joking, I know your faithful, Jack,' Blaise laughed, eagerly searching for his ringing mobile as his colleague entered the shop.

'Hello there my sweet sexy babe,' Blaise answered on recognising that it was Cathy calling. 'Wait; tell me what you're wearing first.'

'Ben, shut up,' Cathy said boldly, surprising him. 'Listen, do you remember you said to me last night that you were looking for some Polish doctor?'

'That's right__ we can't find the bitch anywhere.'

'Well, it might be nothing. I took wee Ben to the vet to have it checked over remember, the vet, she was Polish.'

'Nice one babe, remember me to give you something extra special tonight when I get home.'

'Oh, the minister is here, she wants to know if you fancy a threesome,' Cathy joked playfully.

'Tell her I'll be home shortly then.

211

'I'll bloody cut it off if you put it anywhere near another woman Benedict Blaise.'

'No, that's good, Cathy, I'll pay this vet a visit. That's the one on the Railway Road, right?'

Foetal Attraction

Blaise and Jack Phillips pulled up outside of the veterinary clinic on the Railway Road, both men sitting to smoke a cigarette as they thoughtfully stared at the small building.

'So what do you think, Blaise__ do you think that maybe this could be our woman, given that she's not a doctor as such?'

'Jesus, wouldn't it be nice, Jack. I'm not thinking that it could be the woman we're looking for, she just might know her or be able to tell us where we could find the murdering bitch.'

'Well, anything is possible, Blaise, I suppose.'

'Hey, wasn't there traces of dog hairs found on the victim's, Jack? I'm bloody sure forensics said there were several dog hairs and some other animal or other__ I can't remember what.'

'I think you're right, Blaise,' Jack Phillips sighed, dropping his cigarette to the ground before winding up the window again.

'I think we'll just sit here a wee while and watch for this dark green van that's been witnessed at the murder scenes.'

'I don't think whoever is driving it would be about now, probably after the clinic closes__ what do you think, Blaise?'

'I think we'll go in and have a word anyhow, we can get someone to wait about later on just in case this van does arrive.'

'Ok, you're the boss.'

'Right, let's go and have a look at this woman, Jack. I just hope to God that it is her.'

'We seem to be in luck_ no clients here, Blaise.'

'Right, Miss,' Blaise smiled at the receptionist behind the counter. 'Inspector Blaise, Strabane Police. I need to speak with whoever is charge.'

'That will be Mrs Schultze.'

'Schultze__ is that German?' Jack Phillips asked.

'I think so, I'm not sure.'

'Well, give her a shout and inform her that I need to speak with her.'

'I think she's busy at the moment actually.'

'And you think that I've got nothing do? Get your arse up and tell her I want to speak to her now,' Blaise growled impatiently.

'But she is__'

'If you don't call her now I swear to God that I'll jump over this counter and bloody strangle you__ now get her out here.'

With certain fear and panic, the receptionist rushed into the backroom calling out on Mrs Schultze.

'Jesus Blaise, you're a bad sod,' Jack Phillips laughed.

'What can be so damned important,' the woman complained angrily on emerging from a side door, standing then with hands on narrowed hips, pulling a surgical mask down from her face and removed a pair of slightly bloodied gloves. 'What do you want, I am trying to operate?'

Foetal Attraction

'Sorry about that_ Inspector Blaise, Strabane Police,' Blaise said, closely studying the woman's face. 'Are you of German descent, doctor?'

'Is that what you disturbed me for, Inspector?'

'No, just curious actually,' Blaise said glancing then at his colleague with a slight smile. 'Forgive me for staring, but you look like a woman that we're trying to trace, a Miss Jana Madzia Zaleski,' he continued noticing the surprised expression on the woman's face.

'I__ sorry Inspector, but I don't know anyone of that name.'

'Do you have any identification on you?'

'What__ this is absolutely preposterous. Look, I need to finish this operation, Inspector.'

'Get somebody else to do it, I have a murder investigation to solve and I think that you can help me, Doctor Zaleski.'

'My name is Schultze__ Anna Schultze.'

'You look remarkably like her,' Jack Phillips added as he too noticed the resemblance.

'Give me five minutes to close the wound on this dog then we can talk if you must, Inspector.'

'No problem, but I'm coming in with you, we wouldn't want you disappearing now,' Blaise said, glancing at Jack Phillips.

'You go, I'll wait here, Blaise,' Jack Phillips refused due to his phobia of anything surgical.

Foetal Attraction

Blaise eagerly followed the woman into the small operating theatre, thinking how easily she could perform an operation on a human if needed.

'You look very skilful doctor, like a surgeon,' Blaise said, carefully watching the woman stitch the wound on an injured dog.

'Yes, well, years of practice, Inspector. You can't learn to be a vet just by reading a few text books,' the woman muttered through her surgical mask.

'Those instruments, they look like the same ones that are used in hospitals.'

'Obviously, my God, just what are you implying, Inspector?'

'I'm just making a comment, you carry on there then we get this all sorted out. How long have you been living in Northern Ireland by the way?'

'What__ oh, I've lived here almost twenty years or so, why do you ask?'

'Just making conversation, doctor,' Blaise smiled, noticing the slight agitation in the woman's voice. 'Wouldn't you rather put your skills to that of the hospitals rather than animals?'

'Animals give you less problems, Inspector. Besides, don't you think that animals deserve the best treatment they can get?'

'I'm all for that, doctor. So eh, I suppose you have carried out some abortions on animals. I mean, say a dog having pups and the owner doesn't want them for instance.'

'I am a qualified veterinary surgeon, Inspector.'

'Right, so you are__ so you are,' Blaise sighed, watching then as the woman told her assistant to care for the anesthetised dog before washing at the sink.

'To be perfectly honestly, Inspector, I think that you are making a mistake. I can assure you that I am who I say I am.'

'Well, as I say, we can sort it all out at the station. It won't take long if we can prove who you say you are. You see, I just find it so remarkable that you look so like the woman that we urgently need to speak to.'

'So why do you need to speak with this person, Inspector?'

'We are investigating into the murders of two women and her name came up during our initial contacts with certain witnesses.'

'Witnesses__ so this woman that you seek, she has been seen presumably with these murdered women?'

'Sorry, I can't answer that,' Blaise said. 'I eh__ was talking with your father, well, the father of doctor Zaleski that is. To be honest, the poor old guy didn't look that well.'

'Forgive me, Inspector, but what exactly does that have to do with me,' the woman replied without any sign of emotion. 'Old people often look ill and unfortunately they do die.'

'Right well, love to stand chatting all day, but we need to get to the station.'

'You're so impatient, Inspector,' the woman said, informing her receptionist then to make sure that the clinic was locked up securely before leaving.

Foetal Attraction

A large "WET PAINT" sign hung on the door of the interview rooms as Blaise led Mrs Anna Schultze and Jack Phillips into the first room, apologising immediately for the slight odour of fresh paint. Jack Phillips pulled out a grey plastic chair inviting the woman to sit then seated himself next her. Then, the door opened and Sergeant Bob McMenamin stood with arms folded.

'Can we help you, Bob?' Blaise smiled.

'I'm here with a warning from the DCI,' the Sergeant said bluntly. 'He said to tell you and Jack specifically that under no circumstances have you to smoke in any of the interview rooms from now on.'

'Right, thanks Bob.'

'I'm serious now, the big mad Jock said it's my responsibility and if he smells the slightest hint of cigarette smoke then he's going to do certain things to me that I can't mention in front of a lady.'

'Don't worry, Bob, I'll see that your warning is heeded,' Jack Phillips smiled.

'Right then, let's get down to business,' Blaise said.

'Do you want anyone in attendance, Inspector?'

'No, you're ok, Bob__ this is just an informal interview.'

'Coffees would be appreciated though,' Jack Phillips smiled. 'Coffee ok with you Mrs Zaleski__ sorry, I'm mean Mrs Schultze.'

'Very good, that's was a clever mistake,' the woman smiled, looking rather relaxed as she leaned back, casually stroking both hands over her head to tidy the length of jet ponytail.

'Sorry, it was a genuine mistake,' Jack Phillips said. 'It was when I turned to look at you that you reminded me her.'

'So you still say that your name isn't Jana Zaleski__ what if I said that a quick fingerprint check would perhaps prove it?'

'Sorry, Inspector, that would be impossible.'

'Oh__ and how so?'

'Well, I had an accident some years ago with certain chemicals and my fingerprints were damaged.'

'Oh dear, what a coincidence,' Blaise grinned. 'I suppose this accident occurred at the same time you received your new passport and other documents?'

'Don't be absurd, Inspector.'

'We could always match your DNA with that of Mr Zaleski.'

'You're impossibly persistent, Inspector.'

'Persistence is my middle name__ Mrs Schultze, if that is indeed your name.'

'Are you going to continue denying that you are Doctor Jana Madzia Zaleski?' Jack Phillips sighed loudly. 'This is going to be a long night.'

'Are you married__ any family in Northern Ireland?' Blaise questioned. 'Can you show me any identification?'

'Well, you didn't give me any time to bring my handbag, Inspector_ such is your foolish notion.'

Foetal Attraction

'Are you deliberately trying to wind me up you bi__?'

'Blaise,' Jack Phillips interrupted to calm his colleague.

'Ok, let's continue with this charade,' Blaise said calmly. 'Where were you born, Mrs Schultze?'

'I was born in Leipzig.'

'Is that anywhere near Berlin?'

'Leipzig is 200 kilometres south of Berlin, Inspector.'

'What about your parents, where are they?'

'Heaven, my dear Inspector. Well, if that is where we go when we die, though I don't believe all that nonsense.'

'And I suppose they are buried in Germany? Well, I'll tell you what, Mrs Schultze. If you allow the police doctor to take a DNA sample and surrender your passport in the meantime to one of my officers, I'll allow you to go home.'

'If that is what you wish, Inspector, I shall agree to that.'

'Fine, Jack, would you ask for WPC to accompany Mrs Schultze home and get the necessaries?'

Jack Phillips left the interview room to fetch a uniformed officer and to call for the police doctor.

'Between you and I,' Blaise said leaning forwards. 'You're not fooling me here, Doctor Zaleski, I know you're not who you say you are and I'm going to prove it, should it take me until my dying breath. You killed those two women.'

Foetal Attraction

'You're being ridiculous, Inspector,' the woman again stated. 'If you had any proof of these absurd allegations then you would have arrested me__ am I right, Inspector?'

Blaise knew that at that particular time he couldn't prove the true identity of the woman, not until he had conclusive matches of DNA, which he planned to take from Mr Zaleski, the woman's father.

'Jack, whilst she is in there waiting on Dr Cuthbertson we will take a wee run out to Sycamore Lodge to chat with old Mr Zaleski.'

'Good idea__ and this time we can ask him for a photograph to compare against this Mrs Schultze woman.'

'You get the car and I'll have a quick word with Bob at the desk.'

Foetal Attraction

'You bloody better not have smoked in that room, Inspector,' the duty Sergeant groaned as Blaise approached the desk.

'No, honestly we didn't, Bob. Did you call for the duty doctor?'

'I did, it's Doctor Cuthbertson, he'll be here shortly.'

'Right, ask him to meet me at this address in Sycamore Lodge, I want him to take some samples from the old guy out there.'

'Oh, by the way,' the Sergeant smiled cheerfully. 'I hear congratulations are in order.'

'Oh right, thanks.'

'As a matter of fact, we in uniform have an early wedding present for you. We have just arrested that Johnny Mulgrew, he's in custody now.'

'You big beautiful sod, I could bloody kiss you, Bob.'

'You just stick to kissing Cathy,' the Sergeant laughed.

Blaise called Jack Phillips on the mobile telling him to park up the car again as he now planned to interview Johnny Mulgrew.'

'Bloody hell,' Jack Phillips gasped with surprise. 'Where did he come from, Blaise?'

'Uniform picked him up about an hour ago. I've said all along those guys in uniform are amazing.'

'Aye right,' Sergeant Bob McMenamin groaned with a smile.

Foetal Attraction

'Nice to see you again, Johnny,' Jack Phillips smiled on entering the interview room first. 'We have been looking for you for a while.'

'Mr Phillips__ what's this all about, why am I under arrest?'

'Because we want to talk to you,' Blaise said boldly entering the room then, a manila folder crammed with an assortment of arrest records and statements taken in the past.

'Mr Blaise, haven't seen you in a while, thought you were kicked out long ago,' Johnny Mulgrew smiled as he sat at the table, fidgeting anxiously as he craved a cigarette. 'What's this about; at least tell me why the fuck I've been arrested like.'

'You're not under arrest as such,' Blaise smiled. 'You're just being held because you're such a slippery sod and I really need to talk to you.'

'What about, what the fuck's going on here like? I've done nothing wrong.'

'Why did you run when the officers approached you then?'

'To tell the truth, Mr Blaise, I thought they were going to mug me.'

'Don't try to be a smart arse. Why did you run?'

'I'm allergic to Peelers.'

'I'm warning you, don't mess me about.'

'Just answer the questions, Mr Mulgrew,' Jack Phillips said pulling his chair closer to the suspect.

Foetal Attraction

'Now you're scaring me, are you going to rough me up like?'

'Look, this is a murder investigation, Mr Mulgrew.'

'What! So you think I've got something to do with that woman found in the Canal Basin?'

'Well, have you?'

'Catch yourself on__ why the fuck would I kill a woman?'

'You tell me. Do you own a dark green van, Mr Mulgrew?'

'How would__ I've not got two pennies to rub together.'

'What about any of your friends?'

'No__ look, what's this got to do with me. I never killed anybody so you can forget about me.'

'Right, so I suppose you'll deny knowing Mary-Jo Delaney?'

'Yes__ no, I mean, sure I know her.'

'Oh I know that you know her,' Blaise said, removing the photograph that Jack Phillips had discovered on the footpath of the Delaney home. 'You both look close there__ were you lovers, you both look like lovers?'

'Well, we were seeing each other__ it was mostly just sex, for me anyway. Mary-Jo wanted it too.'

'So you're saying this relationship was based purely on sex?'

'You said you were investigating a murder, what's this got to do with me, or Mary-Jo for that matter?'

'When did you last see Mrs Delaney?' Blaise questioned, removing the photograph of Mary-Jo's murdered body, keeping his hand over it. 'When did you last speak to her?'

'It was eh__ Christ, a few weeks ago. We fell out like.'

'Oh, why was that now?'

'She wanted__ well, Mary-Jo wanted to leave that arsehole of a husband. She wanted us to get a flat together. I mean, she was pregnant__ she said that it was mine, but I knew it was probably his. I'll be fucked if I'm getting stuck with another man's brat.'

'You're all heart, Mr Mulgrew. So how did you both meet?'

'We met one night in the pub, Mary-Jo was out with some friends and we just got chatting like. I bought her a few drinks then we went outside, that's when she told me about having problems with her husband. I only wanted a quickie and ended up with ear ache.'

'So you thought you'd help her feel better by taking advantage of her when she was vulnerable, is that it?'

'Well, she was up for it as much as I was. I mean, we started seeing each other from then on, it suited us both like.'

'You said that Mary-Jo told you she planned to leave her husband and wanted to set up home with you, what did you say to her?'

'I told her we couldn't, I mean, especially when she told me about the baby like. I just told her that we'd had some fun and that was that. I mean, Jesus, who needs to be in that fucking situation. I mean, you know how it is.'

Foetal Attraction

'So what did Mary-Jo say about that, was she angry?'

'She started crying and shit, she kept saying that the kid was mine and she loved me. It was terrible watching her beg. She just kept going on about how she'd make me happy and would do anything for me.'

'I suppose that would've been annoying, I 'd probably have given her a slap too, they can be so annoying at times, eh?'

'What__ I never hit her, Jesus.'

'So eh, if you're not working__ do you do anything on the side to earn a few pound, a wee driving job maybe?'

'As if I would fucking tell you like__ Jesus.'

'I'm not worried about benefit fraud. Do you maybe drive for someone, wee deliveries and so on, for a Polish woman maybe?'

'What Polish woman__ what are you talking about, Mr Blaise?'

'When did you say that you last spoke to Mary-Jo?'

'A few weeks back__ I told her I didn't want to see her again, not if she was into us doing this happy families shit.'

'What about this child, what if it is your kid? I mean, you have a responsibility for it.'

'Fucking catch yourself on__ the brat's not mine.'

'Maybe Mary-Jo just annoyed you to the extent that you got angry and perhaps you hit her accidentally? I mean, it does happen, as we've witnessed on many occasion.'

Foetal Attraction

'I__ never hit her. Why the fuck don't you ask her, she'll tell you, she'll tell you that I never hit her__ ask Mary-Jo.'

'Well, that would be difficult given that she has been murdered,' Blaise stated, pushing the photograph of woman in front of Johnny Mulgrew, watching his reaction to the gruesome image.

'Jesus__ what the f__ is that her?'

'That's the terrible condition that the killer left her in. Some evil sod cut the unborn child from her womb, Mr Mulgrew. I don't suppose you would know anything about that now, would you?'

'How would__ Holy Christ, that's just sick.'

'It sure is. 'Could it be that perhaps you wanted to get back at God for the terrible accident that took your child?'

'Get to__ are you trying to__ fuck off. You're a sick minded bastard if you think that I would do that.'

'Did you kill Mary-Jo Delaney__ did you?' Blaise roared angrily, slapping the palm of his hand hard on the desk.

'Look, all this is just fucking crazy. Ever since__ when my angel passed away I felt like my whole world collapsed. I mean, why would God allow such a terrible thing to happen?'

'It must have been hard for you and your wife,' Blaise sighed.

'We were grand until that. I mean, I know you might think that I'm a piece of scum, but I loved my wife. She just gave up on life too. Christ, she stopped talking to me. Sinead wouldn't even cook a meal or even clean the house. She just sat about the house most of the time, siting with the baby's wee pyjamas in her hand.'

Foetal Attraction

'Maybe you should have helped her instead of going on the drink. I mean, as men we're supposed to be the stronger ones in the relationship.'

'Aye that will be right, it's the bloody women who are stronger, all we do is get drunk and fight.'

'You're right there. Look, to be honest, I don't think that you killed Mrs Delaney,' Blaise said in more friendly tone, which surprised Jack Phillips.

'I wouldn't harm her, honestly. To tell the truth, if I wasn't married I'd probably give Mary-Jo a go, living with her like.'

'About this dark green van, would you know of anyone who has a van of this description__ maybe somebody you've worked with in the past or a friend of a friend?'

'To tell the truth, I can't think, Mr Blaise. Christ, I can't bloody believe that Mary-Jo is dead like.'

'Well she is unfortunately, and we need to find out who killed her and why.'

'Is that photo you showed me real like? I mean, Jesus Christ, what a bloody mess. Who the fuck would be so evil, why the fuck would somebody cut out the baby?'

'Well that's what we hope to find out, and soon. Oh, and by the way, Mr Mulgrew, not a word to anybody about this.'

'Don't you worry about that__ I might be a bit of a bad fucker, but that is just pure evil like.'

'I don't suppose you know a Paddy Flynn?'

Foetal Attraction

'Come on, Inspector__ even if I did.'

'I know, you're not a tout, you wouldn't tell me anyway, right?'

'That's right__ it wouldn't do my Republican soul much good, Inspector.'

'Being a Republican is more important than being a good citizen, is that it?'

'I don't think you want to start a debate now, do you Inspector?'

'You sometimes hang about with Tommy Kelly don't you__ he has a brother, Jimmy right?'

'There you go again__ I can't answer you, Inspector.'

'Right well, time's getting on,' Blaise sighed, checking his watch then glanced at Jack Phillips.

'Right then, you're free to go, but remember, if you hear of anything that may help us catch this sadistic sod let me know.'

'I will do, Mr Blaise. Eh, what's the chance of me getting a lift home then?'

'You'd stand a better chance seeing Scottish guys cheering on England in the world cup.'

'That's a definite no then,' Johnny Mulgrew grinned slightly as he rose from the chair.

Sergeant McMenamin will see you out, Mr Mulgrew,' Jack Phillips said, suggesting then to Blaise that they went to the canteen for a cup of tea before going home.

Foetal Attraction

It was a usual start to a morning in Northern Ireland, a two-hour downpour of torrential rain and bitter wind, and then the skies cleared to allow a brilliant sun to shine gloriously. Yet, that dearly loved sunshine could at any given time, disappear and the ground would perhaps be sodden again, or indeed, covered with snow. All the same, everyone got on with their lives and enjoyed whatever the day brought.

'Now, are you absolutely sure that you're ready for this?' Blaise asked, leading DC Cathy O'Hare towards the red armoured entrance door of the police station. 'Are you sure now?'

'Jesus, Ben, would you stop going on like an old mother hen, I'm fine. Besides, I'll be able to keep a better eye on you,' Cathy O'Hare smiled, taking a deep breath to calm her slight nerves. 'I don't believe how nervous I feel, it's been ages.'

'Look, just because I'm going to let you marry me, it doesn't mean that you can call me Ben. Bloody call me Blaise like everybody else does__ I mean it now.'

'Yes sir, sorry Inspector,' Cathy O'Hare smiled as she saluted.

'Get in there you cheeky tart,' Blaise sighed, gently pushing Cathy inside into the brightly lit reception.

'Hi, Cathy,' Sergeant Bob McMenamin grinned cheerfully. Good to see you back, better than looking at all these ugly sods in here.'

'Thanks Bob, how have you been?'

'Well, sad actually, but now you're here, I'm happy.'

'Hoi, remember that's my intended,' Blaise joked. 'Any messing about and you know what will happen.'

'Cathy loves me really, hasn't she told you, Blaise?'

'All the time, Bob. Is everybody in?'

'The usual suspects are all upstairs awaiting their master.'

'Right, if anyone's looking for me, I'm in the incident room giving a briefing, ok Bob.'

Blaise pushed open the door to a wide applause as Cathy entered, giving a playful curtsey to her colleagues.

'Right, calm down you lunatics,' Blaise grinned, perching himself on the edge of a desk. 'We have two murders to solve, and I want them solved soon.'

'I hear you and Jack interviewed Johnny Mulgrew,' DC Bill Johnson said. 'Did you have any joy with that?'

'Yes and no, Bill. We can rule him out for the time being. Now, you all remember that we were looking for this Polish doctor. Well, my dear intended here happened across a veterinary clinic in the town, and the woman there had mentioned to Cathy that she was from Poland.'

'That's right, I heard you two were getting married,' DC Gemma Galbraith smiled. 'Congrats to the both of you.'

'Aye, congratulations,' the team shouted, clapping loudly.

'Right__ come on you nutters, keep it down,' Blaise groaned.

Foetal Attraction

'Jesus, Cathy, you've got a job on your hands. Although, keep him sweet in the bedroom and promotion is in the bag,' DC Gemma Galbraith joked.

'Right enough of the banter. Let's get serious here folks,' Blaise again insisted. 'When Jack and I questioned this vet, she denied being Polish__ she swears she is German and has documents to prove it, but we can guess where she acquired them.'

'I know this is probably a stupid question, but did you get her documents checked out?' DC Jim Whyte asked.

'Not yet, well, I'm waiting on word from immigration etc. Now, the other thing we need to look out for is the dark green van that has appeared at both murder scenes. It's a Ford Transit, possibly manufactured mid 1990's. The driver apparently wears some kind of balaclava.'

'That's unusual in Northern Ireland, eh?' DC Jim O'Reilly joked.

'This individual is described about five foot seven, wears a long army style khaki coat with hood and dirty denim jeans with some kind of boots or heavy shoes. I can't stress enough here folks, it's imperative that we trace this individual, he could be the one that abducted these two women.'

'What's the situation with Will's murder, Blaise?' DC Bill Johnson asked.

'The DCI wants us to concentrate on these two murders only, Bill. However, you know the score, if anything comes up. We are seriously looking to question a Paddy Flynn, if you happen to bump into him exercise extreme caution; he is one very violent man. He also has an accomplice we think__ a Jimmy Kelly.'

232

'So eh,' DC Gemma Galbraith smiled. 'Whilst we are all out investigating, Inspector__ what will you and Cathy be doing?' The question caused a roar of jeers like a classroom full of teenagers.

'Now children, behave. Cathy here will be on light duties for a while, so she can man the phones and gather intelligence, so to speak__ does everybody know what they're doing, or supposed to be doing?' Blaise questioned, casting his eyes over the assembled team.

There was a loud knocking on the door and PC Billy Kent entered, informing Blaise that there was a young woman at reception reporting that her flatmate has been missing for two days.

'Right you lot go do some detective work,' Blaise said commandingly. 'Bring the woman up here Billy please.'

'Thank God you're here, Cathy,' Blaise smiled. 'I honestly couldn't listen to a woman rabbiting on and crying at this time of the morning__ bad enough listening to you.'

'You cheeky tramp,' DC Cathy O'Hare replied, rising from her chair to join Blaise at his desk.

The uniformed officer led the nervous, trembling young woman over to sit her opposite Blaise, Cathy O'Hare immediately rising to put an arm around the woman's shoulder to comfort her.

'Three teas would be magic, Billy, thanks,' Blaise smiled.

'What's your name, miss?' Cathy asked softly.

'It's Jasmine Doherty.'

'You say your friend is missing__ since when?'

Foetal Attraction

'Two days, we share a flat in the Ballycolman and she hasn't come since she went to visit her sister in Lisnafin, that was on Monday afternoon. She said she wouldn't be long.'

'Are you sure that she isn't with friends, or a boyfriend maybe?' Blaise quizzed.

'I phoned everyone, nobody has seen her. I'm frightened after that woman was found murdered in the Canal Basin.'

'I'm sure there's nothing to be alarmed about, Miss. What's your friend's name?'

'Michele Healey.'

'Right, give me a wee description there, Jasmine.'

'God_ she's about five foot four inches and has short black hair and blue eyes.'

'Right, any distinguishing marks, scars, tattoo's that sort of thing?'

'Eh, she has a lovely peace dove tattooed on her left shoulder. God, I'm just worried because she's about five months pregnant.'

'I see,' Blaise said, feeling a certain sensation tingle his spine. 'How old is Michele?'

'She's just turned sixteen.'

'And she's pregnant?' Cathy O'Hare gasped.

'God I know, that's why she's living with me, she told her parents and they threw her out of the house. Christ, bloody hypocrites so they are.'

'What makes you say that?' Blaise said.

'Well, Michele's parents are never away from the Chapel, always at mass pretending to be Christians. How can you say you're a Christian when you throw your own daughter out onto the street just because she makes a bloody mistake?'

'Take it easy, calm yourself, Jasmine,' Cathy O'Hare said comforting the distraught young girl.

'Where did you say her sister lived__ what's her name?'

'Her sister lives in Lisnafin, just beside the wee shop. Michele's sister is Carol-Anne McGroarty, her husband is called Patrick.'

'Right, we'll see what we can do, Jasmine. Try not to worry, I'm sure she will turn up safe and sound,' Cathy O'Hare encouraged.

'You just fill in your details on that sheet there, write your phone number so that we can contact if we need to. If she does turn up will you remember to call us to let us know please?' Blaise smiled, fearing that perhaps this young girl was to be victim number three.

'Oh, Cathy, would you give Jasmine here a lift home and maybe she could give you a recent photograph of Michele.'

'I've got one__ we just took some photo's the other day.'

'That's good, come on then, Michele, I'll run you home and you can tell me all about it,' Cathy O'Hare said comforting the young girl as they left Blaise alone to ponder with anxious concern on the safety of the missing girl, hoping and praying that she would turn up safe and sound.

Foetal Attraction

The young girl lay curled up on top of the bed, trembling with uncertain fear as she struggled with the bindings that secured her hands tightly behind her back and the makeshift blindfold kept her in complete darkness. Fear and shear panic had caused her to wet herself as she lay sobbing uncertainty, fearing being harmed or sexually attacked and felt afraid for the safety of her unborn child.

Then, in the darkness of her horror, the young girl felt a tender hand touch softly against her cheek, fingers stroking down with caressing purpose until the hand gently cupped her breast over the top of her light blouse. The young girl tried desperately not to make a sound as her unknown captor continued to fondle each breast as though exploring her. Then, as the fear grew, she exhaled a muttered sob, pleading quietly for him to stop, to leave her alone.

'You are so beautiful,' the voice echoed frighteningly in her ears as she felt her blouse being unbuttoned, fingertips caressing her exposed naked flesh, squeezing then more excitedly over her breasts, his panting breath heavier. 'You are such a beautiful girl.'

All hell broke loose within her mind then as she felt hands stroke her bare thighs, slowly pushing the hem of her skirt up until her briefs were exposed. An uncontrollable fear thundered within, her sobbing intense as the kidnapper excitedly gasped, pulling her briefs down then off, his hands forcing her thighs apart. 'Beautiful girl, you're so lovely.'

The stagnant air filled with intense panic and horror as the young girl experienced something that no female should ever experience, and there she lay quivering as he kissed excitedly over her thighs and exposed sex, continually telling her how beautiful she was.

236

Foetal Attraction

'Please__ let me go,' the young girl pleaded through her terrified tears, gasping louder with panic as she then felt the full weight of the man on top of her. 'Please, no__ I'm pregnant,' she begged, surprised then when there was no forced penetration.

'I'm sorry beautiful girl,' the man grunted, sitting then on the edge of the bed, his hand resting on her still exposed stomach. 'I just want to be with someone, I'm so lonely.'

'Please__ will you take the blindfold off, please, I really don't like the dark,' she quietly begged, trying to remain calm.

'Will you promise not to look at me if I take it off?' The kidnapper asked, as though filled with shame. 'Please don't look.'

The young girl opened and closed her eyes continuously as she tried to focus, her heart pounding as she then sighted her kidnapper for the first time, her eyes wide with horrified shock at seeing his deformed, twisted face.

'I told you not to look,' he grunted, trying to cover his face with the balaclava as he stood up from the bed, turning his back to her. Suddenly, and to the young girl's surprise, the man slumped onto his knees on the floor sobbing with shame.

'I'm so hideous__ ugly__ I should kill myself.'

'Oh please, don't cry,' the young girl sighed with all the parental sympathies of an expectant mother, all the fear of being violated gone, all the hatred of her kidnapper vanished as she stared pitifully at the sobbing man before her.

'I__ hate being so ugly__ people stare at me like I'm a freak or a monster__ I disgust them.'

237

Foetal Attraction

'I'm sure they don't,' the young girl said softly. 'It's probably all in your imagination__ you probably think that everyone's staring, but I bet they aren't.'

The man wiped his tearful face as he knelt on the floor, turning his head towards the bed, the balaclava pulled down to cover most of his face. He stared silent, sniffed then rose clumsily to his feet.

'Look, nobody's perfect,' the girl said, still lying partially exposed to the eyes of her abductor. 'Please, will you fasten my blouse and fix my skirt?'

'Ever since I was a child people have had been cruel, making fun of me and calling me a monster.'

'Yes, well I used to be fat when I was at school,' the girl said trying to smile through her fear. 'Can you imagine what name's they called me?'

'But you're not fat now, you__ are so beautiful,' the man said, sitting on the edge of the bed, casting his eyes again over the exposed body of the young girl again. 'You're not fat now.'

'Please__ will you fix my clothes?'

'Do you think I'm ugly?'

'We are what God makes us; I don't like to think of anyone as being ugly. In fact, I think it's terrible to say that about anyone.'

'Mother said that God doesn't exist. Mother said that there is too much evil in the world for a God to exist.'

'It's only people that are bad, just look at the world, it's lovely.'

238

Foetal Attraction

'Do you think I'm lovely__ am I lovely?'

'I__ can't see you properly, it's so dull, and you're wearing__'

'My balaclava,' the man interrupted, touching fingers over the side of his face. 'It's to hide my ugliness.'

'I'm sure it can't be that bad.'

'Mother wants to gather enough money to send me to America where they can do things to my face.'

'Well, there you are then, it will be all sorted for you.'

The kidnapper touched a hand over the girl's stomach again, moving towards her breasts, his breathing increasing as his excitement increased, panting as he said how lovely she was.

'Please, don't,' the girl pleaded, trying to move away.

'I want__ let me__ I need to see,' he panted with increasing lusted desire, roughly pushing up the bra to fully expose her breasts, which he fondled with eager excitement, almost salivating noisily.

'Stop, please don't__ you mustn't, no.'

Like a wild animal, the kidnapper forcefully rubbed his hands roughly over the sobbing girl's partially naked body, desiring her, wanting her with such course passion.

'Oh please__ stop, no, you can't__ don't,' the girl sobbed and squirmed as the kidnapper lost all control of reason as he hurriedly loosened his trousers exposing himself as he then forced in between her legs, his full weight pressing down as he violently thrust himself deep inside the horrified, shocked girl.

Foetal Attraction

The minutes following the viciously barbaric attack hung heavy with angered tension as the kidnapper hurriedly fixed his clothing and knelt on the floor at the edge of the bed, holding his hands over his face, as though hiding his shame.

'Why__ did you do that? That was so horrible. You fucking better not have harmed my baby,' the young girl panted through her tears, struggling anxiously with her bindings, unable to fix her clothing.

'You don't need to worry, mother will sort everything__ mother always does.'

'How the hell can she sort that__ you bloody raped me.'

'It will be all right you'll be like the others soon.'

'What do you mean__ what others__?'

Foetal Attraction

Sergeant Bob McMenamin entered the CID room immediately informing Blaise that an elderly woman had reported seeing a man with a hooded coat carrying a large bundle from his van into the house next door several nights past and that there was a lot of noise in the house.

'That sounds just like our boy,' Blaise said, thanking the sergeant before shouting at his colleagues to drop everything and follow him. 'Jack, you're with me.'

'Jesus, let's hope this is the evil sod, Blaise,' Jack Phillips said excitedly, steering the car through the armoured gates.

'Right, tell the team to wait in the car until I've spoken with this woman,' Blaise said, making his way from the car into the woman's house on Park Road, his eyes watching keenly on the house next to him. 'Right Mrs Callaghan, you say that this man was driving a van, can you tell me the colour of it?'

'Oh God, I couldn't son, but it was a dark colour.'

'Right, so what do you think it was that he carried into the house?'

'I don't know, but it looked big and heavy,' the woman replied almost in a whisper.

'Was this man alone, did you see anyone else entering the house?'

'No, it was just him. They are a bloody odd people if you ask me. They rented the house from Jean and Danny, they are away to live with their daughter for a while in New Zealand.'

'Right, you've been really helpful. Just go inside and leave this to us, Mrs Callaghan,' Blaise said, beckoning on his colleagues to join

241

Foetal Attraction

him. 'There's no sign of the van, let's hope there's somebody at home, eh Jack?'

'Bill, you take Jim and Gemma round the back, Cathy, you shouldn't have come. You stay here with us,' Blaise said in forced whisper, knocking on the front door then. 'You should have stayed at the office, Cathy.'

'He can't be in, especially if the van isn't here, Blaise,' Jack Phillips said, trying to see through one of the windows.

'Maybe he's doing his Wednesday night's shopping?' DC Cathy O'Hare smiled, trying to look through the other window, shielding a hand over her straining eyes. 'There doesn't seem to be a lot of furniture in there.'

'Maybe we should just bloody force the door,' Jack Phillips suggested, sounding eager to enter the house. 'Kick it in, Blaise.'

'Jesus Jack, he's not as young as he used to be.'

'Cathy, I'll kick your arse first, you cheeky tart,' Blaise grinned, taking a step backwards then thrust his foot with great force against the wooden door, causing it to burst open loudly.

All detectives raced into the house that was in darkness, throwing beams of their torches around in search of anyone, Blaise then finding the light switch in the hallway.

'Up here, Blaise,' DC Bill Johnson called out loudly, standing in the doorway to one of the bedrooms, switching on the light.

'Thank God she's alive,' Blaise sighed. 'Call the paramedics. I want her well looked after, and get something to cover the girl.'

242

'Jesus, don't be frightened,' Cathy O'Hare smiled, comforting the sobbing young girl on the bed as she tried to fix her dishevelled clothing. 'It will be ok now pet, you're safe.'

'Is that__ ask her if her name's Michele Healey.'

'Yes__ I'm__ Michele,' the young girl trembled with a mixture of panic and elation as she thrilled in the safe comforting arms of DC Cathy O'Hare.

'Be careful with those clothes, Cathy, we'll need them for forensics.'

'He__ the man who__ took me, he's gone for some food.'

'He'll be well bloody gone by now I'll bet,' Blaise sighed, hearing the wailing siren of several patrol cars approach the scene.

'Listen Michele, did you kidnapper have an accomplice?'

'No, he__ was alone. He__ raped me,' the young girl sobbed, breaking down in DC Cathy O'Hare's arms.

'I really hate bastards like that,' Jack Phillips groaned through gritted teeth, showing signs of uncharacteristic anger.

'That's the world we live in, Jack,' Blaise sighed, glancing his eyes around the sparse bedroom. 'This must be where he holds his victims, Jack.'

'Yes, it looks like it. Let's try to catch this__ well, let's just try to get him before he kidnaps anyone else.'

'Eh, did this person mention anyone else, Michele?'

Foetal Attraction

'No_ he just kept saying that I was beautiful, he touched me and raped me_ it was horrible.'

'It couldn't have been a nice experience, Miss. At least you're alive sweetheart and that's the main thing,' Blaise said, noticing the young girl's briefs lying on the floor at the foot of the bed. He pointed them out to Jack Phillips then.

'Maybe he didn't get time to keep them as he did with the others.'

'Others_ he said others,' the young girl gasped suddenly. 'Yes, he said_ something like I'd soon be like the others.'

'Did he say how many?' Blaise questioned with growing interest, scratching his thumb over his chin. 'Did he mention any names or anything like that?'

'No_ wait, he did say that his mother would sort everything. He said that after I shouted at him in case he had hurt my baby.'

'Bill, come here mate,' Blaise shouted. 'Look, get back to the station; I want you to contact the other divisions, all of them now. Find out about any possible missing pregnant woman_ say over the past two years to start with.'

'Right, will do, boss.'

'So do you think this could be a widespread thing, Blaise?'

'Possibly, Jack. Who knows, these evil sods just may be moving around from town to town.'

'Damn, did your kidnapper wear some kind of hood?' Blaise questioned, hoping for the right answer.

'Yes, we talked about it.'

'You talked about it_ what do you mean?'

'He__ well, he said that he was ugly, that's why he always wore the balaclava thing, he said people made fun of him.'

'So you actually talked with him in a friendly manner?'

'I was just trying to be nice hoping that he'd free me, but the more sympathy I showed him__ well, that's when he__'

'Are you positive that there was nobody else here, nobody at all, Michele. Did he say why he had kidnapped you?'

'No__ he just said I was beautiful.'

'Right, well, the police doctor will need to examine you, Michele, and he'll take some samples that should help us catch this__ person,' Blaise said thoughtful, calling on DC's Gemma Galbraith and Jim Whyte.

'Yes boss.'

'Listen, you two take a car and wait opposite that vet's clinic on the Railway Road, keep an eye for anybody going in or out in a dark green van. The place should be closed now, but you never know,' Blaise whispered so that the young girl did not hear. 'I want this evil bastard tonight before he abducts any other poor soul.'

'Right, so if there is any activity we'll call you straight away.'

'That's it. Wait, second thoughts, if this sod arrives with the van arrest him immediately__ don't take any crap from him__ in fact, you better make sure he is well restrained,' Blaise sighed.

'Will do,' DC Jim Whyte smiled. 'I just hope to God that he resists arrest and I need to use force. I can't stand guys that do things like that to helpless women, especially pregnant ones.'

'Well, just make sure that he is still able to talk to me, Jim.'

'Now, where could that sod be, Jack?'

'God knows, he could be anywhere, Blaise.'

'True, at least we managed to save one soul.'

'Two souls, Blaise__ don't forget that wee unborn angel. Here, remember that old man in Sycamore Lodge told us that his daughter, the doctor, had an imbecilic son. Maybe he just meant that he was physically deformed?'

'Bloody right enough, Jack,' Blaise gasped with surprised recollection. 'I think we will bring this woman in again for questioning, see what she has to say about this, especially if we can catch her son.'

'Right, are you ok, Michele? Cathy will stay with you all the way here. You'll be ok with this, Cathy, uniform are downstairs and forensics should be here soon.'

'Yes, we'll be grand here, won't we Michele? DC Cathy O'Hare smiled, tightly hugging the young girl.

'Right Jack, I'll call the DCI, see if we can acquire an arrest warrant for this doctor bitch. Oh Jesus,' Blaise gasped as he clasped a hand to his face. 'Some bloody coppers we are.'

'Why__ what is it?' Jack Phillips asked with surprised stare.

'When we questioned that doctor woman, we didn't bloody ask her where she was staying, Jack. We forgot to find out for definite where exactly she resided.'

'I'll bloody put any money on it that the bitch is living with her father out in that Sycamore Lodge place,' Jack Phillips said.

'Right, what time is it now__' Blaise said with an exhilarated air of excitement. 'It's only after eight, hopefully that old man will still be pottering about.'

'Let's go then, hopefully the daughter will be there, and that bloody son,' Jack Phillips said eagerly, holding the car keys.

'I bloody mean it this time Jack, if that old sod mucks me about this time__ I swear to God I'll bloody choke him.'

'Here, light a cigarette and calm down,' Jack Phillips grinned, revving the engine.

The moments it took the car to reach its destination in Ballymagorry felt like seconds as the two detectives stood then at the front door of Sycamore Lodge.

'God I love being a copper, don't you Jack?' Blaise enthused rubbing his hands together in certain happiness before giving the door a repetitive loud knocking. 'Open the door sir__ it's the police, open up.'

'It doesn't look as though there's anyone home.'

'Damn it,' Blaise groaned with disappointment. 'Look, it's getting late and we're already doing several hours overtime. Those moaners upstairs will be complaining about the budget.'

Foetal Attraction

'So do you want to leave it until first thing in the morning then? There's sod all we can do for now.'

'We'll do that, Jack. A nice fresh start eh. We'll visit that clinic first, hopefully arrest that bloody woman. Call for someone to keep watch on this place tonight too.'

Foetal Attraction

The morning was just like any other Thursday morning, drizzling rain and mild. The bright blue sky was thick with heavy greyish clouds and every now and then, you could hear birds chirping in the distance. Surrounding the town the mass of farmlands were lush green fields and the trees abundant with leaves and somehow, the cattle and sheep looked content.

Blaise felt exhilarated with energy as he looked forward to the arrest of the doctor, who was now posing as a veterinarian in Strabane for some strange reason that Blaise just could not figure out, but he would find out, he would make certain that once he had arrested Jana Madzia Zaleski, then she would confess all.

Blaise and DC Cathy O'Hare arrived at the station, immediately calling DC Bill Johnson to enquire as to the whereabouts of the dark green coloured van, but there had been no sign of it all night.

'Listen, Cathy,' Blaise sighed on entering the CID room. 'You weren't supposed to be out with us last night. I don't want you going on another shout.'

'Oh be quiet, Ben. I bloody hate to be cooked up in this office all day, no, sod that,' Cathy O'Hare protested.

'Oh dear, are we having a lover's tiff?' Jack Phillips smiled from behind his desk, busily reading his newspaper. 'Blaise is right.'

'Jack__ now you know who's side to be on?'

'I'm definitely with the boss on this, Cathy. Besides, you wouldn't want to risk injury or even a set-back at this stage__ no, you could end up longer on sick leave next time.'

Foetal Attraction

'Look, you need to stay here and man the phones and all that, Cathy,' Blaise smiled, playfully rubbing Cathy's back.

'I bloody hate him, Jack,' Cathy smiled, sitting on the edge of Jack's desk.

'Hey, by the way, Cathy,' Blaise asked. 'What was the surname of that big guy in the film "The Green Mile?" It was John something?'

'Cathy thought for a moment. 'It was Coffee__ yes Coffee.'

'Thanks babe, get one for Jack too.'

'Damn it, the sod caught me out again,' Cathy groaned with a grin.

'Right, so are you nice and fresh, Jack? I bloody hope that we can catch this woman doctor today__ I want her so bloody bad.'

'Oh, and who do you want so badly?' Cathy O'Hare asked.

'Oh, he just wants this other woman,' Jack Phillips smiled.

'There's a bloody vending machine just outside the door,' Cathy quipped. 'I honest to God never saw it when I came in.'

'Ah, that's because you only have eyes for your man there,' Jack Phillips said, turning the page of his newspaper. 'It's new.'

'Right then, once you have finished buying and selling your shares there, Jack, we'll go visit this vet's clinic and arrest her before she opens up. By the way, any word back from the Immigration people on those documents we took from the woman?'

'Nothing yet Blaise, I haven't heard anything. Cathy there can give them a ring whilst she is here today, eh?'

'Yes, and whilst I'm here doing next to nothing,' Cathy smiled. 'I just might do a bit of tidying and rearrange all these files.'

'Don't you bloody dare,' Jack Phillips gasped. 'That's years of organised chaos__ no__ leave it, we know where everything is.'

'Talking of which, is there anything on poor Will's murder, Jack?'

'Nothing yet, but uniform are keeping a good look out for Flynn.'

'Come on, let's get going, Jack. I want that bloody doctor woman today,' Blaise encouraged his colleague.

The drive from the police station to the vet's clinic on the Railway Road took only minutes, Blaise and Jack Phillips thrusting boldly through the door and stared at the smiling receptionist.

'Kindly inform that boss of yours to get out here,' Blaise said loud and commanding. 'Now woman.'

'Oh, I'm sorry Inspector,' the receptionist apologised. She won't be in today. This is her morning off__ she always takes Thursday mornings off.'

'So is she at home then__ where is home exactly?'

'Eh, I'll just check that for you, Inspector,' the receptionist quivered, hurriedly searching in her filing cabinet as though fearing Blaise's wrath again.

'Well__ for Christ sake, woman hurry up, try to tell me before I bloody retire.'

'Sorry, it's Syca__'

Foetal Attraction

Let's go, Jack,' Blaise enthused, not allowing the receptionist to finish as he hurriedly thrust through the exit.

'Wouldn't it be nice if this woman and her son were sitting down to breakfast with daddy?'

'It would be bloody fantastic, Jack. Listen, stop off at that Adult Learning place on the Derry Road, I want a wee quick chat with that manageress again.'

'The big buxom woman you mean? I don't imagine her children went hungry.'

'Christ, Jack, I seriously wonder about you at times,' Blaise grinned, rubbing at his chin with the tip of his thumb. 'What if we're on the wrong track with this doctor, Jack?'

'What__ are you having doubts? It all fits__ she has what looks like a false passport__ she works as a vet and has a mysterious son kidnapping young pregnant women.'

'Right, pull in there, Jack. Aye, you're right, it must be her,' Blaise sighed, staring at the building in front of him. 'You just sit here and have a smoke if you like, I won't be long.'

'You just want that big bust all to yourself, eh,' Jack Phillips smiled, lighting a cigarette.

The manageress met Blaise in the reception as she was chatting with a member of staff, immediately inviting her guest into her office. 'What can I do for, Inspector?'

'I just need some information actually, well, more in hope than anything,' Blaise smiled. 'I'm just wondering did anyone attend

252

your centre here that perhaps had a severe facial injury, disfigured or the likes. A young male perhaps, possibly wearing some kind of balaclava?'

'Oh now, I know that you're investigating a murder so I must give you his name, isn't that right, Inspector?'

'Absolutely, Mrs Duffy.'

'It was John Zaleski__ he was such a nice soul.'

'I don't suppose you would have a photograph of this individual, would you?'

'Oh Inspector, now that would be cruel, he didn't like having his photograph taken, goodness me.'

'I suppose that would be a bit insensitive eh?' Blaise said, quietly saying that he would definitely have his photograph taken with a nice big number, once he had arrested him.

'Did anyone bring him here, his mother perhaps?'

'Yes actually, his mother did usually drop him off. She never once came in with him; she would stop outside then drive off.'

'So you never got to talk with her__ wouldn't she perhaps be required to attend an interview initially?'

'Yes, but that would be with the previous manager, Mr Fitzpatrick.'

'Where could I find him then?'

'Unfortunately he passed away about two years ago.'

Foetal Attraction

'Right, unless I contact a psychic eh?' Blaise smiled. 'So eh, this John Zaleski, how did he come into contact with Mary-Jo Delaney, did she help with his care?'

'Oh yes, Mary-Jo was very good with him, as she was with all the patients. John liked her very much,' the woman continued, giving a little smile. 'He actually told me once that he loved her. It was harmless really.'

'Do you think he was perhaps besotted with her?'

'In his own way I suppose, but Mary-Jo knew how to talk to him.'

'Right, so this elusive mother, you wouldn't happen to know what she did for a living, do you.'

'I'm not sure; I think she was a doctor or something like that. I saw her driving passed me one morning, there was a white coat on the back window of her car.'

'Right, well, you've been truly helpful, Mrs Duffy, thanks,' Blaise said as he shook the woman's hand firmly before making his way back to the car.

'So, how did it go with Busty?' Jack Phillips joked, switching on the engine.

'It definitely looks like this woman and son are the ones, Jack. The son attended here and he wore a balaclava to hide his disfigured face. He also had a wee thing for Mary-Jo Delaney.'

'Bloody excellent, let's go get them then. I'm really interested in what this woman has to say__ and why she has killed these innocent young mothers-to-be.'

Foetal Attraction

'Once we have arrested these two clowns, remind me to call Social Services and have somebody visit that father, the poor old sod shouldn't be living alone, he's too frail,' Blaise sighed thoughtfully, reaching his hand into the pocket of his colleague's jacket for the cigarettes.

'Christ, is that a sign of compassion from you, Blaise?' Jack Phillips grinned. 'Life with young Cathy must agree with you.'

Here we go,' Blaise said sitting upright in the passenger seat on arriving at Sycamore Lodge. 'They bloody better be at home.'

'There's no sign of any vehicles,' Jack Phillips said parking the car opposite the entrance to the house. It doesn't look like there's anyone home.'

Suddenly, a silver car pulled into the driveway and a short grey haired man approached the detectives at the front door.

'Good morning,' he greeted cheerfully.

'Good morning to you,' Blaise replied. 'Are you visiting Mrs Zaleski?'

'I am indeed. Jonathan Patrick Gilmartin, Solicitor,' the man smiled, holding out his hand.

'Detective Inspector Blaise, Strabane Police,' Blaise said, firmly shaking the proffered hand. 'Can you tell me why you are here?'

'It is a private matter, Inspector.'

'Well, I'm investigating a murder case and it would be appreciated if you would tell me, quietly of course.'

Foetal Attraction

'Oh I couldn't breach client confidentiality, Inspector.'

'Look, wee man, I wouldn't like to break your jaw, so, you just tell me why you're here and we'll say no more.'

'I really would tell him, sir,' Jack Phillips said. 'He does tend to get a bit mad at times, and, he does have a witness that would state you did trip on the path.'

'Well, if you put it that way,' the solicitor agreed reluctantly. 'Mrs Zaleski has updated the insurance policies on her son and father, that's all, nothing sinister, Inspector.'

'Did you have an appointment with her?'

'Yes, I was supposed to meet at her the clinic, but the receptionist informed me that Mrs Zaleski was at home.'

'Well, it would appear that she isn't, and we urgently need to talk to her, and her son.'

'You said that Mrs Zaleski increased the insurance policies on her father and son, for how much?' Jack Phillips asked with growing interest.

'All I can tell you gentlemen, is that is a substantial amount.'

'Are you thinking what I'm thinking, Blaise?'

'Oh that I am, Jack__ that I bloody am.'

'As soon as you hear from this Mrs Zaleski, you phone me right away, do you hear?' Blaise said threateningly.

'I certainly shall, Inspector.'

Foetal Attraction

'Right, Jack, I suppose we can head back to the office and go over what we have so far with the rest of the team,' Blaise sighed, watching the solicitor drive off.

'Let's stop off somewhere first and enjoy a real good cup of tea.'

'That's a bloody good idea, Jack. Is there somebody keeping watch at that clinic?'

'Yes, I've got plain clothes to keep an eye out here too. He should be over there in those woods.'

'Good, then a nice cup of tea it is, you're buying by the way, Jack.'

Blaise and Jack Phillips slumped lazily on their chairs after a good lunch, both gathering all the documents relating to the murder investigation. Suddenly, their easy-going manner halted by the somewhat overwhelming appearance of DCI Cruickshank, who perched himself on the edge of Jack's desk.

'How are we getting on lads, any progress? Oh, by the way, bloody good result rescuing that wee lassie.'

'It's just a pity that we didn't capture her kidnapper,' Blaise sighed with disappointment.

'Right, bring me up to speed then, Ben.'

'Do you fancy a coffee, sir__ what about you, Ben,' Jack Phillips grinned.

'Aye, that's a good idea lad__ black with one sugar.'

'This Polish doctor that we're looking for is posing as vet; she works in a clinic on the Railway Road.'

'Did you not have her in for questioning, Ben?'

'I did, she was using an alias__ Anna Schultze. The bitch has also upgraded insurance policies on her father and the son.'

'I see__ I'll get a warrant to search the clinic and her house, see what we can come up with, Ben.'

'It was this woman's son who had kidnapped the young girl, and the dirty sod raped the poor soul, but at least she's alive and well and that's the main thing, boss.'

'So eh, what's the story with this son then, is he the one that killed the two women?'

'Well, nothing definite, but it looks like that, boss.'

'You said the woman bumped up her insurance policies, do you think that maybe she's planning to top her father and son for the money?'

'Probably, it could be that she is planning to get rid of everything that connects to her and is thinking of living her life as this Anna Schultze.'

'Where was the young girl held captive, was it at this Sycamore Lodge place, Ben?'

'No, they had rented a private house from an elderly couple apparently. I think they were using that house as a sort of holding centre, if you get me.'

'Aye, you could be right. I take it the forensics boys are giving it a good going over then?'

'Definitely, I told them to rip the place apart, boss.'

'Now then,' the DCI said with a certain glint in his eye. 'I know you're still looking into the murder of young Will Chambers, anything on that front?'

'We have a definite DNA match on the fingertip that was found in Will's mouth, it belongs to a Paddy Flynn.'

'That wouldn't surprise me in the least that bloody sod is into just about everything imaginable. It's a great shame that he wasn't drowned at birth.'

259

Foetal Attraction

'That's a fact, boss. Uniform's keeping a good eye out for him.'

'You'll need to watch this Polish woman doesn't head out of the country, Ben.'

'I've already contacted the airports, ferry terminals and so on; the bitch won't find it as easy to sod off this time.'

'What about that Johnny Mulgrew, did you question him yet?'

'He's clean as far as this investigation is concerned. I'm convinced more than ever now that this guy in the dark green van is kidnapping these pregnant women for the doctor, who is his mother.'

'What about the father, do you think he knows anything about all this, Ben?'

'I wouldn't think so, boss, I just think that the poor old sod is just too busy trying keep breathing.'

'Right so what are you going to do, Ben?'

'I'm going to brief the team then I suppose it's home time, get a fresh start in the morning, boss.'

'So where is Cathy then?'

'She's at the hospital with the young girl__ Cathy's going to stay with her until we arrest those two lunatics.'

'Right, see you in the morning, Ben.'

Foetal Attraction

The unmarked police car halted in the driveway of Sycamore Lodge in Ballymagorry. Both detectives met the postman, who said that he thought the residents were away as he had been trying to get someone to sign for a registered letter. Blaise knew that the elderly man would be at home; as it appeared, he was too frail to journey anywhere. Then, with his impatience growing, Blaise banged on the front door repeatedly but to no avail.

'Take a look round the back, Jack,' Blaise groaned, lighting one of his colleague's cigarettes. 'I want arrests made today.'

Jack made his way around to the back of house, discovering at the side, a small syringe lying on the ground and carefully covered it with a clean handkerchief, wishing then that he carried several small evidence bags. Jack Phillips continued to the rear of the house, immediately calling out urgently to his colleague.

'What is it, Jack?' Blaise questioned as he hurriedly made to join his colleague at the rear of the house.

'It looks like someone has broken in,' Jack Phillips explained, pointing out the small glass panel on the backdoor, which had been broken to allow the burglar to unlock the door.

'Bloody suspicious if you ask me, Jack,' Blaise said, cautiously pushing the door open.

'Here, look at this, it was lying on the ground at the side of the house,' Jack Phillips said, showing his colleague the syringe.

'Now I'm intrigued,' Blaise whispered, stepping inside followed by Jack Phillips. The two detectives slowly entered the deserted kitchen, their eyes searching, ears listening. Blaise then noticed a black plastic sheet rolled up beside a shovel and several rolls of adhesive tape lay on the worktop.

'What do you think that is intended for, Jack?' Blaise said quietly, noticing a gent's wristwatch close to the kitchen sink.

'Now, surely a thief would take that?'

'Definitely, unless he didn't see it.'

'Did you notice that most of the glass from the door lay on the outside, Jack? The window was broken from the inside.'

'I noticed that too, Blaise. I'm starting to have concerns for the old man.'

'Me too, Jack. I think maybe this evil bitch is planning to collect on her father's life policy.'

Jack Phillips opened two doors that were only small cupboards, but the third door that he opened appeared to lead down to a cellar.

'We'll check that out after we've been upstairs,' Blaise said, searching the sitting room. 'If this was a burglary, the bloody culprit must be blind; he doesn't appear to have taken anything.'

The carpeted stairs creaked eerily underfoot with each cautious step, the air filled with uncertain tension as the two detectives stood silent on the landing, scanning their eyes around until they noticed one bedroom door slightly opened. Suddenly there was a noise from the room, Blaise and Jack Phillips straightened their bodies in readiness as they moved closer to the bedroom. Blaise curled his fingers around the door handle, then, glancing at his colleague, he thrust himself into the room, closely followed by Jack Phillips, both men searching their eyes for any sign of an intruder. The room still and silent, only the constant ticking of the pendulum clock on the wall disturbed the uncertain silence and the cold, lifeless body of the elderly man lay on top of the bed, there on the floor, a cat began to rub against the leg of Jack Phillips, hoping for food.

Blaise pressed his fingertips to the neck of the corpse searching for a pulse, but only felt cold flesh. On first appearance, the scene looked normal, as though the elderly man had just lay on top of the bed and took his very last breath. Then, with keen, investigative eye, Blaise noticed a small bloodspot on the neck of the man, giving the tell-tale sign of an injection having been administered.

'I think we can guess what that syringe you found has been used for, Jack. That evil bitch has killed her father by the looks of it.'

'How the hell could she be so damn callous. I mean, her own father.'

'The lust for money can have a terrible effect on people, Jack.'

'That's for sure; some people can never have enough. Anyway, shall we take a look down in that cellar?'

'First I'll call the forensics team then I'll get the others out to give this place a good going over.'

Blaise and Jack Phillips made their way downstairs into the kitchen again, the hungry cat following. Jack Phillips looked about, searching in cupboards for a tin of cat food, much to appreciation of the meowing cat. Blaise searched and found a large torch, gripping it firmly in his hand as he led the way down the creaking stairs, the stuffy air filled with what appeared to be chemicals of some kind.

Foetal Attraction

The cellar exploded with light as the sensor detected movement, both detectives then staring at the array of boxes stacked against one wall. There, on what served as a workbench, lay several bottles of differing liquids, packs of surgical gloves and masks, assorted medical instruments and a large container of Ketamine.

Blaise pulled open a large drawer on the workbench, discovering an array of literature pertaining to plastic surgery carried out in one particular hospital in the United States of America. What further intrigued Blaise was the small bottle of Potassium Chloride, which looked used.

'I think that maybe this doctor is carrying out some kind of medical experiments, or she could be supplying someone with the foetuses in receipt for money, Jack.'

'So you reckon that perhaps she is doing all this for money in order to perhaps send her son for this surgery in the States?'

'It looks like that; at least, it's the only idea I have for now, Jack.'

'It doesn't look as though there has been anyone else living here except for the old man upstairs, the other bedrooms are covered in dust and what have you.'

'If those two sods don't live here, then where__ Christ, where the hell are they living?'

'Hey, do you remember the caravan park in Newtownstewart, where we found Will's car burnt out?'

'What about it, Jack?'

'Didn't the old guy there tell you that there was a strange couple living in one of the caravans?'

'That's bloody right, nice one, Jack,' Blaise enthused. 'That just could be where those two live right enough. I'll give Cathy a call see who's available.'

DC Cathy O'Hare informed Blaise that only she and DC Gemma Galbraith were in the office. Blaise then asked them both to go to the caravan park in Newtownstewart to check if the doctor and her son were the ones living in the caravan that the elderly witness had mentioned. He told Cathy that he only wanted them to wait and observe, quietly concerned for Cathy's safety should anything occur.

Two large vans arrived at Sycamore Lodge and a small gathering of officers dressed in navy overalls began to unload an assortment of aluminium cases, and sets of bright lights, two forensics officers began to seal off the immediate area, requesting that uniformed officers stand guard at the entrance to driveway.

'Why would she have that sheeting and tape ready if she was looking to collect on her father's insurance, Jack?' Blaise questioned, rubbing at the tip of his chin with his thumb, which never failed to amuse his colleague.

'Maybe it was for something else?'

'I think we should have the grounds dug up, Jack, you never know what we may find__ what do you think?'

'It won't do any harm, Blaise. As you say, you never know. I was thinking too, why would she increase the son's life insurance if she was planning to take him to America for this plastic surgery? It doesn't make sense.'

Foetal Attraction

'Why couldn't she just take out a loan at the bank like any normal citizen would do?'

'It's probably the repayments__ who knows, Blaise.'

'I'd like to know who is paying her for these foetuses, and why in God's name they are so secretive about it.'

'I think these medical people are a strange bunch at the best of times, Blaise. They just believe in their science and don't give any real thought to God.'

'Don't you bloody start quoting the bible at me now.' Blaise laughed.

'I was just saying man, no need to go mad.'

'Listen, don't you forget to give that syringe to forensics for testing, I want to know what that evil bitch injected into her father.'

'That's if it is this syringe, Blaise, it may not have been this one,' Jack Phillips replied, requesting an evidence bag from one of the officers before handing it to him.

'Right, Jack, we'll kick about here until Cathy and Gemma call me back. Hopefully they'll find these lunatics at that caravan then we'll get over there and arrest them.'

'Let's see what we can find then, Blaise.'

32

DC's Cathy O'Hare and Gemma Galbraith steered a leisurely course towards Newtownstewart, both enjoying the unusual burst of sunshine that caressed the acres of green fields either side of the long, stretching road.

'I bet you're glad to be back, Cathy?'

'Too right I am, Gemma. I really hated being cooped up all those months, although it did give me time to get used to living with Ben.'

'Does he not go mad when you call him that?'

'God__ he hates it, but I like to wind him up,' Cathy O'Hare laughed, enjoying the leisurely drive and looking forward to confronting the killers of the two women.

'So, dish the dirt, Cathy. Is he as hot in bed as some of the girls say he is?'

'I'm not telling, Gemma,' Cathy smiled. 'Let's just say that he keeps me smiling, the kinky sod.'

'Oh come on, you're no fun at all, tell me you naughty cow,' Gemma laughed, slowing the car as they neared the caravan Park in Newtownstewart.

'Which bloody one is it, Cathy?'

'I'm not sure, Blaise said it was right beside a post box.'

'That's it over there. Jesus, look, there's the dark green van parked beside the caravan. Should we call Blaise?'

Foetal Attraction

'No__ let's wait until we can see both the mother and son, Gemma. You never know, they may have another woman in there.'

'They wouldn't bring an intended victim to where they live sure?'

'Let's sit here and observe for a while. If the guy comes out and drives off you can follow him and I'll stay here with the mother.'

'Oh Jesus, Blaise said just to observe and call him if they were here, Cathy.'

'Sod that, Gemma, don't you want a piece of the action?'

'Is this going to be a woman thing, Cathy?'

'Yes, why not__ why let the guys have all the action?'

'Oh well, you are the boss's little bed mate,' Gemma teased, fixing her eyes on the caravan directly opposite.

'Why in the hell are they killing these pregnant women anyway, they must be bloody psychopaths,' Gemma sighed, fidgeting behind the wheel from the heat. 'It's really bloody warm today.'

'I know this is seriously the strangest country in the world for weather.'

'We could be sitting here all day, Cathy.'

'Right enough, let's go over and talk to them. We can just ask them a few questions then call Blaise.'

'Sod it, let's go then. First, I'm taking off my jacket before I bloody melt,' Gemma groaned, removing her short jacket and threw it into the backseat.

'Surely if the crazy mother was here then her car would be there too, what do you think, Cathy?'

'Maybe the son is all alone__ we could arrest him, Gemma.'

'I just bloody hope to God that the sod isn't armed.'

'Christ, I never thought about that, Gemma. Was there any mention of these people being armed or anything?'

The two women made a cautious approach towards the caravan, both remaining vigilant and focusing on the door in case it opened suddenly. Even though they were both experienced officers and had made many arrests, neither had ever arrested anyone for murder. A certain nervous tension began to seep into both women as they neared the caravan door, the threat of the man inside being armed very real and caused them both immense concern.

'Jesus, Cathy. If we mess this up Blaise will bloody kill us.'

'Stop worrying, we won't mess it up, how can we?'

'I must admit, you have a nice ass in those grey trousers,' Gemma smiled as Cathy stepped close to the door and wrapped her knuckles on it.

Again, Cathy knocked on the door and it opened only partially, the occupant looking out through the small space.

'Hi there__ our car won't start and we were wondering if you would please jump start it?'

'No, go away.'

'Oh come on, won't you help two poor weak girls?'

'Go away, I can't help you,' the man groaned, opening the door slightly more to take a better look at the two women.

'Hey, I know you, are you John__ I used to work in the Adult Learning Centre in Strabane?'

'No__ please go away,' he groaned nervously, keeping his eyes focused on DC Gemma Galbraith. Unexpectedly, Cathy stepped onto the small step pushing her hand against the door forcing it open and stood face to face with the hooded man. Gemma Galbraith hurriedly stepped up, both women then forcing the man to move back.

'Get out__ get out,' he shouted.

'John Zaleski you're under arrest,' Gemma stated, groaning then as the man unexpectedly punched her directly in the mouth, causing her to stumble backwards into Cathy O'Hare. He pushed the two women to the ground and raced from the caravan to his van, locking the door from the inside as he revved the engine frantically. Cathy stood one side trying desperately to pull the door open as she told him that they were the police. Gemma Galbraith wrestled with the passenger door, ignoring the blood that seeped from her swollen, cut lip.

'Oh shit,' Cathy gasped, watching as the van sped off.

'That ugly fucker has burst my mouth,' Gemma Galbraith groaned, holding the sleeve of her blouse to her mouth.

'Some guys find women with large lips rather sexy,' Cathy joked, comforting her colleague.

'Shit, what are we going to tell Blaise?'

Foetal Attraction

'He'll go bloody nuts. We'll tell him that when we arrived the sod was just about to leave so we challenged him.'

'I suppose that will stop us from getting into shit, Cathy.'

'At least now we can have a look inside, eh?'

'If I had that twat right now I'd kick his balls, the ugly sod.'

The two women stepped inside the deserted caravan, Cathy O'Hare decided that it would be best if she called Blaise and explained what had just occurred, which didn't please him at all.

There didn't appear to be many clothes belonging to the mother but in the single room of the caravan, there were assorted dirty jeans and sweaters, underwear and pairs of socks that gave off a strong pungent aroma, causing Gemma Galbraith to force the windows open.

'Oh Jesus,' Cathy O'Hare gasped with horror as she searched underneath the bed, discovering several pornographic magazines and a clutter of used paper handkerchiefs. 'The bloody dirty perv__ yuk__ he must have a strong right arm.'

'That's why I put on gloves you never know what you'll touch.'

'What have we here?' Cathy O'Hare then remarked, removing a small wooden box from under the bed. 'Oh now look at this, Gemma.'

'Lace knickers__ there's a ruby eternity ring and a brooch with a broken pin. These could belong to the victims.'

'Sick mementos I'll bet, Gemma,' Cathy O'Hare sighed with disgust as she closed the box to leave it on top of the bed.

271

Foetal Attraction

As the two female detectives continued to search inside the caravan, they discovered a white doctor's coat crumpled up inside the washing machine, both noting with keen interest that there were several minute spatters of blood near to the right pocket.

'I'll tell you something, Gemma. That guy must be really sweltered wearing the balaclava thing on a day like this.'

'Christ right enough, Cathy. Did you notice the lumps sticking out of the side of his head and face through the hood?'

'Yeh, no bloody wonder he doesn't like to be looked at. God, can you imagine what he must have went through at school?'

'I've no sympathy for him__ he's a bloody murdering scumbag, Cathy. The sooner he's behind bars the better.'

'I just wonder why his mother removed the foetuses from those two women. I suppose it's what Blaise said, for some kind of secret experiment or something.'

'It's bloody creepy that what it is.'

'What's this?' Cathy O'Hare said loudly, lifting the top of the seat in the lounge area. 'It's a briefcase.'

'Nice one, Cathy,' Gemma O'Hare smiled eager to view its contents as she stood close to her colleague.

'It's passports, one for her and one for him. These are authentic; they're in the name Doctor Jana Madzia Zaleski and John Zaleski. These other two passports are false.'

'What are those papers, Cathy? Christ, that's their birth certificates, genuine ones.'

'What's in the A4 envelope then?'

'Oh lovely,' Cathy O'Hare grinned, removing a thick bundle of £100 notes. 'Nice new crisp ones too.'

'How much do you think's in there then?'

'God knows, Gemma, thousands at least.'

'Oh well, I can guess who's in for a very special treat tonight then,' Gemma Galbraith joked. 'Let me hold that bundle for a minute, I'm not used to holding something as thick.'

'You're bloody terrible, Gemma. Right, let's leave all this stuff on top of one bed so that Blaise can see it when he arrives.'

'Oh yes, why on top of the bed, you naughty tart.'

'Would you stop it, you've got sex on the bloody brain, Gemma.'

'Did you call Blaise, Cathy?'

'Yes, he said he would be out soon as.'

'Oh well, we can wait outside until he arrives then.'

Foetal Attraction

33

Blaise and Jack Phillips arrived at the caravan park, Blaise immediately concerned as to Cathy's wellbeing, then looked at Gemma Galbraith, concerned about her swollen lip.

'So you two half-wits took it upon yourselves to question this Zaleski guy I take it?'

'No, well, he was about to leave,' Cathy O'Hare said.

'Cathy, don't bullshit a bullshitter,' Blaise grinned with a shake of his head. 'So show me what you have found.'

'I've been married almost thirty-five years,' Jack Phillips smiled. 'Not once has my wife lied to me__ and here you are not even married yet and you're lying to your intended.'

'We're not lying,' Gemma Galbraith defended her colleague. 'It's just that we're bending the truth a little.'

'What really happened, and how did you get that lip? I bet you both made to question the suspect and he slapped you both out of the way.'

'That's about it__ the sod was too quick for us, Blaise,' Gemma added. 'At least it gave us the chance to look around.'

'Right well, forensics will be here shortly, their going a bit mad, they said we're keeping them going with overtime,' Blaise said, looking through the documents that were discovered.

The uniform boys are here, Blaise,' Jack Phillips said. 'New passports too, she must've been planning to sod off somewhere, probably to the States eh?'

Foetal Attraction

'That seems likely, considering the literature we found earlier.'

'What do you want us to do, Blaise?' Cathy O'Hare asked.

'Eh, oh you two can go to Ballymagorry, just observe that Sycamore Lodge and see if either of these two nutters turn up. Now I'm warning you both, observe only, do you hear me?'

'Right will do.'

'I know it's being watched already, Jack, it will keep them busy, Blaise whispered.'

'Here's forensics now, Blaise,' Jack Phillips said, lighting a cigarette.

'I bloody hope that you're not giving him cigarettes Jack Phillips?' Cathy O'Hare shouted feigning an angered threat.

'Oh no, Blaise doesn't smoke anymore,' Jack Phillips replied.

'Right come on, you two get off to Ballymagorry. We'll head back to the office, Jack.'

True to form, the unexpected bright sun disappeared as the skies blackened and the cool breeze blew, the rain began to pour down without mercy, causing Blaise and Jack Phillips to race towards the car. Blaise sat in the passenger seat, habitually rubbing the tip of his thumb over his chin. 'What kind of car does the mother drive__ do you know, Jack?'

'Eh__ I don't think it ever came up. Surely to God the traffic boys would spot this dark green van__ there aren't many about.'

'They are looking, they know what to look for, Jack.'

275

Foetal Attraction

Jack Phillips steered the unmarked car through the armoured gates parking then in the allotted car park. The rain had ceased and the wind died to leave the air slightly humid. Blaise wound the window down as both detectives enjoyed a leisurely cigarette as they discussed the events that had just taken place.

'This doctor isn't stupid, Jack. I bet she has a few rented houses about the place.'

'She has certainly planned it well I'll give her that, Blaise.'

'I know what I'll bloody give the bitch. She will be worried now that we have her passports and her money. She won't go far.'

'Unless the crafty bitch has another stash somewhere,' Jack Phillips sighed thoughtfully. Or__ there's somebody else helping her, somebody with connections__ of the criminal type.'

'Yes, somebody that can get their hands on forgery's and so on, like connections to the paramilitaries for instance?'

'That just could be it, Blaise__ that just could be the case. Have you anybody in mind?'

'Most of that stuff comes from the big bad city of Belfast. I'll need to go find some of my touts, see if they can enlighten me.'

'I'll have a word with mine too, Blaise.'

The two detectives left the car and walked across the car park, suddenly, Jack Phillips burst into a fit of laughter upon noticing that someone had put a wheel clamp on Blaise's car.

'Jesus, when I get the clown that did that he'll be sorry,' Blaise laughed. 'That reminds me, I must look for a new car, that's just about on its last legs.'

'You've let it go hell since Julia left.'

'Aye true__ anyhow__ let's get up here and see what the others have to say.'

Blaise was surprised to see that the forensics report was waiting on his desk from the investigation carried out at the veterinary clinic on the Railway Road. The report stated that following a thorough and extensive search of the premises, there were traces of human bone, skin, hair and teeth discovered in the waste pipe and drain, combined with a mixture of animal hairs normally found at a veterinary clinic.

'That bloody bitch is carrying out the murders at this clinic, Jack__ can you bloody believe that.'

'Jesus, why did I not think of that?'

'That's why we found some of those dog hairs on the victims. I blood can't believe that we never gave the clinic a thought, Jack.'

'It's still a damn mystery as to why though. Why is she removing these unborn children then killing the women__ what possible motive could she have for such a horrendous act?'

'Well hopefully it won't be too long before we find out, Jack,' Blaise sighed continuing to read over the report.

'She must be selling these foetuses for money to send her son to America. So far, it's the only plausible explanation. Unless of course, she is conducting some type of medical research herself.

'Perhaps she is researching into whatever condition it is that her son suffers from, know what I mean, Jack?'

'God knows what's going on in her mind. Right, ok she may be doing this to help her son, but the murder of innocent lives can't in any way justify what she has done.

'Let's have a chat with everyone, see if there's any fresh news or witnesses,' Blaise sighed, closing the file and held it under his arm as he rose from the chair.

'Did we ever find out the reason for this doctor having been summoned to appear before the GMC?'

'The sods won't say, Jack,' Blaise replied. 'The Ferret did say that it was rumoured she carried out an abortion on a 15 year old.'

'Come on now, settle down,' Jack Phillips called out to the talkative group seated around the desk as they entered the room.

'Ok ladies and gentlemen,' Blaise sighed aloud, slumping into one of the chairs. 'Does anyone have anything at all that hasn't been discussed__ anything at all people?'

'Eh, I did talk to a woman in the shop on the Derry Road yesterday,' DC Jim Whyte said. 'She remembered the guy was in the shop and he had bought two rolls of duct tape and black bin liners. She said the van had Southern registration plates.'

'When was this, Jim?'

'That was the problem, boss, she couldn't remember exactly what day it was. She's a bit of a scatter-brain if you ask me. Christ, she just kept talking about how terrible the murders were.'

'I don't recall anyone ever mentioning these Southern plates,' Blaise said, glancing through his notes. 'It appears that nobody has ever actually seen the registration plates, he could be using different plates at different times.'

'These people obviously have somewhere to live so we need to check on all rented properties where possible,' Jack Phillips added.

'That's a nice job for you young McKean,' Blaise smiled. 'Also, it would be an idea to check with the Housing Executive, Charlie.'

'I'll get onto that right away, Inspector.'

'Hoi, you won't bloody last long at this nick if you keep calling me Inspector__ it's Blaise, ok.'

'Right, Inspector__ I mean, Blaise__ sorry.'

'Right, listen up you lot,' Blaise said commanding attention. 'About this vet's clinic on the Railway Road, apparently that is where this woman conducted the removal of these two women's uteruses and killed the women. Forensics discovered traces of human bone, fingertips to be precise. There was also human hair and traces of other human organs.

'What about these unborn babies?' DC Bill Johnson questioned.

'No sign of them, Bill. And we have no bloody clue as to why she is doing this, other than guess that it's for kind of medical experiments or something.'

'Bloody absurd if you ask me.'

'Aye well, unfortunately this is the modern world.'

Foetal Attraction

Sergeant Bob McMenamin entered the incident room, carrying a brief handwritten note, his eyes smiling as he glanced at the detectives seated.

'Have you come to see where the real police work is done, Bob?' Jack Phillips joked.

'Jesus, you lot couldn't find your own arses.'

'Right, what's the craic then, Bob?' Blaise asked, noticing the note in the sergeant's hand. 'Is that a love note for me?'

'It's eh, I took a call from some doctor in Altnagelvin Hospital, he informed me that he treated, well tried to treat some guy that came in with damage to his right index finger. The doc said it was missing, but after applying a temp fixing to it, the guy just left.'

'Sounds like our man Paddy Flynn is having a problem picking his nose properly,' Jack Phillips grinned. 'No point in going to the hospital now, he'll be long gone.'

'Right, I'm going back to the desk, unless you need any help here. I mean if you need the expertise of uniform.'

'You're ok, Bob, if we get stuck we'll call you,' Blaise joked.

'Listen up people__ I want everybody out there, look for this bloody green van. This mother and son can't just vanish, they have to be somewhere and somebody must have seen them about. And don't forget, people, keep a look out for this Paddy Flynn.'

34

PC's Billy Kent and Alex Gibson steered a leisurely course in their patrol car, turning off the Derry Road onto the Woodend Road. There was an air of unexpected excitement as they spotted the dark green van in front of them. With the siren on and lights flashing they drove close behind the van, which then sped up, swerving aggressively from side to side to stop the patrol car overtaking.

PC Billy Kent called the registration over the radio; the message relayed back was that the registration belonged to a Red Ford Transit van. The officer then stated that someone should inform Inspector Blaise immediately as the patrol car continued its relentless pursuit of the vehicle.

As the van raced on noisily, it cut off from the Woodend Road and onto Spruce Road, continuing to swerve erratically from side to side in its persistence to keep the pursuing patrol car behind it. Then, quiet unexpectedly, the van skidded and turned round completely before crashing against the barrier along the side of the bridge, hanging dangerously over the edge. The stunned driver thrust the door open, not noticing that he was over the edge and fell, luckily he managed to hang on to a piece of broken barrier as the traffic passed underneath him.

Both officers rushed anxiously from their car, fearing that driver would fall into the path of the oncoming traffic. PC Billy Kent lay flat on the ground at the edge of the bridge without fear for his own safety, desperately reaching his hand down in an urgent attempt to take hold of the driver's wrist, but he was just that bit too far down.

'Alex, hold my ankles and I'll lean over a bit more.'

'Don't be stupid, Billy__ you'll go right over man.'

281

Foetal Attraction

'Hold on mate, I'm trying to reach you,' PC Billy Kent shouted anxiously.

'HELP__ PLEASE__ the driver shouted fearing for his life as he held onto the piece of broken metal.

'Jesus, Billy__ don't lean over too much,' PC Alex Gibson again warned, keeping a firm grip of his colleague's ankles.

Suddenly, a woman screamed as she appeared at the rear of the overhanging van, her eyes wide with fear and panic, then, staring at the desperately struggling officers, she started to back away. PC Alex Gibson could do nothing as he held onto his colleague by the ankles, even though he wanted to comfort the shocked woman. Then, the woman started to run away from the scene, ignoring the shouts to stop.

'Never mind her, Alex, just hold my bloody legs. If I__ could__ just reach over that bit more.'

The driver screamed in sheer terror as his fingers slipped down the piece of broken metal losing his grip, fortunately, the baggy sleeve of his long coat caught on a sharp piece of the metal holding him in mid-air. In desperation to save the driver, PC Billy Kent stretched, but on doing so, leaned too far over the edge resulting in his colleague releasing his grip for fear of falling too. PC Billy Kent fell over the edge, desperate in his attempt then to grab hold of the swinging driver, caught hold of his ankle, causing both men then to fall head first onto the road below. An on-coming articulated lorry unable to stop ran over the two men killing them. Then, as he stood up, PC Alex Gibson thrust himself backwards to avoid any contact with the van that screeched on moving, crashing then onto the lorry, luckily the driver was out of his cab and managed to jump clear.

Foetal Attraction

PC Alex Gibson sank to his knees, horrified and distraught as he stared down to the road with tear-soaked eyes, unable to see his colleague or the driver as the lorry had drove over the top of both men as they crashed to the ground.

Grief stricken and angered, PC Alex Gibson staggered back to the patrol car, lighting a cigarette before calling the station for assistance. A moment of professional training overpowered his grief and the uniformed officer steered the patrol car from the bridge on Spruce Road down to the accident scene on the Derry Road. Immediately he began to divert the queue of traffic around the carnage with the help of several drivers from their cars, the lorry driver continuously apologising to the officer insisting that he was unable to stop as it all happened so quick and unexpected.

Within minutes, two fire engines and three patrol cars attended the scene, and in the near distance, the wailing siren of an ambulance sounded. Then, an unmarked car screeched to an urgent halt and Blaise along with Jack Phillips approached, ordering PC Alex Gibson to their side to give his account of what had happened.

The fire crew and paramedics busied themselves with carefully backing the articulated lorry away from the two men underneath and revealing the true extent of the horrific injuries.

'Christ, this is a bloody mess, Jack. Billy should have just let the sod fall.'

'I told Alex there to go back to the station and make a statement once the paramedic has checked him over, suggesting he go home then__ the poor guy's a wreck as you'd expect.'

'That bloody woman was there too, she'll be going mad now. Pity that Alex had been holding Billy's legs at the time.'

Foetal Attraction

'We could have had them both then, Blaise.'

'Well, at least we just need to concentrate on this mother now. Where in the hell can she be hiding out, Jack. She'll be distraught now, and hopefully slip up somehow.'

'Let's bloody hope so.'

Officers swamped the immediate area, busying themselves with taping off the side of the road and diverting traffic on a one-way system and noting every possible detail of the incident as the ambulance carried off the two dead men. Blaise and Jack Phillips left the scene to return to the station where they would discuss on their course of events.

In the reception area, the duty sergeant called to Blaise informing him that there was someone on the telephone requesting to speak with him. Blaise quietly surprised when the caller stated that she was the wife of Paddy Flynn and that he was at home in a drunken sleep. The woman sounded nervously frightened and urged Blaise to hurry just in case her husband woke up.

Blaise's elation was subdued given the fact of his colleague's death, but he couldn't control his excitement as he urged Jack Phillips to start the car again.

'Sarge, send some back up to Paddy Flynn's house in Sion Mills__ Meadow Crescent, just at that football pitch. It's just precautionary, he may be armed or with mates who are armed.'

'Right will do, Inspector. Hey, is that the guy who killed young Will Chambers?'

'That's him, and I honestly hope he puts up a struggle.'

284

Foetal Attraction

The arrest of Paddy Flynn was disappointing to Blaise, as he didn't get his chance to beat the daylights out of the killer of his young colleague. There, in the interview room, Paddy Flynn sat opposite Blaise and Jack Phillips with a smirk on his face.

'You shot and killed DC Will Chambers in the house at Ash-Pine Manor.'

'Fucking catch yourself on, I wasn't near the place.'

'Look, don't mess me about you scumbag. We have plenty of evidence that conclusively puts you at the house and we have a fingerprint on the handgun that you used to shoot the officer.'

'Bullshit, I wasn't there I'm telling you.'

'Your DNA is on cigarette butts found at the scene; also your DNA is on food wrappers and so on. Look, we have you and everything points to you.'

'You're fucking guessing, you don't have a clue.'

'The DNA doesn't lie and neither does your murdering scumbag friend, Jimmy Kelly.'

Jack Phillips glanced with a surprised look at his colleague, realising then that Blaise was lying.

'Your friend Kelly said that it was you who beat and shot DC Chambers.'

'He's a lying fucker.'

'The thing is, I believe him, because I know what a low-life you are.'

Foetal Attraction

'Your fingerprints are all over the holdall that you used in the robbery of the Post Office in the town,' Jack Phillips added.

'Your mate Kelly is in the cells, he said he would tell us everything that happened and who did the shooting if we cut him a deal, so guess what?'

'That dirty fucker, I knew he was useless,' Paddy Flynn groaned, slumping forwards to rest his arms on the desk.

'Look, you're just wasting time here. The pistol that has your prints on it matches the bullet from the officer, Ballistics are pretty good at that. You shot Constable Chambers in cold blood.'

'If that's what you think,' Paddy Flynn smirked with a shrug of his shoulders, wincing slightly with the pain in his finger.

Suddenly and without warning, Blaise reached across the table gripping the man's bloodied finger causing him to groan loudly with excruciating pain, Jack Phillips then pulling Blaise back telling him to control himself.

'Admit it you scumbag, you killed him__ be a man and admit it you piece of shit.'

'Aye__ ok, I shot the wee fucker.' Paddy Flynn roared with pain-filled anger. 'The wee shit deserved it__ he bit my fucking finger off.'

Blaise gripped both hands onto the edge of the desk, squeezing firmly to control his temper and to stop himself from lunging at the man before him. 'You left your fingertip in the officer's mouth.'

'Keep it calm, Blaise,' Jack Phillips warned.

'Right, sign that there then later you can make a full statement,' Blaise groaned, ushering the uniformed officer to escort Paddy Flynn to the cells.

'That was a nice one there telling him that Jimmy Kelly had implemented him in the murder of young Will, Blaise.'

'It worked eh?'

'Well, maybe you squeezing his injured finger helped,' Jack Phillips laughed. 'So now I suppose we go look for this Kelly and tell him that Flynn is stating that he shot Will.'

'That's it, Jack. I really want to find this bloody doctor woman. I want her behind bars for good.'

'Well, at least there's no chance Flynn will get away with it, it won't take a jury long to find him guilty.'

Foetal Attraction

35

DCI Andrew Cruickshank swaggered into the office with all the boldness of a king then casually perched himself on the desk of Jack Phillips. 'Well, lads, bloody well done to the both of you for catching the killer of young DC Chambers.'

'Thanks boss, Jack Phillips smiled. 'It was a terrible funeral, his poor mother collapsing like that.'

'I bloody hate funerals,' Blaise groaned, slumped behind his desk. Now we have another coming up with poor PC Billy Kent.'

'He was a damn brave boy I'll give him that. I mean, leaning over the edge of that bridge in order to save that scumbag,' the DCI sighed, arms folded across the huge expanse of chest. 'So still no sign of the mother then?'

'Nothing as yet, boss. The evil bitch killed her father for insurance money, can you bloody believe that?' Blaise groaned. 'Ok, the old guy was near to death's door and all that.'

'Maybe she needs money in a hurry for some reason, could be she's planning to flee the country,' the DCI added.

'Well if she is planning to sod off, she will need a new passport because we have the originals and the false ones,' Blaise said, with a note of quiet victory.

'We also have her other documents there, birth certificate, original and the false ones that she was using. Your intelligent little niece found them at the caravan the mother and son rented,' Jack Phillips said, covering a hand over his face then realising that Cathy O'Hare was supposed to remain in the incident room for a while.

'Oh now, don't give him that look, Ben,' the DCI said with that unmistakable glint in his eye that told you he knew all that was happening around him. 'I knew she would bloody find a way to get out and about, she just has to be involved in everything.'

'We were just short of manpower that day, boss. That's the only reason she accompanied Gemma Galbraith to that caravan,' Blaise said. 'I mean, she knows when I tell her to stay put then has to stay put.'

'So where is she know then, Ben?'

'I asked her to type up a few reports for me.'

'I see, so explain then how I saw her leave the station earlier with Bill Johnson. I'll bet they are off somewhere to look for this bloody Polish woman__ she is Polish, Ben?'

'Jesus, what do you do with that Cathy one?' Blaise groaned as he shook his head in good humour. 'Aye, the woman is Polish, boss.'

'This woman, Ben__ did she have any brothers or sisters or was it just her and the Quasimodo son?'

'Jesus, boss,' Jack Phillips laughed.

'You have a lovely way of describing people, Boss,' Blaise smiled. 'There is a brother, he lives in Poland_ he was over once to sort her out when she hit the bottle then he returned home. Apparently, the mother went missing after a boating accident whilst working in Africa. I don't think the body was ever recovered.'

'So eh, how did this woman kill her father then__ did the pathologist get back to you on that one?'

Foetal Attraction

'Eh, well she injected him with Potassium Chloride, according to Doc McElroy; it stops the heart and can't be traced during an autopsy. Apparently, it's produced in the body naturally.'

'I see, so how did you know that she had injected the old man, Ben?'

'Well, Jack and I were at the house looking for her, Jack discovered a syringe lying on the ground outside so we had it tested,' Blaise explained. 'Then, when we discovered the old man upstairs on the bed we checked him out, I noticed a tiny blood spot on his neck and mentioned that to the pathologist and that's what she had done.'

'Right, very good,' the DCI said, almost looking cheerful as he continued to perch on the desk in leisurely fashion. 'So eh, all that remains now is for us is to catch this mad Polish woman and the case is closed, is that right?'

'That's just about it, boss. Oh and we're still looking for eh__ what's his name, Jack? You know__ that guy that helped Paddy Flynn.'

'Oh right, Jimmy Kelly it is.'

'Aye, if we find him then that's it all sorted, boss, both cases.'

'You'll make those sods upstairs smile yet, Ben. So what's on the agenda now for you two?'

'Well actually, boss, Jack and I have a meeting to attend.'

Jack Phillips looked up from report that he pretended to read, giving a look of questioning surprise.

'Jack and I are going to meet a nice big steak for lunch, boss, you're welcome to join us if you want.'

'Too much to do, Ben, I'll talk to you later, boys,' the DCI said then left.

Foetal Attraction

36

The warm, friendly atmosphere of the local Chinese restaurant helped Blaise and Jack Phillips relax as they delighted in the fine cuisine served by the friendly staff, which it would appear could not do enough for you, and that was one of the reasons that Blaise enjoyed eating there. Unfortunately, though, there were certain individuals that Blaise despised seeing there and one in particular was the "Ferret".

The exceptionally slender man, with long pointed nose and narrowed eyes sat at a corner table, dressed in his usual crumpled nylon suit and long shabby raincoat. There he sat hungrily scoffing down a meal probably paid for by some local newspaper for his sewer-like reporting. Although Blaise did not like the man, he did tolerate him to a certain extent due to his keen eye for a story or always knowing what was going on in and around the town.

Blaise continued to enjoy his meal as he tried to ignore the presence of the free-lance journalist until the man spotted him. Then, like a bear to honey, he scurried across the floor towards the two detectives, rubbing thin-fingered hands together in excited, expectant manor. There he stood, nervously twitching and fidgeting waiting for Blaise to acknowledge him.

'Do you see that, Jack? Just when you think that you are enjoying a nice meal you always find that something turns your stomach.'

'I know what you mean, it's like finding a pubic hair in your gravy when you're almost finished,' Jack Phillips sighed.

'Oh now, gentlemen,' the man pretended to laugh in his high-pitched tone, sounding something like a mouse. 'There's no call for that, I thought we were friends?'

'Friends,' Blaise laughed. 'You wouldn't know what a friend was. You must be the most despised man I know.'

'Mr Blaise, come on now. You know I admire you as a fine upstanding holder of Law and Order.'

'You're a scumbag reporter with no morals. I wouldn't piss on you if you were on fire. In fact, every time I look at you, you remind me of something that you accidentally stand in.'

'Listen, about the murders of those two poor women.'

'What about them__ what crap are you trying to stir up?'

'I might just have some information that you might be interested in, Mr Blaise,' the man continued, irritating Jack Phillips as he seated himself down without invite, looking as though he would lick the plates at any given moment.

'What information are we talking about here?'

'Oh now, Mr Blaise__ we both know that Mr John Powers helps to lubricate and loosen my tongue,' the man grinned.

'Well, let's just say that for a teaser I could mention the fact I know you are looking for that Doctor Zaleski woman.'

'Maybe we are, what's so important about that?'

'Wasn't that her son that was killed the other day there on the Derry Road__ along with that poor policeman?'

'What info do you have?'

'Mr Powers, please.'

Foetal Attraction

Blaise reluctantly ordered a large John Powers whiskey and watched the reporter gulp it down with ferocious, greedy satisfaction. Then, to Jack's surprise ordered another.

'Start talking or I swear to God I'll stick this fork right up your arse. What do you know about Doctor Zaleski?'

'Look, what I can tell you is definitely worth a bottle of God's nectar, honestly, Mr Blaise.'

'Well tell me and I'll see if it is.'

'Or we could just jail you for withholding vital evidence,' Jack Phillips grunted, using his elbow to push the irritating man a bit further from his side.

'I've seen her, the doctor__ earlier this morning.'

'Well she will be long gone by now then?'

'Ah, but I followed her, didn't I?'

'To where__ tell me where you followed her to?'

'Eh, I will have another large one thanks.'

'I'm warning you don't push it. Now where did you follow her to?'

'First, I know you lot have been withholding what truly happened to those two women. Give me the exclusive on it and I'll tell you everything I know.'

'Right, ok you can have it. Now tell me you wee shit.'

Foetal Attraction

The obnoxious reporter began to explain that he was visiting someone in Bready when he noticed Doctor Zaleski talking with two men and woman on the roadside. He continued to tell the two detectives that the men and woman looked rather well dressed and their car was a black limousine. Then he described the three unknown persons as looking foreign and that they were waving their arms about and pointing, indicating that they were involved in an argument of sorts.

'You said that you followed her, does that mean that she was on foot__ what?'

'Oh yes, she was walking to where she is living, Inspector.'

'In Bready__ are you telling me that she has a house in Bready?' Blaise questioned with surprise, a certain excitement flooding his every fibre. 'So you know exactly where then?'

'I told you that it would be worth a bottle of Mr Powers.'

'I'll buy you a bloody crate of the stuff if we catch her,' Blaise grinned cheerfully. 'If you weren't such a hideous wee shit I'd bloody kiss you.'

'Does this mean that we're friends then?'

'Christ no, I still think you're a horrible wee scumbag,' Blaise laughed, opening his notebook to take a note of the address.

'That's just as you turn off the Victoria Road onto the Dunnalong Road, Blaise, I know the house,' Jack Phillips said.

'But that's not all, Inspector. I managed to dig up a tasty bit of information on your doctor.'

'Right, go on then,' Blaise said as he felt his body tingle with excitement. 'What else do you know?'

'Well, remember that you said you didn't know why she had been suspended by the GMC?'

'That's right__ 1998 it was, I think.'

'Well, our good lady doctor as rumour would have it was apparently suspended pending investigation into certain malpractices. It wasn't for doing an abortion on a young girl.'

'Like what?'

'It's rumoured that she was removing certain organs from patients that had died on the operating table and that she was rumoured to have given them to persons unknown.'

'Is that right__ why the in hell would she do that? I mean, what bloody reason could she have for doing such a thing?'

'It's back to the theory of medical experimentation I suppose,' Jack Phillips sighed thoughtfully. 'I don't suppose you would happen to know which organs she removed.'

'Not a clue, but why would she do such an unscrupulous thing, unless maybe she was selling them on the black market,' the reporter remarked, pushing his empty whiskey glass towards Blaise.

'Have you anything else for me?' Blaise asked the reporter.

'Well, nothing else yet, but another drink would be nice.'

'Here,' Blaise said, handing the man a £10 note. 'Now sod off.'

Foetal Attraction

'You see, Blaise,' Jack Phillips grinned. 'Even the slimiest, most horrendous of creatures has its purpose in life.'

'True, Jack. I'm bloody glad now that we met the wee shit. Hopefully, if what he says is true, we can catch this bitch at her home and get this bloody investigation over and done with.'

'Christ, Blaise, in all the years I've been in CID I've never come across anything as damned gruesome as this case, honestly.'

'Me neither, Jack, me neither.'

The two detectives hurriedly paid for their meal then left the restaurant, eager in their quest to drive to Bready and arrest Doctor Zaleski for the horrendous murders and mutilation of the two women.

Foetal Attraction

37

Blaise and Jack Phillips raced towards Bready, a sleepy little hamlet surrounded by acres upon acres of farmland. Both detectives were thrilled at the prospect of arresting Doctor Zaleski and closing the murder investigation, not to mention, discovering the reason for the doctor removing the uteruses from the pregnant women.

As the car sped along the Victoria Road just at Ballymagorry, Blaise and Jack Phillips began to laugh as a patrol car followed closely with wailing siren and flashing blue lights. Blaise instructed his colleague to speed up, causing the patrol car behind to speed after them, racing along the road until the patrol car eventually overtook the unmarked car stopping them then at the side of the road. The uniformed officer in the passenger side stepped out of the car and made towards the unmarked car, urging the driver to wind down his window.

'You better tell me that you're a fireman or you were trying to take off there, sir. You were doing almost 80mph, sir.'

'I couldn't have been, I'm not even out ten minutes.'

'Oh a comedian__ Jesus, Jack Phillips isn't it?' The officer grinned stooping to look into the car. 'That was very good by the way, only out ten minutes__ Jesus.'

'Hoi, we are on our way to make an arrest, do you want to assist?' Blaise called out.'

'Right, no problem, Inspector.'

'You better report in and tell them that I've requested you for back up__ just to keep things right__ no lights or siren, ok.'

Foetal Attraction

Both cars slowly pulled up outside of the house on Dunnalong Road, cautiously, Blaise and Jack Phillips positioned themselves at the front door as the two uniformed officers stood at the rear to prevent any possible escape.

Blaise stood close to the front door knocking it repeatedly, his impatience wearing thin as there was no answer. Then, with a surge of anger, he raised his foot kicking the wooden door almost off its hinges.

Both detectives rushed inside, discovering the woman in the sitting room, packing several suitcases. She stared in silent shock at the two officers, trembling slightly as she dropped a folded blouse to the floor, remaining silent as she seated herself on the sofa.

'Doctor Jana Madzia Zaleski, I'm arresting you for the murders of Mrs Alice O'Leary and Mrs Mary-Jo Delaney,' Blaise stated loudly, musing quietly that he had longed to say those words to the doctor.

'I'm sorry,' the woman muttered. 'I won't cause you any trouble.'

'Bloody right you won't,' Jack Phillips added, gripping the woman's arm as he led her outside. Reaching then for the handle of the car door, the woman unexpectedly raised her elbow crashing it hard against the face of the unsuspecting Jack Phillips and ran off along the road.

Blaise rushed from the house, giving chase and calling out to the woman to stop. He began to pant breathlessly as he anxiously followed the fleeing woman, running through several small back lanes and in between houses. Blaise gasped aloud then when the woman began to race across one of the fields, showing her fitness as she effortlessly left the two detectives behind.

Foetal Attraction

'Jesus Christ, Jack__ how could__ you let her escape?'

'She took me__ by surprise__ my bloody face is killing me.'

'She's damn fit__ for her age__ I'll give her that, the bitch.'

'It looks like she's heading for that road over there,' panted Jack Phillips. 'I think that's Cloghboy Road.

Jack Phillips turned to see the two uniformed officers approaching and hurriedly shouted for them to return to the car and go to Cloghboy Road to intercept the woman.

'Christ, my bloody heart thinks it's in another body here. Can you do that CPR, Jack?'

Blaise and Jack Phillips began to run again, forcing their lead-like legs to move as they ran across the field, struggling with several fences, Jack Phillips ripping his trousers on a small wire fence as he clambered over it.

'Ah damn, bloody cow shit__ I've stood in cow shit, Jack,' Blaise groaned angrily, panting heavily as the two detectives continued their chase.

Jack Phillips tried not to laugh but couldn't help himself as he gasped and panted, urging his colleague to continue in their chase.

'I swear to God, Jack, when we catch that bitch I'm going to drown her for making me run.'

'Damn right, especially when we're not that long after having that big lunch.'

'Come on, we're almost there, hopefully the patrol car caught her.'

Foetal Attraction

Blaise and Jack Phillips gave their exhausted body's one more final push as they ran towards the fence, struggling to clamber over it then stood on the road, puffing and panting. Blaise groaned loudly then when the patrol car arrived minus the escaped suspect.

'Hey__ look over__ there,' Jack Phillips gasped. 'I'll bet any money that that bitch is hiding in that barn over there.'

'You could__ be__ right, Jack,' Blaise replied breathlessly. 'Right, let's get over there and__ check it__ out.'

'Do you want us to check it out, Inspector?'

'Aye, if you see the bitch, shoot her.'

'Christ__ Blaise__ you can't do that,' Jack Phillips panted.

'If only. Right you two young bucks get over to that barn, we'll follow__ hopefully,' Blaise groaned.

All four officers approached the isolated barn, then, from a small side door, the woman emerged and began to run again over the field. Blaise found a burst of energy and raced after the woman, diving with arms outstretched and caught both her legs, wrestling her to the ground.

'You're__ nicked_ you bitch,' Blaise panted, kneeling astride the woman as she feebly struggled, Blaise then slapping her face.

'Let me go__ let me go.'

'You're not going anywhere you bitch,' Blaise roared, forcing the woman onto her stomach, pulling her hands behind her back to handcuff her. 'You're a murdering scumbag bitch and you're going away for a long time for what you did.'

38

Both Blaise and Jack Phillips lazed in the canteen enjoying a large pot of tea as Doctor Zaleski lay in a cell. The sudden appearance of the DCI caused a group of uniformed officers to hurriedly finish their tea and exit the canteen quickly.

'Good to see you two working hard,' the DCI quipped as he seated his colossal frame at the table, Jack Philips immediately pouring him a cup of tea. 'What is that bloody smell? It's like__'

'Cow shit, boss,' Jack Phillips laughed.

'How in the name of the wee man did you get covered in dung?' The DCI asked almost showing signs of a smile.

'Chasing that bitch over fields, that's how,' Blaise groaned. 'This is new suit too.'

'So once you question this Polish woman that's this investigation over then, eh?'

'That's it boss, and hopefully the bitch will get a good long sentence too.'

'Right well__ bugger,' the DCI sighed with a shake of his head. 'I bloody knew there was a reason I wanted to talk to you. Jimmy Kelly, that wee rat who helped Paddy Flynn to kill young Will Chambers__ he was arrested in the early hours this morning.'

'Oh now that it is good news, boss,' Jack Phillips smiled.

'Bloody right it is__ let's hope he rots in jail the wee shit.'

'Right then, I'll let you two get on and we'll chat later.'

Foetal Attraction

'By the way Blaise,' Jack Phillips sighed thoughtfully. 'When we arrested your woman in that field, did you notice someone watching us from the roadside, they were using binoculars?'

'No, I don't remember seeing anyone, Jack. It was probably just somebody out walking or one of those birdwatchers.'

'Suppose so__ I'm looking forward to interviewing this woman and finding out why she removed the uteruses of those two poor women.'

'It's definitely a strange one I'll give you that, Jack. I'm just wondering who those people were, the ones that this doctor apparently argued with.'

'Oh right, the ones that the "Ferret" mentioned. It could be someone that has supplied the forged passports and what have you.'

'Or maybe it's the other doctor's that she is supplying with these uteruses or whatever, Jack. Maybe they are looking for more or different types of organs.'

'Surely these medical people wouldn't need to do things like this__ surely they have certain channels that they could use to experiment on bodily parts or whatever?'

'Right well, whatever the hell is going on we'll find out when we talk to this mad woman. We'll give her an informal interview first then let her lie in the cells overnight and give her a full interview in the morning.'

'Once she has tasted the tea and food in here, I'm certain she will be more than willing to confess all,' Jack Phillips sighed, holding a handkerchief to his nose. 'I think you need a change of clothes.'

Foetal Attraction

39

Doctor Jana Madzia Zaleski sat poker-like at the table in the interview room; arms folded across her chest as she gave the appearance of an impatient woman. She sat quiet, as if nothing had occurred or she was about to be questioned on the murders of two innocent souls.

Dr Zaleski combed slender fingers through the length of her black hair before tying it back into a thick ponytail with a red rubber band. Every now and again, she would glance at the uniformed officer guarding her and give a hint of a smirk before staring up at the ceiling as she exhaled a lingering sigh of boredom.

'Sorry to keep you waiting,' Blaise smiled entering the room, a thick manila folder under his arm. 'I hope we haven't kept you from anything?'

'Oh Please, let's not waste time with these idiotic jokes, Inspector. Why don't we just commence with the questioning and my confession.'

'Are you in a hurry to rid your soul of the evils that you have committed, eh?'

'Do you admit that you murdered Mrs Alice O'Leary and Mary-Jo Delaney?' Jack Phillips quizzed.

'No__ I never killed anyone,' the women denied with a cold confidence. 'I'm not the one responsible for their deaths, Inspector.'

'I thought you were going to confess? Just tell me everything and get it off your chest. You owe it to your late son, not to mention those poor souls that you destroyed. Just admit it.'

'I can't confess to murdering someone if I didn't murder them. In fact, my dear Inspector, it is you who is responsible for murder.'

'And just how do you work that one out, Doctor?'

'You and your colleagues are responsible for the death of my poor son. You all caused his death.'

'Look, don't give me that rubbish__ your son kidnapped those two women and you killed them, isn't that correct?'

'You are partially correct, Inspector. You see, my dear son did indeed abduct those women, but I didn't kill them.'

'Right then, let's chat about your father. You killed him with a dose of Potassium Chloride__ you knew it would stop his heart, especially as he was ill. We have the syringe that you used.'

'Yes, my father suffered with bone cancer, he wanted to die.'

'So you thought you'd cash in and up his life insurance policy, is that it?'

'Yes and why not? These insurance people are making millions.'

'You know, you don't look as you give a damn about happened here. You're just sitting there with a look of indifference.'

'Well, it's all been for nothing, Inspector. Everything has been a complete waste since my son is now dead.'

'What do you mean__ are you saying that you killed these women for your son__ explain what you mean by that?'

'Look, I didn't kill those women, Inspector.'

Foetal Attraction

'Listen stop denying it, we found traces of human hair and bone in the drains at your surgery. You killed those women at your clinic.'

'Did you actually see me commit these murders, Inspector? Just because you have discovered human traces, that doesn't imply that I am the killer.'

'Does anyone else use your operating theatre at your clinic?'

'No, but that doesn't mean__'

'Look, don't piss me about,' Blaise interrupted loudly. 'You killed those two women, and you had a third ready__ didn't you? That son of yours had abducted a third pregnant girl.'

'I'm not denying that I did remove the uteruses from these two women, Inspector, but I'm not responsible for their deaths.'

'So who is then__ who killed them?'

'Well, I suppose that my son killed them when he disposed of them. I mean, I had told him to leave them close to the hospital in order that they would receive treatment.'

'That's absolute rubbish__ you removed their insides for God's sake__ how could they bloody survive that?'

'You couldn't possibly understand, Inspector, you are not medically conversant with the workings of the human body are you?'

'What I need to know is why in God's name did you remove the uteruses?' Jack Phillips joined eager for an answer. 'What kind of bloody experiment were you conducting?'

Foetal Attraction

Blaise and Jack Phillips both watched with surprise as the cold, uncaring exterior of the woman faded and a tear rolled down her cheek, as though experiencing a sudden surge of guilty shame and sat nervously twisting her fingers.

'Well, come on, enlighten me please,' Blaise said, opening the folder in front of him, showing the woman the photograph of Alice O'Leary taken by the photographer in the pathology unit. 'How can you try to justify that?'

Doctor Jana Zaleski wiped the tears from her eyes with her sleeve then took a deep breath as she stared for a moment up at the ceiling. She stared directly at Blaise explaining that she took her son to several private clinics in the United Kingdom, Poland and in the United States of America, trying to have her son operated on to rid him of the terrible tumours that had blighted his life since birth, the cost causing the biggest problem. It was at a clinic in America that a woman approached her with a plan to raise the money required for the operations.

This woman had told the doctor that she represented a private group of extremely wealthy people who would pay for her son's operations if she supplied them with several foetuses. Of course, the doctor had refused initially, but after a tortuous struggle with her conscience, she decided that she would do as requested.

The woman representing the private group informed Doctor Zaleski that the group travelled the globe in search of foetuses and that when they travelled to Northern Ireland they would contact her. Several months had passed and the group's representative contacted the doctor with the request for a foetus, which she reluctantly supplied, courtesy of the unfortunate Alice O'Leary.

Foetal Attraction

The doctor explained further that she had instructed her son to take Alice O'Leary to the nearest hospital to receive treatment, but he had killed her and had removed the teeth, fingertips and body hair before dumping the body. The doctor categorically denied any knowledge of what her son had done.

'It wasn't until after I had supplied these people with the second foetus that I discovered these horrible people belonged to a secret group who practised cannibalism.'

'Are you bloody serious?' Jack Phillips gasped with shock.

'Cannibalism__ are you telling me that these bloody people actually ate these foetuses that you supplied?' Blaise questioned with sickened surprise.

'Yes, shocking, Inspector, isn't it? That's why I tried to stop it, I told them that I wouldn't supply them with any more, but they insisted. I was told that if I didn't continue then they would have me killed.'

'This is bloody unbelievable,' Blaise gasped.

'You'll burn in hell,' Jack Phillips groaned.

'These people had information on me. They knew somehow that I was involved in certain illegal experiments. It was nothing too horrific; several of my colleagues were experimenting with certain organs, research if you will.'

'This was the reason that you disappeared in 1998, is that correct? You had removed organs without the patient's or relatives consent and the hospital discovered your sordid practices. You then disappeared for a while before re-inventing yourself.'

Foetal Attraction

'Yes, it was for the good of mankind. Of course, it was unethical but that's why we are where we are today, Inspector. This sort of thing isn't new; it has gone on for nearly a hundred years or so.'

'I suppose so, but it is illegal, Doctor.'

'Yes, but when people refuse to donate organs after their death and there is a shortage, what can you do?'

'Right, we could argue the morals of it all day, Doctor. Look, where are these people__ where did you take the foetus?'

'I took the foetus in a cool box covered with ice to a hotel where this woman would meet with me. I honestly don't know where she went then, Inspector.'

Blaise decided to suspend the interview for a short period when the doctor unexpectedly burst into a hysterical fit of sobbing. He ordered the uniformed officer to escort the doctor back to her cell for a cup of tea, and then he and Jack Phillips made towards the canteen for a calming cup of tea, where they would quietly discuss the doctor's shocking confession.

40

Blaise and Jack Phillips sipped at their tea, trying to make sense of the startling confession by Doctor Zaleski. The DCI approached, looking agitated and angry.

'Blaise, have you arrested this Doctor Zaleski woman?' The DCI asked as he seated his huge frame down on a chair, refusing a cup of tea. 'Have you got her locked up?'

'Jack and I were just questioning her, she has made a full confession, boss.'

'I've just had my bollocks chewed by some clown at Special Branch. They're screaming blue murder because they say that we have jeopardised their entire operation.'

'How the hell have we done that?'

'They say that they have been observing and gathering intelligence for over two years on this group of people, some religious cult or something like that.'

'Apparently they are cannibals, boss.'

'Do you know about these people, Ben?'

'Not as such, we have only just learned about them from the doctor we are questioning.'

'Well, Special Branch is demanding that we stop questioning this woman and surrender everything that we have on her.'

'That will be bloody right__ she's our prisoner, boss.'

'Apparently they have been following these people all over the world gathering information, they're trying to discover who the main man or woman is before they make arrests.'

'She killed on my patch so she'll go to trial here, boss.'

'I'm afraid not, Ben. The Chief Super called me ordering me to co-operate fully with these people. 'I'm afraid that you'll have to hand over all relevant information and your prisoner, Ben.'

'That's just bloody bollocks, boss,' Blaise protested angrily.

'Look, my hands are tied here, Ben. This is a huge operation apparently, it involves over nine different police forces in nine countries and there's absolutely sod all we can do about it, Ben.'

'So am I just supposed to hand everything over and forget about it all__ this can't be bloody right?'

'It's just the way it is, Ben.'

'Why could these bloody people not inform us of what they are doing, especially if it's on our patch__ Jesus Christ.'

'We're just little cogs in the big machine of Law and Order, Ben. We can only do what we can.'

Blaise returned to his office, angered and frustrated at the thought of handing over his prisoner to Special Branch officers, especially after the vigorous effort put into the investigation by his team and now they would have nothing to show for it, except the death of their young colleague.

'I bloody hate all this crap,' Blaise raged as he gathered all the files relating to the case. 'Two officer's dead and bloody Special

Branch get all the glory, sickens me to death, Jack.'

'But at least we know the killers will be caught and jailed, Blaise. I mean, as long as the end result is the killers are locked up.'

'But what about those three other people, I'll bet they are long gone by now.'

'Christ, can you bloody imagine that they're cannibals though. I mean, they actually ate those foetuses. How bloody sick and depraved is that.'

'It couldn't get any sicker, Jack. Call down to the desk and get someone to take these files to the DCI's office.'

'What are you going to do, Blaise?'

'Well, I'm going home but first I'm going for a bloody good drink and stuff everything, Jack.'

'Oh now, do you think that's wise, and what about your Cathy Blaise?'

'Damn_ tell her to meet me in the Chinese at eight o'clock.'

Blaise swallowed his third large dark rum, glancing then at his watch as he quietly complained of having to leave to meet Cathy in the Chinese restaurant. His mind then began to question if he was ready to commit himself completely to her. He wondered then too if he would be able to live as a couple, to consider Cathy before he made any decisions. Then, with the thought of dying alone at some stage in the future, Blaise ordered one last drink then left the bar.

As he crossed the road towards the car park, he was unaware of the black Renault Megane that drove slowly into the car park driving close behind him. Then, Blaise turned to face the car, startled then by the driver, who jumped out pointing a pistol directly at him.

'Kneel down_ get on your knees,' the masked driver shouted aggressively.

'Blaise raised his hands as he reluctantly knelt on the ground, his entire body quivering with immense terror and fear for his life. The gunman stood only feet away as he continued pointing the pistol at Blaise's head, warning him then to lie face down.

'You must have the wrong guy here mate,' Blaise trembled, lying face down as ordered, his heart pounding with such traumatic fear as he knew that death was only seconds away.

'Shut up you arsehole,' the gunman growled anxiously, pulling the trigger, then again, and fortunately for Blaise, the pistol jammed and refused to fire.

In that very instance of realisation, Blaise jumped to his feet and lunged ferociously at the startled gunman, wrestling with him as they fell back against the car, Blaise gripping the gunman's wrist as he tried to wrestle the pistol from him. Then, the attacker raised his knee hard against Blaise's groin causing him to release his grip as he stumbled backwards slightly, the pistol crashed against his jaw sending him sprawling backwards to the ground.

The gunman stood over Blaise, both oblivious to the small crowd that stood watching the attack. Again, the masked attacker tried to fire his pistol, a voice called out loudly warning the man to put his weapon on the ground, again the voice roared then a shot echoed in the uncertain darkness of the evening and the gunman stumbled back against the bonnet of the car before slumping to the ground.

'Blaise felt his heart pounding uncontrollably with fear and gratitude on seeing two uniformed officers that had raced from their patrol car, both pointing their pistols at the slumped gunman.

'You ok, Inspector? Watch him Dave,' the constable shouted, kicking the pistol from the gunman's reach as he then stretched out a hand to help Blaise to his feet.

'Thanks lads, I thought I was a goner there.'

Blaise crouched before the injured gunman, slapping his face to ensure that he kept his eyes open. 'Who the fuck are you_ why are you trying to kill me?'

'Nothing_ personal,' the man groaned, Blaise quickly pulling the hooded mask up from his face, not recognising him, and again questioned the attacker's motives, holding the palm of his hand firmly against the bloodied bullet wound in his chest.

'Why are trying to kill me?'

'It_ it's a hit, mate,' the man gasped with pain, blood then oozing from his mouth as he choked and gagged.

'What do you mean a hit_ why_ who ordered you to kill me?'

'Fuck_ get me an ambulance.'

'Talk to me first_ tell me who ordered the hit_ tell me.'

The wounded gunman exhaled a painfully loud groan as Blaise pushed a finger into the bloodied bullet wound in the man's chest as again he asked who had ordered his death.

'It_ was two foreign_ guys.'

'Who were they, names?' Blaise roared, gripping his hand tightly onto the attacker's jacket as he shook him. 'Who are they?'

'I_ don't_ know. They gave me_ five_ grand to_'

'You must know who they are_ who are they. Tell me_ or you'll fucking die right here.'

'I don't_ know_ they were foreigners, they said they wanted_ you dead_ they said they would send another five grand_ from Argentina when I sent them a photo of your body.'

'Where, send the photo to where?'

'On the_ mobile_ get me to hospital, I'm fucking dying here.'

'Give me names then we'll get you sorted.'

'Inspector,' one of the uniformed said anxiously. 'We need to get this man to hospital.'

Foetal Attraction

'Once I get a name then he can go, constable, and not before,' Blaise growled, slapping at the man's face again. 'Give me a name you fucking clown_ tell me who wants me dead.'

'I've told you_ I_ don't know who they were, fuck sake.'

'I'm calling for an ambulance, Inspector,' the uniformed officer insisted, calling into the station to send for medical assistance, reporting the incident then.

Within seconds, several police cars raced from the police station that was only around the corner from the car park, officers rushing towards their colleagues. The gunman coughed and gagged fiercely as blood spewed and spurted from his gaping mouth and he slid over onto his side. Blaise tried to revive the man but it fruitless and the last breath of life wheezed from his mouth.

'Right,' bellowed the uniformed sergeant. 'Let's tape this area off and get the forensics boys out.'

'Right, no point in me hanging me around,' Blaise sighed.

'You'll need to sort out your report of the incident, Inspector.'

'Stuff that_ it can wait until the morning, sergeant. I'm going home and if anybody wants me, tell them to see me in the morning.'

Just then, Cathy O'Hare pulled into the car park ready to meet Blaise, her eyes wide with shocked surprise on seeing the area taped off by uniformed officers and Blaise then explained what had occurred.

'Let's forget the curry and go home,' Blaise insisted, slumping into the seat.

Foetal Attraction

'But who ordered that man to kill you, Blaise?' Cathy questioned with anxious concern.

'I think it was those foreign people that were paying our Polish doctor for those foetuses. They paid that guy there to shoot me.'

'Christ Almighty, let's hope then that Special Branch and whoever else catch them wherever the hell they are.'

'We'll discuss it with the DCI in the morning, Cathy. Let's just get home and have some made passionate sex.'

'Jesus, somebody has just tried to bloody kill you and all you can think about is sex_ you're a crazy sod, Ben.'

Blaise tried to play down the fact that he was almost shot for Cathy's sake as he slumped in the passenger seat. The moment desperately calling for a cigarette, but Blaise would rather face a dozen more gunmen than Cathy's wrath if he were to light a cigarette in her car, settling then for the last two mints in his pocket.

The journey homeward along the stretching Melmount Road remained quiet and leisurely until the appearance of a black Range Rover. Cathy noticed the vehicle and pulled over slightly allowing it to pass, but the vehicle continued to drive close. Cathy stepped on the accelerator slightly, as did the Range Rover, but this time it bumped into the back of Cathy's car causing her groan.

'Crazy fucker,' Blaise gasped, glancing over his shoulder, watching then as the vehicle revved its engine and bumped into the car again. Blaise urged Cathy to speed up fearing that perhaps it was another assassination attempt.

'Put the foot down, Cathy.'

Foetal Attraction

The more Cathy sped up the faster the pursuing vehicle sped up, continuing to keep close behind and bump into the car. Cathy gripped the steering wheel tightly and pushed her foot right down to the floor, fearing any possible traffic ahead as she continued to speed along the road, closely followed by the Range Rover.

Blaise searched anxiously for his mobile phone, glancing over his shoulder to take note of the registration. The Range Rover sped up and crashed forcefully into the back of Cathy's car causing Blaise to drop the phone, which slid out of reach under the seat. Then, as the pursuing vehicle drove alongside, Blaise's mind pulsated with worrying fear that another assassination attempt was taking place.

As the Range Rover drove alongside Cathy's car, the passenger window slid down and Blaise feared desperately for Cathy as the passenger pointed a pistol. Blaise roared at Cathy to swerve the car and speed up, but the more she sped up the more the Range Rover chased and as it drove up, the passenger began to fire, shattering the back passenger window.

Cathy began to sob with the fear and panic that surged through her, screaming anxiously as again the passenger in the Range Rover fired several more shots, luckily, he missed.

'Where's you weapon_ where is it?' Blaise shouted, pulling open the glove box, hurriedly removing the automatic pistol from its holster sliding out the magazine to check the rounds then cocked it.

Cathy panted breathlessly as she continued to steer the car weaving in between several cars as she raced passed them, the Range Rover continuing to keep up with its persistent chase. The traffic swerving and sounding their horns as the two racing vehicles continued to speed along the Melmount Road.

Foetal Attraction

'Where's your phone, Cathy?' Blaise shouted, grabbing Cathy's handbag from the floor at his feet, searching desperately then tried to dial the number of the police station. The Range Rover raced furiously crashing then forcefully into the back of the car, Blaise sliding down the window to stretch out and fired twice at the pursuing vehicle behind.

The passenger leaned out of his window returning fire shattering the back window of Cathy's car causing her to scream and swerve with fearful panic, Blaise dropping Cathy's phone out onto the road as he tried to shot back.

'Typical, you can't bloody find a cop when you need one,' Blaise groaned, scrambling into the backseat to fire at the Range Rover, trying to recognise the driver or passenger. Blaise pointed the pistol firing twice shattering the windscreen, but the vehicle continued in its relentless pursuit.

Fear and panic pulsated within Cathy as she fought desperately to control the car as it skidded dangerously across the road narrowly missing several on-coming cars as the car took the bend of the road. Two more shot rang out from the Range Rover and Cathy screamed with blind terror as she lost control, the car swerving onto the grassy verge and smashed through a wooden fence. Unable to steer the car it then narrowly missed the small clump of trees before crashing down a small embankment and landed on the edge of the fast flowing river.

Cathy lay slumped against the steering wheel, unconscious as blood oozed from a head wound, Blaise dazed as he thought only of Cathy's safety. Desperately he tried to wake her, rushing round to the driver's door in a bid to drag her out, laying her then on the ground several yards from the crashed car.

Foetal Attraction

Blaise looked noticing that the Range Rover had stopped on the side of the road, the two men now standing staring down. Blaise felt an uncertain closeness to death as he anxiously searched the car for his pistol, unable to remember how many shots he had fired or how many bullets remained.

Blaise's mind raced as his instinct was to shelter behind the car and to shot at the gunmen, but he couldn't leave Cathy exposed. With a deep breath, Blaise raced over to where Cathy lay dazed and uncertain as to where she was, kneeling beside her keeping close watch on the approaching gunmen as they cautiously clambered down the slippery embankment.

With the two men concentrating on their ascent, Blaise heard in the distance the wailing sirens of approaching police vehicles, ceasing the opportunity. He raised his pistol and shot one of the men in the chest, the other diving for cover behind a thick bush.

'Throw down your weapon and give yourself up,' Blaise shouted, knowing that the gunman would not surrender, again he shouted to no avail. Then, just as the man knelt out from the bush with the gun pointed and ready to fire, Blaise fired two shots, one bullet hitting the man on the shoulder and he fell backwards.

Blaise raced towards him, the man hurriedly knelt up pointing his pistol again and fired, Blaise aimed and shot the man in the head watching then as he fell back and lay still and silent, eyes open but seeing nothing.

As Cathy rose unsteadily to her feet, Blaise rushed to her side, embracing her comfortingly as he made her sit down to rest, asking if she was hurt anywhere other than her head, fortunately not.

'My bloody head is killing me,' Cathy sighed, holding Blaise's handkerchief to the wound on her forehead. 'Are_ they dead?'

'Definitely,' Blaise sighed with relief, glancing quickly at each of his attackers to make certain.

Several police cars screeched to a halt on the road above, the concerned officers rushing to Blaise's aid, calling immediately for an ambulance on discovering that the gunman shot in the chest was fortunately still breathing, two officers struggling to keep him alive.

'Let the fucker die it will save the taxpayers a fortune,' Blaise groaned, tending to Cathy's head wound.

'It looks like you're not a popular man,' the DCI's voice thundered as he made his way down the embankment, staring with immense concern at DC Cathy O'Hare. 'Are you ok sweetheart?'

'I'll be fine, sir_ honestly.'

'It's just a bang to the head,' Blaise added.

'Right, well, those two men and that woman were arrested by Interpol the minute they landed in Argentina,' the DCI explained to Blaise. 'When you arrested that Dr Zaleski woman they were watching you. They paid three clowns to kill you.'

'Aye, I think I got that part, boss,' Blaise grinned.

'Oh well, at least your both ok. Hoi, never mind that arsehole, get over here and take a look at my niece,' the DCI roared aggressively at the approaching paramedic.

'The guy's dead so no point rushing with him,' the paramedic replied, giving Cathy a smile as he tended to her wound.

Foetal Attraction

'That was a bit of a scary one for you and Cathy, eh?' The DCI said, resting a huge hand on Blaise's shoulder, almost sounding caring. 'Are you sure you're ok, Cathy?'

'Yes, stop worrying, sir. I just need a change of briefs,' she smiled, standing beside Blaise after the paramedic had finished with her. 'I think you should give us both a few days off sir. I mean, after all that we've been through.'

'You're getting too smart for your own good, Cathy_ I think you've been with him too long,' the DCI replied, almost showing a hint of a smile, suggesting then that both took a few days off.

Case Closed

Printed in Great Britain
by Amazon.co.uk, Ltd.,
Marston Gate.